Darling, All My Love

A 1930s Hub City Romance, Volume 1

Lori Oestreich

Published by Cattail Marsh Publishing LLC, 2020.

This is a work of fiction. Similarities to real people, places, or events are entirely coincidental.

DARLING, ALL MY LOVE

First edition. November 22, 2020.

ISBN: 978-1736140017

Written by Lori Oestreich.

Dedicated to Florus and Don whose love is eternal.

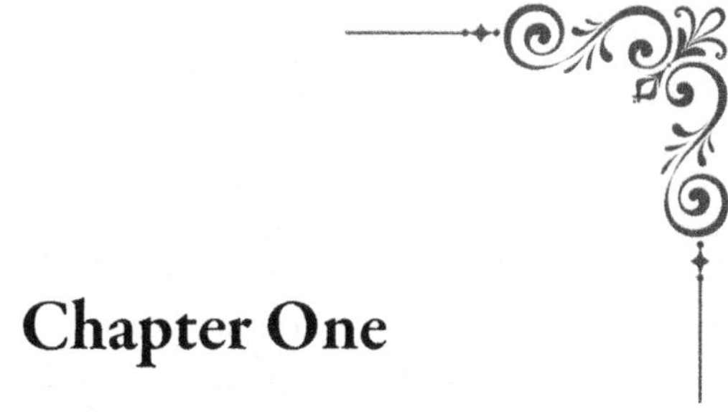

Chapter One

A hat is just one more way to define a person. Lily Vanderhoof appreciated the many styles of hats, but not the symbolism. Women with the fanciest feathers, jewels, flowers, embroidery, or ribbon certainly lived in the most lavish houses. A way of life she could only dream about while sipping iced tea and wearing an old fashioned 1920's cloche from the last decade.

Outside the diner window, the eight-fifteen evening train had arrived in Hub City. Her small town swelled with folks from all over Wisconsin since every track intersected the city like spokes of an old wagon wheel. Travelers paraded across the street in the latest fashionable headwear, piquing her discontent.

The bell hanging from the door chimed and she spun in the booth. A woman wearing a straw hat entered, crossing the black and white checkered tile floor to her table.

"So, you're Lily Vanderhoof? Can't see why you'd catch Ira's eye."

Lily examined her. Under the brim, loose strands of golden-brown hair were similar in color to hers, although much thinner. Yellow flecks streaked the woman's blue eyes, cautioning her as much as the choice words and that smug grin.

"Uh...do I know you?" Lily tipped her head to the side, pushing a loose bobby pin snugly into her hair.

"You should, that's why I followed you to Flo's." The woman stood with her arms folded and her legs stiffly rooted on the floor. "Besides, I overheard you'd be here. I thought it was time you knew." The woman yanked a hand from her tight fold, filling the air with a floral scent. Remnants of talcum powder speckled her forearm. The familiar aroma of Cashmere Bouquet Lily's older sister used. "I'm Bessie. A friend of your fiancé, a very good friend." Her voice lightened with amusement. "In all honesty, he'd be much more than a friend. You see..."

Lily backed away. She wouldn't oblige such an unwelcome gesture. Bessie's demeanor told her everything. A bitter, scornful woman who wanted her out of Ira's life. Lily had been with him for three years. Why now finally show up? Her engagement must have enraged the woman.

"Look at you sitting there in that moth-eaten cloche. You must have played on Ira's good-hearted nature, didn't you? You should be ashamed of yourself luring away a fruitful man." Bessie jabbed her finger in Lily's face, demanding attention. "You are the other woman. The poor damsel in distress waiting to be rescued. Not me." Bessie directed her finger at her own chest. "I was the first. His first."

Lily circled her hands firmly around her glass of ice tea. "His first what?" She glared at Bessie and the dress swaying around her shapely frame.

"Don't you dare question what I've been telling you." Bessie swung her hand onto her hip. "I've got proof."

"I don't need any seedy detail."

"I've seen his scar. Have you?"

Lily's heart sank into the depths of her stomach. *Ira's scar.* The one he'd gotten as a teenager running into a barbed wire fence while a neighbor girl chased him. The mark she'd seen only one time, an inch-long slit right under his ribs. An intimate fact to the woman's story she couldn't push aside. If she would ever use profanity it would be now, but a good Catholic girl couldn't do such a thing. "Leave." Her hand jerked, knocking the glass across the table and dousing the woman's skirt. "You've said enough."

"Ugh! You simpleton." Bessie pushed her shoulders back, displayed a satisfied smile, and exited.

Lily solemnly vowed from then on to detest straw hats. As the surge of adrenaline subsided, her hands trembled and a burning sensation stirred behind her eyes. She ran to the lavatory, slamming the door shut while tears wet her cheeks. Hopes of marriage with Ira shattered over a few words from a stranger. She should have asked when this happened. And more importantly, if their "friendship" was still happening. She blotted her eyes with a tissue. Her assumption the woman told the truth couldn't possibly be right. Ira would disprove the story. If he didn't, she'd be an unfortunate twenty-one-year-old in a similar situation as her unmarried sister.

She stood in front of the oval mirror above the sink. Could he have ignored all the years they'd been together and still be unfaithful to her? The image in front of her reflected definite signs of crying. Her eyelids were puffy, the whites of her eyes bloodshot, and in the center of her blue irises were dilated pupils. The slight brim of her cloche wouldn't hide them. Before Ira arrived, she had to compose herself. She splashed cool water on her face. A few droplets dotted her tan cotton dress and the bow around her neck had loosened. She tightened the knot, held her head high, and marched back into the diner.

Ira sat in their usual corner booth wearing a white button-down shirt and black suspenders. His sleeves were rolled to the elbows, exposing his tanned muscular forearms from manual farm labor. A plaid flat cap, which had compressed the blond curls on his head, rested on his knee. He didn't appear any different.

However, her previous anticipation for the evening diminished, and the smell of homecooked food turned her stomach upside down. The woman mentioned she'd heard Lily would be at Flo's. Could it have been Ira who said she'd be here? Maybe he didn't want to marry her after all. As she neared, she ran her fingers under her eyes. "I hope you haven't been waiting too long." She took the seat across from him.

"Just got here."

A fresh glass of tea replaced her spilled one on the table. "Good. I have something—"

"Wait." He raised his hand motioning at the waitress. "I haven't eaten since dinner."

"Ira." She paused until he looked at her. "I need to talk to you."

He rubbed his stomach. "Can't it wait until we order? Besides here she is. I'll have—"

Lily turned toward the waitress. "Please come back later."

"I'd like the roast chicken dinner with mashed potatoes, corn, and a cola...please." He glanced at her. "Do you want anything?"

"No! I don't want..." The knot in the back of her neck tightened, she placed her hand over the spasm. "I'm sorry, nothing for me."

The waitress walked away.

Ira drummed his fingers on the table. "You're a bit of a flat tire. What's the matter?"

She crossed her legs and tugged her skirt over her knees. "I can't help it when your dame stopped by to introduce herself."

"Dame? What dame?"

"The one with a smashed hat and worn-out lips." Lily covered Ira's hand and the drumming stopped. "She said her name. I don't recall... I think it started with a B."

Ira took his hand away and rubbed the stubble on his chin. "Bessie?"

She swallowed slowly and couldn't force the lump any further down her throat. "How do you know her?"

He shrugged. "She's an old classmate and neighbor of mine. What did she say?"

"That you were intimate." Lily narrowed her glare at him. "She even told me about your scar since I didn't believe her. Is it true?"

Ira's eyes darted everywhere, but at her. "We weren't even engaged then." He bit his lower lip.

"We've been engaged for less than two months. Apparently, any time before that was fine with you." Her skin changed from warm to clammy, and dizziness ensued. She braced her forehead with a shaky hand and rested her elbow on the table to keep from toppling over. Ira exhibited no shame. If it hadn't been for Bessie, he never would have said a thing about it.

"How many times did you? And why didn't you tell me?"

"Once and the way I see it...I could have denied everything, but I didn't." His leg bounced under the table, causing the silverware to rattle. "As far as you know, she could have innocently seen my scar the same way you did on that hot summer day."

"I'm not naïve."

"She's got nothing to do with us."

"Then it should've been easy to tell me about her." Her voice cracked. "How do you think I feel hearing such a thing from a total stranger? Don't you think I wonder what else I don't know about?" She touched the tear falling on her cheek. "Do you love her?"

"Ridiculous." He broke his gaze and peered out the window. "I'm sorry. Is that what you want to hear?"

She waited for him to offer more than two pathetic words of apology, but it wasn't his character. He could have told her he wished it never happened, or it was the worst mistake he had ever made. Maybe he'd given up on them. "I'm not sure you even know what you said you're sorry for. Is there anything else you'd like to say?"

He pulled his cap on. "You can tell the waitress to cancel my order or eat it yourself. Let me know when you've come to your senses. I've said all I'm going to say." He stood. "What more do you want from me?" And he stomped away.

Her hands jerked upward into the air. "Go be with her, you're two-of-a-kind!" She cupped her mouth. Surely, her shrill voice drew attention. A heat burned deep inside like the scorching sun under a magnifying glass. She couldn't face the people in the diner. Holding her hand to her forehead, she ducked out the nearest door in the back.

Each click of her high-heeled shoes ricocheted between the alley walls. Discarded trash along the edges left a crooked path to maneuver under the scarce light of the half-moon. She crossed First Street into the next back street. Her pace slowed, breathing quickened, and an ache arose in the emptiness of her chest. Both shins tingled like a pricked pincushion, while her calf muscles squeezed together as tight as a wringer-washer. The unbearable pain forced her to a standstill. She leaned against the red brick while massaging the knot in her leg.

Across the alleyway was the ladder to her favorite rooftop, a hideaway she'd stumbled upon at the age of nine the day she'd run away from home. By nightfall, the hunger pains made her go home. But the solitude above always brought her comfort. She lifted her skirt above her knees while taking hold of the railing. The cool metal scraped upon her palms. She carefully climbed the first set of twelve steps. Her pulse throbbed. The remaining set of twelve steps left her winded as she eased her way over the wall and onto the roof.

Although the two-story building wasn't the tallest in the city, the lower facade allowed her to sit on the cement ledge. Below rounded streetlights blinded her. On the next block over a dark-colored truck drove through the intersection and turned toward her house. It might have been Ira. Whenever he walked away after a disagreement, he'd always come back. How could he have acted so casual about such a serious act? His proposal to her hadn't erased what he'd done.

She yanked her engagement ring off her finger and held it over the edge. The seconds ticked by. No matter how hard she tried to toss the band, she couldn't. She shoved the ring back on.

A part of her wanted to give up and let him go, but she couldn't do it. She loved him and had grown to count on him to look after her. He had promised their own house on a piece of land from his family's eighty-acre farm. The thought had become a comfortable one, especially since her family had accepted him as a good, faithful, Catholic man. If her family found out about his indiscretions, they wouldn't allow her to make her own decision and their impression of him would be spoiled. She needed time to figure out if her heart could be forgiving.

The hair on her arms stood as chill air ran over them. Clusters of darkened clouds swept in while the wind picked up strength. The sky split open like a ragged seam on a worn pair of trousers. Raindrops pelleted upon the rooftop, and she descended the ladder. The buildings barely blocked the gusts of wind while the downpour stung her exposed skin. Maybe the rain symbolized a new beginning for her like a baptism washing away the original sins of the soul. Her heart needed the purification from her tainted future with Ira. She would never forget this awful night.

Her soaked clothes were heavy by the time she trudged the few blocks home. A shadow from the roof overhang cast the back-porch steps in darkness. As she strolled up the stairs, her parents' voices and figures became clear through the kitchen screen door. An unusual tone in her father's speech caused her to wait on the landing.

"...with the lack of work, once we get this last shipment out, there won't be anything."

Mother picked up the percolator and poured coffee into Father's cup. "Maybe they'll get another order."

"Doubtful. We need to prepare for the worst. It could be weeks, even months."

"We have a little money set aside, don't we?" Mother touched his hand.

"Not much."

"We'll make do. We always have."

"With lard sandwiches?" Father banged the cup onto the saucer. "I hate it when we don't have enough for the children."

"The garden's coming along nicely."

"Don't be so optimistic. We know how much they despise boiled cabbage."

"Frank, please look at me. Try not to be so hard on yourself. We're better off than some."

Father lowered his head. "How long can we continue like this?"

Lily eased her way down the steps and went around the corner toward the front door. Her father's news came at the worst time for their family. One way or another, she had to move out and not be a burden for her parents. The small amount of money she contributed with her job at Livingston's Women's Wear wasn't much. Even her older brother Arthur, who had two jobs, made little to assist with their two younger siblings. A marriage with Ira would have given them relief, but could she still marry him after what he'd done?

A slight creak came from the door as Lily glided through. The overhead chandelier lit the parlor, streaming light into the sitting room between matching tattered chairs. A sewing kit rested on the seat of Mother's chair while Father's had a magazine draped over the arm. A program emitted from the radio in the corner and an unplayed board game lay at the rug's edge. Muffled voices trailed down the hallway along with the lingering scent of supper. She crept up the stairs to her bedroom.

Lily slipped into her nightgown and slid under the covers. Her body tensed on the cool sheets. The events of the night replayed in her head and finding a comfortable position seemed impossible. Could she marry a man who may not be faithful?

What other choice did she have when her family couldn't continue to bear her burden? The situation with Ira and the lack of work in her small town didn't offer many options. She squeezed her lids tight over her swollen eyes, praying for a peaceful night. Finally, her body sank into the mattress with her hands folded together as if she were lying trapped in a coffin.

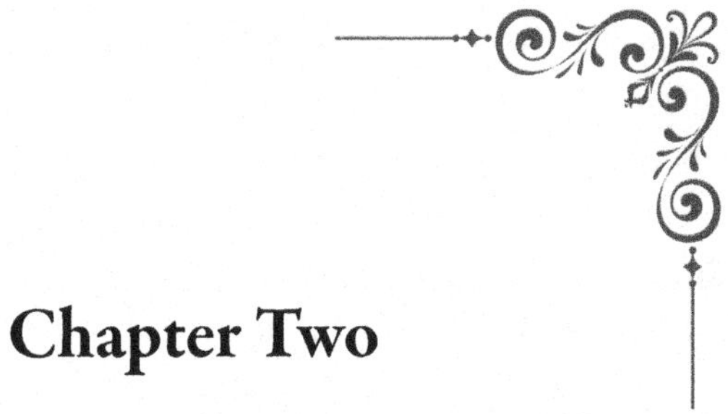

Chapter Two

The early morning church bell rang and Lily sprang forward off the bed. She wanted to keep to herself, but today, May 16, 1933, marked the most important moment of her best friend Anna's life and potentially the second-worst of hers. No doubt Ira would arrive at the wedding as if nothing happened. Playing along with the charade would be the only option in order to not put a damper on Anna and Emmett's day.

Hiding her emotions from her perceptive pal wouldn't be an easy task. The day they met in third grade Anna must have sensed her discomfort on the playground. Their schoolmates wouldn't let her skip rope. No matter how hard she'd always tried to fit in, she never did. Lily was grateful for Anna's friendship. Those trying experiences gained her an emotional strength she planned to draw from when she faced Ira again.

By late morning, Lily had removed the curlers from her hair, ironed the wrinkles from her dress, applied mascara to her lashes, and brightened her lips with rose lipstick. She left her house and followed the sidewalk around the corner to the church. Guests gathered near the main entrance, so she slipped into the side door. Inside Saint John's Catholic Church light streamed through the gothic stained-glass windows. The rays cascaded onto the pews and across the floor. She stopped in the middle of the aisle at the presence of such beauty. Varying hues of red, orange, yellow, green, blue, indigo, and violet illuminated the walls where fourteen Stations of the Cross hung. A sense of warmth enveloped her, lifting her spirit. If anyone could help her get through this day without falling to pieces, it was Him. She always found Him here. God's presence was everywhere and this was the perfect day for a wedding.

Lily opened the door to the bride's room. Anna stood in front of the mirror in an ivory gown that shimmered against her medium complexion and caramel brown hair. The simple design of the dress accentuated her slim curves. An overskirt draping gave the gown a Victorian appearance while the low back exposed her shoulders. She wore a pair of elbow-length gloves with a small bow at the wrist, which coordinated with the one at her waist. The floor-length skirt flowed around her and the veil met her hemline.

"Your dress is remarkable."

Anna twirled around. "You're here!" She smoothed her hand down the side of the dress. "Thank you. I love how well it turned out too."

"The fabric is beautiful."

"It's charmeuse! I've never worn a material so soft before."

Lily glanced around the room. "Is there anything you need help with?"

"Just this nauseous stomach."

"I know the feeling." She pulled Anna into her arms. "Everything will be fine. I'll be by your side."

"I'll always be here for you too."

Lily caught the reflection of her dress in the mirror and cringed. Ruffles flounced across her bustline and hips where she didn't want the added volume. She appeared out of proportion with her petite stature. "I wish your mother found a more flattering material for me. Look at this color! Who else would you have gotten to wear this yellow dress? I look like a banana!"

"Only you could look so fruity and elegant at the same time." Anna covered her mouth as she giggled into her glove. "I do appreciate you agreeing to my favorite color and for trying to calm my nerves with humor."

"Do you feel better now?"

"Yes."

Lily took hold of Anna's hand. "I think it's time to make that fiancé your husband. Am I right?"

"More than ever."

A few minutes later, Lily stood with Anna's parents at the rear of the church awaiting the procession. As children, they'd played dress-up and Lily had loved being the bride. Her visionary husband would be tall, dark, and handsome. Of course, it wouldn't hurt if he could also be a sweet prince charming. The fictitious childhood dream hadn't met reality with Ira and his faults. Before last night, she'd overlooked many things because of his good qualities like honesty and dependability. Now she couldn't get rid of the pungent taste in her mouth over his lack of shame and immoral character. Anna had what she craved with Emmett. He was a man she couldn't live without, a man who adored her, a man... Lily's arm was nudged.

Anna whispered, "Ready? It's time to go. The music is playing."

A classical bridal tune reverberated from the grand pipe organ in the balcony, creating a rich fullness within the church. Lily moved with the rhythm gazing at the happy couples sitting in the pews. One man sat by himself. He wore a spiffy blue suit which was much fancier than the normal churchgoers every Sunday. As she strolled past him their eyes met, only she found herself unable to continue walking. Warmth swept across her face. At her first attempt to proceed, she stumbled. She refocused her attention on the sanctuary, quickening her pace without regard to the tempo of the music. Among the last few steps to the altar, she took a few deep breaths before turning toward the congregation.

All the guests stood facing the back of the church waiting for the bride, except for the man who kept his gaze upon her. His shoulders were wide and strong as if he could toss her right over and carry her out the door. The instant attraction made her uneasy, especially since nothing like this had ever happened to her before. She couldn't turn away from his good-natured smile. A grin came over her, not only to reciprocate, but because his image matched her expectations from long ago.

For the next hour, Lily faced the altar while the beautiful Latin words bonded Anna and Emmett together as one. Once outside the church, in Columbia Park, family and friends gathered celebrating the newly married couple. Lily walked across the street to her house assisting Anna's mother with the meal she'd brought. They carried food over for the crowd, bringing with them a selection of mixed cheese, cucumber and ham sandwiches, a molded potato salad, spiced Seckel pears, olives, and stuffed eggs. Last night's rain produced a muddy mess in the grass creating a spongy walk, especially for the guests in heels. Lily volunteered to take the tea and coffee around to the tables.

A cluster of Emmett's friends sat together at the far table, along with Ira. He had his back to her but his plaid flat cap along with his black suspenders unmistakably stood out. She could have stomped away as he had the night before, but she told herself she could be strong. Slow and unsteady across the soft ground she approached the table. She stopped behind Ira, listening to the conversation. As she peered at the person seated across from him, her heart thumped in her chest at the well-dressed man from earlier. The only fitting name for such a distinguished man would be Mr. Spiffy.

"I get what you're saying, Ira, but I'm a Ford man myself. Why do you like Plymouth V4's?"

Ira held up a finger. "For one they're a fair price." He held up a second finger. "And two, they have increased the horsepower."

"I agree Fords are a little more for the money, but horsepower, you want to talk horsepower? The Ford V8 is putting out sixty-five horses, and the cast-iron flathead will get you seventy-eight miles per hour. Now that's a car. Besides, any car that's fast enough for Bonnie and Clyde is good enough for me."

Lily held in a chuckle. Mr. Spiffy in his fine felt fedora with an extra-wide ribbon certainly could stand his ground against Ira.

"It's not only about the power. It's about the style." Ira tugged the suspender straps off his shoulders. "See these...they're not just for holding up my pants. They're a one-of-a-kind swanky style all their own, just like the Plymouth."

"You may have a valid point, but did you see the new model Ford came out with this year? It's the cat's meow."

Lily never understood why men talked about cars the way they did. Good looking shouldn't refer to a hunk of steel. She moved to the side of Ira, "Would you care for some more coffee?"

"Yes." He looked up at her with a twisted grin insinuating she'd finally come to her senses. "How about another sandwich too?"

Her jaw tensed. "Certainly, I'll be back in a few minutes." She wanted to say something about his request, but there is a time and place for everything...and now was not the right time.

Ira pointed across the table. "My new friend here from the opposite side of town would probably like one too."

She glanced at Ira's new friend.

Mr. Spiffy tipped his hat. "No, thank you. If you don't mind though, I'd like some tea."

"Of course." A light breeze blew a fresh clean scent of him her way. This time the warmth trickled from the top of her head to the tips of her toes. As she tilted the pitcher, a piercing note bellowed out of the band shelter from across the park. She jerked. Her foot slid backward. And her heel sank. The pitcher moved in unison, splashing tea onto the table and barely missing the man's lap.

"Are you all right?" He grabbed a napkin wiping the spill.

"Yes, I'm sorry. Excuse me." She scurried away. This was not the impression she wanted to make. Now he'd think of her as an awkward, clumsy woman. She should have told Ira to get his food, then she wouldn't have to serve him again. He sure had gall asking her to bring him something. She set the coffee and tea on the serving table. The plate of sandwiches contained only crumbs, so she picked up a few slices of cheese and a stuffed egg, placing them onto a napkin. Ira would have to be satisfied with what she could find.

As she approached, Mr. Spiffy didn't look anywhere other than in her direction. She set the food next to Ira's plate stepping behind him. Ira chattered away about the farm, and the man appeared as disinterested in the new conversation as she was. It must be why he stared at her. She couldn't help but stare back. While she smiled at him, he grinned at her. The longer he looked, the more she couldn't take her eyes off him. He had a few gentle crinkles surrounding the dark intensity of his eyes, giving her the impression of a warm inviting personality.

"Did you forget the sandwich?"

She recoiled at the sound of Ira's voice. "They were gone...sorry."

As Ira turned around, she wanted to leap like a frog on a hot tinplate, but she stayed glaring at the ground. A gentle brush on her arm drew her out of her trance.

Anna leaned into her. "Thank you for serving our guests. Emmett and I appreciate all your help."

Emmett pulled a flask from his jacket. "I've got a little something to top off those drinks." He poured a swig into the cups on the table. "Did everyone enjoy the wedding?"

Mr. Spiffy raised his cup. "I wouldn't have stood up, knelt, or sat so many times for anyone other than you two." He laughed and caused the wrinkles to crease deeper around his eyes. "I'm sure you have your reasons for all the movement. At least I can say I'd never doze off if I attended church here."

He's not Catholic. She wouldn't have guessed he belonged to a different church. But St. John's is the only Catholic church in town. Her ideal man on the outside believed differently than her on the inside. How could they ever be compatible? Her church would forbid it. The town would frown upon it. And her family wouldn't permit it. If he grew up as she did, his religion would be a tremendous part of his life too. A relationship with him would be impossible.

The flat pitch of a baritone horn rang out. "If you'll excuse me, my father's getting ready to play." She turned toward Anna and her new husband. "Mrs. Wolff, would you like to come with me to listen to the band?" She snickered. "You can too, Mr. Wolff."

Emmett shook his head. "Keep a seat open for me." He kissed Anna. "I'll meet both of you later. Where will you be?"

"We'll find a spot up close." Lily locked arms with Anna as they made their way through the oak and maple trees toward the red-bricked shelter. Her father, Eddie, sat in the last row of the second regiment band on the pinewood stage. A dozen men tapped their toes while the tune progressed in harmony. A few open chairs were near the front and they paraded toward the seats. She enjoyed listening to the music, but her attention remained focused on Mr. Spiffy. A man whose real name she didn't even know. Maybe for her sake, she shouldn't find out, but her desire made her touch Anna's arm.

"Who was sitting across the table from Ira?"

"Why are you grinning like that?"

"I am?" She covered her mouth with her hand.

Anna's eyebrows rose. "Why are you asking?"

"I almost dumped tea on him." She leaned closer to Anna's ear. "So, do you know his name?"

"Benjamin Claussen. Emmett worked for him at the Ebbe Company after high school."

"He owns the company? I thought he was our age."

"No, his dad and uncle do. He's at least five or six years older than us." Anna tilted her head toward Lily. "It's my turn to ask a few questions."

"Yes, certainly."

"I noticed you're not yourself today." Anna placed her hand on Lily's. "Is there something you'd like to talk about?"

"What makes you think something's wrong?"

"Don't forget how long I've known you. What aren't you telling me?"

"It's not the right time. Besides, it's your day. Let's not make it about me."

"Are you sure?"

"I'm sure." Lily wanted to confide in her about Benjamin, except that meant she would have to tell Anna about what happened with Ira. Besides, she'd made her decision before anything could potentially develop. It's the best choice; the only choice. But how can there be such a loss when she and Benjamin were never together to begin with?

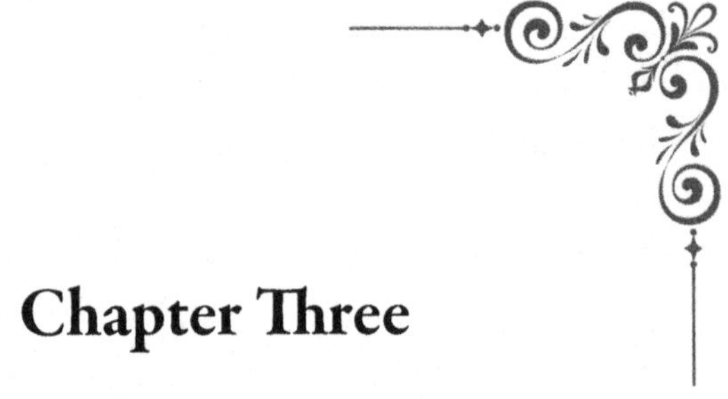

Chapter Three

Benjamin Claussen locked the Ebbe Company's side door. The overcast sky hid the warmth of the sun while the cool breeze chilled him. He flipped the lid on his pocket watch, which displayed a few minutes before six o'clock. He'd never been this late before, and the gang probably started the card game without him.

As he approached his car in the parking lot, Vivian stood next to the fender. If he would have any chance of getting to play tonight, he needed to display the appropriate poker face now. He gave her a grin, revealing his teeth. "Good evening. This is a surprise." He kissed her on the cheek as always. "What brings you here?"

"Can't your girl stop by once in a while?" She squeezed his arm and batted her lashes over sea-green eyes. She was always impeccably dressed and her makeup applied like a movie star on the big screen. "I finished up some shopping in town. I thought I'd stop over."

He glanced around. Never once in the four years of their relationship had she shopped and not bought anything. "I don't see any packages. The stores didn't have anything you liked?"

"They certainly did. My trip was so successful the store is having my packages delivered." Vivian ran her gloved fingers up and down his arm. "Wait until you see the dress I found. It's the perfect shade of blue to emphasize my locks." She swept a strand of her berry red hair aside. "You can tell me how much you like it when you pick me up in a half-hour for dinner."

She's not changing the plans this time. Ever since their engagement this past year she'd insisted on having him do things her way. He was tired of being tolerant. "It's Thursday, the fellows are waiting for me."

"I'm sure you can miss one night of cards." Vivian pouted. "You saw them two days ago at the wedding."

He needed to appease her, so he kissed her on the opposite cheek. "I promised I'd play. I can't go back on my promise now, can I?" His word meant everything. Hers had the sour smell of selfishness.

"You could if you wanted to." She put her hands on her hips. "All you have to do is go there and tell them you can't stay. By that time, I'll be ready."

"I'm sorry." He took her hands in his. "I'll take you out another night. You can wear your new dress then."

Vivian pulled away. "If you loved me, you would take me out tonight. I can't believe you'd choose to spend time with them instead of me."

"How's Saturday? You decide where you'd like to go. I'll make the reservation." The offer came more from obligation than a genuine invitation. Besides, she wouldn't go. She'd be upset for days and not come around until she calmed down. At least then he'd be able to consider his next steps without any pressure from her.

"Make it for wherever you want. I'm not going." She swung around and walked away.

Vivian's heels clicked rapidly upon the ground sounding as if they would break at any second. When the noise faded, Benjamin opened the car door and slid onto the seat. He should be relieved he was able to go, but somehow the situation seemed like the beginning of something worse to come.

Less than four minutes passed until he arrived at Hotel Charles. The main floor housed the restaurant with poker tables scattered near the bar area in the back of the room. A half-wall surrounded three sides of his card pals' usual table but they liked the privacy and the close access to the bar. Benjamin strode through the main dining room amid drifting scents of Thursday's fried chicken special toward Emmett and his cousin Louie. He slipped his hand into his pocket and tossed a handful of change onto the stained felt table before flipping a nickel into the pot. "Sorry I'm late."

Louie grumbled. "You told me you were leaving more than a half-hour ago."

"I forgot about the numbers that needed to be done before the morning. Besides, Vivian stopped by after you were gone and wanted me to take her out tonight."

Louie flicked his cigarette over the ashtray. "That explains a great deal."

"You sound bitter." Benjamin pulled out a padded chair. "What did she ever do to you?"

"It's not what she's done to me." Louie took a puff and blew a cloud of haze into the air, merging with the scents of cigar and pipe smoke. "It's what she's doing to you."

Emmett pulled the cards together into a pile. "I think we should play." He laid them next to Benjamin as he took a seat. "Besides, I'd guess your lateness has more to do with your father grooming you harder than Louie's to take over at Ebbe. Either way, you're both set up pretty sweet for running the company."

Louie snubbed out his cigarette. "All right now, my father works me just as hard as Benjamin's. Ask him who works longer when it comes to fishing season. He's the first one out the door."

"It's true." Benjamin dealt a round. "Five card stud aces high."

"Take it easy on me tonight." Emmett picked up his cards. "I need to come home with some money or I'll have some explaining to do."

Benjamin fanned out his cards. "I'll do my worst." He grinned. "Tell me, the lady in the frilly yellow dress at your wedding...who is she?"

"Lily Vanderhoof. You're not interested in her, are you?"

Louie tossed a coin to the middle. "Of course, he's not. He's got the lovely Miss Vivian tied to his money clip."

Benjamin glanced at Emmett. "She brought me some tea. We never did get around to introductions." He turned toward Louie. "And Vivian doesn't have her hands on any of my money."

"Well don't take this the wrong way, but take a look at Vivian's mother." Emmett pushed two nickels into the kitty.

"You're both plotting against me now?"

"I'm pointing out her mother acts like she's a queen." Emmett cracked his knuckles. "I'm sure you've heard what they say about apples and trees?"

Louie tapped on the table. "One rotten apple spoils the whole tree."

"Both of you are wrong. She's nothing like her mother. And Louie, you mixed two sayings with different meanings again." Benjamin lifted the edge of his card. "I thought we were here to play poker. Not analyze my fiancée."

"You know I'm only pulling your arm."

"Leg." Benjamin tossed in two nickels and raised another.

Louie swept his cards together on the table. "You know me. I don't understand women at all anyway. I'd be lying if I said I did."

Emmett matched the bet. "First fold of the night. You know what that means, don't you, Louie? It's your turn to get the drinks."

"I'm going."

Benjamin was familiar with Louie's harsh comments, but Emmett had never spoken up before. Maybe he should consider their frankness since they both noticed Vivian's altered behavior. It was becoming more apparent these last few months the issue might not go away. He couldn't continue to ignore the problems with Vivian.

"Are you still in?"

Benjamin had three diamonds showing and one in the hole. "Yes, I'm in." He rolled two more coins into the pile.

"Now that Louie left, is there more to the story with Lily?"

"I found her intriguing."

"And?"

"And it's only been a couple days since we met, but there hasn't been a day I didn't think of her." Benjamin put his hand up between them. "Before you say anything, I know I'm engaged. Believe me, I know."

"I don't envy you one bit. The ties you have with Vivian's family...well, any man would dread making the wrong choice."

"I've made my share of bad decisions lately. On the day of your wedding, Vivian was ready to go and at the last minute she changed her mind."

"Why?"

"I told her maybe she could get some ideas from the small wedding you were having. I think it may have annoyed her."

"How come?"

"She said there was no way she'd be seen in a Catholic church, friend of mine or not."

"Well, this friend likes her less and less."

"She always makes more out of everything I'm trying to say. I only tried to remind her of our original plan at First Presbyterian." Benjamin stretched his arms out as wide as they'd go. "Now, it's turned into a gigantic social event."

"Princess Vi doesn't seem too far-fetched, does it?"

Benjamin chuckled. He spun a coin on the table. "I guess not."

Louie returned and pulled out his chair. "Since I lost the first round, I got each of you an extra drink." He pointed to the short waiter headed their way balancing a tray on each of his palms.

"Let's finish this up." Emmett turned his card over showing a pair of kings. "What do you have?"

Benjamin flipped his card over.

Emmett's jaw dropped. "A flush?"

"Luck must be on my side, at least in cards."

The waiter set the tray of drinks on the table and left.

Emmett took out his flask, sloshing some gin into each glass.

Louie passed out the drinks and raised his highball glass. "Here's to three musketeers, all for three and three for all."

"It's all for...forget it." Benjamin grinned and put his glass down. "Let's play. I don't want this luck to cool off."

After an hour, Benjamin's pile of money towered on the green felt. He struck a match and touched it near the bowl of his pipe while taking several gentle puffs. A good smoke always relaxed him, and the challenge of worthy opponents energized him. "Are you in or out, Emmett?"

"Out. This hand was awful. I'm down to the last of my change. My wife isn't going to like this."

Louie tossed his cards on the table. "You sure are on a streak tonight. There's about six dollars in that mound of yours."

Benjamin reached forward, knocking his head on the stained-glass fixture above. The light swung back and forth across the table while he drew the pile of winnings toward him. "We could quit now." He grabbed the shade, centering it above the table.

Emmett grimaced. "One more, I have to win some time. Five-card draw. Deuces wild."

Benjamin picked a coin off the heap and threw it in. "All right, ante up."

Louie matched the bet and stood. "Wait for me, there's quite a dish over there I've had my eye on."

Emmett shouted as Louie lumbered away, "Hurry up, we don't have all night."

"It won't be long. He'll say something wrong like he usually does." Benjamin laughed.

Emmett picked up his hand spreading the cards out between his thumbs. "Do you think you could let me win this last round so I can at least go home with a couple dollars?"

"Now that wouldn't be fair to Louie, would it?" He peeked at his hand. Three tens, a deuce, and the four of diamonds. "Besides, would you even feel good about winning if you knew I let you?"

"Sure, I would."

"Let me see what I can figure out."

Emmett finished his drink and crunched on a piece of ice. "You know there's a way to get the scoop on whether or not Lily mentioned you."

"If you want." His lips curled into a smile.

"Where's your poker face now?"

Benjamin gulped the last of his drink. "It's gone when it comes to Lily. She's so easy on the eyes."

"Shh!" Emmett pointed at the waiter wiping off the next table. "That's her brother Arthur."

"Splendid, all I need is for this to get around town."

"I'm back." Louie slid the chair toward the table. "What don't you want getting around town?"

Benjamin slapped Louie on the arm. "The fact you got shot down again."

"Witty. I knew it ran in the family." Louie rubbed the welt on his arm.

"All right you two, let's play." Emmett held the deck in his hand. "How many you want?'

Louie bent his cards slightly off the table. "I'll take one."

Benjamin wanted to fold for Emmett's sake, but not yet. "One for me too." He tossed away the diamond.

"I'm taking three." Emmett discarded his onto the pile and dealt himself three.

Louie doubled his bet. "I've got a good feeling about this one."

Benjamin couldn't fold now. Besides, if Louie spoke up, he knew he wasn't bluffing. "I'll match your bet and raise you another nickel."

Emmett folded. "Too much for me."

Louie tossed in another nickel and laid his cards out.

"Good hand." Benjamin slowly spread his hand across the felt. "But my full house beats your straight."

"Well, at least I've got a few dollars left, unlike Emmett. Your wife isn't going to be pleased." Louie picked up his coins.

"I should have quit several hands ago." Emmett stacked the cards and slipped them into the box. "I doubt she'll be upset."

"You'd be wrong for sure." Louie flipped a coin in the air, caught it, and slapped in on the backside of his hand. "If a woman says to bring money home, she means it. Heads or tails? Tails, I'm right."

"That's not a proper wager." Benjamin waved a dollar in front of Louie. "I'll bet Anna won't be mad at Emmett."

Louie lifted his hand off the coin. "Heads. All right, we'll play your way. I'll take you up on that bet. There's no way she won't be angry."

Benjamin handed Emmett a dollar. "We'll let him hold the money."

"All right, I'm in, here's mine." Louie put his dollar on top of the other one.

Benjamin winked at Emmett. "This one isn't much of a gamble. With the luck I've been having lately, how can I go wrong?"

Louie stood placing his winnings into his pocket. "You may not be lucky in everything."

"How do you figure?"

"You know how the old saying goes...lucky at cards, unlucky in love."

Benjamin laughed. "For once you said it right."

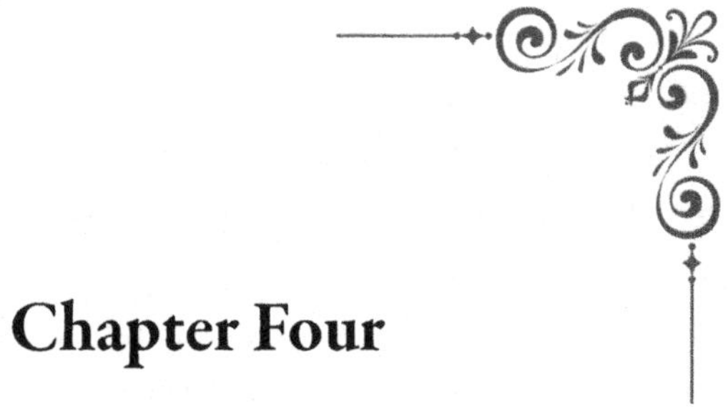

Chapter Four

"Oma?" Lily knocked on the door. "Oma, it's Lily. I'm here with Celia."

"Just go in, Oma probably can't hear us knocking."

Lily opened the door and her sister followed through the foyer into the dark living room. "Oma, are you here?" The drapes were drawn shut creating a dreary aura in the room. Ever since Opa had passed, the house didn't seem the same. Even the scent of his pipe smoke faded each time she visited. She slid the material apart. Particles danced through the rays while the smell of dust tingled in her nose. "It's odd she's not here on a Friday morning."

Celia motioned with her hand. "I think I hear her in the kitchen."

Lily followed through the hall lined with pictures of family members she'd never met. Oma told the best stories about all her ancestors and she could imagine being there with them. As they neared the entryway, Oma stepped in front of them.

"Child!" Oma placed her hand on her chest. "You scared me half to death."

Oma's stark-white hair was tightly drawn around her crown with braids. Lily bit back the giggle forming in her throat. Oma's appearance flawlessly matched her frightened-half-to-death comment. "We didn't mean to. Celia came with me for a visit."

Oma pushed Celia's wheat blonde bangs to the side. "It's good to see you. Let me get a good look at you. I've missed those rare gold-flecked green eyes of yours." She put her hands on either side of Celia's hips. "You're skin and bones. Don't they feed you at the restaurant?"

"Of course they do." Celia laughed. "I work most of my meals off by running to get everyone else's food. I'm eating, please don't worry."

"Both of you sit." Oma pointed to the chairs surrounding the table. "I made some Apfelkuchen this morning. Just the right amount of sugar to fatten you up."

Lily gazed around the yellow painted kitchen. The cakepan cooled on the counter underneath the open window. In the corner, the apple corer had remnants of the last apple peeled. The high cupboard door above was open with the stepstool her short, stout grandmother used to reach the shelves. She pulled out the wooden chair. "I thought I smelled baked apples. I love your apple cake."

Celia sat across from her sister. "I miss your cooking, but that's only second to your tales of the olden days."

"You're here now, eat." Oma set an enormous slice of cake at each place. "What would you like to hear about?"

"You and Opa." Celia picked up her fork. "As long as it doesn't make you sad."

"It's becoming easier now to talk about him and not shed a tear or two. You know, we were happy together for almost fifty years." Oma put a dollop of whipped cream on her slice, passing the dish to Celia. "Not to say times weren't hard, but I wouldn't change any moment spent with your Opa. We made a good life together here. Just look at you two."

Lily scraped the last of the cream from the bowl. Maybe weeks ago she could have pictured one day saying the same about her and Ira. Not anymore. Now she had to become more like her sister and learn to fend for herself. "When did you and Opa get here?"

"The spring of 1883."

"Mother was only one year old." Celia moved her chair closer to the table causing the legs to screech across the tiled floor. "I'm not surprised she never mentioned the voyage. Was it frightening leaving Germany?"

"Yes, but your Opa had a cousin who would write to us from America. We heard of the rich land in Wisconsin, the freedom to practice your religion, and the communities forming among our culture. What Germany lacked, flourished here. So many families had already abandoned their homes and farms. Our small town at the foot of the mountain only had one shoemaker and your Opa still didn't have enough work."

Lily reached out, touching Oma's arm. "Was it harder than these last several years?"

"Much worse. Those times were as tough as an old piece of leather. If it weren't for your Opa's cousin, we'd still be there. I'm indebted to his generosity. You see, he not only sent us news in those letters, but they also contained money." Oma's soft smile widened and the wrinkles around her mouth faded into the larger creases.

Celia's left eyebrow rose. "To come to America?"

"Yes, child. One afternoon a traveling salesman arrived at our door. Not the kind you don't want to see, but the nice kind." Oma snickered.

Lily and Celia laughed.

"I meant he was nice in the sense of helping us with coming to America because we didn't quite have enough for the full fare."

"He sold it to you anyway?" Celia put the last bite in her mouth.

"After your Opa convinced him he needed a new pair of shoes." Oma stacked the plates together. "We left three weeks later." She carried the plates to the sink.

Lily's sister had left home last spring, partially to aid the family with more money than she could make here. The secret other part was a man her maternal cousin thought would be perfect for her in Milwaukee. He wasn't. Yet Celia stayed, figuring her chances in the big city were better both monetarily and romantically. If Lily's family could make it across the world, and Celia could move hundreds of miles, she certainly could find her way.

Luckily, Lily didn't have to travel so far in search of romance. She smiled as her stomach did that funny backward summersault again. Ever since she'd interrogated Anna about Benjamin, something always happened to remind her of him. This time it was the salesman. In Benjamin's line of work as a purchaser, he must deal with a lot of them. From what she'd experienced with him ribbing Ira about cars, he must be as quick-witted as her Opa.

"Lily."

She squinted at Celia.

"What's got you so lost in thought?"

She whispered, "Nothing."

"I don't believe you."

"Ahem!" She glared at Celia with pursed lips.

Oma placed the coffee on the table and set a stack of three saucers with cups next to them. "Pour yourself a cup if you'd like." She sat. "What have you done with yourself in Milwaukee,

Celia? It's a big enough city. You must have found a decent suitor by now."

Celia's shoulders rose as she sucked in air. She sighed. "No Oma, I haven't met anyone yet."

"You can't go through life on your own, child. Doesn't it worry you when you finally decide to settle down, you'll be too old to have a family? You're already twenty-two."

Lily slowly pulled the coffee cup across the table. As long as Oma didn't find out about her estrangement from Ira, she would be safe from her questions. She poured the steaming liquid into her cup and took a sip while peeking over the rim at Celia.

"I'm twenty-three Oma. I just haven't found a good one."

"I think good means a bit different for you. As long as he's a Catholic man who can provide for you, he's good." Oma picked up the percolator. "Need I remind you, the longer you wait, the less chance you'll find a good man."

"No Oma, you shouldn't have to." Celia shrunk in her chair a little.

Lily shrunk even more in hers. Ira met Oma's expectations except she wouldn't be the one to marry him. Oma was the last person Lily ever wanted to disappoint. But could Oma be wrong about what makes a good man's character? Right now things were different than when Oma decided to marry Opa.

"I trust you'll heed my advice." Oma filled her cup. "It comes from my love for you child."

Celia pushed against the chair seat with her hands, straightening the curve in her back. "I understand."

"Your little sister found a good man, isn't that right?"

Lily sprinkled a teaspoon of sugar into her cup and stirred while the liquid swirled around like a devastating tornado. If she withheld the truth from Oma, it wouldn't be right. Except after her strong warning with Celia, her decision could go either way.

"Lily?"

"Yes, Oma."

"Did you hear me? I said Ira's a good man."

The coffee churned under Lily's spoon, mimicking the sensation in her abdomen. In Oma's eyes, he might be good but she wasn't so sure anymore. "He...he's...he was—"

"Spit it out, child."

"Oh, all right...he was a good man."

Oma's eyes widened. "Why? What has he done?"

Lily sighed. "Believe me when I say he's not the man I thought. Right now, I don't know the outlook of our relationship. If I truly state how I feel...well, I'm afraid you'll tell me I'm not getting any younger either. Could we talk about this later?"

"I've lived a long life. I've seen my share of heartache. My words may be harsh, but I only want the best for you and your sister." Oma placed a hand over each of theirs. "Forgive an old woman."

Celia squeezed Oma's hand. "There's nothing to forgive."

"You're not just any old woman." Lily placed her other hand on top of Oma's. "I see you as a wise, mature woman." She smiled.

"I'm pleased to hear you say so." Oma returned the grin. "There are a few items on the matter I'd like to address. Don't be too quick to dismiss Ira. At one time, you agreed to a marriage with him. I can't imagine what could have happened for your feelings to change faster than it takes for a yeast cake to rise."

Lily wanted to spout out how Ira had dismissed her three days ago. He had no regard for her feelings in the least bit. With Oma, she'd always held back. Probably because Oma never seemed to be wrong about anything. Maybe her knowledge came with age, or maybe she was just born with righteousness. Either way, Lily's comments would never sway her grandmother.

Oma shook her head. "Everyone makes mistakes and you certainly don't want to find out yours was too hasty. There is something wrong with this younger generation. A commitment isn't something to make light of in the least bit." Oma pushed her chair away from the table. "It's almost time for my women's church group."

If Oma believes everyone makes mistakes, maybe she does too. And just maybe now Lily had a glimmer of something hopeful in case she ever needed to convince her grandmother. She stood and wrapped her arms around Oma's shoulders. "Thank you for the visit. We'll see ourselves out so you can get ready."

"I'm not sure when I'll be back again." Celia leaned over kissing Oma on the cheek. "I'll try to come back before too long."

"Don't forget to eat a little more while you're away. A man does like a plumper woman." Oma chortled.

"I'll try." Celia followed Lily through the hall to the front door. The latch clicked. "Is Oma getting sterner with age?"

Lily stepped on the stones lying in the grass until she met the sidewalk. "You know she means well. I think she's hiding how hard it is not having Opa around. Didn't you smell the dust? She never used to have a speck of dirt in the house."

"Of course she misses him. However, the way she talked to you about Ira. If she knew what a two-timing man he is, she wouldn't think you should stay with him."

"I couldn't bring myself to tell her what Ira did. She wouldn't understand his promiscuity as we do. Somehow, I'd be blamed since I didn't marry him the first time he asked. And that's the last conversation I want to have with her again. Besides, I would hope Oma wants us to be as happy as she was with Opa." Lily stopped at the corner before crossing the street.

"I'm sure she does. But do you honestly believe love can only be found with a Catholic man who provides for you?" Celia ran in front of her and turned around, promenading backward. "That may have been what Opa was to her. You have to know you need an undeniable love too. How can you love a man who isn't faithful to you?"

"That's why I've been struggling. I loved Ira with all my heart. You know me, once I fall in love, I fall hard. I just don't know if I can get beyond the pain he's caused."

"There is one sure way to get over a love."

Lily stopped walking. "And I'm sure you'll be the one to help me out with that, won't you?"

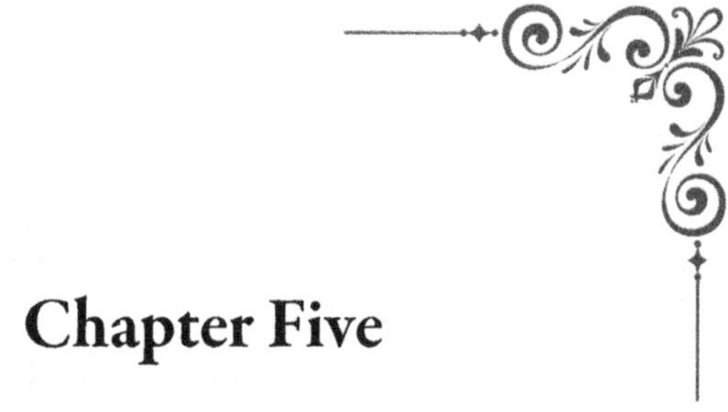

Chapter Five

The bell chimed on the cash register at Livingston's Women's Wear totaling twenty-eight dollars and thirty-five cents. The most money Lily had ever spent on her wardrobe. She chose twelve dresses, two coats, one slicker, one plain brimmed slouch hat, four pair of hose, along with two chemises. She'd saved for this day for months but hadn't been sure if she should spend all of it on herself. Celia could be quite convincing, especially when using the same tactics as Oma. Her sister insisted if Benjamin pursued her that she needed the proper fashion to meet his expectations. Lily wasn't sure it mattered since he hadn't taken his eyes off her in the dreadful banana dress. Besides, wouldn't he have tracked her down in these last four days? She'd heard nothing from him.

Rain splattered against the storefront window. She pulled her new slicker on, hid the packages underneath, and went out the door. The large awnings hanging over the sidewalk provided some shelter as the rain whipped through the air.

At the intersection, puddles already pooled. Keeping water out of her shoes would be tricky. She hopped over the rushing stream. Away from the shelter of the buildings, the wind propelled her around like a rag doll. The brown paper packages slipped under her raincoat. She squeezed them tighter against her body. A few more blocks stood between her and home.

Near the edge of the last busy street, she glimpsed a black car turning the corner headed toward her. She took a split second to move away from the curb, but the car hit the puddle directly in front of her. Water shot up underneath her slicker. The rush of cold water forced her arms horizontal like a stone statue. Her packages fell to the ground. She shrieked.

The car came to an abrupt halt and reversed to where she was standing. As the passenger door flung open a deep masculine voice spoke from the shadowed interior.

"I'm so sorry, are you all right?"

"Of course I'm not all right! I'm soaked!" How could he have not seen her? He'd barreled right at her. She turned her back and knelt, grabbing one of the packages by the twine. The paper had reacted like a sponge, pulling filthy water from the ground.

"Let me help you." The man crouched down gathering her scattered wet purchases.

At least he had some common courtesy to assist her. The rain hadn't let up one bit. She needed to get the clothes out of these packages soon. Worst of all, if the water soaked into her silk chemises they'd be ruined for sure.

The lapel he had tugged up tight against his neck and the hat he'd pulled down around his ears hid his face...until he turned toward her.

Their eyes met. She squeezed the package tight to her chest.

"Lily, I didn't recognize you."

How could it have been him? She opened her mouth. Nothing came out.

"Let me introduce myself." He moved forward extending his hand. "I'm Benjamin Claussen. Remember? We met at the wedding. I'm a friend of Emmett's."

She must look like a drowned animal. Why did it have to be him? A shiver ran through her, not from the cold but him.

"You do recall who I am?" He grinned.

"Of course, I almost spilled tea on you." Lily wiped water from her face and recovered her poise. "Is this repayment?" She smiled.

"No, definitely not."

She held out her hand and he took it in his. The warmth of his grip sent a flicker of electricity through her like the lamps at the park in a storm.

"Will you let me give you a ride home? It's the least I can do."

"Yes, thank you." She released his hand slowly, enjoying the strength and warmth.

Benjamin opened the back door and placed her items on the seat. "You're shaking. Allow me." He removed his jacket, placing it around her shoulders. "Hopefully this will warm you some."

The material of his suitcoat had a much softer feel than her father's. The earthy, musky wood scent wrapping around her smelled heavenly. Lily pulled both sides of the lapel tighter to her neck, she pushed her new garments over on the seat and slid in. "My house is over on Chestnut." The pipe smoke in his car had the same sweet scent as her Opa's. She smiled. However, the dark scent of a strong sweet lavender mixed with vanilla seemed too feminine for Benjamin. The embedded perfume had to be from the fiancée Anna mentioned. She buried her nose in his jacket shoulder, avoiding the smell.

"All right." He shut the door and went around to the driver's side hopping into the seat. "Is that across from the park where the wedding was?"

"Yes."

He adjusted the mirror. "If it's not too forward, I have a question for you."

She took the cloche off her head shaking the water onto the floormat. "What is it?"

"Why did you sit in the back instead of up here in the front?"

Had he wanted her to sit up front with him? "Etiquette, I imagine. I've always sat in the back except when I'm with relatives."

He pulled away from the curb. "What are you doing walking out in this weather?"

"I didn't have much choice." She held back a grin. "I would have been fine in this slicker if it hadn't been for the man who almost drowned me with his car."

"I said I was sorry."

She laughed. "My regular Saturday morning shift ended at Livingston's."

"It's a women's clothing store, right?"

"Yes, today of all days I decided to buy a few things." She touched her soggy parcels on the seat. "I should have waited for nicer weather." She might just have to resort to her old clothes to impress him if these ended up being stained.

"If I ruined any of your things let me know." He downshifted and turned the corner. "I will pay you for whatever is damaged."

"Thank you for the offer." He had a genuine kindness, unlike Ira. Without a doubt, he was the most striking man she'd ever met. His endearing smile warmed her inside while his character so far had been nothing but magical. She stiffened, bracing herself for the last turn. "My house is the white and green one here on the right."

Benjamin pulled over.

"Thank you for the ride. It was wonderful to see you again."

"Please allow me to open the door for you."

"Certainly." His politeness was a refreshing change. Her eyes followed him around the car until he reached the door and opened it. As she stepped out Mary ran toward her. What was Ira's sister doing here? Ira had never involved her in their disagreements before. Something had to have happened. "Mary, what's wrong?"

"It's Ira. He's sick."

An ache struck her throat and sank to her chest. No wonder she hadn't heard from him. She intended to meet him tomorrow after church at their usual time in the restaurant. Too much time had passed since their disagreement and a decision about their future needed to be discussed.

"Is he going to be all right?"

"The doctor thinks so. I knew you'd want to come out to see for yourself. He's been confined to his bed since yesterday."

"Benjamin, this is Mary." She picked up her items from the back seat. "I'm going to run into the house and get out of these wet clothes. Mary, can you wait here? I'll go back with you to your house."

"Nonsense. I will take you both in my car." Benjamin held the door open for Mary. "We'll wait here for you."

Lily took a few moments to open the packages and hang the items before changing into dry clothes. She hurried as fast as she could, slipping on the first dress she grabbed and ran down the stairs out the door. Benjamin met her at the car. She scooted in next to Mary. "I appreciate you taking us."

"You're welcome."

"Their farm is on the road past the mill. Do you know which one I'm talking about?"

"Yes."

Lily turned her attention toward Mary. "What happened?"

"The doctor thinks it's a combination of influenza and overexertion." Mary twisted her fingers through her hands. "He was chopping wood out back when he collapsed."

"How long had he been out there?"

Mary's eyes welled with tears. "It couldn't have been too long. Maybe a half-hour until I went out there to get him for supper." Her voice cracked. "I'd taken him some water earlier. He seemed tired, but he didn't want to quit working. I should have stayed with him."

"Shh! It's not your fault." She caressed Mary's shoulder. When Lily's brother Arthur had come down with a fever, she'd been beside herself with worry too. Mary and Ira were just as close. "No one knew what was going to happen."

Mary sniffled. "Ira doesn't know you're coming." She wiped her cheek on her coat sleeve. "He asked me not to tell you."

"I see." Ira wouldn't have mentioned the quarrel to his seventeen-year-old sister who liked to be the center of attention. "What reason did he give you?"

"He didn't want you to see him like this."

"How come?"

"He thought he'd come across as weak."

"I wouldn't think that. He's sick." Lily patted Mary's hand. "I'm glad you didn't listen to him. It will all work out, you'll see." *A little white lie can't be so bad, especially if Mary's conscience is put at ease for now.*

"I hope you're right." Mary pointed at Benjamin and whispered, "Why did he bring you home?"

"It's not what it appears. He accidentally splashed me so he offered me a ride."

"That's all?"

"Yes." Lily certainly had no intention of telling Mary about her brother being such a nincompoop and how Benjamin had been nothing but a gentleman around her. She peered out the windshield at the little brown two-story house. "Benjamin, it's the farm here on the right." Her nerves heightened as he pulled into the driveway, stopping near the front porch. He shut off the engine and got out.

Benjamin opened the back door. "I'll wait here until you're through. Take as much time as you need."

Several minutes later Lily held onto the railing, easing her way up the narrow stairs toward Ira's room. She wiped sweat from her hands onto the waistline of her dress. The house appeared tidy as usual but stale warm air mixed with a medicinal odor made breathing a bit unpleasant. Each step her foot shook before it landed on the short treads. Ira had never been sick enough to be laid up like this. Nerves pulsated throughout her body and she halted multiple times. Would he be angry she'd come to see him?

As she reached the landing, she turned the way Mary mentioned. Her insides twisted like an old rag wrung out to wash the floor. If she didn't go in now, she feared the ache would never go away. *Ira's too young and healthy to have anything seriously wrong.* Or had that idea come to mind to comfort her? She held the doorknob until the knot faded, turning just enough until it unlatched. The door opened slightly. She whispered through the crack. "Ira?"

"Who is it?"

She opened the door a smidge more. "It's me, Lily. May I come in?"

"Wait a moment."

The bed creaked a few times and it went silent.

"You can come in now."

The doorknob slipped from her sweaty hand, flinging the door open the rest of the way and striking the wall. She flinched. Ira had the sheets pulled up to his neck even though his mussed-up blond hair was damp around the edges causing the curls to sag. The usual pinkish coloring of his face didn't exist as his complexion matched the whiteness of his sheets.

"I hope you're not upset I'm here." She pulled a chair near the end of the bed and sat, hoping Ira didn't notice her shaky legs. "I had to come and see for myself you were all right." She glanced around, noting the room had dark wood halfway up the wall. Above, creamy-light colored wallpaper depicted varying scenes with houses, trees and people in the outdoors. The room, although a little dated, seemed to suit him.

"How are you?"

"I'm fine. I've told everybody, but it doesn't matter. All this fuss is foolish. Mary wasn't supposed to tell you anyway." He folded his arms over his chest. "I'm surprised you even came."

He didn't appear fine to her. "Your family cares about you... I do too, or I wouldn't have gotten so...never mind."

"You embarrassed me in public with your questioning."

"I didn't mean to."

"Everything should have been over when I said I was sorry." He folded the covers down around his waist revealing a sweat-dampened striped pair of pajamas.

"I'm sorry for humiliating you." Lily tucked her hands between her knees. "How long do you need to stay in bed?"

"Doc said it could be up to a week until I get all my strength back. It's not right for me to be laid up like this with so much work around here. The hired hands can't do all the chores. I have to get out of this bed."

Ira had been lucky their family farm had done so well during these times. Her life would be different if they got married but she didn't doubt he could take care of her. "I'm sure your family would agree it's best to listen to the doctor. Take it easy for a while. If you push yourself too fast, what good are you then?"

"Will you come out and visit me if I stay in bed?" He tilted his head. "I've missed you."

Lily couldn't speak. Her mouth was drier than a scouring pad. He certainly had a way of pulling her in with such a sad expression.

"Fine, I will rest for one week, except then—"

"Good, now tell me what happened."

"Not much to say other than the heat got to me."

"You've worked in the warmth before; besides it hasn't been very hot yet." A stench she'd never smelled before lingered in the air. And it wasn't the distinct scent her family members had when they'd come down with influenza. "Are you sure that's all?"

"Well...I suppose it could be something."

Lily scooted off the seat and strolled behind the chair to rest her palms on the back. "What else has been going on?"

"I've been tired lately. I figure it's on account of all the extra fieldwork." He braced his arms on the bed rising upward onto the pillow.

"Did you mention it to the doctor?"

"No." Ira shrugged his shoulders. "I didn't think anything of it till you asked."

He didn't seem as concerned as she was about the diagnosis. "It might mean something for your condition." She still wasn't so sure she'd been told everything. Maybe he made light of it to ease her from worrying. Although, that didn't seem like something he would do. More than likely, he didn't ask the doc any questions about his illness.

"Don't get sore, but your hair's looking awfully shabby."

"Why would you say something like that?" She put her hands up in the air. "Didn't you hear it raining? As soon as I heard, I rushed here to check on you and make sure you were fine." Heat radiated from her cheeks to her ears. "Now that I have, I'm going to go. You need your rest."

"Lily, I didn't mean—"

"I don't want to slow your recovery." She moved the chair against the wall.

"You're not walking home, are you?"

"No." *Why is he asking about my well-being? A minute ago, he didn't seem concerned.* "Emmett's friend gave me a ride. He's waiting for me. I should go." She went toward the door.

"So that's how it is now that I'm stuck in this bed."

"No, that's not how it is. I'm not Bessie and he's not you."

"Clever." Ira straightened himself to a sitting position. "Does that mean you'll be back?" His bottom lip jutted out.

Lily took a deep breath and slowly exhaled. "I'm not making any promises." She waved as she glided out the door.

After speaking with Ira's family, who appreciated her stopping by, Lily exited onto the porch. Benjamin sat in his car with his hands draped over the steering wheel. Twice in less than a week, chance had brought them together. The first time he captivated her by his charm. Today she experienced the most kind-hearted man she'd ever met.

Benjamin got out of the car and approached her. "Sorry, I didn't see you. Are you ready to leave?"

"Yes, I am." She proceeded down the porch stairs. The rain had let up enough she wouldn't get too wet in the short walk. "Thank you for waiting."

"My pleasure." He opened the back door.

Lily crouched down and sat on the seat while he held her hand. As she glanced up, she caught his gaze and turned away. The skin on his hand was so soft, so uncalloused, she could hold onto it forever.

"Lily."

Her eyes fluttered up at him.

"I'm going to have to let go of your hand."

His deep brown eyes held her concentration. "Yes." And she allowed her hand to slip from the warmth of his grasp.

"You'll need to bring in your leg too...so I can shut the door."

"Of course." She moved over to the center of the seat and hoped he hadn't noticed her foolishness. He shut her door and got in. What if he had noticed her reaction to him? Did he feel the same connection when they touched? A connection that could be right, but also wrong in so many other ways. She wouldn't be like Bessie. She couldn't. He could only be a friend and she'd make sure that's how he saw her. Friends just like how Ira talked to him. "How long have you had this car?"

"This ol' girl?" He slapped the dash. "I picked it up last year. Got a good deal since she'd been in an accident. My cousin Louie helped me fix her up." He pulled out of the driveway. "It's a fine ride, and I even saved some dough."

"What type is it?"

"Model A Ford Sedan with a two-o-one."

"What year?"

He ran his hand across the dash. "Twenty-nine."

"That's the year I graduated from McKinley. She can't be that old of a girl."

"For her it is. She's lived half her life already." He patted the dashboard and moved his hand to the steering wheel. "As for you, you're far from old. If I thought you were old, I'd be ancient. I graduated in twenty-three."

"Oh my, you are ancient." She laughed.

He stopped at the intersection. "You didn't say how Ira was doing?"

"I think he'll be fine." No need for her to get into any of the concerns she'd had for Ira. Maybe she was wrong thinking there was more to his condition. She certainly hadn't studied like the doctor had to get his degree.

"That's good to hear."

The mention of him changed the air. Why had Ira made such a rude comment? Lily tried to push his words from her mind. She scooted between the two front seats moving her head from side to side and checking her reflection in the rearview mirror.

Her hair laid a little flat, but Ira had seen worse. Benjamin's eyes appeared in the mirror looking back at her.

"Is Ira a relative of yours?"

She swallowed several times. "Ira was my...he is my fiancé." Benjamin moved his head and she could no longer see his eyes. "I'm not sure what he is anymore." She placed her right hand on the back of the passenger seat.

"Sounds like we're in the same dilemma."

"You're engaged too?" Anna had told her about Vivian and even though she didn't like hearing him say it, she was glad he told the truth.

"I am, but lately I've had concerns."

"Does she know how you feel?"

"No, it doesn't appear so. It's not for a lack of trying." He downshifted. The car slowed as they reached the city limits.

Lily covered her mouth. "Achoo."

"Gesundheit. Hope you're not catching a cold."

Vivian's perfume tingled in her nostrils. She didn't want to talk about the subject of their fiancées anymore. "Where do you work with your father?"

"At the Ebbe Company."

Hopefully, Benjamin didn't notice the slip-up of her saying he worked with his father. "That's on Main Street, isn't it?"

"Yes, I work with my father's cousin and his son Louie."

"The one who helped you with the car?"

He nodded. "My father and my uncle went into a partnership with Hans Ebbe. When he died in the early twenties, they took over the company." He shifted gears. "Louie and I are next in line to take over."

"How is it working with family?"

"For the most part, it's good. My father likes to have things done a certain way." He turned his head slightly toward her. "I should say, his way. That's why it's difficult sometimes because you have to know what he's expecting you to do."

"I can see that would make things a little challenging." She rested her hand on the seat as they turned the corner onto Chestnut. "You're blessed to have a profession you like."

"That is true. I'm grateful, especially in these times." He coasted to a stop, set the brake, and got out.

Lily waited until he opened the door. He offered his hand and she took hold. "I appreciate you taking me home twice, but maybe the next time you'll watch where you're driving." She raised her face toward him as he drew her out of the car.

He smiled. "I sure will." He steadily pulled her hand while the distance between them inched shorter and shorter. He shut the door and moved into her personal space, towering above her.

The rich chocolate tones in his eyes deepened toward the center, drawing her in like a tunnel to his soul. She teetered on the edge of falling into his arms and allowing him to caress her lips with his. Time seemed to stand as still as her feet. Within the closeness, his warm breath fell upon her face. Neither of them stirred.

"Halloo, Lily!"

She jumped back, letting go of his hand and turning toward the direction of the shout. Her older brother Arthur sat on the porch chair with his elbows positioned on his knees and his hands tucked under his chin. His interruption had saved her from making a horrible mistake. She doubted Arthur even realized what might have happened. However, if he had sensed an attraction she needed to find out and make certain he said nothing. "I should probably go in."

"Now that you know where I work, you can stop in." He gave her a warm, inviting grin.

"I'm not so sure."

"Please just stop in and let me know if any of your clothes were ruined. I wouldn't feel right if I didn't pay for the damage. You'll do that, won't you?"

"All right, I can't promise, but I will think about it."

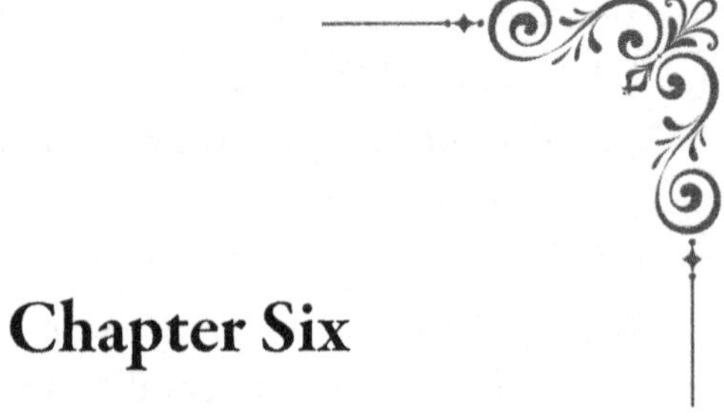

Chapter Six

Vivian DuCate turned the china plate over, carefully rubbing her index finger across the red manufacturer's stamp. The symbol of a wreath bordered a capital M with the words "Noritake" above and "Made in Japan" below. She tipped the plate over again checking her reflection in the glossy finish. On the front side of the ivory dish, a gold band surrounded the edge with a bordered pastel design in a floral print. A perfect image of her face cast back. Only special occasions brought out the twelve-piece china setting. Decoration Day marked a traditional celebration for her family as well as all the guests they invited to commemorate it. Ever since she found a niche in designing an elegant table, the task became hers.

She stacked the plate along with the others on the walnut sideboard. Sliding open the serving drawer, she pulled out the ivory lace linen tablecloth. The flower design within each six-by-six-inch square was hand-stitched together to complete the elongated tablecloth, a favored family heirloom, and the foundation for all the additional items set on it. She draped the cloth on top, running her hand across the material, smoothing the wrinkles as she sauntered around the table. The delicate lace caught her ring at the edge of the last corner. She stopped to unhook the string. A half-inch run appeared. She touched her fingertips on either side to pull the material taut. The appearance didn't change. Her mother wouldn't be pleased, but Vivian would be the one who needed to accept the imperfection. As soon as she married Benjamin, the heirloom would be hers.

Twisting the engagement ring back and forth on her finger, she tried to catch the light just right to make it sparkle. The day Benjamin asked to marry her she hadn't hesitated. Even though the ring hadn't been the precise one she wanted. Instead of his grandmother's ring, he'd bought an art deco design in 18k white gold with a round center diamond in a square setting. Along the sides, a beaded row ran through the middle surrounded by intricate scrollwork. The man meant more to her than the ring she hadn't received. He came from a quality family of good beliefs and held a position that could support her in the manner she'd grown accustomed to. She regarded herself as one of the fortunate women to discover a man of his caliber.

At each place setting, she carried over the required pieces of china, silverware, and stemware, situating them an equal distance apart. Atop each plate, an ivory linen napkin in the shape of a boat finished the commemorative look she desired. All that remained were the final touches to dress up the table: some candlesticks of varying sizes, hand-drawn name cards, along with a few well-positioned fresh-cut flowers. She moseyed through the kitchen and into the back entryway, grabbing the garden shears on her way out the door.

The stone path alongside the house led her under the wooden archway of overgrown violet and pink morning glories with hydrangea bushes lining the edges. People who went by probably didn't realize such a lovely garden existed beyond the dense shrubs. She wandered through the winding pathway toward the center of the garden where all the paths met at a tall stone obelisk. The perfect flowers would symbolize the day, along with emitting a wonderful fragrance. There were so many to choose from.

Within twenty minutes, she gathered enough cut flowers to fill a large centerpiece vase. The bouquet consisted of red garden roses, white astilbes, and blue clematis. She gathered them into a pile, placing them in the crook of her arm. As she exited through the archway onto the stone path, Benjamin ran up alongside the house opposite to her course.

"Vivian!"

She continued on her way. The thorns were poking into her skin. She released her hold as much as she could without dropping them.

"Vivian, wait!"

She stopped and laid the flowers onto the ground. "I heard you the first time. I can only imagine what the neighbors are thinking. What is so urgent?" He'd better be here to apologize for not taking her out to dinner.

"I wanted to catch you before you went into the house." He took a few short breaths. "What are you doing with all those flowers?"

This didn't sound like the apology she was looking for. "They're for the dinner party tonight. You're still planning on coming?" If he didn't, she would be the only one without an escort. "Or did you forget?"

"No, it's the reason I came by. What time should I be here?"

"Five. I'm quite certain I mentioned that last week."

"If you did, it slipped my mind." He bent down, gathering the bouquet. "I can help you with these if you'd like."

"That's sweet of you." She placed her hand on the back of his arm as they strolled down the path. "Father told me yesterday he figured a way for Fredrick to cater our wedding dinner."

"When will he find out for sure?"

"With any luck, soon. Once we have available dates, we can move forward rather quickly." She put her other hand on the front of his arm and squeezed. "I'm becoming rather excited the closer we get."

"It's not too overwhelming for you, is it?"

"You should know me by now. I enjoy planning."

"I just thought you might be under too much stress. A smaller wedding might be better." He stopped walking. "The one you couldn't attend was pleasant."

When will he learn to keep those comments to himself? "Our list is still growing." She wanted everyone possible to attend her day. "A small one won't work for what I've envisioned."

"Then I'll leave it up to you."

As they approached the back-porch steps, she caught sight of his car out on the street. Something about it didn't seem quite right. "How come your silver piece is missing from the middle of the tire?"

"Is it?" He turned toward the car. "It must have fallen off when I hit a puddle in the downpour and ended up giving a lady a ride home."

"A lady?" She had better be unattractive and old. "What lady?"

"The unfortunate one I soaked when I wasn't paying attention." He stared at the ground and shuffled his feet. "I couldn't leave her out there, especially since it was my fault."

"Who is she?"

"Lily Vanderhoof. Have you heard of her?"

"No. Where does she live?"

"By Columbia Park."

One side of her lip curled. "Now I understand why I don't know who she is. She's one of *those* families who live north of the tracks."

"She's a fine person." He rubbed his jaw. "After what I did, she was still pleasant to me. I'm sure I ruined some of her clothing."

"I will socialize with my own kind. I suggest you do the same." She took the blossoms from him. "Ouch! I need to go in and finish the table. Don't be late."

At half-past five, the housemaid led Benjamin into the front room where everyone gathered. She should have told him four-thirty. At least then he would have arrived well before the other guests. He sauntered through the crowd shaking hands and stopping to chat. He'd given her time to take a few deep breaths. Perhaps that was his intention. She sensed he knew she couldn't stay angry with him for too long. Particularly not when he appeared in his luxurious gray herringbone suit with a crisp white handkerchief tucked into the breast pocket.

She grinned at him as he approached. "Glad to see you made it on time."

"Sorry, just a little late." He showed her a small space between his thumb and index finger. "Your dress is delightful. It's festive for the occasion." He surveyed the room. "It seems your parents invited a good crowd to dinner this evening. There are a couple of new faces I've never seen before."

A compliment about her dress and an apology helped to dismiss his lateness. "The man in the brown suit is Mr. Johannes, a neighbor from around the corner. I don't think you've met him."

"No, I haven't."

"The couple near my father is the Hansens." She took his arm as he turned toward them. "Harvey is the new bank manager who came to town last month. On his right is his wife, Nettie." She leaned toward him. "Father said it's best to be friendly with the bankers since you never know when you might need them."

"That's true."

"In any case, there's a scandal about the Hansens."

"You know I don't approve of engaging in gossip."

Vivian fluttered her eyelashes.

"All right, what is it?"

"First let me say if people didn't want others to talk about them then they shouldn't behave inappropriately."

"It may not be true."

"It is. I'm convinced of it."

He shook his head. "All right. What did you hear?"

"Nettie worked for Harvey as his secretary before coming to town." Vivian lowered her voice to an audible whisper. "A little more than an employee from what I heard. Harvey had a fiancée at the time too." She placed her hand on the side of her mouth, leaning closer to his ear. "The fiancée found out about Nettie. Apparently, the fiancée didn't want to give up too easily and told Harvey she was carrying his baby. Definitely a bad idea on her part. I don't know what she was thinking letting everyone know she'd given in to temptation. Well, for the fiancée it worked since Harvey fired Nettie and hired a new secretary."

"I presume the fiancée wasn't pregnant."

"That's right. After three months, Harvey found out about the fiancée's deception and ended it for good this time. Not long after, he went back to Nettie. When the position became available here, they thought it best to move to a different town."

Benjamin didn't say anything.

"It's quite the disreputable story," Vivian smirked. "The way I see it, they all got what they deserved. The fiancée ended up marrying a poor man and the Hansens were sent out of town. What goes around comes around."

"Well, I imagine it's better Mr. Hansen figured out how he felt before he ended up marrying the wrong person."

"You're defending his actions." She folded her arms, scowling at him.

"I'm not, but marrying someone you're not truly in love with isn't a good plan either. As a matter of fact, this story only proves my point."

She could feel her face heating up. "It's obvious to me he didn't take his commitment to the proposal very seriously." Her temple throbbed.

"Vivian." He took her hands. "Look at me."

"How can you condone what he's done?" She tensed her hands against his.

"I was only trying to give you another perspective."

"I know what he did to her." She stomped her foot. "Infidelity is deplorable."

Let's not argue." Benjamin pulled her closer. "I understand what you're saying, but people are staring." He stroked her hair. "We can discuss this another time."

Vivian's lip quivered. "Fine." *He can be reprimand later.*

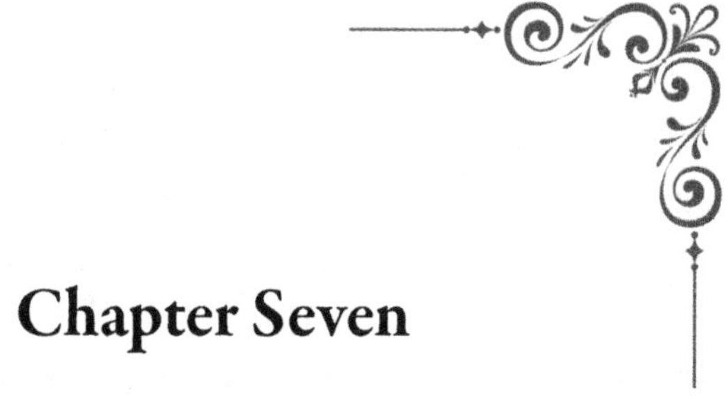

Chapter Seven

Benjamin sat at his desk with his suit jacket draped on the back of his oxblood leather office chair. He turned the dial on the copper calendar to display the month and day of the week—June and Wednesday. The last trainload should arrive sometime this afternoon. The timing varied depending on how many rail cars the switch car needed to bring into the docks. He checked his open orders as he expected the supply of hay, grain, and feed along with flour, potatoes, coal, lime, and lumber. In recent months, the Ebbe Company advertised they would arrange the financing as part of FDR's New Deal program on lumber for home building and remodeling projects. As a result, he'd increased inventory counts several times per week to accommodate the ordering demand.

The second hand on his pocket watch had stopped moving. It read four-forty. He turned it over to open the back. On his first day with the company his father had given him the timepiece with an inscription on the cover—*Time spent wisely is time well spent*. As of tomorrow, on the fifteenth, it would be ten years.

Back then, he almost didn't accept the position since he'd wanted to go out on his own like his older brother Robert who'd become a traveling salesman. Being the last son in the family, the odds were against him choosing his own path. Any attempt would have earned him the same distress his brother went through. More than eight months passed before his parents and brother reconciled. Benjamin didn't have the heart to cause them added pain. Neither had his younger spinster sister when she'd assumed her role in the bookkeeping department several years later. Despite his parents' demand, working at Ebbe turned out to be good for him. However, their insistence on courting Vivian four years ago wasn't turning out so well.

Benjamin inserted the key hanging from the watch chain into the hole and wound the pocket watch clockwise. Familiar shuffling footsteps echoed in the hall, approaching his door. That noise could only be his cousin Louie, who never picked up his feet or a woman for that matter. Still, most people assumed they were brothers, not cousins. Probably because of their similar dark features and stature but that's where it ended. Not only did he walk the opposite of his cousin, with long decisive steps, but he had a far better sense of humor. "Louie, I figured it was you. Do those cuffs on your fancy pants weigh you down and make you drag your feet?"

"Ha, ha. You're one big jokester this morning." Louie leaned against the doorframe crossing his arms over his chest.

"Do you have the time?"

Louie tugged the watch from his pants pocket. "Ten-twenty give or take a few minutes." He tapped on the glass face. "Sometimes she runs a little slow."

Benjamin turned the watch crown clockwise, adjusting the hands. "Well, ten-twenty it is."

Louie motioned with a tilt of his head. "I see your father-in-law's in the office. Can't wait till we're one big happy family around here."

Benjamin rolled his eyes upward. "Officially, he's not my father-in-law—yet. I still call him Walter." If everything went the way he'd planned, Walter wouldn't be his relation and Ebbe wouldn't be affected by his decision. It was one thing to choose for himself, but the business affected his whole family. Vivian's father had professional ties with the family well before Benjamin started working for his father. Even before their business association, a church group, The Presbyterian Brotherhood, played a significant role in his father's relationship with Walter. Benjamin could only hope the long history between his father and Walter would stay intact.

Louie approached the desk and grabbed a piece of paper off the edge. "Well then...any idea what Walter's working on with Uncle Christian?" He glanced at the document for a moment and tossed the paper back onto the pile.

Benjamin tucked the watch into his vest pocket. "A large bid two counties over." His father gave Walter the lowest markups due to his personal connections even though their business practices were on opposite spectrums. Walter's deals were based on how much his wealth would increase, not on how people would be impacted. "It sure is hot in here."

Louie placed his hands on the desk and leaned toward Benjamin with a peacockish grin. "Am I making you uncomfortable with your pending nuptials?"

"Nope, not at all." Benjamin rolled his shirt sleeves up to his elbows and loosened his tie. "Once the arrangements are finalized, you'll see."

"I'll see what?" Louie pulled a handkerchief from his inside jacket pocket and tossed it to Benjamin. "Take this and clean up your obvious signs of nervousness."

"I shouldn't have said anything, but you're going to find out soon enough." He hoped Louie could keep this to himself. "Once the negotiation is done with Vivian's father, I'm breaking my engagement."

"That's the best news I've heard all year and then some." Louie rubbed his hands together. "What took you so long?"

"You look like a prospector who found gold." Benjamin shook his head. "Try to contain yourself."

"Oh, I can't contain myself." Louie tipped his head toward the ceiling and made kissing noises into the air. "I'll bet you're going after the girl in the frilly dress from the wedding. Lily, isn't it?"

"Can't you ever be serious? If anyone could understand how complex of a situation this is, it should be you." Walter may very well not conduct business with them ever again but Benjamin had to take that chance. Lily had shown him a glimpse of what he deserved for his future and Vivian fell short of those expectations. "This chat is only between us."

"Of course. You know, I'm only ribbing you." The front door chimed. "Got to get back to work."

Maybe it was too quick on his part to tell Louie about his pending plans, except saying it aloud made his decision concrete. One step closer to making his own choices. No matter how much Mother wouldn't like it, he needed to be stronger than a house's support beam. Eventually, she would come around. Probably. It was hard to tell since Vivian's mother, Deloris, and his mother were friends. But a life with someone he no longer loved would be much worse than the short time of awkwardness his mother would have with her friend. Besides, he'd gone along with everything else his parents wanted him to do, especially his mother.

She doted on him. Would he remain in her good graces if he went against her wishes or would he end up like his brother, begging for forgiveness? More importantly, could his mother accept someone other than Vivian for his future?

"Benjamin, someone is here to see you." Louie stood in the doorway with a goofy grin. "I insisted she sees you instead of me relaying her message." He motioned for the person behind him to stroll in.

"Lily! What a surprise." Benjamin got up from the chair. If he would have placed a bet she'd stop by, he would have lost. Her hesitation three weeks ago seemed more like a fold than a bluff. "Please, come in."

Louie pulled the door shut, giving a thumbs-up through the pane of glass. He twisted around, displaying his backside while running his hands up and down his sides as if he were having the kiss of his life.

Benjamin bit the smirk on his bottom lip. The gestures of approval from Louie didn't shock him as much as Lily did. He couldn't stop staring. She was breathtaking. "Have a seat. I'm pleased you stopped by." His legs were weak and unsteady like the giddiness from an unexpected gift. He hurried around to the front of the desk and leaned against the corner while she settled in the chair before his desk. The frilly lace around her neck harmonized with the gentleness in her heart. Only a couple of feet stood between them. "I like your dress. Is it one of your new ones?"

Her cheeks instantly pinked. "Thank you, it is." She brushed her hand across her lap. "It's wonderful to see you again too. I didn't want to bother you, but Louie insisted you weren't busy.

You certainly can tell the two of you are related. I suppose you've heard that before."

"Yes, I have." She looked amazing in that greenish-blue dress, but she could wear anything and he'd still have to clench his jaw so it wouldn't fall open. Her outward appearance drew him in. What made her so special though was the beauty from within. Never had he met someone who captivated him as she did. On the day he'd soaked her, it could have turned out worse. Instead, she'd been such a good sport. "Please tell me what I owe for my reckless driving."

Lily clutched her shiny black purse. "Nothing, no damage. The packages were just a little wet and everything washed up without leaving any stains. I would have stopped sooner, but my sister came to town for a few weeks."

"Oh?"

She squirmed in the chair. "Actually, to be honest with you, my sister convinced me I needed to at least be courteous of your request to stop by." She crossed her tanned stocking leg over her knee.

The soft sheen of her skin glistened over the contour of her round calves, which seemed a perfect size to the rest of her. Those legs definitely were an added attraction. "Well, you must thank her for me. How far away does your sister live?"

"Milwaukee. Her waitressing job at Childs keeps her busy. I don't see her too often since she moved last year." Lily's head drooped. "Sometimes that's a good thing."

Benjamin rubbed his chin. "I've heard of Childs. They're a restaurant chain in many of the bigger cities. I had their flapjacks in Chicago once on a business trip." He tilted his head, making contact with her robin-egg colored eyes. "Don't you get along with your sister?"

"I do. Except when she insists her way of thinking is right. I've endured that with a lot of my family lately. They all seem to pull me in different directions."

Could the meddling possibly be about her fiancé? Benjamin certainly could relate to her dilemma. "Family sometimes has a way of thinking they are helping when they are not. It's usually how they would handle a situation, not necessarily how the decision is the right one for you. You're the only one who can decide what you want to do. It's taken me a while to come to that conclusion."

"Well, there's another good piece of advice I'll have to consider." Lily straightened in the chair, placing her shoulders back. "Everyone seems to have their own notions when it comes to Ira."

Why would her family make it even more difficult for her? "I'm assuming though, you are glad your sister's been around for you during this time with Ira. Did she go with you to visit him?"

"No, we didn't see him." Wrinkles formed between her eyebrows. "The last time I was there, you were with me."

Had she ended her relationship with Ira? Is that why her family had not been agreeing with her? Their visit was so close to the news he'd heard. "I'm relieved."

Lily uncrossed her legs. "That's an odd choice of words." She shifted again in the chair, seeming a bit flustered.

He didn't want to make her uncomfortable. But by revealing his feelings of relief, he had. Nevertheless, she must realize how disastrous the situation could have been. "It may not be appropriate to say, but you were fortunate. Only a short time passed after you left before the doctor quarantined the house."

Lily slapped her hand to her chest. "You must be mistaken." She jumped out of the chair. "What happened?" Her words were halting and shaky.

What had he done? "I'm sorry. I thought you knew." Benjamin steadily pushed himself off the desk and stood. "The week after you left, Ira's neighbor came into the store. I wish I didn't have to be the one to tell you but...it's polio."

The color drained from her face. "It can't be Ira."

"Sadly, it is. You're looking unsteady, are you all right?" Benjamin took a few steps toward her. If she fainted, he wanted to be close enough to catch her. "Maybe you should sit down."

"I don't want to sit." Lily grabbed onto his arm. "What else do you know?"

The desperation on her face pained him. "That's all I heard, I'm sorry." He'd only spoken with Ira one time, but he seemed to be a strapping fellow. "He's strong. If anyone can get through this he can."

A tear flowed down her cheek, another followed. "I wasn't there for him. What type of person am I to abandon him when he needs me?" Lily leaned into his side, hiding her face.

Benjamin sensed Lily didn't want him to see her cry. "You didn't know." Her sweet floral scent tickled his nose. He wrapped his arms around her, pulling her closer. She fit perfectly right next to him. Instincts seemed to be taking over his intelligence. "You're the kindest person I know."

He squeezed tighter as her shoulders moved upward with each sob. The warmth of her trembling breath made his skin tingle with tiny bumps. Or had it been her closeness? Was he wrong to comfort her? A woman crying always troubled him, except with Lily her tears tore at his soul. Somehow, he had to ease her discomfort. He rubbed her back from the lower curved dip up toward her shoulders. Each long stroke seemed to help her relax.

She nestled one side of her face into his chest.

Benjamin wanted to protect her heart. Still, he feared no matter what, it was going to break anyway. "I know it's difficult not to worry, but please try." He brushed the back of his hand across her cheek.

Lily tilted her head up.

Her lashes were clumped together and the sadness in her down-curved lips made him regret being the one who told her. "You won't know how Ira's been affected until he pulls through."

"Take me to him."

A tightness balled his gut. "What if he's still contagious? I couldn't live with myself if you were exposed." Benjamin ran his thumb under her eye, tracing the top of her cheekbone and wiping the last bit of tears.

Her lashes blinked rapidly. "I'll go across the street to Doc Spencer's. He'll know if I can see him. Promise me you'll take me if he approves."

The gaze of her blue eyes mesmerized him, and he found himself agreeing. He forced a nod. "Of course, I will." Benjamin ran his hand down her arm, grabbing onto hers.

The setting of her engagement ring bit into his finger and he let go.

He couldn't deny his connection to her, but right now all he could be was a friend. She had to decide her fate with Ira. If it didn't work out, he'd be there for her as long as she wanted. If she wanted more, he'd be more than happy to oblige when his relationship ended with Vivian. "I can drive you once the afternoon train is unloaded. It should only take an hour and a half. Will that be all right?"

"Yes, that will be fine." Lily made her way toward the door. "If Doc doesn't want me to go, I'll stop back. Otherwise, I'll wait for you at home." As she took hold of the doorknob, she turned and looked over her shoulder in a pained stare. "I do appreciate your kindness again, taking me all the way out to the farm."

"You're welcome." He waved. "See you soon."

Lily whooshed through the doorway, leaving behind an aroma of velvety flower petals.

Benjamin leaned back onto the desktop, viewing the bare entrance. What did it mean Lily hadn't seen Ira for almost a month? Had their relationship been over until he'd given her the bad news?

More importantly, what did it mean she wanted to see Ira? He should have had the watch inscription etched in his brain by now. If he had, maybe the time he spent with her would have been wisely spent.

Instead, now her emotions might take over her head and drive her right back into Ira's arms. Pity could do some strange things and he didn't want this to be the case with Lily. But he was in no position with his engagement to offer her anything more than a platonic relationship.

Resisting everything when it came to Lily had been the hardest. And today he was stuck with physically driving her right back to Ira.

Again.

He had been a fool.

A hazy smoke wafted in from the hall as he caught a whiff of an expensive cigar. He stood and straightened, awaiting his presumed future father-in-law's appearance. Devious and shrewd were the best words to describe Walter, and Benjamin needed to be cautious he didn't divulge anything before the deal finalized. Keeping up the facade a little while longer would hopefully pay off in the long term. The empty doorway filled with Walter's tall, portly figure.

"I see you're alone now." The cigar pinched between Walter's lips muffled his words.

Benjamin's stomach clenched. Walter was the last person he wanted to see. He'd rather daydream of Lily. "Yes. How can I help you?"

"Has your father told you about the new job I'm bidding on?" Walter rolled the cigar a half-circle in his mouth while a cloud of smoke hovered over his head. "It will be a tremendous opportunity for both of us."

"Yes, Father mentioned it's one of the largest we've had in a long time." Benjamin backed up to the desk. "I will do whatever I can to help secure a good outcome." He tightly grasped the edge of the desktop.

"Glad to hear. You're a smart boy for the most part." Walter wolfishly grinned. "Except next time, you may want to pull the blinds."

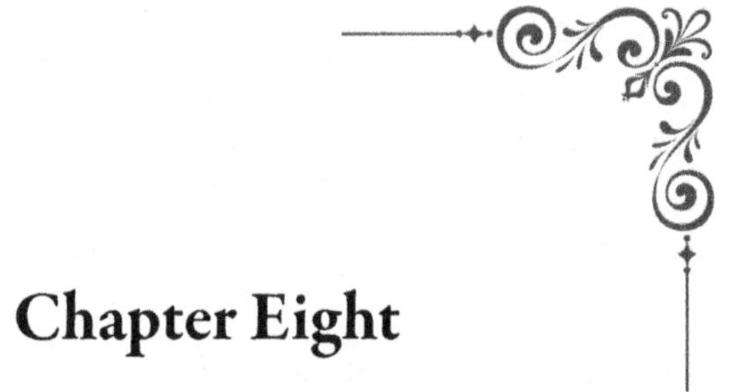

Chapter Eight

Lily's heart thumped harder against her chest the closer she came to Ira's porch. She glanced over her shoulder. Benjamin stood outside his car and gave her a reassuring smile. On the entire ride to the farm, she couldn't stop talking about everything and anything that didn't even matter. All that mattered right now was Ira.

Her nerves were wound up as tight as a head full of bobby pins. So many people had died contracting polio. Thank the Lord Ira didn't. There wasn't any rhyme or reason as to who got it or how bad he or she was left with the effects of the disease. A couple of years ago a priest who couldn't breathe from the virus had been saved by a new machine called an iron lung. The newspaper stated the cost was as much as a fifteen-hundred-dollar house. There would be no way their small town would have that for Ira if he needed it.

Lily stalled in front of the first step. Ira hadn't wanted to see her the last time. For sure, he wouldn't want to see her this time. If he had, his family would have contacted her about his condition. Even now, the living room curtains seemed to be waving her away through the open window.

"Lily."

She turned toward Benjamin.

"I can come with you if it will make it any easier."

How could she turn down such a sweet invitation? "If you can assist me to the door, I'm sure I'll be fine."

He hurried to catch up with her, extending his arm. "I'll stay with you until you don't require me anymore."

Lily slipped her arm around his. The tone of his voice soothed her and she lifted her foot onto the step. With him by her side, her heart thumped for joyous reasons but the timing sure seemed wrong. Her focus should be on Ira despite their troubles. He would need her now more than ever to get through this illness until he became strong again. Even if he didn't want her there, he'd need to overcome his stubbornness. She had an obligation as his fiancée to help him get well again. There was no doubt she needed him just as much too. Her family had been burdened with her upkeep long enough.

As she approached the screen door, a set of footsteps echoed off the wooden floor inside and a face appeared.

"Mary, I just heard about Ira. May I come in?"

The closer Mary got to the door the more guarded she appeared.

"The house is in a bit of disarray." Mary hesitated before opening the door and Benjamin followed Lily in. "As long as you don't mind."

"I don't mind. You had no idea we were even coming." Vinegar mixed with a scent of lemon drifted through the air. In the dining room, the chairs were upside down on top of the table. Lily kicked her shoes off onto the braided rug. On the opposite side of the entryway, all of the living room furniture had been pushed to one side of the room and the floor appeared damp. "How is he?"

Mary wiped her hand across her stained apron and took Benjamin's hat. "As well as can be expected considering what he's gone through." She hung his fedora on the rack and turned toward Lily. "What have you all heard?"

The usual tidy bun in the back of Mary's head drooped. But it wasn't only her disheveled look that seemed alarming. It was more the cold way Mary had greeted her. Lily could understand Ira's illness taking a toll on his sister, but she didn't understand Mary's lack of affection toward her. "Only that your family was under quarantine for an outbreak of polio. Why didn't anyone get word to me?"

"I'm sorry, Lily. This time I promised not to say a word."

"But why?"

"I'm going to leave that up to Ira." Mary gestured toward the dining room. "I'll take these couple of chairs down, please have a seat. I just made a fresh batch of lemonade."

Lily stood at the edge of the oak table. "I can help with the drinks if you like. You look like you've been cleaning all day."

"I have. Top to bottom for weeks, trying to keep the germs from spreading." Mary went toward the kitchen. "It's just a couple of glasses, I'll get them."

Benjamin pulled out a chair for Lily. He leaned close whispering, "Do you want me to stay?"

His breath tickled across her ear. "Yes." The reply came without a thought. She wanted him here. Maybe that was a little selfish on her part, but after the reception from Mary, she needed Benjamin at her side. She faced him on her right. "I have an idea Mary's not telling me something about Ira's condition."

Benjamin sat. "You might be right. Mary did change the conversation rather quickly."

Lily glanced in front of her into the long galley kitchen. Sun brightened the area from a double window over the large sink below. The remaining portion of the wall space had floor to ceiling built-in white cabinetry. On the opposite wall, the iron stove took up the majority of the room along with a rectangular table. The far wall at the end had a door out to the back and the icebox where Mary stood.

The icebox door closed and Mary inched toward them with two full glasses. "I just came downstairs from taking Ira a glass of lemonade when you got here. I'm hoping he's awake when I go up this time." An inviting sense of warmth seeped from the slight grin on her face.

Lily reached for the glasses, handing one to Benjamin. "Don't wake him if he's resting."

"You've come all this way." Mary came around the table. She placed her hand on Lily's back and leaned in closer. "Are you sure?"

The gentle touch along with Mary's calming voice had finally given Lily the reassurance she wished for. Mary did want her here. She twisted to one side toward Benjamin. "How long can you stay?"

"I'm in no hurry to be anywhere. Take all the time you need." He set his half-empty glass on the table. "Besides, this lemonade is quite delicious."

"I'll be back before long." Mary headed for the stairs and disappeared down the hall.

"You're right, Benjamin. Mary is hiding something." She picked up a napkin and placed it under her drink. "Your friendship means a lot to me and I take solace with you being here."

"Maybe my presence is part of the problem for Ira and his family. I brought you here last time and I'm quite certain I caught Mary's glare of disapproval when I walked in this time."

"Oh my gosh! How could I be so insensitive? I should have just gotten the bicycle from home and came out here myself. What was I thinking?"

"I'll try to smooth everything over with Mary while you visit with Ira. I'm certain she'll understand after I explain. You're going through a lot right now." Benjamin patted her forearm. "I wish your circumstances were different. And if by chance there's something Mary's not telling you, I'll be here." He gave her a comforting smile.

The small lines that formed around his soft lips when he smiled were endearing. "Thank you for trying to ease my mind, but it's difficult with all the upheaval in my life." She cupped her hand around the glass. "Did I mention my father lost his job?"

"No, where did he work?"

She took a sip of lemonade. "At the cigar factory. It's always only a matter of time before he goes back. Father said it's like a seesaw these last few years. We hoped the worst was behind us. Fortunately, my job contributes a little and my mother does seamstress work when she can."

Mary came downstairs. "Ira's awake. You can go up whenever you're ready."

Benjamin squeezed Lily's arm. "I'll be waiting for you right here."

Lily made her way toward the stairs. She had a new outlook on the important things in life. Ira's admirable quality of forgiveness would go a long way in working through any troubles. He would forget about the prior month and welcome her back—she had no doubt. She entered the hall and Ira's door stood slightly ajar. The antiseptic smell floated in the air. Her legs wobbled at every step toward his room. Peeking through the crack in the doorway, she noted the crisp white sheets wrapped tightly around his legs. She knocked on the doorframe.

"Yes."

Lily poked her head closer to the gap in the door. "Is it all right if I come in?"

"It's only you, right?"

Mary must have mentioned Benjamin came with her. "Yes, just me." She pulled a chair across the floor within a few feet of the side of the bed. "It sure is hot up here."

Ira wouldn't look at her. Instead, he stared down at his clutched hands. "You didn't come to talk about the weather, did you?"

The sharp tone of his voice warned her he was irritable. Her words faltered. "No, I...ah...thought you might...ah...want some company."

"Is that why Benjamin came too?"

Well, of course, that was the real reason he snarled at her. She took a deep breath. "I'm truly sorry for bringing him here again. I wish someone in your family would have gotten word to me. I had to hear about you through the grapevine. Benjamin was there and he knew I was in no condition to make it out here on my own. That's all there is to it." She leaned into the back of the chair and exhaled.

He glanced at her for a second before turning his attention back toward his lap. "Fine. It doesn't matter how you got here anyway. I just want to know why you are here."

The quick glimpse of his face made her heartbeat quicken against her chest. His skin had a grayish tone. His eyes were dull. Even his usual vigorous figure seemed smaller and frail. His condition had to be bad. She swallowed slowly. "Because I would want people to visit me."

"I don't need anyone's pity." He crossed his arms.

"That's not why I'm here." Lily sat up straight in the chair. "I'm not trying to say the wrong things. There must be something I can do for you."

"No."

"I know you're not pleased with me about confronting you in public at the restaurant." She leaned forward, pulling the chair closer. "I should have waited until we were alone. I'm certain we could have talked it out."

"Why now? What changed your mind?"

"I've had time to think about what matters." She placed her hand on his upper arm. He shrugged his shoulder away. No matter how negatively he responded, she had to convince him he could rely on her. "I want to help you through this. I know you'd do the same for me."

He made direct contact with her eyes. "You have no idea what I'm up against."

She widened her eyes at the intensity of his stare. "Whatever it is I want to be there for you." The lack of strength in his arm along with his reactions frightened her. What was he hiding? The heel of her foot tapped rapidly against the wooden floorboards. "Talk to me."

"I'm stuck in this bed."

He obviously was still weak from the illness. "You'll be out soon enough."

"No, you don't understand."

She clung to the last bit of hope while listening to the tremble in his voice. "Please Ira, tell me."

"How can the doc be right? I'm a man, a strong man. I used to be able to work from dawn 'til dusk farming as well as anyone of my neighbors. What's going to happen to our farm now? We can't pay the help to do everything and my father isn't getting any younger. I'm not any good since this damn disease knocked me down." He pulled on the sheets, squeezing them into a ball under his fists. "I can't get up."

"You're scaring me."

"It's polio." His downcast eyes didn't look at her. "I can't feel my damn legs." He whipped the sheets off. "Look! They won't move."

Lily inhaled. His feet were turned inward and his knees were curved outward. The muscles seemed to lack shape under his wrinkled skin. She covered her mouth.

"I won't ever walk again." He pulled the sheets over his legs. "Every passing moment tethers me tighter to this bed."

Lily lunged toward Ira, wrapping her arms around him. "I'm sorry." Tears flowed into the crook of his neck. "They don't know you as I do. You can beat this. Don't give up."

"Stop. I can't change anything." He pushed her off of him. "It's out of my control."

Her heart ached. "You can't just give up so easily." She caressed his forearm. "I will come out here every day no matter what it takes until you walk again."

"I'm not giving up, but I have to do this by myself."

Her heel tapped faster as her voice rose. "Why won't you let me help you?"

"I'm going to do the only thing I'm capable of doing right now. I've made a decision about you and me." Ira put his hand on hers, stopping it from rubbing.

She wiped at her tears. "Then we should talk about it."

"No! I can't marry you anymore."

She gasped. "What did you say?"

"You heard me."

"Why?"

Ira hit the bed with his fist. "You see what I look like now. I'm crippled. How can you even ask me that question? I'm thinking about everyone, not just us. My family's farm is uncertain, and marrying you will only make the situation more intense. Besides, how do you expect me to take care of you? I told you I can't feel my legs."

"You could get better."

"The odds are against me. I won't ask you to wait." Ira picked up her hand. "You deserve to be happy and a life with me won't do that."

A happy life. It was supposed to be a happy life. He'd said so when he proposed. Lily pulled her hand away. Her heart pounding in her ears deadened the words coming from Ira's mouth. She caressed her white-gold engagement ring. A lone mine-cut diamond with a small detailed channel on the shoulders.

The day he'd asked her to marry him had been beyond what she'd envisioned. Right down to the church bells ringing as he hoisted her upon his horse and they rode out of town. He'd only told her he had a surprise for her and she would have to wait. The entire way she held his waist, taking in the scent of his spicy cologne. They finally stopped along a meadow of wildflowers which stretched out over the hillside. Ira helped her down and led her to a shady spot under a giant tree. He reached behind the oak and pulled out a picnic basket. As he laid the checkered blanket down, his hands trembled. Ira assisted her to the ground but as soon as he knelt in front of her with his hands cupped over each other, she'd held her breath.

Her breath escaped her now in small quick gasps. Her neck muscles seemed to be squeezing her like a noose. She had to get out of here.

Lily pulled the ring off and placed it into Ira's palm. She managed to get up and shuffle across the floor toward the doorway. Her actions seemed slow and staggering as if each motion were frozen in time on a strip of film. The rhythmic side-to-side movements between the walls propelled her toward the bottom of the stairs. On the final step, she collapsed, hiding her face in her hands. She wailed.

"Lily. What happened?" Benjamin put his arms around her. "What's wrong?"

She couldn't catch her breath.

"Lily, look at me." He pulled her into his side.

She couldn't.

Benjamin sat on the steps next to Lily and squeezed her shoulder. "I'm here for you and so is Mary. What can we do for you?"

Lily shook her head. "Nothing." Her body was numb.

Mary squatted in front of her. "I'm sorry you had to find out about my brother this way. We are still holding onto the hope he will regain feeling in his legs. You mustn't lose hope either."

Lily's breathing slowed. "What did Doc Spencer say?"

"The next six months will be crucial to his paralysis. Right now, he has a small chance of walking again." Mary opened her arms. "You look like you could use a hug." She leaned forward.

Lily embraced her. "I'm going to miss you." Her eyes filled with tears.

"What do you mean?" Mary rubbed her back.

Lily backed away. "The engagement is off. Ira doesn't want to marry me anymore."

"I'm so sorry. I had no idea." Mary blinked away the tears forming in her eyes. "I'm going to miss you too."

Benjamin grabbed hold of the railing. "Stay here. I need to speak with Ira."

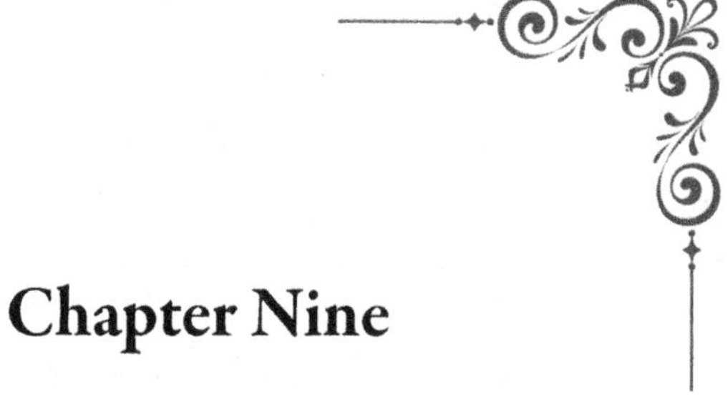

Chapter Nine

Vivian rounded the corner in the downtown morning light of Hub City. Last night's heavy rainfall put a chill in the air, making the six-block stroll tolerable. Sneaking through the side streets allowed her to avoid almost everyone from seeing her tousled hair. She glided her hand into her dress pocket, touching the folded piece of paper, a tonic advertisement she'd recently torn from a magazine.

Sallie's Beauty Parlor stood at the intersection of Third and Main. Floor to ceiling windows faced both streets with the newest beauty supplies on display. Browsing through the window, she didn't find the tonic from the ad. Staying on top of a regimen would keep her looking her best for as long as possible. Every woman knew beauty enticed a man to marry and her time was running out.

These past four years, Benjamin had been led to believe she was only one year older. In fact, she had begun school one year late and needed to repeat the fourth grade. A story she had no intention of retelling anyone. She'd been able to stay looking young, but lately, her skin's appearance had some fine lines. Marriage couldn't wait any longer. In less than six months, thirty would catch up to her.

Entering the salon, an odor of burnt hair drifted through the air from the permanent wave machine. Some women lost chunks of hair trying to glamorize under the curling mechanism. She never intended to attempt such a venture on her perfect waves. The chairs were all empty as she was the first patron to arrive on Saturday morning.

"Good morning, Vivian." Sallie stood near the beauty chair in her rose-colored uniform, motioning her hands with excitement. "Come right over. I'll get you started. What would you like done today?" Her gum popped like a hot kernel in a kettle of grease.

Vivian untied the scarf and removed it from her head. "I want the full treatment—a shampoo, set, style, manicure, and facial. Are you able to squeeze it all in by early afternoon? I have a dinner date this evening."

"We should be able to accommodate, however, let me check with the girls and see which one can do your manicure." Sallie chewed again while pointing toward the empty seat. "I'll be right back."

Vivian pulled the hanging drapery to enclose the area on both sides of her and sat. Now no one would be able to view her from the front windows or the other parlor chairs. She examined her reflection in the mirror, moving her head from side to side while running her fingers through her hair. Her locks could use a trim, maybe she could add it in too. Only Sallie would need to work fast. She had to be the chattiest lady who could babble on about any topic, but her skills as a hairdresser were the top in town.

Sallie wiggled her fingers in the air with excitement. "Good news, we'll get you in for the manicure." Her full crimson lips matched the color of her moon manicure.

Vivian liked the look of both the tip and the natural crescent at the cuticle left unpolished. Maybe this time she'll try the same style for her nails. "Delightful, I want to look exceptional this evening." She reached into her pocket, pulling out the advertisement. "Do you have this tonic?"

Sallie read over the information. "I don't carry this particular one. I have heard of it though. I'm sure I can mix up something comparable. Do you want me to try?"

"Yes, I do." She rubbed her forehead. "My skin's shiny and slightly oily right here."

"Let me take a look." Sallie touched above her brow. "I've got a little something I can put on if the tonic doesn't do the trick. I'll mix it up first, we'll shampoo after. What do you have planned for tonight?"

"Benjamin asked me to dinner this evening. I'm finding it difficult to contain my enthusiasm." She could count on one hand the number of times he'd taken her anywhere these last months.

Sallie chose rose essential oil, added it to a dish, and picked up witch hazel. "Is tonight something special?"

"I certainly hope so. It's been a while since he's surprised me with anything. That's why I scheduled the full treatment. Of course, your beautician expertise always makes me look my best."

One of Sallie's pencil-thin eyebrows arched. "You're too kind." She took the cap off the lavender oil, sniffed it, and dripped a few drops into a small stone dish.

"I love the smell of lavender." Vivian waved her hand in a circular motion, leaning into the aroma. "It's always been one of my favorites."

"Mine too. The herb is calming and helps with headaches too. Usually, all of the tonics I mix contain at least a drop." Sallie picked up the chamomile bottle, added a little to the concoction along with a dab of vegetable glycerin. "I'll do my best to help you get ready for this evening. Tip your head back while I rub this in."

She sucked in a quick breath of air. "It's cold. Will this help with blemishes too?"

"Yes, it's another benefit to using lavender. Relax now for a bit while I clean this up. Then I'll begin on your hair."

Vivian had no interest while Sallie talked nonstop about her family. They didn't seem any different from anyone else's. Her eyelids drooped. *Snap.* Sallie's gum brought her back to consciousness and the reality of this evening. The last time they should have gone to dinner, Benjamin chose playing cards with the men over her. She expected him to make up for the slight even though he didn't know it yet. He should bring a lovely gift, followed by flowers, along with her favorite assorted chocolates in the tin box. Of course, they would go to the nicest restaurant in town. She would have the best meal on the chef's menu. At this point, she could forgive him...just a little. Besides, there would be a lifetime for him to make it up to her.

Everything was coming together now since Fredrick agreed to cater the wedding. Luckily, she worked well under pressure since the ceremony would be next month as it was the only available date. She could make it work and Benjamin would have enough time to get an astonishing suit. Whatever surprise he had planned for her tonight wouldn't surpass her news about the wedding date being moved up.

Sallie lowered the chair. "Your set is ready to go under the dryer."

Vivian followed Sallie to the next phase of beauty. The hairdryer looked like such an odd apparatus. It not only warmed her head, but her entire body became uncomfortable under the heat. The worst part was the constant hum in her ears, making it almost impossible to hear anyone speak. Everyone knew the finest gossip happened at the parlor. She didn't want to miss any of it. If she had to be stuck under the soaring temperature, at least she would have time to glance through more beauty magazines. They helped her keep up with all the glamour articles, especially any new products by Elizabeth Arden.

Vivian flipped through the pages. No story seemed interesting. Probably because Sallie had asked if they were celebrating something special. She wouldn't be caught off-guard about an important day in their relationship. On their first date, the leaves had turned to bright yellows, reds, and oranges. That timeframe didn't fit. The day he asked her to go steady didn't coincide either. Nor did either of their birthdays—hers in December while his in September. The day he proposed, they had gone to dinner. By the time they were done, the snowfall exceeded the prediction. They had ended up stuck for over an hour. Benjamin shoveled around the entire car to get them out of the drifts. It couldn't be then either, but it might be their first kiss. Her diary would confirm it as soon as she got home.

After a half-hour, Sallie reached under the dryer, patting the hair around her head. "We're ready to put the hair clips in."

Vivian grabbed another magazine and followed her to the chair. A boisterous woman's voice carried on from the other side of the curtain. The whole parlor must be listening to the conversation about her daughter's upcoming wedding with a distinguished oil company's son. Whoever the woman was, she had every right to brag about such an accomplishment for her daughter. The son she spoke of fit the description of only one man, Tom. Vivian courted Tom the summer between her junior and senior years of high school until her mother decided he wasn't the right man for her. In the following years, she lost all hope of ever finding a man with a similar status until she met Benjamin. This time she wouldn't give up so easily.

As the clips scraped across Vivian's scalp, she flipped to the next article which seemed rather interesting. The title "Beauty Routine of a Hollywood Starlet" revealed dark reds, maroons, and raspberry lip color becoming the most popular, according to the Hollywood stars. With her hair color and olive skin tone, the best choice would be the dark red. The voices on the other side of the curtain rang out again and she awaited another gossipy story. The high-pitched voice of the hairdresser on the other side of the curtain had to be Sallie's cousin working on the boastful lady's hair.

"A few more rolls and you'll be ready to go under the dryer."

"I don't suppose you heard about the Blanchard farm under quarantine for polio." Mrs. Boastful posed the question, not for an answer.

"No, how did you hear?"

"My husband did at the butcher shop. I sure hope it's an isolated incident. You remember what happened the last time it swept through the town...all the schools closed."

"I sure do. Have you heard how the family's doing?" Sallie's cousin sounded sympathetic more than inquisitive.

"The son is paralyzed."

"That's awful."

"What's worse is his fiancée was seen in the arms of another man." Mrs. Boastful raised her voice for the juicy tidbit so everyone could hear.

"Shameful. Let's get you over to the dryer."

Vivian figured out Mrs. Boastful's daughter was Agnes Jones. She was a lucky one to marry Tom but certainly didn't seem his type. In school, she was a quiet girl with looks so plain she hadn't attracted any of the boys. Why Tom would find her interesting, let alone marry her, showed his bad judgment. Agnes must have a lucrative dowry, be a floozie or there had to be some family business connection. This story didn't have any rumor worth repeating.

On the other hand, the engaged woman in another man's arms would be one to consider. For sure, she would keep this scandalous story from Benjamin. If the tale of the prestigious banker with a comparable status didn't persuade him about making a commitment or breaking one, it's doubtful a well-off farmer's fiancée would make any difference. Quite certainly, a recurrence of the same argument wouldn't be on her agenda this evening.

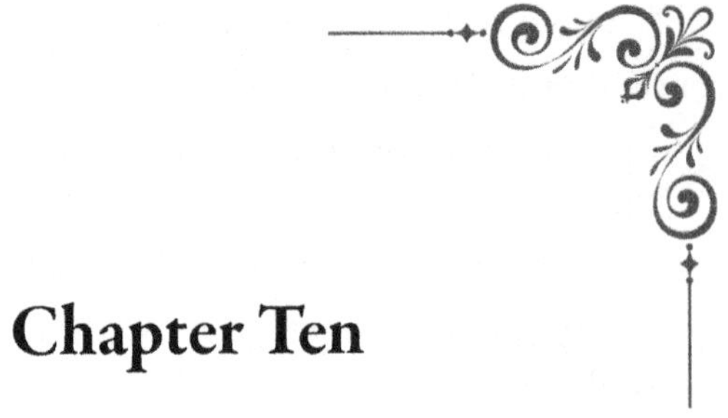

Chapter Ten

"Hurry, we're going to be late for dinner. If you wouldn't have waited until the last minute to pick me up, we wouldn't need to rush like this." Vivian slipped her right hand around Benjamin's arm as he shut the car door. She loathed not being on time and he knew that. "We wouldn't need to be parked three blocks away either."

"I didn't mean to be so far behind schedule." He smiled politely. "Work turned out to be quite hectic today. I'm sure you heard your father won the bid yesterday, so we need to get all the supplies promptly."

That smile was meant to pacify her, she'd seen it before. How dare he. She'd spent the whole day getting ready for him and he couldn't even leave work a little sooner. "Well, congratulations on the job. Although, you should realize I'm more important than work." Vivian touched the stubbles on his face. "You didn't even shave."

Benjamin placed his hand on top of hers, lowering it into the crook of his arm. "I'm sorry. I should have been ready on time and more presentable." He pulled out his pocket watch. "We have five minutes. If you don't want to be late, our only choice now is to run."

"Fine, but I hope you won't put me in this situation next time."

His long strides pulled her along with him.

Vivian's lengthy floral dress hadn't been designed for a dash down the sidewalk. Nor were her black leather pumps with a strap across the instep. She held her oversized ostrich feathered hat in place with her left hand. After a couple blocks, she panted, "Slow down. I can't keep up."

He changed his steps to a quick march. "Your dress looks swell, is it new?"

"Yes, it's the one I told you I bought." The one he could have seen a month ago if he would have agreed to take her anywhere that night but instead chose a pointless card game. He sure seemed to know how to provoke a reaction from her this past year, just like purposely rubbing a cat's fur the wrong way.

"I thought it might be."

Darn the man, he didn't even sound the least bit out of breath. "I'm pleased I finally have somewhere to wear it," she hissed. The dampness under her arms would likely leave noticeable stains on the delicate silk. She'd probably never wear this dress again.

He reached for the Hotel Charles' door handle.

She yanked his arm. "Wait! I know you may not care how presentable you are, but I do." She ran her hands down the sides of her dress, adjusted the hat on her head, and tucked any loose strands of hair back in place. His eyes were darting between the door and her fussing. "Do you have a handkerchief?"

"Yes." He pulled it from his breast pocket. "Really, you look fine."

"I want to appear more than just fine." She dabbed the cloth on her face and neck, handing it back to him. "All right, I'm ready."

His lip curled slightly. He stuffed the moist hanky into his jacket pocket and opened the wooden door.

The restaurant owner at Hotel Charles greeted them at the entryway. "Glad to see you again, Mister Benjamin." The proprietor nodded. "Miss. Your requested table is ready. Come, follow me." He led them to the far corner of the restaurant to a private table partially hidden by a half wall. The owner pulled the chair out for her. "Your waitress will be over soon. Have an enjoyable evening."

Vivian kept her gaze on Benjamin from across the table, waiting for him to look at her, but he didn't. His cheeks were flushed and short, coarse dark hair protruded around the jawline and lips. Any kisses wouldn't be the romantic ones she'd envisioned for tonight. What would it have taken him, five lousy minutes? Now his sandpapered face would rub her delicate skin raw and the tonic treatment she received earlier would be wasted.

He picked up his water glass, took a long drink, and stared into the dining room. His thoughts seemed occupied elsewhere. Why was he ignoring her presence? "Benjamin."

"Yes?" He finally paid her the attention she deserved.

"What has you so quiet?"

"I can't believe how many people are here."

"If you'd taken me here more often, maybe you would have noticed how busy this place can get."

Benjamin's brow furrowed.

"Well, they have the best food and it is the weekend." They better not run out of the meal she chose. They really should have had reservations earlier than six-thirty. "I don't know why you seem so surprised. Isn't this the same place you play your card game?"

"Yes, but Thursday nights aren't so full." Benjamin tugged the knot back and forth on his silk green necktie. "Your hair is curlier. Did you get it done today?"

At least he still noticed the small things she changed about herself. "Yes, my nails too." She held both hands above the table. Her new white filigree bracelet slipped forward. "The color is cornflower blue. Doesn't it go well with my new dress?" She paid attention to his changes too. He seemed a bit on edge tonight.

"Yes, they go well together." He glanced at the menu. "Do you know what you'd like for dinner? We should probably decide before the waitress comes over."

Vivian picked up the menu. Although Benjamin didn't bring her gifts, he did take her to one of the most expensive restaurants in town. She loved how the tall walls were decorated with lovely floral wallpaper on top, but accentuated by dark wooden beadboard at the bottom. Each of the tables was lit with a single candle. He couldn't have been more dashing in the flickering light. A double-breasted brown plaid suit complemented his complexion and hair. She could probably ease up a little on his money tonight and order a less expensive meal. "I'll have the dinner special."

"Good choice, I think I'll have the same."

Vivian put the menu aside and placed her hands in her lap. "At the parlor today, Sallie asked if tonight was something special and I told her I didn't know." She awaited a reply, but he said nothing. This night was special for her. She wouldn't have sat in the parlor half the day if she hadn't looked forward to being with him tonight. Maybe he was so reserved as to not ruin a surprise. After all, they were seated at a private table. She couldn't wait any longer. Apparently, she'd have to try and pry the secret out of him. "Is there any reason in particular?"

"Reason?" His eyes rolled upward as if he were searching for an answer. "No, nothing special. We haven't been to dinner in a while."

"I thought it was about time too." She gave him a half-smile. He wasn't going to make finding out what he was hiding easy on her. "It has been *way* too long." She accentuated the word as a hint and hoped he'd make a mental note. With any luck, next time wouldn't be too far off. "Did you know in a few days it will be the anniversary of our first kiss?"

"Our first kiss?" His head jerked back and he appeared caught, like a mouse in a trap. "Hmmm, our first kiss. You don't say."

A tall blonde-haired woman approached the table with a pad of paper and set down a basket of warm rolls.

Benjamin pointed to the item on the menu. "We'll have two dinner specials."

Blondie gave him a smile and a wink. "I'll get your order going right away. Anything to drink, sir, other than the water?"

"No, the water is adequate."

The waitress waltzed away with her hips swinging to and fro as if she were in a seductive dance contest.

Vivian turned away from the waitress's illicit behavior, but Benjamin's glance seemed far too long. She held her index finger above the table and waved it in the air. "Do I have your attention? We were talking about the importance of the upcoming date before the interrupted rudeness. I speculate you forgot." She touched his hand firmly. If he didn't remember who he came with, he should now. "I can overlook you not knowing since I recently had to verify myself."

Benjamin unrolled the utensils from the napkin and placed the cloth in his lap. "You're right. I hadn't remembered the exact date."

She brushed at her attention-getting feather hanging off her hat. The fluffy quill usually captivated people but not so tonight with Benjamin. He'd better at least get the answer to her question right. "Do you at least recall where our first kiss occurred?" That night had been momentous for her. If he couldn't come up with the correct answer, the evening might be ruined.

He sat up straight in the chair, clearing his throat. "A few blocks before your house after I walked you home from the fair."

Vivian could hardly contain her enthusiasm. He had passed her inquiry for the most part. "Almost, it was only one block. You are right though; it was the fair. I'm so delighted you remembered." She tilted her head and fluttered her lashes. "For me, I fell in love with you the night you kissed me." She took her napkin from the table, placing it in her lap. "Is that how you recall the night?"

"I know it had been a swell night."

"Swell indeed." Vivian took a roll from the basket and pulled the top away from the bottom. "I'm famished, what is taking them so long? A dinner special should be quicker than this." She took a bite of the bread.

"I'm sure it won't be too much longer."

Vivian hadn't appreciated how the waitress winked at Benjamin. Even her voice sounded kittenish, maybe it was the reason her tail wagged so much. Perhaps Miss Wiggles needed more of a clue Benjamin belonged to her. If Vivian caressed her face with her left hand, the candlelight would surely catch the diamond on her ring finger. There would be no way Miss Wiggles could mistake the twinkle from her engagement ring. Vivian stuck another piece bread in her mouth.

A clanging noise erupted from across the table. Benjamin had been fiddling with his silverware and the butter dish.

"Benjamin!"

"Yes?"

"Those are for eating. Not playing."

One of Benjamin's eyebrows rose into a disapproving arch. He moved the knife and spoon back into its proper place and bit into the buttered roll.

She rocked her left hand in the glimmer of candlelight playing on her diamond ring. "I have some lovely news."

"Tell me."

"Fredrick agreed to cater our wedding." Vivian placed her diamond hand over her heart. "The best part is he has an opening on the Fourth of July."

"That's only two weeks away. I couldn't possibly—"

"Seventeen days to be exact." The stunned expression on his face gave her slight concern. "I can help you with your suit. There's no need to worry." If she could have everything else ready, why should he be worried? "Besides, Fredrick only had one opening left for a summer wedding and I told him we'd take it."

"What?"

"Think about it this way, the date will be easier for you to remember." She adjusted the napkin on her lap. "Here comes our food."

"Two dinner specials." Miss Wiggles set a plate in front of Vivian and then served Benjamin. "Be careful, the plates are a little hot. Are we all set here or can I get either of you anything else?"

Vivian bounced the fingertips of her left hand on top of her cheek.

Benjamin tilted his head at Vivian. "Do you have an itch?"

Vivian glared at him with pursed lips.

He glanced back at the waitress. "No, this will do."

Miss Wiggles winked again. "All right, I'll be back to check on you in two shakes of a lamb's tail."

Benjamin grinned.

Vivian couldn't believe he was going along with Miss Wiggles' flirtations...and right in front of her too. "I cannot believe how you smile with that come-hither look after she winks at you."

"I thought it was funny. Her lamb's tail comment made me think of Louie except he would have said sheep, goat, or pig." He chuckled.

"I don't find humor in this at all." Vivian took a bite, swallowed, and dabbed her lips. "At the very least, the waitress must be looking for a good tip from you. I can't believe how many times she has winked at you. I'm sitting right here. She hasn't even looked at me once."

"I'm sure it's not only me." Benjamin cut into the slice of roast beef. "I'll bet she's friendly with all the patrons." He slid the forkful into his mouth. "Maybe we should change the subject and talk about something else."

"Women who flaunt themselves around attached men are a name I'd rather not say." Vivian put her fork down. "I'm too much of a lady."

"Please don't get upset. That's the last thing I want to happen this evening." He gave her a sidelong glance. "You're not done eating, are you? I thought you were hungry." He stabbed a few green beans. "You've barely touched your food. Don't you like it?"

"Yes, except I lost my appetite." Tonight hadn't gone at all how she wanted. Especially since she didn't receive the reaction she sought regarding the wedding news. A summer wedding fulfilled her dreams and everything had fallen into place perfectly when Fredrick suggested the holiday wedding. There would be no way she would wait until next year. Marrying after she turned thirty would be out of the question. She had to figure out why Benjamin appeared out of sorts. He hadn't spoken much and seemed starving by the way he'd gulped down his food. No matter what, he would need to see things her way. He always did and this time wouldn't be any different. But why did he need to make it so exasperating?

Benjamin wiped his chin. "I hope you're saving a little room for dessert. One of my favorites was on the board at the entrance when we came in." He tipped his glass up toward his lips. "The waitress is on the way over now." He polished off the remaining water in his goblet.

"Maybe I'll have a bite or two of yours."

Miss Wiggles filled the water glasses. "How's everything tasting?"

"It's all delicious." Benjamin adjusted the napkin on his lap. "I'd like a piece of Portsmouth orange cake."

"Good choice, I'll be back shortly." Miss Wiggles swung her oversized hips toward the kitchen.

"See, I told you." Vivian shook her finger back and forth. "She didn't look at me once or ask if I wanted any dessert."

Benjamin picked up a roll and soaked up the remaining gravy on his plate. "Would you like some cake?"

"No."

"How about having some coffee with me? We can have it with dessert."

"A cup would be fine." The food smelled rich, especially the creamy mashed potatoes. Vivian picked up her fork, taking a few small bites. "I thought we could go for a drive after dinner or if you'd prefer maybe a stroll downtown." They needed quiet so she could find out what was on his mind.

"Yes, maybe. We'll have to see what the weather is like." Benjamin placed his silverware on the plate. "I heard it might rain."

Miss Wiggles placed the plate between them. "Here's the orange cake. I took the largest piece I could find. That way the two of you can share." She winked at Vivian. "I'll take your plate, Miss. Looks like you saved some room for dessert. Is there anything else I can get for you?"

Benjamin turned Vivian's coffee cup over. "Some coffee for the lady." He placed his cup right side up on the saucer. "Make it two cups, please."

"Coming right up." The waitress sashayed toward the corner table with the brewing device.

"Did I see her wink at you?" The side of his lip curved upward.

Vivian picked up her fork, hacking through a small corner piece of cake. "She did, the hussy. I'm sure she's hoping I get fat eating the dessert." The forkful slid between her lips.

He shook his head and his mouth formed a tight straight line. "If you'll excuse me, I'll be back in a moment."

She could not care less if he'd been bothered by how she perceived the waitress's actions. He was her man and now she'd indulge in more cake. The orange flavor was sweeter than expected and the cake itself so moist each crumb stuck to the fork. Every serving made her crave more. She could understand why it had become his favorite, but not why he seemed so emotionally aloof tonight. Benjamin's abrupt response to the wedding and the small talk afterward led her to believe he was conflicted. Or maybe the large new job with her father put him under too much stress. She needed to find out either way. Before long a scanty couple of bites remained.

"Coffee, Miss?"

"Yes, please."

Miss Wiggles filled her cup.

"Thank you."

"Anything else you'd like?"

"No, that will be all." The fork cut through the last piece, slicing it in half. As she put it in her mouth, she savored the delicate morsel. Perhaps she should take Benjamin lunch at work next week. The tension he had been under must be from there. Marrying her had to be the best thing happening to him right now.

She put her hand under her chin, fixating on the small cake piece. Time ticked slower than the minutes under the hairdryer, waiting for him to return. Her fork poked into the last crumbs and she glided the cutlery through her lips. As soon as she located Miss Wiggles, she would order another piece. She turned her head, focusing on the path Benjamin had taken through the dining room. Several minutes passed until he approached. His hands rubbed intensely up and down on his wool pants. Her heart palpitated. Whatever he had to say, she'd reassure him. If the wedding news had given him the jitters, she'd tell him he'd be a fine husband. If he had stress from work, she'd help him relax.

Benjamin plopped onto the seat, stared down at the empty cake plate, and unbuttoned the top button on his yellow shirt. "I don't know where to start." He straightened his tie, glanced at her, and back to the table. "So, I'm just going to let you know how I feel." He took a deep breath and slowly exhaled. "I haven't been happy for a long time."

"Is something wrong at work?"

"No." He scratched at his skin under his shirt collar. "It's us."

Her stomach tightened around the cake, turning it into a hard ball. "Us? I have no idea what you're talking about—you haven't said anything to me—ever." Her mind raced for an answer. "I'll order you another piece of cake. I shouldn't have eaten it all."

"It's not the cake." He rubbed his hand vigorously across his forehead. "I've tried many times to say how I've been feeling." The tone of his voice dropped. "But you didn't listen."

"We can work this out." Her chest tightened.

"I'm sorry."

What? He's sorry? He can't mean he's leaving me. No, she had to fix this. "If you're nervous about the wedding I can ask Fredrick for a later date. We can get married in the fall or even the winter. A white wedding would be fine with me."

"No." His posture stiffened against the chair.

She couldn't bring enough air into her lungs. "Why are you doing this to me?" Her palms pushed hard against the table. Oh, God, this wasn't happening. Not to her. "There's someone else, there has to be. I'm right, aren't I?"

He reached across to touch her hand. "Please calm down."

Vivian yanked her hand away as heat spread from her neck up to her face. "Calm down? You want me to calm down? Obviously, you had every intention when you brought me here to end our relationship in front of all these people. Now you want me to calm down? I won't. You can't make me."

The dining room had become quiet.

She pointed at the hushed crowd. "You have their undivided attention. Tell them how much you detest being with me." He should be the one embarrassed by his horrific actions.

Benjamin leaned forward, voice low. "Please, Vivian, don't make this any harder than it is. I brought you here because at one time we were both in love. I wanted to show you I still care about you even though I don't think we should get married. I hoped we could remain friends—"

"Friends?" Her lower lip started to quiver.

Benjamin offered her a handkerchief.

There was no way she would give him the satisfaction of seeing her cry. She grabbed her shawl and bolted from the table, weaving her way through the packed dining room toward the front doors. A stinging sensation eased its way from her nose upward to her eyes. Every step she took was aimed at the intention of not humiliating herself any more than she already had. Than *he* had.

She chose a path to the left, but a man stood blocking the way. Circling the table, she headed through the passageway toward the entrance until a highchair obstructed her. She readjusted her exit.

The tears were filling her eyes no matter how rapidly she blinked. Her throat constricted as if someone were strangling her. She scurried around the next row of crammed tables. The dining room was like a never-ending maze of gaping faces and whispers behind hands.

A new pathway became bleary through her tear-soaked vision. A man in a white busboy uniform closed off the only way out. She attempted to forge through anyway. As she squeezed by, she caught her foot on a chair leg and stumbled. She grabbed hold of the busboy's jacket tail. They tumbled to the floor along with a stack of plates. Dishes flew in multiple directions, falling around them in a rhythmic clamor and shattering into tiny pieces.

Something cold, wet, and slimy covered her face while her back pressed the floor. She wiped at her eyelids and it oozed into her hair. As her eyes focused, the busboy was pinning her down and blowing hot breath two inches above her face. His cheek dimples and round face made him look like a baby. "Get off me."

"Are you all right?" The busboy's voice shook with each word. He lifted himself off of her and knelt by her side.

She sat and brushed pieces of lettuce salad off her dress. The sliminess matting down her hair must be dressing. "What did you do?" He'd ruined her dress, that's for sure. She shook her hands, splattering dressing and food bits onto the floor.

The busboy handed the feathered hat to her. "I'm so sorry."

Everyone had been out to humiliate her tonight. She couldn't swallow the sob trapped in her throat. All around her, a circle of legs had formed. She placed her hat on her head, tugging it down as far as she could. Her stomach roiled. Everyone in the entire place closed in on her. Convulsive gasps shook her body.

"Vivian."

As she peered out from under the brim, Benjamin stood above, offering his hand. Between the sobs, she gathered enough wind and wobbled onto her feet. Shielding her face with her hand, she fled out the door onto the sidewalk. People parted like the Red Sea while she ran through the crowd, but she had to stop at the intersection.

"Vivian, Vivian!"

No explanation from Benjamin would suffice. She haphazardly crossed through the oncoming cars as their horns honked and tires squealed. *Friends!* She'd show him friends. *Jackass!*

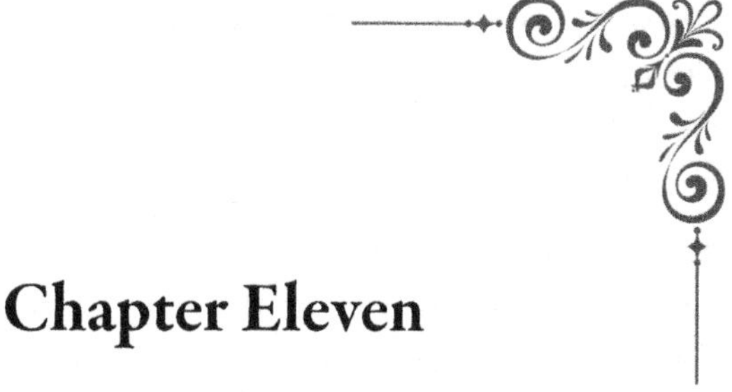

Chapter Eleven

As soon as Lily's regular Saturday morning shift ended at Livingston's, she climbed the stairs in the alleyway to the rooftop above the store. Her favorite place stretched only two-stories high along Main Street but seemed so close to the heavens. On a clear day, the countryside sprawled for miles to the north of town where the rolling hills met the sky. The train tracks divided the center of town with the majority of shops, restaurants, and hotels dotting the middle of the city to the south. The sun would be setting shortly and the view was spectacular. She loved the peacefulness of the rooftop and many times she'd found clarity here.

More than ever, she needed it again and had asked her friend to meet her. If she could share her thoughts, maybe everything would start to make sense. She sat next to Anna on the cement ledge with her feet dangling over the pebbled rocks below. "Thank you for coming." She smiled. "I hope you haven't been waiting long."

"No, about ten minutes." Anna wrapped her arm around Lily's shoulders. "How are you doing?"

"I've spent the past three nights praying the rosary for answers." Lily folded her hands in her lap. "Wednesday night after parting with Ira, the rest of the day was a blur. I blamed him mostly for not having enough strength to continue building a life with me."

"Oh, Lil."

"The next morning, I thought about how I'd abandoned him too easily in his time of need. Maybe if I hadn't pushed him away first, he wouldn't have done the same to me. By the end of the day, I figured I deserved to be isolated and alone forever." Lily's lip quivered.

"No, you don't. And I'm so sorry I was out of town when you needed me."

"I know you would have been here if you were able. Yesterday did get a little better. I actually had some good memories of the times I'd spent with Ira." Lily's eyes filled with tears. "But he will never be the same again." She wiped at her cheek. "There's nothing I can do to change the fact the disease chose him."

Anna squeezed her shoulder tighter.

"This morning my mind filled with unanswered questions. What made me believe I could have taken care of him? And could we have made a happy marriage together?" She sniffled. "What was his reasoning to end the relationship? Has he saved me from making a rash decision to stay with him? Or did he decide selflessly to set me free?"

"I think your questioning is normal under the circumstances." Anna rubbed her hand across Lily's back. "I'm not sure if you'll ever know the answers."

Every single question brought her more guilt than the last. She still had a chance to live life to the fullest, even though right now it didn't seem possible. "I can't continue with my life and harbor any resentment toward him. That's one thing I know for certain."

"Of course, you wouldn't. You're the most forgiving person I know."

Lily twisted around and put her arms out toward Anna. "I could use a hug."

"Certainly." Anna pulled Lily into an embrace.

Lily placed her chin onto Anna's shoulder. The world had turned into a lonely place without Ira. Below on the street, people were oblivious to her as they went about their daily lives. A commotion across the street in front of the Hotel Charles pulled her out of her misery. A woman in a blue floral dress with a matching ostrich feathered-hat ran down the sidewalk in a contrary direction. People scattered like drops of water in a hot pan of lard. The unhappy scene appeared all too familiar as an apparently remorseful man pursued the fleeing woman. The lump in her throat descended slowly. Ira literally and figuratively wouldn't be chasing after her anymore. Her heart ached. She had to stop her grief for what might have been. There had to be something better ahead. Maybe she should recall some pleasant memories instead.

The red-bricked building of Hotel Charles held an enjoyable experience, her first job. The summer before high school graduation, she worked as an elevator operator. Hearing the stories of faraway places from the people who stayed there fascinated her. Passion for travel had ignited in her as every place sounded more interesting than her small town. No promising future held her here anymore, and Celia had mentioned she would have a decent chance at finding a job in Milwaukee. A new place could do good things for her.

Lily glided off Anna's shoulder. "I think I know what I need to do."

"Great! Tell me. What is it?"

"You know how I've always wanted to see what's beyond Hub City?"

"Umm..." Anna appeared perplexed. "Yes, but what does that mean?"

"Now might be the time to find out."

Anna blinked rapidly. "You mean leave town? Are you sure that's the right decision?" Her eyes filled with tears. "Maybe you should think about this a little longer."

Lily didn't want to cause Anna any heartache but apparently, she had. "I won't be going right away. I'll need a couple of months to save money for the trip to Milwaukee." If she hadn't spent money on the new clothes, she could have left sooner. "That should be more than enough time to think everything over." She had to do something to make a change in her life. Gazing at the buildings across the street, tears stung in her eyes.

"Milwaukee?"

Lily swiped at the tear falling down her cheek. "Yes, with Celia. I might even be able to work with her at Childs." She shifted her eyes from one location to the next. Each spot held a fond memory. "Hub City will always be my home, and nothing will come close to the feeling I get on this rooftop." The sun painted a beautiful glow at the edge of the earth. "But I think it's about time for me to be more independent. Leaving will help me do that."

Anna swung her feet on top of the ledge and bent her knees toward her chest. "Please don't go, Lil." Her swollen red eyes peeked out from under her lashes.

Lily's heart ached even more. "What am I supposed to do?"

"I wish I knew."

"If I could stay, I would. My family has to come first right now. Everything would have been fine if Ira and I were getting married." Lily rubbed her bare ring finger. "I can't even be angry with the man. I'd be a terrible person if I spoke harshly of a man who can't walk anymore."

Anna hugged her legs. "Maybe his illness is clouding your memory."

She pinched her brows together. "What do you mean?"

"Your relationship with him was like riding a teeter-totter. One time you're up and the next you're down stuck in his manure." Anna put her feet down and twisted one of her brown t-strap shoes into the roofing pebbles. "And the times you've been down were much more lately. You have to know I'm right." She patted Lily's leg. "If I were to guess, he had something to do with the mood you were in on my wedding day."

Lily's mind ran through the scenes. When she'd spoken to Anna a few days after the wedding, she didn't mention how serious the disagreement with Ira had become. She wanted her friend to remember her wedding day as a happy one. Instead, she'd inquired about Benjamin. But finding out he had a fiancée only solidified another reason they wouldn't be right for each other.

Anna placed her arm across Lily's shoulders again. "If you've discovered anything through all this, you have to know how strong of a person you are."

"I don't feel that way." Her posture sagged as she hung her head.

Anna leaned forward, causing her corkscrew curls to bounce in the breeze. "Look at me." She made eye contact. "You have the strength. It's in there." She pointed to the center of Lily's chest. "I know it is. How about the G.A.A.?"

Lily tilted her head. "What does the athletic association have to do with this?"

"The *girls'* athletic association," Anna emphasized the word. "It has a lot to do with you and who you've become. You didn't care if a sport was boyish. If it wasn't for all of your encouragement, none of the girls would have played. Don't you remember? We never would have had a team for hockey or rifle."

"Maybe one time I had some courage."

"We beat the pants off of those boys." Anna touched Lily's hand as it rested on the ledge.

Lily nodded. "We sure did." That day she was so proud of how hard they all worked together as a team. The boys' team had brushed off the result, saying they hadn't even tried to win. She didn't believe any of them. They were a bunch of sore losers.

"Pants!" Anna slapped her leg. "I almost forgot. What about the day you started a new fashion?"

"I didn't want to freeze to death." Wearing a dress in the middle of winter was foolish and women should be able to cover up their legs with warm pants just like the men.

"Well, no one else would have worn their brother's waist overalls to high school. The whole place went into an uproar and you didn't care what they thought." Anna laughed. "Your parents even bought you a pair for Christmas that year, remember?"

"I did set a new trend, didn't I?" Lily half grinned. The ensemble brought with it a lot of teasing from her classmates. She had built a tough exterior over the years, but the name-calling and snickering still sensitized her core.

"Yes, you did." Anna squeezed her hand tight. "I'm sure you're overwhelmed right now. But you can overcome whatever lies ahead. Give yourself time to work through this. I'll be here for you and Emmett will too."

Her friend always found ways to make her heart light again. "Thank you, Anna. I don't know what I would do without you."

"You deserve to be happy, Lil. Don't settle for anything less."

Ahooga!

Lily glanced below just as a car swerved to avoid a collision. Had she settled for Ira? If she'd been honest with herself, she would have to agree. Something unexplainable between them hadn't quite fit. Like an irregular puzzle piece forced together, creating a distorted picture of happiness. Why hadn't she realized this before? They didn't belong together.

Anna was right; next time she wouldn't settle for anyone other than her ideal someone. He'd be attentive, considerate, value her opinion, and above all—trustworthy. Of course he would also meet the physical characteristics of tall, dark, and handsome.

To find one man with all she aspired seemed farfetched, especially since she had already met him. Well, for the most part. She didn't fit into Benjamin's affluent life and most importantly not his spiritual one. Her luck of finding an exact man seemed as rare as spotting a four-leafed clover in a meadow. She turned her head toward the touch on her shoulder.

"You're off somewhere again."

Lily didn't belong in Benjamin's world. But why had her attraction to him been so undeniable? "I'm just trying to put everything into perspective." She moved the pebbles around under her feet.

"You know, there are many things out of our control." Anna rubbed up and down on Lily's arm.

"I just wish I knew the right thing to do." Lily placed her hand on top of Anna's. "I'm at such a crossroads. I don't want to make the wrong decision." Moving away would certainly separate her not only from her family and Anna but any possibility with Benjamin too. She gazed at Anna who appeared absorbed in deep thought.

"You know I believe everything happens for a reason. Maybe you were never supposed to end up with Ira anyway." Anna squeezed her upper arm. "I'll bet your destiny lies somewhere else and you just don't know it yet. Choose the path that's right for you." Her seriousness softened into a grin.

"So, you'll be fine if I decide to move to Milwaukee?"

Anna nodded slowly. "I'll be sad, but it's your decision. If you choose to stay or leave, I know either way will bring you to your destined place. It's just a matter of how you get there." She looked up at the sky. "Of course, God is the highest power and He already knows. It wouldn't hurt to ask *Him* for an opinion."

Lily's heart had been wrapped in reassurance. Her friend truly wanted the best for her, even if it meant she wouldn't see her as often. As far as believing in destiny, Anna would need to convince her a little more. "I have another question for you. Ever since I met Benjamin at your wedding, I've found his presence appearing just at the right time." She shifted herself on the ledge to face Anna. "Not once, but twice. Would you consider him being there at times when I needed a friend destiny or luck?"

"Absolutely destiny!" Anna's face lit up like a decorated tree on Christmas Eve. "Don't forget friendship can always turn into long-lasting love."

"Don't get any ideas." Lily covered the grin spreading across her face with her hand. She couldn't fully give in to a smile yet with the tinge of guilt in her heart. "You know he's already engaged to someone who is better suited for him than me."

"You may say that. However, I can tell you're attracted to him."

Her stomach fluttered. "But it doesn't mean he feels the same about me."

"Lil, why do you think he drove you home in that rainstorm? You even thought he was going to kiss you before he left."

"I'm sure I misread him."

"Emmett thinks—"

Lily's mouth formed an O. "You told him?"

"I'm sorry." Anna gave her a supportive squeeze on her shoulders. "I'm sure he won't say anything."

"And what did he say after you told him?"

"Benjamin would be lucky to get such a great gal." Anna quirked her left eyebrow. "And do you know what I think?"

"No, what?"

"Maybe he'll be the reason you stay around."

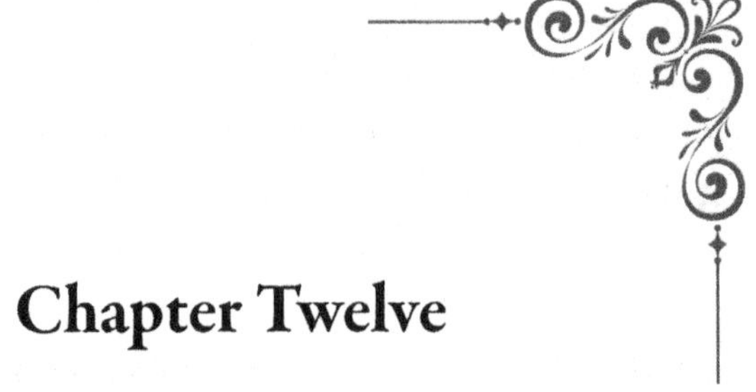

Chapter Twelve

Benjamin placed his feet with his two-toned brown and tan oxfords on the walnut desk's edge, covering the stain worn from years of propping his shoes just there. While Monday's workday neared the end, he'd earned time to catch up on the weekend news. Unfolding Friday's *Hub City Times* newspaper, he read the caption under the date June 16, 1933—"*FDR Signs into Law Banking Recovery Act.*" Most everyone agreed having banks insured eliminated the conflict of interest between investment and commercial banking, a protection that should have happened long ago. With all the rehashing news from four years ago, his father inadvertently revealed this morning he'd lost some money in twenty-nine due to the crash but wouldn't share any further details. Benjamin had been sworn to secrecy since divulging the information even now could cause unwarranted concern for the family and Father wouldn't let that happen.

"You're looking quite comfortable."

He peered over the top of the paper at his sister. Eva's black-framed glasses hung near the end of her nose. A pair of white sleeve protectors established her position as a bookkeeper against her dark suit jacket. But her thin pressed lips set off alarm bells.

Eva zipped into the room. "Walter might be stopping in your office."

Benjamin dropped his feet to the floor and his chair sprang him forward. "He's here?"

"Yes, he just went into Father's office."

He pitched the newspaper on the desk. "This can't be good. I thought Vivian's parents confronting ours in the vestibule at yesterday's church gathering would have sufficed."

"Are you fantasizing?" Eva's hands flew up in presumed disbelief. "There's no way a brief exchange at services would be the end. Especially since Walter dragged Deloris away hollering. That, my dear brother, is the calm before the storm."

"I can't change what happened at the restaurant nor how we've grown apart." Vivian should have understood. He'd wanted the chance to explain and an opportunity to soothe her afterward. Instead, she'd ignited like steel on flint. "My hopes are Vivian and her mother will settle down as the months continue. As for Walter, Father said it would be best if he managed the situation."

"You can daydream all you want." Eva placed her hand on the back of the guest's chair. "But the reality is Vivian and her mother spread news faster than a declining balance. I'm sure however they tell their version of the story, you will be the ass."

Benjamin rubbed his jaw. "I know you're only watching out for me and perhaps you're right that there is more to come. After I told Vivian how I felt, I never saw her at such a loss for words nor has she ever given up so easily. Father and I will do whatever we can to protect the business. All I can do now is be apologetic for the public display of humiliation I caused. And if I'm branded the *ass*, I'll deal with the consequences. I knew my decision wouldn't be without complications."

Eva sidestepped around the chair and approached the desk. Her voice lowered. "If you want to avoid Walter, you could make a trip to the post office for me. I have payments that can't wait another day." She held a stack of envelopes in her hand. "It's a good excuse to leave since the mail needs to be there by four."

Benjamin picked up the square cast iron paperweight and grabbed the envelope beneath it. "Set them here on the desk with this apology letter I wrote Vivian. Hopefully, she'll forgive me." He put the paperweight down and reached into his jacket, opening his watch. "I'll leave shortly."

"Thank you, I appreciate it, and let's hope your letter calms Vivian." Eva placed the mail in front of him. "Mother's expecting me home soon anyway and I have a few entries to finish in the books before I'm done."

A train whistle blew, a thunderous clash of metal, and a long-drawn-out screech echoed in his ears. The walls shook against the filing cabinet. The floorboards vibrated under his feet. "The train's derailing into the building!" Adrenaline shot through his tensed muscles. He dashed off the chair and grabbed Eva, shoving her out toward the hall. "Come on, we've got to get out of here!"

"Holy crap!"

Benjamin tugged on her hand. "Outside, now!" Eva's fingers slipped away. He took her by the arm. "You have to stay with me." They ran past the flour sacks piled half-way to the rafters, the pallets lining the wall, and out the side door into the parking lot before the screeching died away. The cars on the side-street were at a standstill. A crowd was gathering along the sidewalk.

Chaos stirred among the onlookers as he approached a man in a brown derby hat and matching suit. "Can you tell me what's going on?"

The man pointed at the temporarily incapacitated train. "Another foolish one thought they could beat the steam engine. When will they ever learn?"

"Is everyone all right?"

"I presume. The fool got out of the car, waddling like he was on a good bender." The derby hat man stumbled and flailed his arms in demonstration. "I would imagine he couldn't help it after he spun around the way he did when the front end got clipped."

Metal pieces were scattered about. The cars' engine appeared pushed off to one side with smoke billowing off the radiator. The mess would probably take hours to clean up. "He's quite the fortunate fellow."

"Indeed." The derby hat man sauntered away into the mass of people.

Eva touched Benjamin's arm. "The danger appears to be over and the building is unscathed. I'll go in and get the mail and meet you at the car."

Benjamin followed Eva until she climbed the steps and he continued around the corner. The train stretched past the next intersection, blocking the exit onto the street. He would need to go another route several blocks out of the way. If he took the square around the park by Lily's place, there would be less congestion and he might make it in time to the post office.

Benjamin took long strides toward his car. Lily was consistently on his mind. He struggled with the idea of checking on her. Emmett had kept him updated with as much information as he could share about her these past few days. But, until now, he hadn't been in the right emotional state. His desire to see her grew stronger. He put his hand on the door handle and a pat on his back caused him to turn around.

"Here's the mail." Eva placed the envelopes in the palm of his hand. "I hope you have time to make it."

"I've got a plan. The timing will be close, so I'd better be going." He slid in, pulled on the emergency brake, advanced the throttle lever on the right of the steering wheel, and pushed the spark lever upward on the left side. Then he opened the gas valve under the dash, turned the ignition key, rotated the choke clockwise, pulled back the choke rod, and depressed the start button on the floor. The engine sputtered as he adjusted the choke. "See you at home later." He let out the clutch and waved through the window.

As he pulled onto the road, the smell of fresh bread drifted through the air from Becker's Bakery on the corner. He downshifted before the next intersection, stopping a few feet from the yellow stop sign. The street had cars lined up for several blocks to his left. On the next block, homes occupied one side while the opposite was inhabited by the park. Lily's place stood halfway down on the right.

He proceeded to cross the congested road straight onto Chestnut. He accelerated after the intersection. An object struck his windshield. He stomped on the brake and hit the horn.

Ahooga!

He veered toward the edge of the road, coming to a halt while a small dark-haired boy raced toward him on the sidewalk. On top of his hood lay a wooden airplane. He lowered the door latch, the hinge opened, and he reached for the toy. "Is this yours?"

The boy stood still, glaring at his feet. "Yes, sir."

He shut the door, scooting around the front of the car and onto the sidewalk. "What's your name?"

"Frankie."

"Well, Frankie—here is your airplane." He handed him the toy.

Frankie's chin trembled. "Thank you, sir." A small tear rolled down his cheek.

Benjamin crouched to the boy's eye level and patted his back. "You'll be all right. The plane isn't broken."

"It's my favorite." Frankie wiped his arm across his face. "I don't know what I'd do—"

"Excuse me, what's going on here?"

Benjamin craned upward. A face blocked out the sun and the glow shined around her like an angel, if his faith would allow him to believe such a presence. "Lily!" His heart palpitated rapidly, spreading a warm sensation throughout his chest. "What a surprise."

"It certainly is." Lily placed her hand on Frankie's shoulder. A radiant grin stretched across her lovely pink lips. "I see you've met my little brother. What kind of trouble has he gotten into now?"

Benjamin caught an aroma of her flowery perfume through the slight breeze. "No trouble." He stood. "The airplane caught in the wind, blowing it onto my car. Everything is fine. Right, Frankie?"

"Yes, sir."

Benjamin grinned. "Your brother's a nice young man."

Lily ran her fingers through her brother's tousled hair. "What brings you by this way?"

"I'm on an errand." Benjamin unclasped the lid on his pocket watch. "It's getting late. I need to be going."

"I won't hold you up." Lily took Frankie's hand. "Come, we're going home."

Benjamin couldn't let this angelic woman dash away. Now was his chance, especially when she seemed to appear from above. "Go for a ride with me." He held out his arm.

Lily peeked over her shoulder. "I thought you were in a hurry." Her voice bubbled with hopefulness.

"I am, but it's a short trip to the post office. We can go for a longer ride afterward." Benjamin took a couple steps forward. "Please accompany me."

Frankie tugged on her arm. "I'm big enough to walk home by myself."

"It seems like I have no choice." Lily let go of Frankie's hand and wrapped her arm in the crook of Benjamin's. "I'll allow you to be my escort."

The sun above seemed to shine brighter and Benjamin had a hard time containing the smile spreading across his face. He opened the backdoor for Lily. As she beamed at him, her blue eyes glistened like the dew on a cool morning. Short wisps of light golden-brown hair curled along the edge of a tight-fitting hat. He closed the door and leaned into the open window. Her perfect mouth curved slightly at the edges. "Are you comfortable?"

"Yes."

"All right, we better get going." He dashed around the car, moved a few levers, and pulled into the street. "Ever since I've been trying to make it to the post office, one thing after another has delayed me. First, it was the train—"

"I heard the racket and the squeal. What happened?"

"Someone didn't stop soon enough and hit the train, but I heard he's okay."

"I'm glad no one got hurt."

"Everyone got lucky." He put his arm out the window, pointing toward the ground and signaling left. "I was in my office with my sister. The noise and shaking were terrible. I thought the train derailed and was headed into the building."

"Your office is right next to the tracks." She situated herself in between the front two seats. "What did you do?"

"My sister and I ran out into the parking lot." He turned left, honking through the uncontrolled intersection. "If the train hit, our escape would've been too late."

"Thank the Lord you're both safe. If anything happened to you, it would have been a tragedy."

She made the hope in his heart ascend like mercury in a thermometer on a hot summer day. He parked in front of the post office. "Do you mind waiting here? It shouldn't take long."

"No, go ahead. I'll wait."

He dashed around the car and up the stairs. As soon as he mailed these payments, he could be back with Lily. He couldn't wait to find out if she shared the same feelings now that they were at liberty to choose each other. Both of the lines in front of the long counter had people waiting. He chose the shortest line.

The woman in front of him appeared to be finished. He moved up behind her. The woman backed into him and his envelopes fell to the floor. "Sorry, I didn't mean to run into you." The woman glared at him before she tromped away.

Benjamin bent down, gathered each piece of mail and stacked them together. As he handed them to the clerk, his eyes narrowed on the payment envelope with Walter DuCate's address. "Is it possible to have these go out today?"

The clerk pulled out his watch. "They're late." And pointed at the time.

"I know." Benjamin slid in closer whispering, "Please. I'm certain you don't want to hear any excuses as to why I'm a few minutes past four. All of my envelopes are ready to go with the stamps on them."

The clerk scrutinized each piece of mail.

"I'd be grateful."

"Wait here. Let me see what I can do."

Benjamin stepped back from the counter, turning toward the large window. At this angle, he couldn't see Lily or his car. He wandered closer and peeked through the pane until her figure appeared in the backseat. His average day had gotten better. In a few moments, they would drive the hill past the hospital and into the open field overlooking the city. The view there had to be the best spot, except for the proximity to the cemetery.

"Mister."

Benjamin twisted around, stepping back toward the counter.

The clerk's fingers rapidly tapped a pen against the wooden countertop with a hurry-the-hell-up beat. "I was able to catch the truck for your out-of-town mail."

"Wonderful, thank you." Benjamin strode toward the exit. After the last delay with Lily's brother and the airplane, he hadn't held out much hope in the timeliness of the payments. However, his luck sure seemed to change with the sweetest woman he'd ever met waiting for him.

He pushed the handle down on the front car door and slid onto the seat. "It took a little longer than expected." He pivoted toward the back. "I thought we could take a drive to overlook the city. Would you care to see it?"

"Sounds lovely." Her eyes widened. "The last time you brought me home, I don't think I properly thanked you. I do appreciate everything you did for me that day. You're a kind man."

"That's nice of you to say, but you certainly make it easy to be with you." Benjamin hoped she could sense how much he wanted to be with her. He put the car into gear and pulled onto the street. The last two drives involved him taking her to see her fiancé. Ira's disability, unfortunate as it was for the man, opened up the possible chance of a future for them. One thing for certain, Ira's situation reinforced the meaning of his watch inscription. He had every intention of wisely spending all the time he could with her if she'd let him. He glimpsed at Lily in the rearview mirror. "How have you been doing?"

"Better now, thank you for asking." She gave him a soft smile. "I'm sure it couldn't have been easy on the way to my house last week. I only said a few words to you during the whole ride."

"Completely understandable after such a shocking experience." He shifted into a higher gear. "I would have done anything to help you, but I could tell you weren't ready for a conversation. However, if I can do anything for you now, I gladly will."

"I think you can."

Benjamin's heart leaped blissfully. "How?" He viewed the mirror again.

Lily's eyebrows rose into a curious arch. "You can tell me what happened when you went upstairs to see Ira." She scooted forward on the seat.

That's one piece of news he needed to proceed on carefully. "Mostly, he talked about how much his illness changed his life."

Benjamin shifted gears and a grinding noise rattled into the car. He should be able to double-clutch properly without conscious thought. "And how his current situation forced him to decide to break the engagement." But he hated speaking about the situation that had to be painful for her. "I'm sorry it ended that way."

She rested her hand on the back of Benjamin's seat near his shoulder. "I've come to realize the relationship wasn't good for me...or him."

Her alluring scent pleased his senses. "I see." Maybe Vivian would conclude the same about them someday. As he approached the incline, he pressed down on the accelerator pedal. "The spot I want you to see is just over the crest of this hill." The remaining part of the conversation he'd had with Ira, Lily should hear from him face to face. She deserved the courtesy. Especially if there would be any hope for her to understand his position. He put his arm out the window, bent his elbow ninety degrees, and put his hand up in the air making the right-hand signal. "Have you ever been here before?"

"Not here exactly, but I visited some relatives at the cemetery across the street."

"Aah...the departed have quite the view of the city from up here."

Lily laughed.

Benjamin pulled up near the edge of the hill, set the brake, and shut down the engine. "We can see better from outside." He closed his door, opened hers, and offered his hand. "I think you'll like it here." They strolled to the front of the car. He swept his arm wide from the left to the right. "This is such a peaceful place to think."

"Yes, it is and a beautiful sight of the city." She stepped near the edge of the cliff. "It's much quieter here than where I go."

"Where is your place?"

"On the rooftop above Livingston's." Lily backed away from the edge, rotating on her heel. "I can't see all this the way you do, but I truly enjoy the moments I've had there." She placed a hand on her hip. "I'm assuming you brought me to this tranquil site to tell me something I may not like."

"You certainly are perceptive." He tapped his palm on the hood of the car. "Would you like to have a seat?"

"I'll stand." She ambled next to him, facing out toward the cityscape.

Benjamin leaned his thigh against the car. "There is no easy way for me to say this, so please bear with me while I try to explain the best I can." Lily's face already had a wary appearance. "When Ira spoke with me, I think he wanted a clear conscience for the decision he'd made in letting you go."

Lily twisted and turned her fingers together.

He sensed her nervousness at the conversation. "I'm quite certain Ira observed how affected I'd been when I met you the day of the wedding. In case you hadn't noticed, I was at a loss for words." He had her attention by the steady gaze in her stunning eyes. "I could tell you were someone special from the moment we met." He cautiously awaited a reaction from her, but she performed as well as he did when playing poker. "And I think I sensed you were attracted to me too." He licked his lips with cautious hope. Damn. Had he read her wrong? Dryness tickled the back of his throat. He coughed. "Anyway, Ira must have noticed something too because he asked me for a favor when I saw him last."

She raised her brow.

Benjamin swallowed and took a deep breath. "He wanted me to promise to take care of you."

Both of Lily's hands clasped her hips. "I can take care of myself," she huffed. "It's not his place to pass me off to the next man that comes along."

"I'm certain—"

"Certain the two of you get to decide my fate, huh?"

"No, it's not like that."

"And I have no choice in the matter? Let me tell you this, I don't need a man. As a matter of fact, I'm moving to Milwaukee as soon as I have enough money saved. That doesn't sound like a woman who needs a man to look after her, does it?"'

He shook his head. Where had the conversation gone so wrong? Should he try to have her understand or would it be best for him to keep quiet? He hadn't done so well with Vivian either.

"Besides, you're engaged. I'm not going to be the cause of someone's relationship dissolving. I have too much integrity."

"I'm not anymore. Our engagement is over."

"What?" Lily gasped.

Every ticking microsecond her facial expressions transformed from hopeful to dreamy to joyous until they were doubtful and wary and hopeless. His stomach sank like a boulder in quicksand.

"All this seems way too convenient for both of us." Her hands fell to the sides. "Don't you agree?"

Benjamin touched her arm and traced his fingers down to her palm. "I don't want to waste any time." He gently squeezed her hand.

Lily's eyes closed as she took a few deep breaths. "I'm not certain if I can carry another heavy burden knowing what this could do to your ex-fiancée."

"We've been given an opportunity." Benjamin's heart fluttered. "The circumstances, for the most part, were beyond our control. A relationship takes two people who are devoted to their love. Neither of us had that in the people we were with." She had to know he spoke the truth even though it may sound harsh. "Shouldn't we at least figure this out together?" He raised her hand, placing a tender kiss on her ivory skin.

Lily pulled her hand away. "This is all way too fast." She placed her palm out in between them. "Please stop, I want you to take me home."

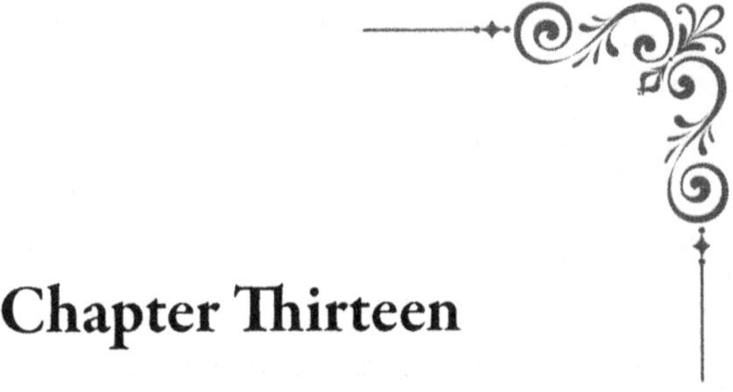

Chapter Thirteen

The aroma of popcorn wafting in the air made Lily's stomach yearn for the delicious kernels coming from Mr. Hell's wagon. The attendant, her brother Arthur, emptied a batch from the spurting hot kettle into the tray below. He had an ideal setup, drawing in the moviegoers on their way to the Relda Theater half-way down the block.

Anna dug in her coin purse for some change. "We'll take two bags."

"What are you two girls going to see on a two-for-one Tuesday tonight?" Arthur presented Lily with two overflowing bags of salty buttery goodness.

"We're on our way to see *King Kong*." Anna handed Arthur ten cents.

He dropped the coins into the till. "I heard that one is getting to be popular."

"What is it about?" Lily held out a bag to Anna.

"A giant gorilla falls in love with a young woman." Anna grinned. "It is a bit far-fetched, but maybe the idea is more about love overcoming obstacles."

"Is this your clever way of bringing up Benjamin?" Lily ate a kernel from the bag.

"To tell the truth, no. But you brought him up earlier and I know you're probably still thinking about him. Who wouldn't be? He's a handsome man."

Arthur cleared his throat. "Hold on a moment. He's the one who plays cards with Emmett, right?"

Anna's eyebrows rose. "Umm...Yes."

"Well, sister. It took me a while to put two and two together. He's the same man who brought you home from Ira's." Arthur roguishly grinned. "The one who almost kissed you."

Lily abruptly twirled toward him. "I thought you said you weren't watching?"

"I can't disclose everything. I never know when I might need that information." Arthur chuckled. "Must be the reason why I never told you what I overheard at the card game." He rested his folded arms on the counter.

"Spill it, if you know what's good for you." Lily shook her fist at him. "Don't forget, between Celia and me, you've always been outnumbered with the secrets we have on you."

"Gee! I didn't say I wasn't going to tell you. Anyway, at the hotel last month, Benjamin said something about you being interesting." Arthur leaned forward out the popcorn stand's window. "Emmett even hushed him up. So, it had to be good."

Lily chucked a piece of corn at Arthur. "*Interesting*...that could mean a lot of different things."

Arthur smiled and exposed his cheek dimples. "No, not *interesting*. It was... easy on the eyes. Yes, that's what he said."

The edges of Lily's lips curved upward. Benjamin must have told the truth yesterday about his feelings. He liked her before Ira overstepped his obligations and made Benjamin give his word to take care of her. "Anna, did Emmett tell you anything about this?"

"No, he didn't."

"See you at home, Arthur. Your secrets are safe...for now." Lily waved as they shuffled toward the theater. "You know I never said I didn't find Benjamin attractive. I do, but after what I've gone through with Ira...well, I couldn't do the same thing to his fiancée."

Anna halted. "They never would have gotten married anyway. Not from what Emmett told me. Benjamin had problems with Vivian well before he even met you." She elbowed Lily. "Trust me, he won't be an eligible bachelor for long. Especially if you don't let him know you're interested. All those unwed hovering women certainly will."

"Ha! Well then, maybe we really aren't meant to be." He could have his pick of so many others. She didn't like it, but Anna was right. A group gathered in front of the theater. Lily settled onto the bench next door underneath the department store's candy window. She whispered, "Perhaps my destiny is Milwaukee." Did she even deserve this chance with him? She set the popcorn bag down and tucked her skirt around her legs. "Benjamin possibly choosing to be with me sounds wonderful." If only he were Catholic. "But I'm not certain now would be the right time."

Anna scooted in next to her. "Is it still too soon after Ira?"

"No, it's not that." She couldn't stop guilt from bubbling inside. Ira's life implied a hell on earth. Even worse, he'd nobly released her from a possible life sentence of purgatory. And now the man who's mutually attracted to her has become available. "After everything that's happened with Ira, it doesn't seem fair to have a chance at happiness." *Do I deserve this opportunity after failing so miserably with Ira?* She bit the edge of her lip. "Don't you think I'm being too selfish?"

"Of course not."

"Then why do I feel so bad?" Lily glanced at Anna and back to her hands resting on her lap. "What will everyone think if they see me around town with someone else so soon?"

"Honestly, why does it matter what other people think?"

"Well, I care." Lily crossed her arms. "Don't you remember what I went through in grade school? Those mean girls all thought I wasn't as good as them. And even though I've grown stronger, that doesn't mean those times still don't bother me."

"Yes, I remember." Anna rubbed Lily's back. "People can be so cruel and you shouldn't have been treated that poorly. I'm sorry for what happened to you. Please don't be sad."

Lily's body tensed at the memories. "It's probably best to avoid situations that could potentially cause me aggravation." A new start would be simpler than dredging up the past. Her neck muscles tightened. "Benjamin and I are so different. I just don't think he's the right one for me."

"I can understand you wouldn't want to intentionally place yourself in that type of position." Anna moved closer to Lily. "But should you always let what happened in the past affect right now and your future?" Anna rested her hand on Lily's knee. "I hate to say this, but Ira wasn't always the nicest to you. Sometimes when people aren't treated kindly, they are led to believe that's the way they should be treated. Do you remember when I mentioned on the rooftop the other day that you deserve to be happy and shouldn't settle for anything less?"

Lily nodded. "I'll try."

"Good. I want you to keep that in mind." Anna twisted toward Lily and adjusted her skirt, covering her knee. "You said you don't think Benjamin's the right one, however, he could be. I know he is a man who will treat you well." She placed her hands on Lily's shoulders. "And since you're leaving town anyway, why shouldn't you enjoy yourself a little?"

"I suppose you could be right." Lily rolled her head, loosening the muscles. She had a couple of months yet to save for the move. "When you say it like that, I guess there's no harm in finding out if Benjamin could be the one for me."

"Glad to hear." Anna pulled Lily into a hug. "I'll be here for you if you run into any trouble." Anna gave an encouraging smile. "We'd better get going to the movie before all the good seats are taken."

After a short wait in line, the usher with a fancy bowtie led Anna and Lily into the theater. A light flickered across the room as the newsreel played on the screen surrounded by majestic red-velvet curtains. A set of large marble columns were anchored on both sides of the tied-back drapery. And an art deco design garnished in gold rose above the center of the screen, sprawling onto the ceiling.

At the foot of the stairs, Anna paused in the dim glow, glancing at people in the crowd. She pointed at a man waving his arms as if he were landing a plane. "Usher, we will go in the back there on the left."

Lily poked Anna's arm. "Is that Emmett?"

"Yes."

Lily trailed behind up the steps. Why hadn't Anna mentioned her husband planned on coming? Something didn't seem quite right. Each filled row of theater seats blocked the view of the figure next to where Emmett stood. All that peeked out was a dark sleeve on the armrest. The style fit that of a male jacket. If she were to wager, the nicely tailored arm belonged to Benjamin. *He sure is sneaky, getting Anna to bring me here.*

No wonder Anna had asked her to come out tonight. The usher helped Anna up the last step and into the line of seats.

Benjamin's eyes widened as Lily appeared. He rose, letting Anna pass by to sit on the other side of Emmett. A twinkle gleamed in his chocolate brown eyes.

Her heart raced faster and it certainly hadn't been from the climb up the stairs. The usher held Lily's hand while she exited the walkway into the row, taking the last seat next to Benjamin. She rested the popcorn bag on her lap. "So, we meet again."

The huge grin on his face made it seem like he was up to something. "I'm glad you're here."

Her stomach flip-flopped. Had she misread his smile as shenanigans? Or was he being coy with her? "Did you know I would be here tonight?"

"No, I thought I was only going with Emmett."

Considering he wasn't aware she'd be here, the scheme must have been planned by Anna and Emmett. "I thought it would be just us girls going out to the movies too." Lily pointed with her thumb past Benjamin. "I'm certain they were the ones who tricked us."

"I can't say I'm not happy they did." His eyes glanced between her head and neck. "You look beautiful tonight. I like how the polka dots match."

"Thank you. I cut material from the scarf and wrapped the crown so they looked like a set. A plain hat, such as this, allows me to easily transform it into something new." Lily slid back into the cushioned chair. Her decision wouldn't be an easy one after these next eight weeks if he kept exuding so much charm. "Popcorn?" She held up the bag.

"Maybe later."

He liked her, he wasn't engaged, and as Anna would say, maybe fate's playing a hand in keeping her here. "Would you like to continue the conversation from yesterday? I promise not to end it abruptly with you this time."

"Yes, I would." Benjamin shifted in the seat facing her. "My excitement got the best of me yesterday and I should have been upfront right away about Vivian. I broke it off Saturday. We never would have been happy together. I know that now." He leaned closer. "You've given me hope with our friendship and I want very much for us to be more than acquaintances."

Everything he's saying sounds perfect. Her head slanted toward him.

"I can see you're thinking about my proposal. If I told you again how I couldn't take my eyes off you when we met, would that sway your decision?" His gaze penetrated hers.

All the blood in her body rushed to her face like a raging river. She couldn't take her eyes off of him either. Not now and not the day they'd met.

"I'm choosing you because I like you." He held out his hand to her. "This moment would have happened even if Ira hadn't asked me to take care of you. I wanted to get to know you since I saw you in that frilly dress." A definite coy smile spread across his face.

He chose her because he wanted to, not because he was told to. How could she resist?

"I know you said you'd listen, but I'm getting nervous you're not saying anything." He stood. "If you want nothing to do with me, I'll go." He put his hand out towards her. "Lily, please! We can take this as slow as you want."

The film danced across Benjamin's figure while his shadow stretched over the screen and up the ceiling. People rustled in their seats while others called out for him to sit down, creating even more of a ruckus. His figure seemed to mimic the King Kong movie poster at the theater entrance. One giant gorilla falling in love with her. Lily snickered as she reached out, placing her hand in his.

"It's about time," the man behind bellowed. "Can you sit down now so I can see the rest of the previews?"

Lily tugged on Benjamin's arm and he plopped into the seat.

"So, you're agreeing to get to know me better?" He raised his eyebrows repeatedly in a quick flash imitating Groucho Marx on the movie clip.

Witty and so handsome. Lily grinned. "I agree with your persistence."

"I think you're saying I have a bit of charm...I like that." His thumb caressed the top of her hand. "I could certainly get used to this. What would you like to do tomorrow?"

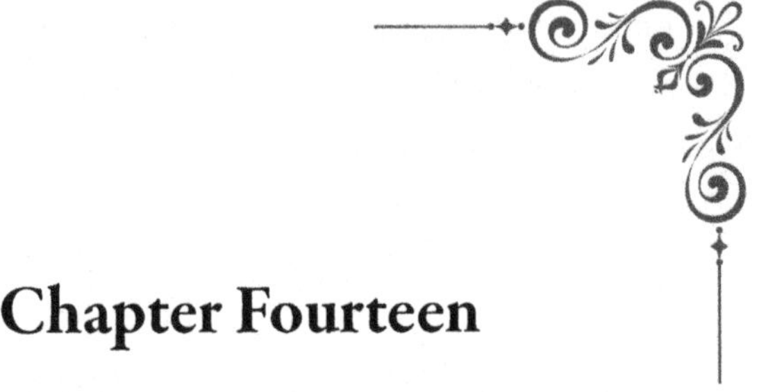

Chapter Fourteen

Lily tossed her bathing suit on the bed. "What was I thinking suggesting we go to the pool? Don't you think this stretchy material and lack thereof is rather revealing?"

"You'll fit right in." Anna plunked onto the mattress. "Besides, Benjamin will be in swimwear too. Don't you want to see those long legs?"

"You're incorrigible."

Anna chuckled. "I encourage you—I think that's what you mean."

"Yes, of course, that too." Lily picked up the one-piece green suit and laid it against herself. "I still can't believe how incredible Benjamin is." She twisted back and forth. "He knows all the right things to say."

"I'm happy you're happy. We're going to have such a good time together." Anna rubbed the palms of her hands together. "Anything you'd like to tell me about last night?"

"We didn't get much of a chance to talk after the movie started." Lily laid the suit on the towel and rolled it into a ball. "Benjamin held my hand the whole night and every time his fingers brushed mine, I couldn't focus on the movie. Instead, I imagined what my life would be like with him."

"Oh, and how was it?"

"Peaceful, like we enjoyed the ordinary things in life." Lily placed her hands to her heart. "Spending time together going to the corner market or eating in the kitchen or taking a drive." She squeezed her arms tighter to her chest. "I enjoy going with him in his car. It's a shame he walked to the theater. Not that I didn't appreciate Emmett driving me home last night, but my time with Benjamin ended so soon."

Anna clapped her hands together lightly at the fingertips. "Everything's moving along quicker than I hoped."

"I have known him for a while already. As far as how we met last night—you're not absolved from being so sneaky."

Anna unveiled a cheeky grin. "Would you have gone if I told you he'd be there? I don't believe you would. You said it yourself—you're happy."

"I am, but I also want to make decisions in my own time. You're the one who believes in fate." Lily stuffed the towel under her arm. "If we are meant to be together, wouldn't it happen on its own?"

"I suppose so, but not if you're off in Milwaukee and he's here."

"I plan to get to know him better these next couple of months. We're going to take the relationship slow. I'm trying to be realistic, so please don't get your hopes up. If things don't work out at least I can still leave town. Nothing has changed since the discussion we had before the movie." Lily opened the bedroom door. "Let's go enjoy our time at the pool."

The first day of summer had turned out to be a perfect day for the grand opening of the pool. If it hadn't been for FDR and his New Deal, the community of Hub City would only be fanning away the heat. Lily propped her head with her hands while lying on the cement edge next to the pool. She loved swimming but her last handstand hadn't ended so well. She'd swallowed a bunch of water and couldn't quit coughing.

Anna seemed to be having an enjoyable time despite trying to get away from a bunch of young boys at least ten years her junior. Surprisingly these boys must have thought splashing was some form of endearment. She stood. Leaving Anna alone much longer to fend for herself wasn't a good idea. Besides, so far there wasn't any sight of the men coming to their rescue, although the hour had to be close to the end of their workday. Lily jumped into the pool, weaving her way toward Anna.

"Nice to see you come back into the water, Lil." Anna bobbed up and down, rippling the water around her. "Are you feeling all right?"

"Yes, thanks for asking." Lily joined in the quick movements, creating even more waves. "I watched how you kept swimming away from those annoying boys. I think they like you."

"I'm not so sure." Anna's neck stopped at the water level and she popped back up like a spring. "You know I'm an old married lady now."

"With lovely green eyes."

"Oh my! That's sweet of you."

Lily stopped bouncing. "The next time those boys splash around us, I might have a way to make them quit."

Anna pointed. "Now is your chance, here they come."

Lily made a circle with her thumb and index finger, stuck them in her mouth, and blew. A piercing whistle louder than the lifeguard's echoed over the people in the pool. The boys stopped and swam in the opposite direction. "Look at that Anna, it worked."

"Hey, are you whistling at us?"

Anna turned in the direction of the inquiry. "We sure are."

"Thanks, sweetheart." Running to the edge, Emmett lunged into the air grabbing his crossed legs before hitting the water.

A whistle blew from the lifeguard's stand. "No running!"

Emmett shot up and appeared right in front of Anna.

"Nice one." Anna wiped the water off her face. "Lil and I were just talking about how males show their affection."

Lily laughed.

"Come on, Benjamin." Emmett motioned with a flick of his hand.

Benjamin shook his head. "I think I'm going to sit here on the edge for a while." He lowered himself onto the ledge, dangling his feet into the water.

Lily faced Anna and Emmett. "You two can swim if you want. I'll go over and keep Benjamin company." She took several strokes, kicking her feet toward the long-legged man. Anna sure was right about getting a gander at those legs.

She swam to the side of him and stood while he swooshed his long feet through the water. His feet appeared double her size six, and his stark-white, slightly hairy legs hadn't seen a ray of sunshine in quite a while. Although his well-defined thigh muscles were absolutely swoon-worthy.

Her legs wobbled as she braced her hand on the ledge. "You look like you're ready to go swimming." He wore a wide horizontal striped black and gold top paired with black shorts trimmed by a white belt. "Are you planning on coming in and joining the rest of us?"

"Maybe in a little while. I'm still trying to get used to the water. Besides, it's enjoyable now that you're here."

"It is?" She smiled. He's such a sweet charmer.

Benjamin's eyes twinkled through the squint of his lids. "I couldn't help but notice how well you swim. You sure make it look easy."

She squeezed water from her hair. "Thank you. I spent many summers at Anna's grandparents' pond in the country. They had a large oak tree that had a rope tied to an overhanging branch next to the water. We'd swing out and let go. I had to learn fast how to dog paddle, otherwise I would have sunk to the bottom like a rock."

"I'm certain I would sink. I never learned how to swim." He fluttered his feet back and forth. "As long as the water's not past my chest, I'm fine."

"You're half-way there." Lily pointed to his feet. "That's exactly how you move your feet in the water and keep your lower body afloat. The paddling of your arms keeps your head and chest portion buoyant. Whichever section begins to sink is where you need to either kick harder or paddle faster."

"Sounds simple enough."

"The technique is one of the easiest to learn but can be quite exhausting for long distances." She skimmed her hands across the water. "Aren't you getting warm sitting there?"

"You're right, the sun's baked me enough. It's time to cool off for a while." He lunged forward into the water, creating a small splash. "I have to admit I hesitated a little when you suggested coming to the pool." He patted the ripples on the water drifting below his waist.

"As soon as I mentioned my plans, I did too." Everyone in town had waited a few extra weeks for the pool to be filled due to the pea plant needing the water. The opening had been the talk of the town. Why had she chosen such a crowded public place for meeting? "However, I'd suspect not for the same reasons."

He rubbed his chin. "For me, I would have rather done something I'm good at."

"So..." Lily tilted her head. "Do you think you need to impress me?"

Benjamin chuckled. "Of course, shouldn't I always try?" He cupped his hands together just below the water's surface and squeezed rapidly, forcing water to cascade into a fountain. "Why were you reluctant? And don't say it has anything to do with what you are wearing. Emerald green is flattering on you."

A sudden rush of warmth spread to her cheeks. Lily cupped her hands, trying to create a fountain with the water but every time she squeezed her hands together, nothing happened. "Both of us were engaged not that long ago to other people and there are many folks here from our small town." She smacked her hands together swiftly and water spurted out. "Being a part of anyone's gossip is something I'd rather avoid."

"I will defend you to anybody." Benjamin took her hands in his. "You have nothing to be ashamed of. Unlike me. I should have known better than to break off the engagement in public. Vivian didn't take the news as well as I'd hoped. The whole restaurant witnessed the aftermath. I'm certain Vivian was utterly devasted by her exit. I tried to stop her as she went outside, but she ran down the sidewalk before I could catch her." He rubbed her skin lightly with his thumbs. "When we went for a ride the other day, I mailed her an apology for everything that happened."

Lily swayed their arms back and forth. "That was kind of you. I'm sure your words will provide Vivian some comfort." He had said all the right things for her, including how he'd stand up for her. She never had someone in her corner before. And his concern for Vivian revealed his genuinely caring character. Her brow wrinkled. Could the woman in the fancy blue ostrich hat be the same person? The likelihood of what she'd witnessed Saturday seemed to coincide with his story. "Which restaurant were you at?"

"The one in Hotel Charles."

"Oh, no! I was on the rooftop across the street and saw the commotion."

Benjamin's left brow arched. "What happened inside was even worse."

"That's too bad." She compressed his hands gently. "I'm sorry the two of you had to go through such a traumatic event."

"You and I have gone through a lot too, yet if we hadn't, we wouldn't be here together now." He inched closer, bringing their hands up toward his chest. "I think there are a lot of reasons you've come into my life. Right now, I can think of one good example, but I'd need your assistance."

Lily craned her neck upward. His gentle gaze tranquilized her. "Yes. How?"

"About five years ago I fell in the water while fishing on a boat and almost drowned. The vest I was wearing had several holes in the vinyl and the fiber inside got saturated, weighing me down. If Louie hadn't been there, I wouldn't have made it out of the lake. I think you'd be the perfect person to teach me how to swim."

"Of course I will. Let's go over here to the edge of the pool." Lily bounced in the water following Benjamin. "We'll make sure you know how to kick before we try to swim. Hold onto the ledge keeping your body horizontal in the water. Your legs need to be straight, with your toes pointed." She stood on the side of him.

He grabbed hold and started kicking, but his legs were working as if he were riding a bicycle.

"Try to relax."

Benjamin quit the motion and his body hovered just below the surface of the water.

Lily took hold of his feet, glancing across his long and lean frame. A pleasant shiver ran through her spine. "I'll help you." She moved his legs up and down. "It's like you're chopping with each limb alternately." She let go. "Good. Try to stay close to the water's surface."

"I think I have it now." Benjamin peered over his shoulder.

"Yes, you do." He couldn't have had a sweeter expression. "Let's try to do the stroke with your arms. We'll practice in the air."

Benjamin rose and faced her.

"Follow what I do. You'll want to stretch your arms above your head, cup one of your hands like you're holding a baseball and keep your arm straight, bringing it in front of you, then down toward your thigh. All right, good. Now flatten your hand and sweep in reverse above your head. Continue with the opposite arm using the same motion and keep alternating. Yes, like that."

"Should I try in the water?"

"Very well, but it's not easy coordinating your arms and legs at the same time. Don't get too discouraged. It's similar to patting your head and rubbing your stomach at the same time."

He chuckled.

"Concentrate on the arm movement like you're picking an apple and putting it in your pocket. See if you can swim from this edge to the one over there." She swept her arm from one point to the other. "I'll watch from here."

Benjamin pushed off the pool bottom with his feet, taking a few strokes, and kicking fast. The first few times, he'd only swam a short way before standing. Each time though he'd go a little farther before stopping.

Benjamin trusted me. Another one of his many admirable qualities. All their times together were effortless. She could be herself and he liked her just the way she was. And according to him, she was beautiful.

So far on the swim back, he hadn't stopped. He was either a quick learner or she'd been a good instructor. Either way, they suited each other and if their relationship continued so easily, she doubted she'd be headed out of town.

"Did you see that? I swam the whole way back."

"You were great. I think I mastered your fountain too." She squeezed her cupped hands together, spraying a stream of water directly into his chest.

"Whoa!" Benjamin lowered his hands in the water and aimed. He gave her a mischievous grin as he shot the water right into her face.

"Aah! You do like me."

He laughed. "Don't ever doubt it. So, do you think I'm ready for the Olympics?"

"Well...no. They haven't included the dog paddle as an event yet." Lily giggled. "There is one more thing you could learn in case you tire out while swimming."

"Oh. What's that?"

"Everyone should learn how to float. When you're too tired to swim, you can relax in the water until you catch your breath."

"Aren't you just offering yourself to the sharks?"

"There aren't any sharks around here." She shook her head. "You're being silly. Let's go near the edge. That way you can grab onto the side in case you think you're going to sink."

Benjamin knelt next to the ledge. The water level fell just below his broad shoulders.

"I think this depth will be good. I'll stand behind you and ease you back until you're level with the water. It will be hard to hear once your ears are underwater so I want to mention a few things. Relaxing by deep breathing is the best way to stay afloat. You can also kick lightly to keep your legs horizontal. When you're comfortable, let go of the ledge and I'll hold onto your head so it doesn't go under. I won't let go until you tell me."

"All right. Are you ready?"

Lily braced her hands on his back. She nestled closer to his earthy musky scent. "Go ahead." Her hands slid from his back, up his neck, and onto his head. His dark coffee-colored eyes were open as his head sank into her palms. She smiled.

Benjamin relaxed so easily, he seemed to be a natural at floating. Maybe his trust in her helped him feel comfortable. He slipped his hand off the ledge. The center of his body descended slightly as his legs dipped down. His eyelids locked shut. Panic spread across his face.

"Breathe." She wasn't sure if he'd heard, but he finally took a deep breath and then another. His core rose back to the surface. He kicked his legs, making them parallel. His eyes opened.

She nodded. "Good." Being this close to him brought that shiver to the nape of her neck.

A shadow cast over them.

Benjamin's eyes widened and his mouth dropped open.

Lily peered at the person hovering above. She followed the smooth legs upward to the torso covered by a yellow suit. An oversized green straw hat protected the perfectly made-up woman's face. Tight red-pigmented lips and daggered green eyes shot a coldness to the pit of Lily's stomach.

"Vivian!" His body thrashed in the water.

Lily shuffled backward and her hands slipped off his head.

Benjamin's core plummeted. His limbs formed a *V* shape. He writhed under the water.

Lily reached for his flailing arms, catching his wrist. She tugged.

His feet struck the bottom and he torpedoed to the surface. Coughing, he held his hand to his chest as he hunched over. Water spewed down his chin.

Lily patted his back. "Are you all right?"

"I...think...so." His words gasped between the breaths and coughs. He straightened his back and rotated toward Vivian.

"Nice to know you still get choked up seeing me." Vivian's eyes shifted to the side of Benjamin and fixated on Lily. "Let me guess, this must be the damsel you saved in the downpour. Lily, isn't it?"

Lily couldn't shake the sense of déjà vu. The last confrontation she had with a woman had been the start of her whole relationship with Ira unraveling. Another public display was exactly where she didn't want to be. Maybe she could be exceptionally sweet. She bobbed to the edge. "Pleasure to meet you." Lily held out her hand.

Vivian's nose rose in the air. She crossed her arms over her chest and locked eyes on Benjamin. "My instincts were right all along." Her laced sandal tapped against the concrete. "You ended our relationship for someone like her? A poor Catholic church mouse."

Why had Vivian stooped to name-calling? Lily had endured the same malarkey at school. How childish was this woman? Lily may be poor and Catholic, yet she wanted to prove she wasn't as mousy as Vivian thought. But she needed to let Benjamin handle this quarrel with his ex-fiancée.

"That's enough." Benjamin put his arm across Lily's shoulders.

"And to think I thought the letter you'd sent meant you had finally come to your senses." Vivian waved her hand up and down Lily's figure. "Apparently not. That will never happen if she's around distracting you."

Benjamin pulled Lily closer. "What happened between us, was between us. Keep Lily out of it."

Lily didn't want to be seen as the 'other woman.' But in Vivian's eyes, it was reality. And since Vivian had no issues with public displays, the whole town would know about her in no time. One of her worst fears seemed to be coming true.

Vivian posed with one hand on her hip. "Well, I know I would have never allowed you to wear that swimsuit. You look like a wasp with those black and gold wide stripes. What were you thinking?"

"I was thinking I had a day planned with an amazing caring lady." Benjamin took Lily's hand and led her away. "The air in this direction will have a bit less tension."

"Don't think this is over." Vivian bellowed.

Lily leaned into his side. "Sorry for letting you sink."

He pulled her closer. "You pulled me to safety. I'm grateful. Sorry you had to endure Vivian's foul attitude."

Never had Lily encountered a woman with such intense nastiness. "I might have spoken too soon about there not being any sharks around here."

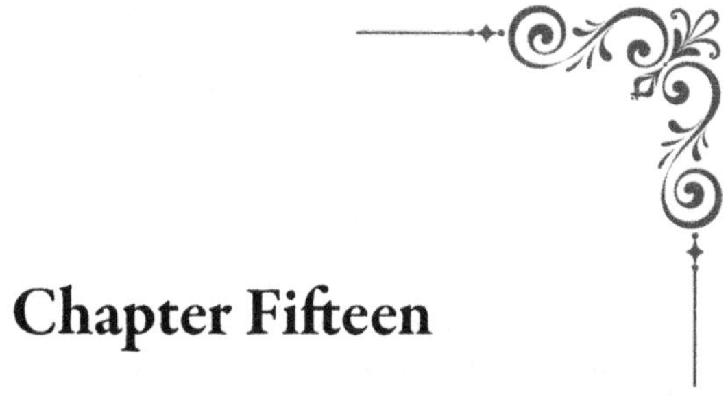

Chapter Fifteen

Vivian strolled into her favorite place, the sun-parlor. A nice breeze blew between the opposing cluster of windows. Sun rays enhanced the cheery yellow-painted walls. This was a place to impress anyone who entered. Her family had Hub City's finest collection of artwork, stately furniture, and prized possessions.

The housemaid had prepared the room for afternoon tea but Mother had asked her to inspect the servant's work before their guest arrived. A wise decision since one of the embroidered pillows on the red upholstered armchair appeared flatter than it should be. She gave it a fluff and scanned the pillow in the matching chair. The quaint set was the most comfortable wing-backs in the house. Not to mention in the most elegant style of Queen Anne, having slender legs covered by decorative gilded florets and *S*-shaped scrolls. She turned on her heel. If the pillow hadn't been sufficiently fluffed, what else would she find where the incompetent maid failed?

The gold-striped settee anchored the far wall and faced the chairs. In between nestled the tea table with four creamy-golden, carved cabriole legs holding a distinctively shaped mirrored top. Beneath the mirror, a base featured a wooden scrolled basket of roses.

Placement of the dishes and utensils were of the utmost importance. Vivian approached the tea table, viewing the arrangement as their guest would. On the far left of the table, the ornate china teacups from Hammersley and Company had been organized in a row. The edges of the cups and saucers were trimmed in gold. Each was decorated with four roses in orange, yellow, red, and lavender. Uniquely, one of the four colored roses adorned the inside of the cup. She repositioned the center teacup over slightly, aligning the row into perfection.

Next to the teacups, spoons had been fitted inside each other along with a stack of forks. Dishes of cream, sugar, lemon wedges, and spiced syrup along with a covered slop bowl were centered on the table. The brass bell ringer sat near the edge, with remaining space on the far right empty to hold the teapot.

On the side of the settee, a round table covered in a lace doily had a stack of plates layered with napkins in between alongside the silver, three-tiered food stand. The light meal consisted of a small top tier with thinly sliced, toasted English bread and butter. The middle layer hosted a mix of open-faced sandwiches dolloped with either pimento butter and brie cheese or maple cream and chopped nuts. The largest tier was filled with her favorite assorted frosted cakes. Vivian licked her lips.

Behind the food, a crystal flower vase displayed shades of orange and red roses, enhancing the tea service. A few flowers didn't cascade in the correct direction. She pulled the stems, sniffed the blossoms, and rearranged them. Everything was complete.

Vivian chose the farthest wing-backed chair from the doorway. She crossed her legs at the ankles, straightened her spine, and adjusted her white dress skirt dappled with red, blue, and yellow circles.

She turned her head toward the clicking of heels approaching on the wooden floor. "Good afternoon, Mother." Her red hair was pinned away from her face, giving Mother a youthful appearance. Sometimes people would comment they looked more like sisters. The compliment always made Mother happy. Although, Vivian figured people were just trying to be nice.

"Have you made certain we are ready for our guest?"

"Yes, Mother." Vivian touched her wrist. Her new bracelet should have been there for the occasion. She hated losing anything and especially since she'd only purchased it a month ago. The white stone would have harmonized well with her dress. The last time she had the bracelet was at Hotel Charles. She must have lost it somewhere between the time she left the dinner table with Benjamin and before she got home that night. Hopefully, someone at the restaurant found it.

Deloris touched the painting by Georgia O'Keeffe and tilted the frame upward. "Now remember, when Constance arrives let me do all the talking. You'll get too emotional."

"Yes, Mother." Her mother had crafty ways of controlling most any situation. If she pushed too hard though, Benjamin's mother would wrap him up tight like a baby in a blanket and they'd never convince her to align with their wishes.

Deloris glided across the floor, balancing her navy Edwardian hat stacked with plumes of feathers. She settled herself onto the settee and jiggled the handbell. "Our goal here is to have Constance assist us in making Benjamin see how poorly he's behaved. If you go off on a tangent, what reason will Constance have to help you?"

"I understand." Vivian tucked a wavy strand under her white-laced hat and covered her burning cheek with her hand. How could Mother say that to her? Mother had been the one who had the outburst four days ago at church. Vivian had been humiliated in front of the whole town and now would have to bite a hole in her cheek and say nothing to Constance. Mother always had to reign above her.

The grandfather clock in the hall chimed three times as the housemaid brought in the teapot.

"Anything else, ma'am?"

"No, that will be all." Deloris slid the teapot closer. "Don't look so dismal, Vivian. Put your shoulders back and sit like a proper lady. I'm certain Constance will understand your position. Our friendship spans quite a lengthy period. I trust she'll do the right thing."

"All right, Mother."

The housemaid appeared at the entrance. "May I present to you, Mrs. Constance Claussen."

Vivian bowed from her chair. Inside the arched doorway, Benjamin's mother soared almost to the six-foot doorframe, but her height didn't intimidate Vivian. She gazed at Constance's peach dress with puffed quilted detail on the bodice and sleeves that hung snuggly around her slender frame. The embellished neckline dipped into a *V* with a decorative pin accentuating the narrow point. Her hat brim curved upward in the back, exposing her black hair, and a purple ostrich feather in the front emphasized her impressive outfit. Benjamin certainly had her dark features. Constance gracefully walked across the room, between the wing-backed chairs and the tea table, outwardly prepared as a worthy opponent to her mother. Vivian rose, crossed over the oriental rug, and approached Constance near the tea table.

"Lovely to see you, Constance." Deloris' orange-red lips curved into a smile. "How would you like your tea? With lemon as usual?"

Constance smiled warmly. "Yes. And add some spiced syrup too, please."

"Wonderful choice." Deloris drizzled the syrup into the cup, poured in the hot tea, and added a wedge of lemon along with a spoon and fork.

Vivian held the saucer and escorted Constance to her chair. Not once acknowledging her.

Constance sat and crossed her legs at the ankles, smiling politely. "It's good to see you, Vivian."

Vivian handed her the tea. "Likewise." She twisted her fingers through her white-gloved hands. Constance's critical tone echoed in her ears. *Where does she get off judging me for what happened?* Her mother definitely had a battle on her hands.

Constance gently squeezed the lemon wedge with the fork. "The weather's been pleasant if you like it a bit on the warm side."

Deloris picked up her teacup. "Let's drop the idle chitchat and get down to the business at hand." She took a sip.

"All right." Constance lifted her chin. "I'm listening."

"I am going to assume you're well aware of how Benjamin publicly ended his relationship with my daughter. And I will conclude you had no idea he planned on doing such. If this is incorrect, don't let me continue." Deloris placed her saucer and cup on the table, studying the woman opposite. "Good. Then I know you would have intervened."

Constance frowned. "Of course. I never would have condoned such behavior."

"Have you spoken with him about his rationale?"

Constance swirled her spoon through the tea. "I have."

Vivian's throat constricted. She tugged on her boatneck collar. Would Benjamin have told his mother something different than he'd expressed to her? If he'd given his mother the same implausible tale, had she believed him?

"Honestly, I felt he was holding something back in his explanation." Constance laid the spoon on the saucer and set her tea on the side table. "He profusely apologized if his actions caused any unpleasantness in your and my relationship. I believe my son is truly sorry for any repercussions due to his decision."

"That's all fine and good, however, my daughter is still in love with your son. The town is talking about how disgraceful your son's actions were and I would think you wouldn't want your family's reputation tarnished any more than I want ours to be." Deloris sternly glared at Constance.

"No, I do not." Constance's brow furrowed. "I hope you're not suggesting my son's the only one responsible for what happened. Your daughter could have handled the situation with a little more grace."

Vivian squeezed her fingers around the armrests. Was Benjamin's mother delusional? She tried to leave without causing a scene. None of what happened was her fault. What had Benjamin told her?

"I think you need to explain yourself." Deloris crossed her arms.

"You know as well as I do a relationship takes two people who are willing to work hard. In this case, that would be my son and your daughter. I know my son; he wouldn't just call things off on a whim. And you have to know your daughter can't be completely innocent. Have you asked her about the circumstances surrounding the broken engagement?" Constance tipped her head slightly toward Vivian.

"Well, I really don't like what you are insinuating." Deloris' cheeks reddened. "Vivian did tell me what happened. I think you're the one with blinders on. If your son's so innocent in the matter, why would he have sent Vivian an apology letter?"

Vivian twisted in the chair. Benjamin's letter reiterated how he'd cared for her and how sorry he was for ending their relationship. This obviously validated the fact that if Lily wasn't around, she'd still be with Benjamin.

Constance straightened in the chair. "Benjamin is remorseful, but that doesn't mean he is the only guilty party in this fiasco."

"You'd better be careful as to what you're saying. It seems to me you don't have control over your son at all. Don't you remember what happened with your son Robert? You let him have his way and now he's a lowly traveling salesman. Let's not forget my husband has given a lot of business to Ebbe. You wouldn't be as affluent if it wasn't for him." Deloris steepled her fingers. "I suggest you rein in your son before it's too late."

Constance's shoulder slumped forward. "What do you propose?"

Vivian smirked. Benjamin's mother caved as expected.

Deloris gestured Vivian toward the tiered tray. "It may be a touch more complicated getting them back together than you think. Are you aware of Benjamin meeting someone else?"

Vivian gritted her teeth at the mention of Lily as she picked up the goodies.

"That cannot be." Constance slowly shook her head. "I would have heard."

"Oh! But it is." Vivian held the tray in front of Constance and handed her a plate.

"It is not that I don't believe either of you." Constance transferred a maple cream and nut sandwich onto her plate. "I simply have a hard time considering my son would do something like this."

"Especially since we're engaged to be married."

"Vivian!" Deloris scrunched her face into a disgusted expression and returned her focus to Constance. "I assure you I have first-hand knowledge this is true. Never would I have fathomed your son would disrespect my daughter like this."

"I am so sorry, Deloris. Who is she?"

"Lily Vanderhoof."

"Vanderhoof? That family name is not familiar." Constance took a nibble of the sandwich.

Vivian presented her mother with a plate and offered the tray. Certainly, Benjamin's mother hadn't heard of her. Why would she? Little Miss Lily Flower was only one rung above a woman of ill repute.

"Probably not, they are not of our notability." Deloris chose a morsel from each of the trays. "Benjamin drove this deplorable papist home several times."

Constance covered her mouth.

"Vivian dismissed his actions as a gesture of friendship. However, we've recently understood his candor covered up his deceit."

"Benjamin will not disgrace our families like this. And with a Catholic too!" Constance's face flushed. "My son has not been raised to treat such a young vibrant woman like your Vivian this way."

Deloris grinned. "I am pleased you are seeing this from my vantage point."

"Don't worry, it is *our* position. Especially since we were the ones who encouraged them to initiate the relationship. I will do whatever I can to influence my son."

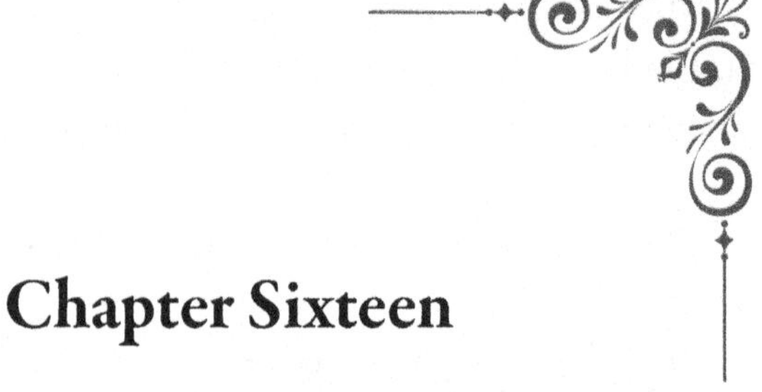

Chapter Sixteen

Benjamin opened the door to the local roller rink, situated on the outskirts of the city park. As he stepped in, wheels thumped across the wooden floor slats. The circular motion of the skaters created a wind tunnel inside, blowing around humid stale air. Similar to how Vivian's hot air had burst into his lesson at the swimming pool three days ago. Lily had handled herself graciously like a lady despite Vivian's temper tantrum. He admired her calm demeanor and the way she could inject humor into the situation. Scanning people near the tables and around the rink, he noted neither Emmett nor the girls were here yet. It had to be close to seven o'clock when they'd planned to meet. As he pulled out his pocket watch, he flipped the lid, noting the time at ten minutes till the hour.

A pipe organ across the room vibrated a familiar musical tune. He hadn't been here since last summer, but a few practice glides should keep him steady on his feet. In the corner an open table was large enough to seat all of them. He sat, untied his skate laces, loosened the nut with the key while he pulled the plate apart so he could slip his shoe into the opening. Once adjusted, he squeezed the metal together and tightened the nut. Repeating the process with the other shoe, he tied both laces and buckled the skate straps. He stood and pushed off with one foot across the floor toward the empty corner. As he got closer to the edge, he spun around and skated backward. His wheels tapped the floor along with the beat while he rolled next to the wall. He enjoyed this thrilling activity and it suited him, which would undoubtedly allow him to dazzle Lily with his skills. A few complex turns boosted his confidence; he'd be ready for sure when she arrived.

Benjamin skated to the table and braced his hands on the back of the chair. Saturday nights were always busy at the rink and tonight wasn't any different. With so many people, the high-pitched roof rebounded all the commotion like thunder rolling in on a stormy night. Twenty-foot-high poles lined the sides of the rink, supporting the roof and making people disappear for brief moments. While the crowd circled, the constant swirling movement of the clothing colors could make any sober person feel dizzily drunk.

As he followed the skaters, Lily appeared alongside in a sky-blue dress walking right at him. Everyone else faded from view. She seemed to be hovering toward him as if she were a dream. His body tingled. She was even more beautiful than the last time he'd seen her. There had been a way about her he found tremendously captivating. He waved his hand, drawing her attention.

Lily walked faster than Anna and Emmett, leaving them trailing behind. She smiled. "Good to see you again, Benjamin."

"It seems like days."

"Let's see...it's Saturday and the last time was Wednesday...so yes, it's been three whole days. What have you been doing without me?" She laughed.

"Please have a seat." Benjamin pulled out a chair. "I've kept my nights busy, so I tried not to miss you too much." He winked.

"Last night I had a meeting at the Good Fellows Club. And the night before that I played poker with Emmett and Louie."

Lily tilted her head. "Hmm...and you still found time to miss me?"

"Did you miss me too?" Emmett slapped his hand on Benjamin's back.

Benjamin lurched forward while his skate wheels rolled back and forth. His arms flailed as he spun around. He stopped twirling in front of Lily and held his arms open wide. "Ta-dah!"

"Wow!" Lily clapped her hands.

"He's much better at catching himself from falling than I am." Anna sat in the chair next to Lily. "Usually the next day I have a purple bruise on my backside."

"I'll try to keep you from falling, sweetheart." Emmett leaned over and kissed his wife.

"I can promise that I'm much better at skating than drowning." Benjamin chuckled. "However, I had such a good swimming coach it might end up being a toss-up with some more practice."

Lily grinned. "Well, I'd better get my skates on then." She took a shoelace which held a shiny silver skate key from around her neck.

"I'm glad you decided to come anyway, Anna." Benjamin shook his thumb at Emmett. "Maybe he can help you out as Lily did for me. He was bragging at poker how at the marathon last summer he could skate circles around everyone."

Emmett rolled his eyes upward.

"You fell more times than I did." Anna shook her head.

"That's only because of all the spiked punch." Emmett held out his hand. "Come on, this song has a good beat."

"Hang on to me and go slow." Anna wrapped her hands around Emmett's arm. "I don't want you yanking me down."

Lily stood, skated backward, and motioned with her index finger for Benjamin to follow her. "Let's go, I can't wait to see those fancy moves."

"Looks like we'll be great partners." Dampness formed on his palms. Impressing her should be easier this time. At least here, he wasn't an anchor at the bottom of the sea. He wiped his hands across his pants and pushed each leg backward while picking up speed toward Lily. Holding his hands out, he reached for her. "Let's show 'em what we've got."

She nodded.

As they touched, a tingle ran through him, pulsating every nerve in his body. Benjamin smiled and gave her hands a slight squeeze. The thumping of his heart kept pace with the rapid tempo of the waltz. "Ready to try a few steps?"

"Sure."

He pulled her close, pressing his fingertips against her shoulder and applying light pressure on her back guiding her. He glided her backward across the wooden floor while gazing into her eyes. She had a natural beauty makeup couldn't create. Her darkened lashes and raspberry colored lips simply enhanced her allure. They zipped around the rink weaving between the skaters. The wind blew the curls around her tight, knit cloche.

He swept her to the right, twirling in circles. Her head tipped back and she giggled. The scent of her flowered perfume wrapped around them as her skirt whirled in the breeze. He held her closer, swaying along with the melody. She was comfortable in his arms. He could certainly hold her like this forever.

In the third routine, he spun her in the opposite direction. An intensity connected their eyes while their bodies formed a natural rise and fall along with the rhythm of the song. They were both in such perfect tempo. Everyone else seemed to disappear. Her quickened breaths pulsated on his fingertips. He'd never had such a powerful connection with anyone.

Gracefully, they soared across the floor from one side of the room to the other. Their wheels clicked on the wood as they twisted around each other. His heart raced as the song neared the end and he slowly turned her. They rolled to a stop in a tight embrace. His breath quickened. Her moist lips seemed to be awaiting his and he inched closer.

Her lashes fluttered and she tilted her head.

Applause erupted.

Benjamin pivoted. A group of bystanders encircled them. He bowed, waving towards his partner.

Lily curtsied.

He grabbed her hand. "It's warm in here. Would you care to go outside to cool down?"

"Sure. I wouldn't mind getting some fresh air."

They took their skates off, setting them under the corner table. He led her through the side door and out into the night. A sliver of moon hung in the dusk sky. Farther, light from a small window above illuminated an empty bench. A row of high bushes blocked the view into the parking lot. "Please sit." He held her hand while she lowered herself onto the bench. Muted music set an inviting atmosphere. He scooted in next to her. "At least we can hear each other easier out here."

"Where did you learn to skate like that?"

"Aw...so you thought I was good?"

"Yes, of course. I never doubted you would be." She smiled.

"You're not so bad either. We made a pretty great couple out there." He grinned. "I guess all those summers I spent skating with Louie were successful. The street he grew up on happened to be a dead-end, good thing, since my mother didn't like it if I played in the street. Anyway, we played our version of hockey. Since there were only two of us, you were either the goalie or on offense. Sometimes we got other kids in the neighborhood to join us. Either way, it was fun. What kind of games did you play?"

"Your story reminds me of when I played kick the can. However, we played it on the street." Lily smirked. "And it wasn't a dead end."

"Good thing you're still here to tell the story."

"It sure is." She tucked a few loose strands under her hat. "But playing in the streets wasn't the most dangerous act I ever did."

He twisted toward her and rested his elbow on the back of the bench. "Don't stop there, what happened?"

"Remember the water tower they took down three years ago in Columbia Park?"

"Yes?"

"Well, from my upstairs bedroom window I'd always wondered how gorgeous the view would be from the top of that tower. So, one day, when I was around fourteen, I finally decided to find out. I crossed the street into the park and stood frozen at the bottom of the ladder. The rungs seemed to have multiplied along with the height. But something about the long climb beckoned me. I pulled a bench over to reach the first rung and shimmied my way up to the platform surrounding the tower. I walked completely around the entire circle. You could see over the top of all the buildings and for miles beyond the edge of town. It was magnificent."

"I'll bet." He leaned in. "Were you scared when you climbed down?"

"No, not until the car pulled up with the copper."

"You're teasing me."

She shook her head. "No, I'm not. He took me in, fingerprinted me, and stuck me in a cell until my father came."

"He probably wanted to put a good scare into you."

"I'm sure you're right. I never scaled that tower again, but it didn't stop me the day I found the ladder to my rooftop."

"At least that climb is much safer." He picked up her hand, rubbing his thumb across her skin. "I'm enjoying the times we've gone out."

"Me too."

"I've been thinking..." He didn't know if he should ask but now seemed an appropriate moment. At least they were alone. "I'd really like to take you somewhere without our chaperones. What do you say, next time I'll stop by and pick you up?"

"Well..."

Had he pushed her too fast? They'd only planned two events together. He glanced into her blue eyes. "We don't have to. I just thought it might be nice."

"I wouldn't mind. However, my father has a strict rule on meeting any man I'd spend time alone with. I thought you might think the whole family encounter might be a bit premature. Especially since we don't know everything about each other yet."

"I know you're sweet, kind, considerate, and obviously beautiful."

Lily's face flushed. "You're all those too. Handsome, I mean." She laughed. "I know my father will ask about your family, what you do for work, and other probing things like that. Are you all right with those types of questions?"

Benjamin brought her hand up toward his face. "Yes. I will go through any inquisition for you." He kissed the back of her hand.

"Thank you. But maybe you should answer a question I've been wondering." She arched her brow. "Do you mind telling me what religion you practice?"

"I'm Presbyterian."

Her eyes widened. "I presumed you weren't Catholic like me."

"Will that be a problem with your folks?" He placed his other hand on top of hers and scooted closer till their shoulders touched.

"I'll make sure they understand we're not running off to get married." She peered up at him from under her lashes.

"Yet." He chuckled.

"That doesn't sound like a slow relationship." She shook her head with a playful smile. "I don't think the family would find humor in that comment like we do."

"Did I say I was joking?"

"No." She nudged his arm. "But if you're in so much of a hurry...why don't you stop by tomorrow after church and meet them? Say around twelve-thirty?"

"Perfect. And afterward, I'll take you out to a place I think you'll like."

"I can't wait!"

A couple hours later, Benjamin walked up the backstairs of his house. The evening had gone better than he could have imagined and tomorrow would be an exciting day. He reached for the knob, opening it into the dim-lit entryway.

"Good evening, Benjamin."

He spun around toward the kitchen. "Mother, I'm surprised you're up this late."

"I need to speak with you. Come, sit."

Benjamin walked in. Her tone sounded serious and he sat across from her at the parquetry topped breakfast table. He hardly ever saw her wearing that silk purple robe and the last time she waited up this late, it wasn't good. "Should I be concerned you're drinking coffee and staying awake for me?"

"It's decaffeinated, but even so, I wouldn't be able to sleep anyway. Not without talking to you. You've been keeping yourself quite busy lately. If I didn't know any better, I'd think you're trying to avoid this conversation." The coffee cup clanked on the saucer. "What have you been doing with your time these last few days?"

His back stiffened against the chair. He certainly couldn't tell her about Lily now. Not with this mood. "Just the usual. Cards and a club meeting." Mother had to be aware of something, but what?

She studied him. "I had a chat with Deloris the other day."

Uh-oh. "I see." He shifted in the chair.

"Vivian was there too."

His muscles tensed. "How is she?"

"As well as can be expected." Her eyebrows rose. "She loves you, Benjamin."

"That's not love," he mumbled.

"What?"

"Nothing. I'm sure she's upset with me and she has every right to be. But I've made my decision. Besides, we aren't suited for each other."

"Nonsense! You don't know what's good for you. Vivian may be a little rough around the edges with her attitude, but it isn't anything you shouldn't be able to handle. You've done just fine these past four years."

A heaviness settled in his stomach. He should have expected Mother would think he couldn't decide what was right for himself. If he'd stood his ground sooner, he wouldn't be in this predicament. Vivian wasn't the woman for him and the sooner his mother understood that the less complicated his life would be. "That may be true. However, lately, everything has changed with her."

Her eyes narrowed. "Or with you?"

"What does that mean?"

"Twice in the last week you've disgraced our family. First with the absurd public display, which I forgave you for because I thought you only needed some time to figure things out. But now, I find out the real reason you've given up on Vivian."

"I explained why."

"Benjamin Kenneth! Lying to your mother is not something I will tolerate."

"I didn't lie."

"When you don't tell the whole truth...it's still a lie by omission. Keeping Miss Vanderhoof's existence out of the equation has certainly played a factor in whether or not you would work things out with Vivian."

A jolt of coldness struck his core. *She believes them.* "I'm not lying!" His voice softened. "I'm your son. I've given you no reason not to trust me and I'm telling you Lily had nothing to do with my choice to end things with Vivian."

"I will not tolerate any further humiliation for our family. Miss Vanderhoof is not the one for you." She slapped her hands on the table.

He jumped.

"We have a business reputation to uphold in this town. As long as you are under this roof, you will do as I say."

"Then I'll move out!"

Mother gasped.

"You don't even know Lily. She's special." His words halted. "I care about her." He slowly exhaled. "Don't you think Vivian and her mother have a biased opinion?"

Mother sprang upward. *Smack!* The chair struck the tiled floor. A vein throbbed in the middle of her forehead. "I'd think long and hard about trying to make it on your own. Your brother had a very hard time financially. We've arranged everything for you to be successful." Her facial expression soured. "You know what you need to do. You've made this mess and compounded the problem with a Catholic. The sooner you make amends with Vivian, the easier your life will be."

How had he let his parents dictate his life for so long? There was no reasoning with Mother. He stood, turning toward the backstairs. Mother unquestionably made her point clear, but somehow, he had to figure a way out of this dilemma.

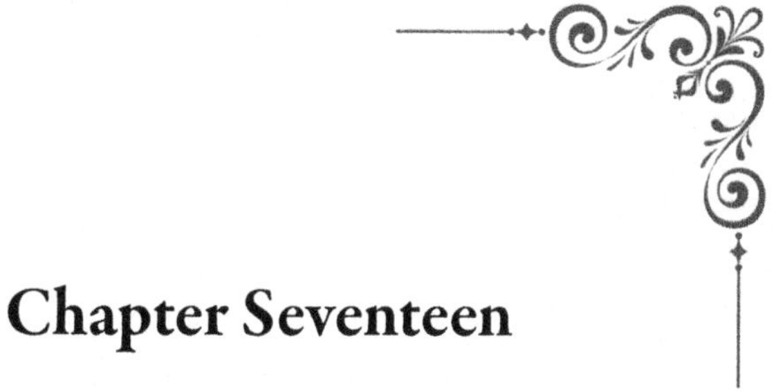

Chapter Seventeen

B*ong! Bong! Bong!* Every day the church bells rang in the neighborhood at six in the morning, then noon, and again at six in the evening as a reminder to pray. "Hail Mary, full of grace, the Lord is with thee; blessed art thou among women, and blessed is the fruit of thy womb, Jesus. Holy Mary, Mother of God, pray for us sinners, now and at the hour of death. Amen."

Rushing through the familiar prayer, Lily grabbed the canister of soap flakes, shaking them into the dishwater. Benjamin would arrive in a half hour to meet her family. They had retired into the sitting room, praying the Angelus honoring our Lord and His Blessed Mother. Oma had decided to stay after lunch once she found out about the new admirer. Lily hadn't been concerned about Benjamin being quizzed by her parents, but Oma had no tact. Hopefully, Benjamin would understand Oma's good intentions if something candid slipped out.

The private time Benjamin had planned today eased her mind. Meeting his ex four days ago only enlightened the reasons he ended their relationship. She sensed Vivian would have a hard time letting him go. Honestly, that would be the milder side interpreting Vivian's character; she was truly off one's nut. To her surprise, last night in the seclusion of the bushes she was sure Vivian should have popped out from somewhere. Luckily, she didn't but the more she could stay away from Benjamin's ex-fiancée, the better.

She rinsed the plates and piled them on the far side of the enameled sink. Squeezing out the dishrag, she wiped the crumbs off the table. Oma had brought over a loaf of delicious graham bread and the tiny remnants were all that remained. She loved her grandmother, but her stomach roiled that bread recipe over the notion of Oma learning Benjamin wasn't Catholic. In no uncertain terms, Oma had always insisted the family remain faithful to their religious beliefs. If Benjamin was her intended person, there would be a struggle on her hands. Not only with Oma but her parents too. If this relationship turned into love, could she find the strength to stand up to them? If not, she could possibly lose him forever.

Lily untied the apron and slung it over the hook on the kitchen door. She strolled through the hall, stopping several feet before the front entrance. Above the entryway a crucifix hung, to the right of the door a font was filled with holy water, and underneath, a statue of the Virgin Mary holding baby Jesus. Did Presbyterians have similar traditions?

"Staring at the door won't bring him any sooner, honey."

She gazed into the sitting room. "I know, Father."

He motioned to her. "Come in and rest for a while."

Oma patted the ottoman in front of her. "It's the Lord's day and resting is what you are supposed to do."

Lily went in, taking the seat by Oma. She nibbled on her thumbnail.

Her mother rocked in the opposite chair. A needle pursed between her lips, she held Father's sock in one hand and a light bulb in the other. She stretched the sock over the top of the bulb exposing the hole and spoke around the needle, "Why are you so nervous?"

"I've never met someone like Benjamin before. He has been such a gentleman and so considerate of me." Lily twisted her hands. "I just hope all of you will like him."

"If he's as good as you say, your mother and I will." Father moved a piece on the board game he was playing with her younger siblings. "We've noticed how happy you have been these last few days."

"I haven't seen you as often as I should." Oma touched her back. "But you certainly have been doing your fair share of smiling today."

"I'm pleased Benjamin has been there for you." Mother pushed the needle through the material. "He seems to have given you comfort during this difficult time."

"Thank you, everyone." *Thud!* Lily craned her neck. The sound had to be a car door shutting. She shuffled over to the picture window. "It is true, he came into my life at just the right time." She smiled.

Benjamin walked toward the front porch. He was handsome in his dark blue pants, white button-down shirt and straw boater hat. In his left hand he held a bouquet of flowers in orange, pink, lavender, yellow, and white.

Her rose-colored cotton dress would be perfect with his casual appearance. "He's here!" She rushed toward the foyer and opened the outside door. "You're right on time. Everyone is waiting for you."

Benjamin's eyes sparkled. "You look lovely." He raised the bouquet near his chest. "Even more exquisite in comparison to these flowers."

Her face warmed. "Oh my, thank you." She moved to the side, pushing open the door. "I'm excited to know what we're doing today."

"You'll just have to wait and see."

"That's not nice keeping secrets from me already." She pouted.

"Not even that pretty puffed lip will make me tell you." Benjamin grinned as he came through into the entrance. "Who will I be meeting today?"

"My parents, grandmother, younger siblings, Frankie—who you already met, and Ruby." She held her hand out. "I'll take your hat."

"Well, at least with the little ones the conversation won't be too intense." He winked. "Actually, parents usually love me, and I hope your mother finds these flowers just as beautiful as I think her daughter is."

Heat prickled her cheeks. "You're so sweet. I'm sure she will." She shouldn't have forgotten how much of a charmer he can be. "I did let them know all of your good qualities. Are you ready?"

"Lead the way."

Lily led Benjamin into the sitting room and stood in front of Oma's chair. "I want to present my grandmother, Mrs. Goslein. This is Benjamin Claussen."

Oma held her hand out. "I've heard good things about you, young man."

"Thank you." Benjamin shook her hand. "Your granddaughter is a special lady."

"Good answer." Oma let her hand slip away.

He pulled a lavender-petaled flower from the bunch, handing it to Oma.

"Nice gesture, young man."

Lily walked Benjamin toward her parents. Father held his shoulders back and his chest out, standing next to Mother who was relaxing in the corner chair. So far Benjamin's magical charm worked with Oma. "Mother, Father, this is Benjamin Claussen. Benjamin, my parents Ruth and Eddie Vanderhoof."

Father reached his hand out toward Benjamin. "Pleasure to meet you. Claussen, is that the same family who owns the lumber yard?"

Benjamin took his hand. "Yes. My father and uncle operate the business together. I work there too purchasing the items for the store."

Father rocked forward on his tiptoes, elongating his stance. "I've been there a few times." He nodded with a pleased smile. "It's a fine place you have there."

Lily grinned. Her father wouldn't be able to elevate more than a mere few inches compared to Benjamin's soaring height.

"Thank you, sir." Benjamin offered Lily's mother the cluster of flowers, but he removed one flowering stem.

Mother took them. "Beautiful flowers. I love the pastel colors. Thank you." She smiled. "Where do you live, Benjamin?"

"With my parents, Christian and Constance on South Cedar."

"That's a pleasant neighborhood and it must be quite close to your work."

"Yes, ma'am. About three-and-a-half blocks."

Mother smelled the bouquet. "You seem like a thoughtful gentleman. No wonder my daughter fancies you."

Lily's cheeks warmed. "Oh, Mother." Benjamin had positively earned her parents' respect by how he presented himself. She guided Benjamin to the other side of the room near her siblings sitting on the floor. "Benjamin, my sister Ruby."

"Hello, Miss." Benjamin knelt, handing the flower to Ruby. "I saved the prettiest pink flower just for you."

Ruby grasped the stem. "Pink is my favorite color."

"Mine too." Benjamin laughed. "How old are you?"

"Six. My birthday was last month."

"Well, happy birthday."

"I'm eight." Frankie stood. "Do you remember me?" He stuck out his hand.

"I certainly do." Benjamin grabbed hold. "You have quite a grip."

"I've been practicing." Frankie pumped his arm up and down. "Father says you can tell a lot from a man just by how firm of a grip he has."

"Your father's a smart man."

Frankie let go and squinted his eyes. "Where are you taking my sister?"

"It's a surprise, so I can't tell you right now."

"Aw, please." Frankie softened his expression.

Ruby chimed in, "Please?" She folded her hands under her chin.

"Children." Mother got up from the chair. "It's not appropriate to keep asking."

Lily touched her brother's shoulder. "I tried to find out too. He's not going to surrender. I'll have to tell you both all about it after I come home."

Frankie skidded his foot on the floor. "I suppose."

Ruby copied her brother, kicking her foot across the floorboards.

"I apologize, Benjamin." Mother came closer. "The children tend to get excited when they meet new people. They've been rambunctious ever since they got out of church this morning. It's hard for these little ones to be quiet for so long."

"I understand." Benjamin smiled. "I have nieces and nephews who are the same way on Sundays."

Mother's brow furrowed. "I don't believe I've seen you at St. John's. Where do you and your folks belong?"

"The First Presbyterian Church."

"Oh?" Mother's vocal pitch rose and her fingers splayed across her chest.

Lily searched past Mother near the corner chair. Father's shoulders had slumped, and his hands hung loosely at his sides. She swiftly rotated toward Oma whose face had fallen slack and slightly pale. *Please, family, don't say anything embarrassing.*

"Yes, it's the one near the post office." Benjamin's lips tightened into a straight line.

Lily gazed at Benjamin. Her stomach quivered. Everything had gone so well up until now. "Well, I think we'd better be going."

"Lily?" Oma scooted to the edge of the chair. "Come closer."

She stared at her shoes until reaching the ottoman.

Oma whispered, "You knew, didn't you?" A bitter smile fell heavy on her lips.

Lily's heart had a dull pain. "Yes, Oma. I'm sorry." Although she sensed Oma's disappointment about Benjamin not being Catholic, she was grateful for her discretion.

Oma cleared her throat. "Well, I couldn't let you leave without your crucifix necklace. Where is it, child?"

Lily touched her neck. "I must have left it in my room." She understood Oma wanted her to have the protection of the crucifix, but Benjamin probably had no idea of the symbolism.

Oma pointed toward the stairs. "Ruby, run up and get it for your sister."

Ruby bounced across the floor.

"It's on my night table by the bed." Lily wandered over to Benjamin and placed her hand on his elbow. It was time for them to leave.

"Wonderful meeting all of you today." Benjamin presented an easygoing grin while turning toward her parents and grandmother. "I hope to see you again soon."

"It was a pleasure meeting you too." Mother graciously smiled. "And thank you again for this bunch of flowers." She gave Lily's arm a light squeeze. "We'll talk when you get home. I'm going to go put these in water before they wilt." She strolled out of the room.

Lily expected nothing less than a deep conversation from her mother which would have absolute influence from Oma's perspective.

"I appreciate you coming by to meet the family." Father patted Benjamin on the shoulder. "Have a nice time this afternoon."

And she had no doubt Father would be right there for the discussion too. Although he appeared alarmed earlier, his friendliness toward Benjamin seemed like approval to her.

"Be sure you drive carefully with my granddaughter." Oma wagged her finger as she gazed at him with a watchful eye.

"Yes, ma'am. I will take special care of her." Benjamin glanced at Lily. "Shall we?"

Ruby bounded down the stairs. “Here.” She handed Lily her necklace.

Lily strung the chain around her neck. She walked with Benjamin to the font, making the sign of the cross over her head, chest, and shoulders. A natural Catholic action she'd done almost every day for protection she'd only now keenly become aware of. What was Benjamin thinking as she did it? “I'm ready to go now.”

Five minutes later, dust rolled out from behind the car and created a trailing cloud, covering the vanishing city in the mirror. Lily had given Benjamin her consent when he asked if she wanted to ride up front with him. Their first date alone seemed so much more genuine while he sat beside her. He maneuvered around the holes. The unfamiliar dirt road didn't give her any clues as to where they were going, nor how soon they would get there. Mostly, this side of town was forestland with very few houses. “How much longer until we get there?”

“Only a few more minutes. I think you will like this place.”

“I've never been out this way before.”

“It's well worth the ride. You'll see.”

“How about a little hint?”

“No, sorry. Not even a clue.” He shifted the gears. “How do you think everything went with your family meeting me?”

“You impressed them.”

“Up until they found out I was Presbyterian. I couldn't help but notice your mother's voice going up an octave.”

“Mother was surprised. I probably should have mentioned your faith before you came.” Truly, she hoped they hadn't found out so soon. Maybe it was better this way. They'd have some time to think about it before they confronted her.

"I hope your family will get to know me." He turned toward Lily and smiled. "If they do, they'll learn this Presbyterian is smitten with their daughter."

"Smitten, huh?" Lily's face burned. She leaned on the door through the curve as he downshifted, turning off the road onto an area with tall grass. The car jostled across the bumpy trail while a few tree branches scraped against the sides. Before long, they couldn't go any further. She tightened the scarf knot at the nape of her neck and pushed the bobby pins along her hairline. "Is this the place?"

"This is where we need to stop." He turned the engine off. "We'll need to hike the rest of the way. It's not too far. Are you up for it?"

"Sure."

Benjamin came around the front of the car and opened the door for Lily. He offered his hand, guiding her out. "I need to get a few things from the luggage trunk."

"Would you like some help?"

"Yes. That would be fine."

She followed him to the back of the car.

He unbuckled the straps and flipped up the latches. Reaching into the trunk, he pulled out a fishing rod. "Would you like to carry this for me?"

"Aha! We're going fishing."

"You're a regular Dick Tracy." He laughed. "I guess I can't trick you."

Lily giggled. "No, you can't." She took hold of the pole. "Is this one of your favorite fishing spots?"

"It sure is. So you'll have to keep the spot a secret." He pulled out the tackle box. "Let's walk this way. Even though the area is remote, people still seem to find it somehow. The last time I came out here a group of boys were stump fishing. They hightailed it out of here as soon as they saw me. I think they all had enough belts in them; they were rather bent."

"I guess this would be an out of the way place, so they don't get caught with alcohol. What is stump fishing? I've never heard of it before." She swiped at the long grass with the pole, making the stalks sway. "Does it mean there are a lot of dead trees where the fish are?"

"It could, I suppose, but I mean fishing without a pole." He stepped over a rock in the path. "You use your hands, or so-called stumps, to catch the fish. Once the fish bites onto your hand, you yank them out of the water."

"Wouldn't that hurt?"

"I've never tried it, but I'd think so. Maybe that's why they were drinking, to dull the pain." He held a tree branch back until Lily passed.

She stomped the grass down in front of her. "These weeds are almost as tall as I am."

"I can see where you get your stature from after meeting your family. Your father was only a few inches taller than your mother and she's even shorter than you are."

"I know, and if Oma would have stood, you would've seen she's the tiniest of all. This is getting pretty thick in here. Do you think there are any snakes around?"

"I'd bet there would be some, but we're rustling the grass so that should scare them away."

Lily jumped on top of the closest rock. "I don't like snakes. You didn't tell me there were any snakes."

"If it makes you feel any better, I've never seen one."

"Well, why did you say there were snakes?" She moved her foot off the rock and let it hover in midair.

"I should say I haven't seen a live one." He held out his arms as far apart as they could go. "I've only seen a skin about this long."

Lily put her foot down on the rock.

Benjamin laughed.

"Are you telling me the truth?"

"I am." He offered his hand. "If you're still scared, I can carry you."

"Well, if we see a snake, you will need to keep me off the ground to get me out of here." She stepped off the rock.

Benjamin led the way through the narrow path and a group of trees into a clearing. "So, what do you think?"

The sun sparkled off the water into the surrounding lush shades of green in the trees. Lily strolled closer toward the pond. The clear water appeared like glass straight to the sand on the bottom. Along the edge, frogs were croaking and leaping among the lily pads which waved across the top of the water. Underneath, small schools of fish darted between the stems. She peered across the water. Cattails were so dense they hid the edge of the pond. To the left and the right edges, a narrow river led in and out. She turned toward Benjamin and placed her hand upon her heart. "It's breathtaking."

"So glad you like it. I enjoy how peaceful it is here. It's one of the reasons I find this my favorite spot for fishing. Have you ever fished before?"

"No."

"Well, then this will be an exciting experience for you." Benjamin set down the tackle box. "All right, would you like me to teach you?"

"Yes, I would."

"Please hand me the pole." He grabbed hold. "I've already attached the hook along with the cork bobber, but we'll need to put on a worm. Would you mind getting the jar inside the tackle box?"

Lily flipped up the lock, opening the lid. Taking out the jar, she held it up, gawking through the glass at the worms wiggling their way through the dirt.

"Do you want to learn how to bait the hook?" He held the line in his hand. "Or would you rather have me do it?"

"I'll try."

"Well, first you'll need to rub your hands on the ground a couple of times. That way you won't leave your scent on the worm."

Lily bent down to the ground, scraping some loose dirt together in a pile and scooped it into her hands. Eagerly, she rubbed them back and forth until all the dirt fell out through her palms. Taking the jar in her hands, she unscrewed the cap and held up a worm. "Ready. How do you put this on the hook?"

He handed her the line. "All right, push the hook through one end of the worm and then shove the end to the top of the hook where the string is attached."

"I think I've got that."

"Looks good. Now the next poke you'll want to leave a little loop dangling." Benjamin moved closer toward Lily. "Not too much of a loop or it will be easy prey but not too tight either otherwise there won't be enough wiggling action to attract the fish."

"Like this?"

"Yes, it looks like you have the hang of it."

Lily glanced at him. "So, I just continue the small loops?"

Benjamin met her gaze. "Mm-hmm, keep going until you reach the end. I like you don't mind getting dirty fishing. Yet, I can't help but notice the movements your lips make every time the worm wiggles when you poke it. If it bothers you, the next time I can chill them first."

Lily let go of the hook. "No, it doesn't bother me. How can you chill them when you said they need to wiggle to attract the fish?"

"Don't worry. Once they hit the water, they wake up and start wiggling again." Benjamin chuckled. "I chilled them for my sister one time, but it wasn't long enough. After the first poke, her finger got wrapped up with a huge nightcrawler. She dropped the pole and screamed so loud we ended up not catching anything that afternoon. Afterward, whenever we went fishing, I ended up baiting the hook for her."

She swung the pole toward the water. The bobber popped up only five feet in front of her. "Well, that didn't go too far."

"No, it didn't and the water is fairly shallow there. The hook is probably laying on the bottom, so you'll never get a fish to take a bite. Would you like me to show you how to cast?"

"I suppose that would probably be a good idea."

"Pull up on the pole and wind on this lever."

She tugged on the pole, winding the line from the water. "Is your sister older or younger than you?"

"Eva is twenty-five, two years younger than me." He moved behind her. "I'll help guide the pole while you cast." Placing his hands on both of her arms, he rotated her sideways to the pond.

"Stay relaxed. We will make one smooth, quick motion. When the pole is aimed toward the water, release your finger from the line." He turned her slightly to the right and then quickly back to the left. The line flew through the air about twenty feet farther than her cast. "That's a good spot. The depth is just about right there for the setting of the bobber."

"Yes. Much better." Being in his arms was so much better too. She leaned back a little until the warmth of his chest pressed against her back. Her shoulders eased. The touch of his hands lying lightly on top of her arms triggered a few goosebumps. Or was it the musky scent of his cologne? Winding the line slightly made the bobber sink under the water for a second and pop right back up again. She leaned back a little more; his chest rose and fell with every breath. Did he sense how she continued to inch closer to him? His warm exhale moved her hair slightly. Between his breathing and his hands, the goosebumps multiplied. The bobber dunked under, along with most of the line.

"Give it a tug." Benjamin slid his hands underneath her arms and drew them upward. "Now wind in the line. I think you've hooked a big one. Look at how the pole is bending."

"This is exciting!" She spun the reel quickly.

"All right. You're almost near the edge of the pond. Pull up on the line to bring the fish out of the water."

Lily wound the line around one more time, yanking the pole hard. The fish flew into the air and accelerated like a pendulum toward them. She jerked the pole to the right. The fish swung around them, making circles. She lost her footing and twisted around, facing Benjamin. He fell backward, taking her down with him. Her arms flung forward as she landed on her hands and knees over the top of him. Her crucifix necklace smacked him in the nose and swayed centimeters above his face.

"Holy Moly! Are you all right?"

"I think so." She sat off to his side.

"Here, let me help you." He got up, brushed off his hands, and offered them to her.

She gazed upward at him as she rose. They stood toe to toe. Her heart raced while she imagined him moving closer, but he didn't stir. The timing was perfect for a kiss. Why didn't he? Had he been as mesmerized by her as she was with him? She smiled at him. "I won't stop you if you'd like to kiss me."

"I'd love to." He leaned closer. "But..." He pointed at her neck. "Jesus seems to be watching us...it's a bit unnerving."

Lily giggled. She tucked the crucifix under her dress collar.

Benjamin crouched and gently brushed his lips across hers. He placed his hands alongside her face, running a thumb above her slightly puckered lips.

A tingling sensation ran through her.

His fingers traced her jawline and he tilted her head, laying his full lips upon her mouth. The kiss lingered at the center of her upper lip. Slowly, he caressed her lips between his. He varied the intensity from one side of her mouth to the other.

She melted into him.

His lips glided along her cheek, earlobe, and the pulsating place near her neckline. The tips of his fingers trailed down the sides of her neck, tracing over her shoulders, across her arms, and around her back, encasing her like a cocoon in the warmth of his arms.

He held her tight against him, straightening his stance while raising her upward. Their lips firmly sealed together as her feet dangled above the ground.

She wrapped her arms around him, embracing him. No one had ever made her sense such passion before. Nor kissed her so deeply, signifying his craving for her.

Gradually, he lowered her to the ground releasing her from the kiss. Their eyes focused on each other while he rubbed her arms. His eyes widened. "I'm so sorry."

"There's no need to apologize."

"It seems I have wiped dirt all over your beautiful face." He stepped back. "And your dress is covered as well."

She signaled a circle with her finger. "Turn around."

He rotated on his heels.

Lily laughed. "My handprints are marked on the back of your white shirt too."

"I guess fishing can be quite a dirty pastime." He grinned. "At least you can say you didn't let the fish get away."

"I sure can. In more ways than one." She couldn't have imagined their first kiss being any more perfect. Had he fallen for her during their embrace as she had? If his kiss was any indication, she'd have to say yes. Why had she ever doubted their connection? Nothing could come between them now.

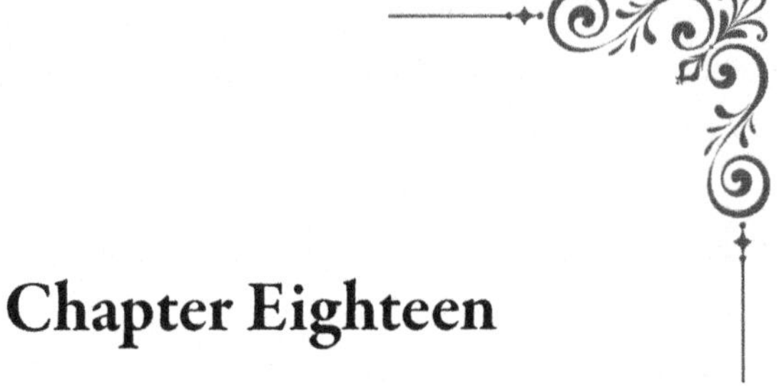

Chapter Eighteen

The early afternoon light disappeared as the heavy wooden door slammed shut behind Vivian. Hotel Charles was the last place she ever wanted to step foot in again. Tirelessly she'd searched for the bracelet all the way here, but no luck. Some greedy slob had found it and kept it—*May they rot in hell!* —or it was still here somewhere. Her nose crinkled as the stale odor of smoke drifted from the poker room. Everything in this place reminded her of Benjamin and that dreadful night he expressed he just wanted to be friends. *Friends? Idiot!* Did he even know how ridiculous that sounded? They were engaged to be married for the rest of their lives.

Drapery covered the only windows on the north side of the room. But a light from an open door illuminated the dining room just enough for her to weave through the tables. The place sat empty except for whoever was making the noise in the kitchen. Someone whistled a tune while pots and pans chimed a tinny sound. Whoever it was better be able to help her, so she didn't ever have to come back here again.

She stood in the kitchen doorway. A short man dressed in navy wool pants and a blue shirt scrubbed away at a stack of dishes with his back to her. "Hello?"

He didn't move.

She took in a deep breath, "Hello?"

The man jerked back and swiveled around. "Can I help you?" He shook his hands over the sink and rubbed them across his apron.

That round baby face with those cheek dimples. She squeezed her eyes shut and opened them. "It's you!"

His look twisted into a puzzling gaze. "It is me." He moved closer. "Who are you?"

She put her hands on her hips. "You don't recognize the woman you knocked to the ground and humiliated eight days ago?"

"Forgive me, your face was covered in French dressing and lettuce." He squinted and lifted his head, studying her. "Yes, I can identify you now."

She huffed. "Well, aren't you going to apologize now that you know who I am?"

"Oh?" He stepped a few inches closer. "I thought maybe you were sorry for yanking on my uniform while I innocently tried to serve a salad."

Her chin rose. "You certainly are no gentleman. What's your name? I need to report you to the owner of this place."

"My name is Arthur." He stuck out his hand. "Pleased to meet you."

She rolled her eyes and shook her head. "A gentleman never offers his hand to a lady unless she initiates the handshake."

"I've never met a lady as cross as you." Arthur bowed. "Forgive me, ma'am." He rose and a smile spread on his lips indenting those dimples even more.

"Now you're just trying to appease me." She let her hands slip from her waist. "But at least you have a tiny bit of manners."

"So, Miss, what is your name?"

"Vivian."

"Well, Miss Vivian, how can I help you?"

"I came to find out if anyone found my bracelet."

"What does it look like?"

"A large white stone in the center and the band is silver in art deco." She traced her finger on her wrist. "The clasp must have broken the night I was here."

"I don't know what art deco is."

"A design." She pointed to her engagement ring. "Like this."

"Come with me." Arthur zigzagged through the tables, into the poker room, and behind the bar. "All the lost items are over here in a box." He dug around. "Why are you still wearing that ring? I heard your engagement was off."

"You mind your own business and keep looking." He'd stuck his wide nose into her personal life after she left that night.

He tugged on a few things and swiveled around, holding a shiny chain between his fingers.

"My bracelet." She grabbed at his hand.

Arthur pulled away. "Hold on a minute. How do I know this one is yours?" He slid his fingers through his black hair, sweeping the strands to the side.

"I think I'd know my filigree bracelet."

He cupped the jewelry in his palms. "I'm not sure this is yours. It doesn't look filigree to me and you never mentioned that it was before."

"Do you even know what filigree is?" She doubted he was sophisticated enough.

"Nope."

"Hand it over." She held her palm open.

Arthur grinned. "I'll need your last name in case someone else comes looking for this and it turns out not to be yours."

Was that his real reason or did he have another motive? "You first." She stared down at him.

"Vanderhoof."

A storm of adrenaline rushed through her body. Was he related to Lily? "DuCate." She wiggled her fingers. "Come on, I gave you my full name."

"I can put the bracelet on for you." His right eyebrow arched.

Is he flirting with me? Vivian held out her arm. "Fine." The way he spoke to her, he sounded annoyed, but now she wondered. Was that just his way of showing her he liked her? Maybe he'd have some valuable information if he knew of Lily. She needed to play this just right. "Thank you, kind sir." She forced a smile. "Vanderhoof...where have I heard that name before?"

Arthur straightened his back and stood tall. "We're from the Columbia Park Vanderhoofs. Originally of upper Austria, Frankenburg to be exact. And my father, or I should say Vater, is the great cigar wrapper of this here city." He squeezed the clasp shut.

"My, oh my!" Vivian waved her hand vigorously in front of her face. "I had no idea I was in the accompaniment of such high society." She curtsied. "How many princes and princesses are there to take over the prestigious tobacco throne besides you?"

"One younger prince, one older princess, and two younger princesses." He held out his arm. "Let's go sit and chat for a bit."

"Lead the way, Prince Arthur." She wrapped her hand into the crook of his elbow. "I do love how your accent goes in and out." She followed him around the bar.

Arthur tapped his lips with his finger. "Oops! Excuse my articulation. I should try harder to conceal my identity. It just causes issues for the ordinary people." He smirked.

"Thank you for putting on my bracelet." He was no match for her. She kept her tone soft. "What is your older sister's name?"

"Celia." He pulled out a chair at the poker table.

"Hmm." Maybe Lily would be younger than her. "What about your other two sisters' names?" She sat.

He pushed her chair in. "Ruby and Lily."

A bitter taste filled her mouth. "How old are they? You said they were younger, right?"

He took the chair opposite. "Ruby's eight and Lily's twenty-one. My older sister is twenty-three." He laughed. "My mother had her hands full with the three of us only being a year apart."

She turned her head away, facing the dark paneled wall. How could she use his fascination with her to her advantage? He seemed willing to tell her anything she wanted to know, but she still needed to make this conversation seem casual. She took a deep breath, "I've always wanted a sister. Lily's close to my age, what is she like?"

He threw his head back and laughed. "Even my oldest sister isn't close to your age. You've gotta at least be in your thirties."

"I am not!" She stared at the red and white stained-glass fixture above until the tightness in her jaw eased. "Besides, a lady never tells how old she is and a gentleman never asks nor tries to pry it out of her." His social graces were as short as his stature.

"Well, don't worry, your secret's safe with me...I already know." He playfully winked and picked up a deck of cards. "I'm good at predictions."

The twanging cords in her neck pulled her posture rigid. "Keep your thoughts about my youth to yourself." If he'd been so good at predicting things, he wouldn't have given up information about his sister. How did he not see the connection?

"I like how perfectly aged and feisty you are." He snickered. "I've got a trick I can show you. Want to see it?" He bent the cards, making a half-circle, and whirled them back together into a straight pile.

Her head minutely shook. He was crass. She was astute and she had him right where she wanted him. "If you must." She waved her hand above the table. "Go ahead with your little trick, I doubt it will impress me."

After shuffling a few more times, he placed the first card face up on the table, followed by several more. "Celia and Lily always got the best of me, but that's why I have insight when it comes to women."

"You're so self-absorbed."

"Me? Ha!" As he finished laying the cards into piles, none of them had the same amount.

Vivian sighed. "What do you do for a living besides annoy people who come in here?" She leaned forward, studying the cards as he kept making stacks. "How's your memory?"

"I work in Mr. Hell's wagon near the theater. You should stop by sometime and I'll give you a few treats." He winked. "As for this trick, you don't think I'm memorizing all these cards?"

"Maybe? I wouldn't put anything past you." She concentrated and tried not to blink so she wouldn't miss anything. "Do your sisters have jobs too?"

"They sure do. Celia is a waitress in Milwaukee and Lily's across the street at Livingston's." Arthur slapped down the last card. "As you can see, I have twelve piles here. Now I'm going to turn them all over in case you think I've memorized any of them. I'll even go one step further and let you place them in another spot." He turned his back to the table. "You can move the piles anywhere you'd like."

Interesting...Lily's at the women's clothing store. She pushed each stack to a new location on the table. "Ready, you can turn around now." He made prying so easy...like taking candy from a baby face.

He motioned with his hand like a magician over the top of a rabbit hat. "Out of all the piles which nine would you like me to pick up?"

"I would like..." Vivian pointed. "...this one, and this one, and these two..." until three remained. "Your sisters must be fairly shrewd if they're able to have an advantage over you."

"Well, they came up with a lot of harebrained schemes together that made me look bad." He pushed the remaining piles into a single row. "Out of these, I want you to choose which two will have the top card turned up."

"Turn over the one on each end." She needed more information about Lily. "I'm not sure I'm following what your sisters did. Can you give me an example?"

Arthur flipped over the top cards, one a three and the other an eight. "For the trick, I will tell you what the remaining top card is." He gathered all the cards except for the three piles in the row. Quickly, he laid one after another card face up, until he'd gone through the entire deck. "It's a ten." He flipped over the card.

Vivian's eye's widened. "How did you do it?" She smiled with closed lips. "Do it again."

"First, let me tell you about the doozy that almost got both of my sisters in trouble with the law."

Perfect performance right into her hands and he thought his trick was so good. She leaned in. "Go ahead, I'm listening."

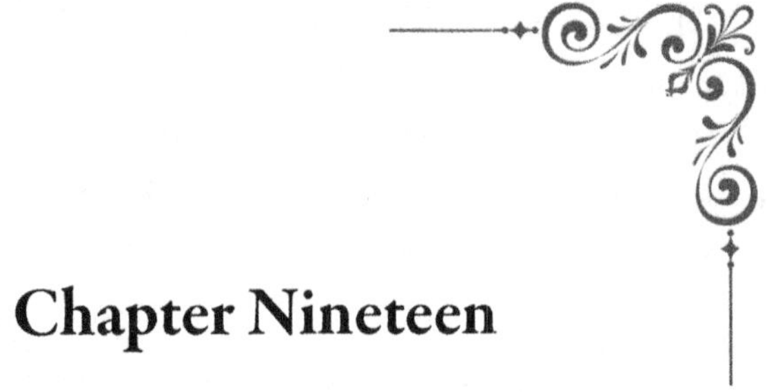

Chapter Nineteen

Lily's toes pushed against the wooden porch planks, moving the swing slightly. The sultry evening air cooled as dark clouds whirled overhead. Hopefully, Benjamin would arrive before the storm blew in.

At the beginning of the week, her fishing excursion with Benjamin ended with the best kiss she'd ever had. But when she got home, her parents weren't pleased with her disheveled appearance. First, Mother warned her about charming men with cars and how easy it would be to get in the family way. So she had to explain what happened while casting, leaving out the romantic parts. However, hours passed before the inquisition subsided. Finally, her parents' frame of mind changed and they seemed to believe Benjamin was still an honorable man. She tried further easing their minds by promising she would continue to take their relationship slowly.

However, those words she'd used to convince her parents presently sounded more like concealing a secret to her. She loved him. And from the way he'd held her in his arms, he loved her too. Until now, she hadn't ever encountered such genuine affection. Her heart couldn't deny her life had forever changed. She had no idea how long her excitement would remain unnoticed within her family. Without a doubt, her parents would think loving him would be way too fast.

All day today, she'd been in a wonderful mood because he had made plans for them tonight. Another new exhilarating adventure which he called Friday fist fight or some thingamajig like that. Although she'd never attended such an event, she didn't care what they did as long as they were together.

Smack! Lily glanced up as the screen door slammed shut and her mother approached.

"Do you have a moment? I need to speak with you before you leave."

"Yes, of course."

"I've thought and prayed about how to approach this subject all week." Mother pulled the wooden rocking chair closer. "Your father and I are glad you've found Benjamin."

Lily grinned.

The expression on Mother's face turned serious. "We know what happened between you and Ira was probably one of the hardest times you've had to go through."

Why would Mother bring up Ira now? Her brows knitted together.

"Your well-being is important, however, so is your spirituality." Mother stared intently into Lily's eyes. "And before you get too serious with Benjamin, our responsibility as your parents is to make sure you understand a lifelong commitment of marriage is impossible with a man who is not Catholic."

"Oh?" Her eyes narrowed. "I didn't say we were getting married."

"Good." Mother patted her forearm. "I'm sure you also realize marriage is a sacrament." She rubbed her hand back and forth across Lily's arm. "The church wouldn't welcome you if you were to get married to someone outside of our faith."

Her heart sank. Mother couldn't be right, could she? "Benjamin believes in God."

"I don't doubt he does." Mother's tone softened. "But Presbyterians and Catholics don't worship in the same way. Certainly, his family would feel the same. I can almost guarantee they wouldn't like that you are Catholic."

"Why wouldn't Benjamin's family like my sister?" Ruby peeked through the doorway.

Mother swiveled in the chair. "How many times have I told you not to eavesdrop on other people's conversations?"

"I'm sorry, Mommy." Ruby pouted. "But why is it wrong to be Catholic?"

"It's not." Mother motioned for her to come closer.

Ruby scampered over and climbed onto her lap.

"My, you're getting big." Mother positioned Ruby squarely on her knees. "There are other religions, like Presbyterian, and what they believe is not the same as we do." She tucked a blonde curl behind Ruby's ear. "When two people get married, they tend to marry someone of the same religion. It's easier to raise a family that way."

"But why did you say Presbur...Presburtrys don't like Catholics?"

"Presbyterians." Mother smiled. "Well...a long time ago, Catholics were not always good to people of other religions. It's a hard thing to forget when something bad has happened." Mother held Ruby's chin, turning her face upward. "That is one reason why I tell you to be nice to everyone."

"I really try."

"I know you do, sweetie." Mother pulled Ruby into her arms and kissed the top of her head. Then she scooted her off her lap, patting her bottom. "Now run inside and play nice with your brother."

"I will, Mommy." Ruby galloped away.

Lily placed her feet on the porch, making the swing wobble cattywampus. Her relationship with Benjamin had so far been effortless, except for the complications with their exes. But nothing compared to the seriousness of their religious differences. In hindsight, she should have anticipated this discussion would happen. "Everything sure seems simple when you're little."

"The right decisions are always harder, no matter how old you are." Mother's lips twisted into a grim shape. "I wish the situation could be different and so does your Oma."

"Oma?" Of course, she had something to say. "She's always expressed the need to marry a Catholic man." Benjamin hadn't declared thoughts of marriage unless she considered his cheeky response after she mentioned them running off—not yet. *Had he meant it?* Until he seriously stated such a commitment, she won't be the one to say anything.

Ahooga!

Lily jumped. "He's here! I have to go." She exited the swing.

Benjamin waved out the car window, rolling to a stop. He got out and hurried around the front of the car toward the passenger side. "Hello, Mrs. Vanderhoof."

Mother waved. "Nice to see you."

Lily darted down the steps onto the trampled grass path. She twirled around in the gusty wind toward Mother. "I might be a bit late tonight, goodbye." Holding the large brimmed slouch hat on her head, she ran toward him.

Benjamin stood next to the car, leaning on the open door. He was dashing in that feathered fedora with matching chocolate pants. His wide smile welcomed her. "You look lovely, as always."

"What a wonderful compliment." She slid onto the seat. "You're such a gentleman."

He hung over the top of the door. "Did I ever tell you blue is my favorite color?"

"I thought you told my sister it was pink." She giggled. "Besides, my dress isn't blue."

He grinned playfully. "I'm talking about those captivating eyes of yours. I could stand here and stare into them for hours."

The apples of her cheeks warmed. "What about the frightening fight night?"

"I think you mean Friday fight night?" Benjamin chuckled. "Since I promised I'd take you somewhere, we'd better go." He shut the door and strolled to the opposite side.

Every time without fail her face flushed by the words he'd chosen to say. She couldn't resist his charismatic ways, nor did she want to.

The car door shut. "So, tonight's boxing match should be a good one. Our local boxer, Jimmy the Kid, is up against a German by the name of Maximillian." Benjamin shifted the car into gear. "Do you know much about the sport?"

"No, nothing. But when I told my brother he said the experience can be quite thrilling. I'm hoping he's right. You didn't get to meet Arthur, did you?"

"I have." He signaled with his arm bent out the window. "At Hotel Charles when I play cards on Thursday nights."

"Of course." That's where Arthur overheard Benjamin say she was easy on the eyes. Her hand quickly covered her mouth as she tittered.

"What's so amusing?"

"Just something I remembered my brother said." She smiled. "Once you get to know him, you'll find he has his ways of being rather candid."

"Seems our brothers are alike." Benjamin turned the corner onto Second Street. "Years ago, my older brother Robert left home after a serious disagreement with my parents. I'll just say his frankness didn't go well. It took a lot of guts to do what he did and go out on his own. I have a great deal of respect for him."

"Have you been able to keep in touch?"

"He'll call the office once in a while." He shifted gears. "Robert's a traveling salesman and doesn't stay put in one place for too long."

"Oh, I see."

He pulled into a parking area behind the armory. "Wow! This place is going to be packed like a bunch of dill pickles in a jar." He cranked the wheels, easing into an open spot. "There's got to be people from all over the county here tonight."

"I had no idea this type of event would be so popular."

"I'm appreciative of your willingness in trying things that interest me. I can't tell you how good it makes me feel just being myself when I'm with you." He shut off the engine and cranked the window closed. "Nevertheless, if you're having any second thoughts, we don't have to go in. This isn't a typical place I'd take a lady such as yourself and I certainly don't want you to be uncomfortable."

"Well, I mentioned I wanted to try the things you liked to do. So, I'm as ready as I'll ever be." She had a funny quiver in her stomach that mirrored both nervousness and excitement. What would it be like to watch two people hit each other in the face on purpose? Money, without a doubt, can make people do some strange things. Her door opened. She took hold of his hand, stepped out, and stood facing him.

He nudged closer, maneuvering his face under her brim, and kissing her smack dab on the center of her lips.

The kiss was soft, slow, and sensual. Her knees buckled a little. Luckily, he'd held her close with his powerful arms. She opened her eyes as his lips broke the caress, his face only a mere inch away. Her eyelashes fluttered against his warm breath. Would he sneak another quick one? She wanted more. Maybe he just needed a little nudge. "That was a nice surprise. Did I ever tell you how much I like surprises?"

"Glad to know. I'll save a few more for you later." He turned, placing her hand in the crook of his arm and swung the door shut. "We'd better hurry before the downpour gets here." He pointed at the clouds along with a sheet of rain moving toward them.

They evaded the storm and within several minutes entered. Inside, a throng of people lined all sides of a square, raised mat in the center of the room. Their chairs were in the fifth row, eye level with the bottom of the ring. Three thick ropes were strung horizontally between each of the four poles. At two of the corners, men sat crossways from each other while another paced in the middle. The high ceiling above rebounded the chatter below.

Benjamin had been right when he stated they'd be packed in. There must be hundreds of people in this small building. She could barely move her arms without touching the man next to her. Even worse, the heat soared ten or fifteen degrees higher than outside and the stench of sweat hung heavy in the air. Maybe that's the reason the boxers only had shorts on. This sport seemed particularly peculiar since men at the swimming pool wore more to cover their exposed skin.

Benjamin squeezed her hand and leaned closer. "Keep an eye on our local favorite in the black trunks. That's the one we want to win." He pointed to the left. "He may not look like a tough contender, but he's quick on his feet and has one helluva hook."

"All right. I'll root for Jimmy." He seemed a bit slender in the waist, but his legs and arms were muscular. She'd heard Arthur say stamina is an important factor and just because you're the strongest doesn't mean you'll win the match. If so, Jimmy certainly had a chance against the well-defined build of Maximillian the goliath.

A bell rang. The two men exited each corner, walking into the center near the only man fully dressed. The referee made gestures with his hands while speaking to the boxers. After a brief minute, he motioned them back into their corners. Jimmy the Kid danced back and forth on his feet while his opponent beat his gloves together.

Ding!

Lily's heart pounded as Maximillian shot across the ring toward Jimmy who held up his gloves warding off the flurry of blows. One struck him in the kidney and he flinched. Eventually, he got his opening and swung striking goliath squarely on his right eye. Blood sprayed from the gash on his brow. The wallop knocked his opponent onto the springy ropes, showering blood droplets and perspiration into the rows.

Lily covered her eyes with fanned fingers as he bounced back toward Jimmy. They jabbed at each other as they shuffled around the ring from side to side. Every so often one of them got lucky and ducked. But the majority of punches made direct contact jerking their bodies apart.

Neither let up.

Lily grabbed Benjamin's arm, holding tight. Maximillian wildly pummeled with his fists, while Jimmy held his gloves close to his face and seemed to wait for his chance to strike. The Kid made another hit to his opponent's swollen eye, which appeared almost completely closed now. Goliath staggered.

Lily squealed, "Get 'em!"

The Kid swung his left glove, striking the opposite side of Maximillian's face and in a split second threw his right onto the angle of his opponent's jaw. Goliath crashed backward to the floor, whacking his head against the mat.

Jimmy danced around Maximillian, but he didn't stir.

"One." The referee signaled the count with a chopping movement of his arm. "Two." He walked around to the other side of the splayed body. "Three."

Slowly, Goliath rolled from his back onto his side.

But the referee's count continued. "Four."

The crowd rose to their feet shouting, "Jimmy the Kid! Jimmy the Kid!"

"Five."

Benjamin jumped up, pulling Lily with him. "He's going to win!"

Lily bounced on her tiptoes.

"Six."

Maximillian squirmed sluggishly onto one elbow and then the other.

"Seven."

Lily held Benjamin's hand as their arms waved overhead along with the multitude. They chanted along shouting, "Jimmy! Jimmy! Jimmy!"

"Eight." The referee crouched over the boxer.

Goliath braced one fist on the mat, but his arm gave way and he fell sideways.

The warmth of adrenaline rushed through her.

"Nine." The referee swept his hand down in a deliberate manner.

The crowd roared. She'd never had such a connection with so many people.

"Ten." The referee grabbed Jimmy's wrist, hoisting his arm in the air.

"Hoorah!" Benjamin applauded. "What an exhilarating match."

Lily cupped her hands around her mouth. "Attaboy! That was exciting, except way too short. Why don't they go any longer?"

He grinned. "I'm so glad you enjoyed yourself. But they didn't even make it to the end of the first round. That was called a knockout."

"Oh? No wonder everyone had so much enthusiasm. Then I guess Jimmy did great."

"Yes, he did. Usually, the matches last much longer. It could be up to fifteen rounds and if they box till the end it's about an hour."

"I see."

"Do you want to leave?" Benjamin picked up his fedora. "We could stop by Nightingale's for some pie."

"I'd love to." Lily hooked her hand around his arm as they followed the mass of people who were pushing their way toward the door. "Jimmy must be overjoyed having so many here rooting for him."

"It wasn't always like this for him." Benjamin held her tighter while the path became narrower. "You see, his motivation for boxing came from a time when no one seemed to like him much."

Lily's eyes opened wider. "Do go on."

"Well, my brother once mentioned Jimmy had a hard time during high school with the fellows. They'd made him an outcast because of how he looked. Back then, he didn't have the physique he does now." Benjamin placed his hat on his head as they shuffled through the doorway. "What he's accomplished since then is impressive. Especially with a record of ten wins to three losses and he's getting better all the time. He sure showed those brutes."

"That is an inspiring story." Jimmy had changed his life and proved himself worthy. He fought for what he wanted and didn't let anyone or anything stand in his way. That took a lot of courage.

The storm left scattered puddles behind while the sky flickered in the distance. Benjamin opened the car door. "I think we're going to be stranded here for a bit until it clears out." He craned his neck toward the back of the car. "Besides, I'm blocked in by a Buick." He offered his hand, easing her onto the seat and went around the front to the driver's side.

She turned toward him as he slid in. "Thank you for taking me tonight."

"You're welcome." He smiled. "I've never dated a woman who enjoyed the same things I do. First fishing and now boxing. We make the ideal pair."

"Yes, we do." Lily had been amazed by Jimmy's tenacity. His experience at school, although horrible, gave her hope. She'd struggled with rejection too, but hadn't handled it as well. The time had come for her to take more control of her life. And she'd start with her future. If it turned out Benjamin loved her too, she would fight for them to be together.

Benjamin touched her arm. "What has you so deep in thought?"

"I was thinking about how Jimmy had been treated at school."

"Oh?"

She fussed with straightening her dress skirt. "I can relate to what you told me. A group of rich girls in grade school tormented me. Nothing I did was good enough for them."

"I'm sorry. That must have been awful."

"It was. I've decided all that's my past and wallowing won't benefit me at all." She turned toward him with a smile. "So, I've decided to be strong like Jimmy."

Benjamin tossed his hat on the dash. "That's great. However, remember you wouldn't be who you are today if it wasn't for the experience. And I love who you've become." He twisted in the seat, leaning closer. "Didn't I mention saving something for you later?" His gaze met hers and he gradually lowered his eyes to her lips.

"Mm-hmm." Her heart pattered. *He loves who I am.*

"I think it's later, don't you?" He placed his finger under her chin, tilting her head ever so slightly. "You're beautiful."

Her skin tingled at his light touch. She so desperately wanted a long-lasting kiss. "Let's pretend this is a knockout and you have to kiss me for a count of ten to revive me."

"A slow count of ten or a fast count?" His brown eyes twinkled.

She grinned. "A long, slow count."

"I'm certain I can accomplish that." He swept across her jawline, grazing his fingertips against her neck, into her hair, and knocking her hat onto the floorboard. As he drew her closer, his lips hovered above barely touching hers.

She counted the electrifying seconds.

He covered her mouth. Tenderly, he cherished every inch of her lips.

She reached for his arm, which held her firmly near him. Her hand softly ascended along his bicep, across his shoulder, and traced every defined ripple until her fingers curled around the back of his neck. Their connection intensified with each other's grasp.

Lightning lit the sky.

His hands climbed further into her hair, releasing the grip of her bobby pins. He glided his sweet-tasting lips in the most perfect way.

Thunder rumbled low.

Her heart filled with his soul-binding affection. She inhaled his masculine scent as her breath hitched.

He tipped her head back as he trailed a few nibbles down her neck. Fleetingly, his lips rose again placing numerous kisses upon her cheek. His shaky breath sent shivers prickling her skin. He released her and gazed into her face. "Your skin is aglow. I'm pretty certain I've revived you."

"Oh, yes. You certainly have."

"Well then, are your lips ready for another round?"

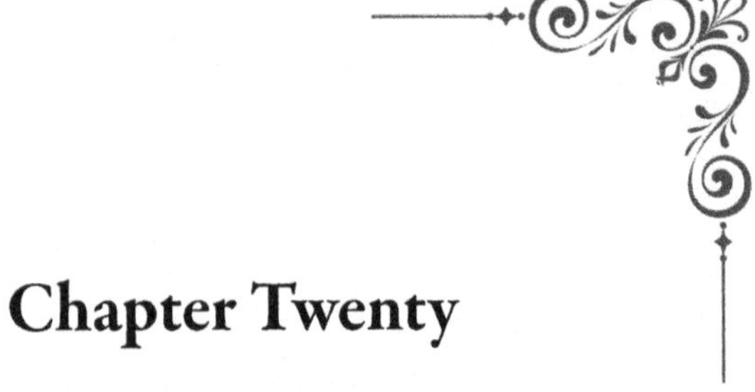

Chapter Twenty

Benjamin tapped the pencil on the clipboard while Louie weighed the penny nails. The day before holidays were always slow at the store and Independence Day hadn't been any different. So he made good use of the time for inventory checks. He had a system in place for ordering all the binned hardware based on how many pounds were remaining. On average, a customer would buy a set number of pounds depending upon the type of nail, screw, bolt, or nut. He would review the sales figures from the last three months and be able to calculate how much to stock. Of course, these types of items were in higher demand during the building season so he had to keep that in mind too.

"Eighty-d is two and three-quarter pounds." Louie unhooked the chain hanging from the scale and dumped the contents into the wooden bin. "That's the last of the nails. What do you want to weigh next?"

"How about the nuts." Benjamin leaned over the counter, writing the tally in the appropriate column.

"That reminds me of your ex-fiancée. A nut who doesn't fall far from the tree." Louie slapped his leg and laughed. "You haven't seen her since that time at the pool, have you?" He grabbed a handful of nuts and dropped them onto the tin scoop.

"It's an apple, Louie. Are you ever going to get that saying correct? And no, I'm hoping she'll stay away. Lily doesn't need to keep running into her when we are in public." Benjamin sat on the stool. "The last couple of times I made certain we didn't cross her path."

"Don't you realize she's still carrying a torch for you? I think you shouldn't have let her off so easy the first time she came prowling around. Did you ever wonder how she knew you were even there? She probably hired a dick to keep tabs on you." Louie hung the scoop on the scale. "Three-quarters a pound for the quarter-inch nuts."

"You slay me! A private dick, really?" Benjamin chuckled. "Vivian would never go that far. She's done nothing remotely close that would make me any more cautious than I already am. What's the next size you have there?"

"Five-sixteenths and there's only two."

"Benjamin!" Hefty footsteps clomped about on the wooden floorboards in the back area. "Benjamin! Where are you?"

He twisted on the stool. "I'm out here, Father."

"I need to speak with you. Come back to my office." Father spun around, treading heavily in the opposite direction.

Louie pulled off his glove and tapped his finger on his lips. "What have you done now?"

"I have no idea, but from the sounds of it, he isn't in a good mood. I'd better get back there." Benjamin hustled over and gave Louie the clipboard. "Here, this will keep you busy so you don't eavesdrop outside the door."

"I don't need to be a spy. I'll leave that up to Vivian."

"Humph! Just concentrate on the inventory, will you?" His heels made a one-eighty as he hurried toward the office. He'd learned at an early age when his father was displeased to get it over with as soon as possible. Otherwise, the stewing might make matters worse. But he couldn't imagine what he had done wrong. He stepped into the doorway as Father jammed a handful of papers into his desk, banging the drawer closed.

Father jerked his head up. "Shut the door." His chair rolled closer to the desk.

Benjamin took a couple of paces inside. Slowly, he swung the door until the latch clicked. His father's present irritated reaction caused more of an alarm than when he initially called him. He walked over toward the chair situated in front of the desk.

"Have a seat, son."

He rubbed his sweaty palms across his pant legs and sat near the edge while awaiting a reprimand.

Father's lips were pinched in a straight line. He rested his forearms on the desk, leaning forward. "Your mother and I have given you a good life, haven't we?"

"Yes, you have."

"And you know we depend on you to take over here."

Benjamin's eyebrows drew together. "You're not sick, are you?" Anxiety tightened around his abdomen.

"No, it's nothing like that. But someday we all pass on." Father straightened his spine. "This place is your legacy, along with Eva's."

A wave of relief allowed him to breathe easier. "I appreciate how hard you've worked all these years. I'll try and make you proud when the time comes." Father couldn't have called him back here for this. Nothing was making any sense. "You seemed agitated before. I know something is bothering you."

"I think that intuition is what makes you such a good businessman. Your brother didn't hone in on his as we wanted." Father sighed. "Instead, he found it easier to be reckless and obstinate." He shook his head. "And now, you're going down the same path."

"What?"

"Your mother told me how you lied to her."

"I didn't."

"You haven't been completely honest with Miss DuCate regarding your broken engagement and another woman, have you?" Father's tone sharpened. "Our reputation is important. So is the DuCate family's. Sowing your wild oats elsewhere wouldn't be the right choice."

"It's not like that with Lily." Benjamin's heartbeat resounded in his ears. "I don't understand where all this is coming from. Two weeks ago, you said you'd handle everything. What's changed?"

"I've already explained it to you. I can't be any plainer. What happened with Robert can't happen again." Father's jaw clenched. "Your uncle pulled us out of the predicament last time and we don't have any more family members willing to do the same."

"What do you expect me to do?" As soon as he asked the question, tunnel vision set in and he didn't like who awaited him at the end.

"Exactly what you were intended to do all along." Father stood, towering over the desk with a stern intensity about his reddened face. "Marry Vivian."

"You can't be serious." He rubbed an unsteady hand across his forehead.

"End of discussion." Father yanked down his sleeves. "I've got some work I need to tend to. Please see yourself out."

Benjamin stood. Nothing worthwhile would come of attempting to continue the conversation. Father had spoken. He rotated the doorknob and swung the door open. Until he figured out Father's reasoning, he couldn't address the situation any further. He wandered past Eva's office into the parking lot. The sun shone on his face and he held a hand over his brow while the other clung to the metal railing. He wanted to run down the stairs and never come back. That would show his parents they couldn't dictate his life. Robert didn't let them, so why should he? The discussions between both parents seemed too coincidental. Each of them had mentioned his brother when they brought up his future. What could that mean? Had Mother finally convinced Father to accept her rationale? He couldn't just leave like this. There had to be a way to straighten out this mess. He may be defeated right now, but the war wasn't over.

Turning around, he gradually meandered inside toward his office. Why was this happening right now when he'd finally found Lily? His head hung low while he stared at his feet as he walked through the hall and into his office. A figure moved. He lunged backward. "What the—!"

"Shh!" Eva motioned with her hand. "Close the door."

"I'd rather be alone." He gave the door a shove and it clicked shut.

"I'll bet I can guess why." Eva stood in his pathway. "You look awful."

"Thanks for letting me know. What do you want?" He sidestepped around his sister, heading toward his desk.

"Tell me what happened with Father."

He plopped into the chair. "If you only came in here to snoop, you can leave now."

Eva leaned against the corner of his desk. "I'm here to help—not pry into your personal life."

"How do you know what Father talked to me about then?" His eyes narrowed. "You had to be listening."

"I wasn't, I swear." She traced an *x* over her chest with her fingertip.

"All right, you have one minute to convince me of your good intentions." He pulled out his pocket watch and pushed the latch release on the crown. "Go."

"Walter." She crossed her arms.

The hairs on his arms stood. "What about Walter?" He closed the lid on his watch and stuck it back into his pocket.

"Father had a heated conversation with him." She fiddled with the dial on the desk calendar. "As soon as he left, you were called back to Father's office. My guess is whatever was said had to do with Vivian."

His brow furrowed. "I didn't see Walter come in. Besides, Louie and I were out front all morning. And why didn't I hear either of them yelling?"

"Walter used the side door to the parking lot right outside my office. As for you not hearing them, I can only assume if their speech was muffled for me through the adjoining wall, you'd be out of earshot out front." She pushed a stack of papers aside and sat on the edge of the desk.

"What you're saying sounds logical." He leaned backward in the chair. "So, what did they say?"

"Honestly, I heard only bits and pieces but enough to understand Mr. DuCate had an agenda. The conversation lasted only a few minutes. And at one point, Walter raised his voice like he had authority over Father. I heard the word *agreement* but that's all I could make out. I went closer and Walter mentioned you and Vivian. But by then, he must have finished because it was quiet. Until Father's office door slammed. I got startled and almost tripped over my feet backing away from the wall."

Benjamin rubbed his chin. "What you overheard can't be a coincidence to what happened with me afterward. Father had the audacity to order me to marry Vivian." His chest tightened. "There is no way I'm making that woman my wife. Not after experiencing what love really should be. Lily's more important than any legacy."

"I'd vote for love over Vivian any day." Eva slid off the desk. *Whoosh!* A stack of papers cascaded off after her. "Oops, sorry." She bent over, gathering the pieces. "Even if Walter told Father you had to marry Vivian, why would he listen? Father never changes his mind after he makes a decision. Besides, didn't he tell you he'd take care of the issue with the DuCates?"

"That's what doesn't make sense." Benjamin scratched his temple. "Three minutes with Walter and Father surrenders. What could he have over Father? Do you think he threatened him? But with what?"

"You're the one who goes to all the movies." Eva sorted the papers in one pile and the envelopes in another. "What kinds of devious schemes have you seen?" She tapped an envelope on her palm.

He flung forward, sitting up straight in the chair. "Maybe it's like that new movie coming out. You know, the one about the con artist and the botched blackmail scheme."

"*Hold Your Man*?" Eva placed the envelope on top of the others. "Don't you think you're letting your imagination get away from you?" She laughed.

His gaze followed the envelope and an idea popped into his mind. "No. I might be on to something, and you can help. Remember when you had me mail the payments?"

"She nodded."

"There was one in there for Walter."

"So?"

"Why would the company send Walter a check? He buys from us. We would get a check from him." He grinned. "Can you look into how many times we've sent Walter money and how much we've sent him?"

"Sure, I'll get right on it." Eva twirled around and exited the office.

Maybe, just maybe, this idea of blackmail was far-fetched. But right now, it was the only thing that was a plausible explanation as to what had just happened. If Father was paying money to Walter, he had to figure out why. And if Father did give Walter money—what dishonest, immoral, or unjust thing could Father have done? That part in his theory didn't add up. Father was honest, moral, and just. Except for this one time with him when Father had been completely unfair. No matter what, he couldn't give in. He couldn't give up on love. And he couldn't lose Lily. Not now.

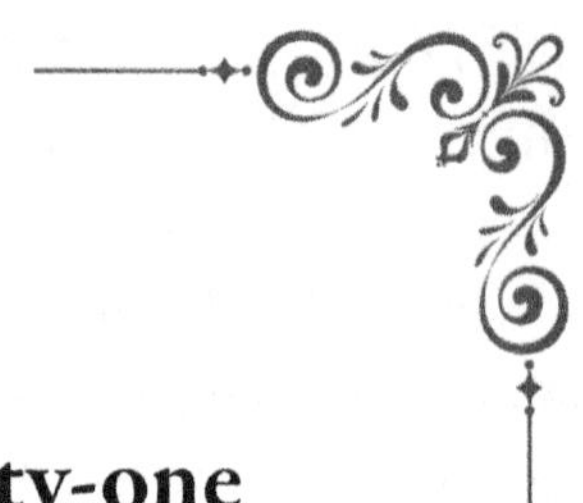

Chapter Twenty-one

Lily angled her face toward the sky, basking in the sunlight. Columbia Park filled with neighbors who had arrived for the Fourth of July celebration. Every year the block picnic seemed to grow along with the variety of food as each household brought a dish to pass. She enjoyed tasting all the delicious recipes, especially the desserts like green tomato pie, icebox brown sugar cookies, and the lady across the way's chocolate spud brownies. Those were her favorite.

Next to her, Anna had sprawled on the blanket they'd tossed over the sparse grass. The rays pleasantly tanned Anna's skin while her pale coloring undoubtedly freckled. A leisure day, such as this, made her appreciate the time she could spend with her friend and their handsome gentlemen. Except, their men had decided to engage in a game of football beyond the cluster of oak trees, leaving her alone with Anna.

She tipped her head forward and opened her eyes. Father Toeller, the priest from Saint John's Catholic Church, passed by several feet in front of her carrying a plate of sandwiches. She returned his smile. Maybe she should have taken the opportunity to ask him why she couldn't marry a man who wasn't Catholic. But now wasn't the right time. Besides, the act would be too forward and presumptuous for her. Although she'd tried to push her mother's words aside regarding their religious beliefs, she couldn't. Benjamin had to be in her life, destined to be her true love. Anna had told her as much.

Her friend rolled over onto her side. "There is such a positive connection between you and Benjamin." Anna grinned. "I take it everything is going well with you two."

She was thrilled they were together, but would they be able to endure the difficulties undoubtedly coming their way? "I couldn't be happier with how our relationship has been. We've gone to some fascinating places, but not exactly where I thought we would." Lily crossed her legs and tucked her dress skirt around her knees. "I asked Benjamin to share his interests with me. Mainly because I wanted to see what his everyday life is like and learn whether or not we'd be compatible. And of course, how I would fit in."

"So, do you see what I see?"

"I can't believe it! We are perfect for each other." Lily's heart fluttered with giddiness. "I don't know why I ever doubted we were right for each other."

"I knew it."

"There's one major problem. And I'm not sure how either of us will be able to overcome the issue." Lily pulled her knees to her chest, hugging them tightly. "Mother mentioned the church won't allow marriage with someone who's not Catholic. Have you ever heard of such a thing?"

"No, but I'm not at all surprised. The church has lots of rules we need to follow and they're not always easy." Anna propped her head with her hand. "What are you going to do if it's true?"

"I'm not sure yet. If Benjamin doesn't ask me to marry him, it's a moot point." Lily touched the crucifix on her necklace and slid the pendant back and forth. “I have to believe everything will work out. I love him.”

Anna shot up, throwing her arms around Lily. “I’m so happy for you. What did he say when you told him?”

“I didn’t.”

Anna pulled away. “Why not?”

“He didn’t say it to me.” Lily grinned as if revealing a secret. “But I can feel the love in his kiss. In the gentle way he holds me close. In the caress of his fingers as they trace upon my cheek. And in the warmth of his breath across my ear.” She tilted her head, peering into the sky. “I’m as certain of the fact he loves me, as the earth will be lit by the moon tonight and the sun tomorrow.” She held her hand to her heart. “I read that once in one of my mother’s romance books, but it’s exactly how I feel about him.”

“Well, then.” Anna’s brow arched. “He is your soulmate!”

“I hope I’m not fooling myself into thinking we’ll get through this difference between our faiths.” Lily fiddled with her necklace. “Am I?”

“Every couple has issues. Fate brought you together, but love is what will get you through the rest. You have to hold onto that. I do. Some days are harder than others, even for me. But then I remember why I fell in love with Emmett in the first place.” Anna mirrored Lily earlier by placing her hand over her heart. “We are better together than apart. When you love someone, don’t ever give up.”

“That’s such good advice. I’m sure it’s easier to say than to live up to, but maybe that’s when you know you’ve found your true companion in life.” Lily craned her neck at the sound of snapping twigs. "They're on their way back and it looks like they're bringing us lunch."

Emmett and Benjamin set the multiple plates they'd brought onto the blanket.

"We grabbed a variety of food." Benjamin knelt next to Lily. "All of it looked so good. Thanks for inviting me."

"I'm happy you didn't have to work." Lily smiled. "Bringing over the food was sweet of you. It's the little things like this that count in a relationship."

"My pleasure." He smiled.

"I heard Benjamin took you to a fight on Friday and you liked it." Emmett glanced over while taking a mouthful of fried chicken.

"There wasn't much time not to enjoy the fight." Lily picked up a roll with ham spread. "Did you hear Jimmy caused a knock over?"

Benjamin turned toward Lily. "The term is knockout." He grinned.

"Well, he did fall over." Lily laughed. "How did you two do in the football game?"

"We lost." Emmett licked his fingers. "None of our fellows could catch. So, it didn't take too much effort from the other team."

"I stood there like this." Benjamin waved his arms in the air. "I was wide open many times, but no one threw it to me."

Anna popped a stuffed olive into her mouth.

"That's because there were always two men on defense hovering around you." Emmett held out the plate of sandwiches. "What did you expect?"

"I could have dodged them." Benjamin took an egg salad sandwich. "Besides, most of the time our quarterback either got tackled or tossed away the ball."

"Maybe you could have." Emmett set the plate down. "Guess it doesn't matter either way."

Anna dabbed a napkin on her lips. "Remember the last time we were all here together?"

"I sure do." Emmett kissed Anna. "It was the best day of my life." He put his arm around her shoulder, pulling her into his side. "Maybe the next time we're all here together, it will be your turn, Lily."

A big smile spread across Lily's lips.

Benjamin's cheeks flushed a shade of crimson. He pulled the sandwich away from his mouth and swallowed. The egg content squashed out between the bread, dropping onto his shirt, and plummeting directly on the crotch of his pants.

"Goodness sakes!" Lily grabbed a handful of napkins and gave them to Benjamin. "Is there any egg left in that bread?"

Benjamin flopped the two pieces open. "Nope. All of it seems to be on my pants." He wiped at the mess, but the spot seemed to get larger.

"Looks like you could have used the bread and done a similar job. Sorry to put you in the hot seat, my friend." Emmett chuckled. "Here, try this leg instead."

Benjamin took the chicken piece. "I guess I'll just have to add this encounter to my list of egg stories." He cheerfully grinned and took a bite.

Had Emmett apologized to throw her off? Lily gave him a few more napkins. "By the way you're smiling, it has to be almost as funny as this time." She giggled.

Emmett slapped Benjamin on the shoulder. "Tell the girls about the one with you and your brother, that one is the best."

Benjamin stuck a napkin in his collar and laid another over the obvious stain below. "Wish I would have done that earlier." He smiled. "Well, Robert and I used to spend our teenage years every Saturday helping out in the store. We learned a lot. Not just because of the work, but also from the men coming in to buy their goods. A weekend never went by without a story about hunting, fishing, drinking..." He coyly grinned, "...and especially women. Those were the ones Father made us promise not to tell Mother. He said most of what they were saying wasn't true anyway and they just liked to talk big. Of course, we never said a thing. If we had, Mother would have put an end to our fun."

He pulled some meat off the bone and ate it. "Anyway, one of the funniest tales had to do with Elmer. He would always come in bragging about something or another. But for a month straight we listened to him about his chickens. He'd always tell us how many eggs they would lay and he said it had all to do with a certain kind of feed he gave them."

"So Robert and I snuck out to the farm. We added a few eggs to the nest during the week and when Elmer came in, he claimed he wasn't surprised at all by a few more. He boasted again at how well he could make his chickens lay eggs. The next whole week, we added a dozen every day and when Elmer came in telling everyone, they all said he'd been giving us a tall tale. Of course, he insisted he didn't. But he seemed a bit more surprised than the previous week. That's when my brother came up with another plan."

"Are you sure it wasn't you?" Emmett peered at him suspiciously.

Benjamin wiped his fingers on the napkin. “Maybe, but more than likely we both conjured up what happened next.”

“What?” Lily’s eyes widened. “Did he finally catch you putting all those eggs in there?”

“Nope. For the next week, we put hard-boiled eggs in the nest.”

Anna snorted and covered her mouth.

Lily laughed. “I’m guessing Elmer figured out the two of you were in on it.”

“Yes, but Elmer had the last chuckle. He told everyone about his marvelous egg mash and said it was so good his chickens had laid eggs ready to be eaten. And it was all on account of the young Claussen boys who helped out with special key ingredients. For a while, Elmer had some people believing our feed would do the same for their chickens.” Benjamin turned the chicken leg, took another bite, and swallowed. “That is one of my finest eggstraordinary tales.” He grinned. “Cracks me up every time.”

Anna snorted again.

Lily held her stomach, roaring with laughter.

“You told it well this time.” Emmett slapped his palm across his leg. “Well, I wish we didn’t have to go but I promised my family we’d stop over. They planned a small get together with a relative we haven’t seen in a while.” He stood, offering his hand to Anna. “Let me know soon when we can go out again.”

“I’ll figure something out. Why don’t you stop by the office at the end of the week and I’ll run it by you?” Benjamin held out his hand, shaking Emmett’s.

“Probably be there about three-thirty Friday. Will you still be around?”

Benjamin nodded. "See you then."

"Bye, Lily." Anna waved.

"See you later." Lily gathered the plates while they walked away. "I'll throw these out if you want to fold up the blanket. Or would you rather stay here for a while?" She stepped onto the grass.

Benjamin tossed the blanket in the air. "I'd like to go home and change my pants. We could go for a drive afterward."

"Oh, yes. I like that idea."

Five minutes later, Benjamin shifted the car into gear. "The road south of town is scenic through the winding bluffs. How about going out in that direction?"

"Sounds pretty." Had he been surprised by Emmett's hint of marriage? Is that why he dropped the egg salad? Or maybe he'd said something to Emmett about her while they played football. The clue of marriage could have been directed at her so Benjamin could watch her reaction. She'd questioned for weeks how their connection would progress. If she truly wanted to find out, there would be only one way before she lost her nerve. "Where do you think Emmett got that idea of us getting married?" She peered over at him.

Benjamin grinned. "I'm quite certain he can tell how taken I am with you. You also heard me say earlier how men talk about the women they find attractive. I'm thinking we are not the only ones who do though." He stopped at the sign. "Don't you tell Anna how handsome I am?" He winked.

"Absolutely." Lily's brow rose as a curious sensation came over her. Benjamin must have mentioned something since he didn't disagree. Hopefully, his parents wouldn't think the same way as hers when it comes to marriage. "Will I be able to meet your folks?"

Benjamin drummed his fingers on the steering wheel. "No, sorry. Father planned on taking Mother to the picnic at the Good Fellows Club. They haven't had one in the past few years and the club parties usually last until late in the evening. We'll have to set up another time for you to meet them." He accelerated into the intersection just as fast as he clarified his answer.

She'd never heard him talk like that before. Apparently, he must be nervous for her. *He's so sweet.* "That would be wonderful." Her parents had made Benjamin feel at ease. Hopefully, his would do the same for her. Although she was disappointed, maybe he could tell her a little about them. When they finally did meet, her nerves wouldn't be so jittery. "I don't know much about your parents, what are they like?"

Benjamin turned onto Cedar. "Well, they've known each other for most of their lives since they grew up neighbors back in Waupaca. The first few years they were married my father farmed with my grandfather and in the winter, he'd travel to the lumber camps. He intended on saving money and buying a farm, but mother had enough of that kind of life. Instead, they moved here and Father started working with Hans Ebbe."

He pulled into the drive and parked next to the house. "There's no need for you to sit in the hot car. Why don't you come in while I change? Then I can show you around."

"I'd love to see the house."

Benjamin led the way through the back door. He motioned to the right. "Here's the kitchen and over there the door opens into the dining room. Why don't you wait in there? I'm going to take these stairs and I'll meet you shortly."

"Fine. I'll see you in a little bit." Lily stepped into the huge kitchen. There were so many cupboards and drawers along two of the walls, she had no idea what could have filled them. She passed by the breakfast table with the geometric design on top and through the swinging door.

"Look at that!" She sucked in a quick breath and covered her mouth. On one side of the room, a long table had enough chairs for ten people with a matching filled china cabinet situated on the wall directly behind. She gently ran her hand across the straight-grained table with hues of green and purple. Along the edge, a sideboard coordinated with the other pieces including the identical etched glass design of the cabinet. She'd never encountered such deep chocolate wood before. The color emulated Benjamin's eyes beautifully.

Across the room, a similar dark wood edged a tiled fireplace. She moved closer, peering at the assorted glass items from one end of the mantel to the other. There were plates with scenic pictures, fancy colored vases, brightly painted figurines, and, at the center, an old ticking clock. Above, hung a square mirror almost equal to the size of the fireplace. She caught a glimpse of herself and tiptoed backward until her full length appeared. Picking up the sides of her skirt between her fingers, she pulled her dress away and bowed. The elaborate dinner parties must be wonderful here. She twirled around, walking past the open staircase which protruded beyond the short wall. Benjamin would probably come from there when he finished changing.

The outside wall housed four expansive windows which extended from almost the top of the twelve-foot ceilings all the way to the floor. Near the last window, a wooden shelf was tucked into the corner by the stair wall. As she came closer, the glass shelves displayed different breeds of porcelain dogs. There must be almost a hundred of them. An adorable black, tan, and white dog posed in a sitting position. She picked up the canine, turned it over, and in ink the word Japan was written on the bottom.

"I see you have found my collection of dogs."

Lily jumped. That voice wasn't Benjamin's.

"They're fragile!" The steps creaked. "If you wouldn't mind placing it back on the shelf where you took it from."

"Yes, of course." Lily gently set the piece back and circled around. "I'm Lily Vanderhoof." She walked toward the stairway. "You must be Mrs. Claussen. Sorry, if I startled you. Benjamin didn't think anyone would be home." His mother's features were similar to his. "Nice to meet you." She held out her hand.

With a pinched face and unpleasant expression, Constance daintily touched her hand. "I certainly wasn't expecting anyone." She held her purple silk robe together at the top. "Where is Benjamin?"

"He's upstairs." His mother looked fashionable even in a garment not intended for company.

"I see." Constance stepped off the last stair. "If you will follow me, we can have a seat in the front room and wait for him there."

Lily trailed behind her as they walked through a living room and set of double glass doors into the front room. From what she was wearing, along with her tousled black hair, his mother appeared to have been resting. Maybe she'd been embarrassed, but it didn't excuse her from not smiling even once.

Constance closed the doors.

A small knotted lump tightened in her stomach. She followed Benjamin's mother into the room and sat across from her in a floral embroidered chair. Taking a long deep breath, she slowly exhaled. "Your son is a very nice man."

"Thank you, he is special to me too. I'm not sure what Benjamin has told you about his family, but I have always been the one to look out for my son's best interests." Constance's coral manicured nails tapped on the wooden arm of her chair. "I know him better than anyone. If he hasn't told you, we have a very close bond." Her eyes narrowed like a piercing dagger to the heart.

Lily's apprehension grew as his mother's face pinched together again. "Yes, he's told me only good things about his family." She shifted in the chair. Her parents hadn't made Benjamin this uneasy. Maybe his thoughts earlier of meeting his family weren't out of nervousness but utter fear by how his mother would react. Her body shuddered with a chill.

"His last relationship ended not long ago. I'm concerned he's not ready to begin a new one." She cocked her head and slowly shook it to and fro. "Surely, you do not want to get hurt."

Her insides quivered like a gelatin mold. "I don't believe Benjamin has any intentions of breaking my heart." *Doesn't she realize he's old enough to make his own decisions?*

Constance clenched the material at the top of her robe. "He may not have a choice. Did he mention we are a deeply faithful Presbyterian family?"

"Yes." Her voice shook slightly.

"I have to say, a long-term relationship with a Catholic is improper." Constance's tone sharpened. "I'm surprised your family has not mentioned the same."

Lily glanced at the doorway. Time seemed to have slowed. "We've talked and there are some concerns." Her heart burned as it tore in two.

"Good, then you agree." Constance forced a smile, but it quickly slipped away. "I'm sure you're a very nice young lady and you come from a caring family, but you cannot deny our differences go beyond religion."

Lily stared past Constance at the phonograph situated atop a small table. She couldn't observe the unpleasantness in that woman's face any longer or she might break down and cry.

"Socially my dear, your family is from the north side of town and that won't work for my son." Constance's voice projected over her. "He's expected to take over the company from his father and marry Vivian. You don't want to come between what he is destined for, do you? He shouldn't have to choose between you and his future with Ebbe."

She resented the intimidation and needed to get out of here. Constance made it clear Lily was not good enough for her son by belittling everything about her. How could she have been such a fool believing she could fit in? *Click.* She glanced at the door.

Benjamin's somber gaze darted between her and his mother. "There you are. I've been looking all over for you." He rushed over to Lily. "Are you all right?" His hand slipped onto hers.

She nodded. His usual soft caress seemed tense.

He cocked his head toward his mother. "I'm surprised you're home. If I knew, I would have introduced Lily properly. Hopefully, your discussion has been a pleasant one so far."

"If you'll excuse me, I think you two should just go. The timing is all wrong." Constance placed the back of her hand onto her forehead. “I have a horrible headache. I’m going to go back and lie down.”

Lily uttered through gritted teeth, “It was nice meeting you.”

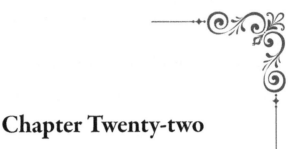

Chapter Twenty-two

The trees whizzed by as Benjamin glanced at Lily's solemn face in the passenger seat. She hadn't spoken but a few grumbles since they left his house and headed out of town toward the bluffs. What had happened behind those closed doors? He could only imagine how cruel his mother must have been to make her so upset. His thumbs strummed a rhythmic beat on the steering wheel. He'd seen this quiet side of Lily before when he tried to explain how Ira wanted him to take care of her. He didn't want to repeat that situation, so he needed to approach with caution. "Lily, please talk to me."

"Am I a wicked person?"

"No, of course not. Did my mother say that to you?"

"Somewhat. If you're not Presbyterian or an affluent woman, then you're not good enough for her son." She glanced away toward the side window. "Did you know she felt that way?"

"Um...well, no. Not like that exactly."

Her downcast eyes flickered back at him for a brief second. "Then what did you know, exactly?"

He swallowed the lump rising in his throat. "Mother's not pleased I broke the engagement with—"

"Apparently."

He sensed frustration in her raspy voice. She needed an explanation of the facts. "I don't think I mentioned my mother's friends with Vivian's mother. They have been for a long time. Anyway, one day the two of them must've gotten together and decided Vivian and I were the perfect pair. Everything went smoothly for quite a while. Until recently, when it didn't. I don't know what happened between us except we didn't get along anymore. Nothing seemed to make Vivian happy unless it was her way. And then I made the connection. I couldn't let another woman manipulate me exactly like my mother had all these years. And you know the rest of the story."

"That explains some of your mother's feelings, but not how she views me. Why wouldn't she just want her son to be happy?"

He'd been beyond happy lately and his mother should have noticed. Lily was right, but she'd never had to cautiously tiptoe around a matriarch like his mother. "I can't grasp why Mother's adamant I marry Vivian either. I've tried figuring out a resolution for almost two weeks now. Just yesterday, Mother convinced Father to side with her."

"Both your parents?" Her hands abruptly shot in the air. "And you've known for weeks and didn't tell me?"

"I didn't want to concern you." His stomach constricted around his picnic lunch. "Besides, most things subside eventually."

She twisted her body in the seat, facing him directly. "Do you honestly believe something like this will just go away?"

He peered at her reddened face. "Aah..."

"Not when you are destined to only marry Vivian and run the company. And if you don't, according to your mother, your future won't be at Ebbe."

"They won't do that. It's an empty threat. They've always regretted running my brother Robert off; I know they won't do that to me. They need me."

"Your mother certainly convinced me she intended on carrying out all the words she said. You need them more than they need you. Don't you see that?" She shook her head. "If you don't take over the company from your father, it's you who will be without a job."

"That's one way to look at the situation. Still, my father always said Ebbe's my legacy. And I can't believe he'd take that away from me over some persistence from my mother about Vivian who has nothing to do with the company. Besides, Father knows how hard I've worked." He had to bank on the truthfulness of his statement. Father had always been fair. He just needed to figure out why he wasn't now.

"Maybe if you were this stubborn with your mother long ago, you wouldn't be in this predicament." She twisted to face the front. "Please, just take me home."

His grip tightened on the steering wheel. He'd done exactly what he didn't want to do...ticked her off again.

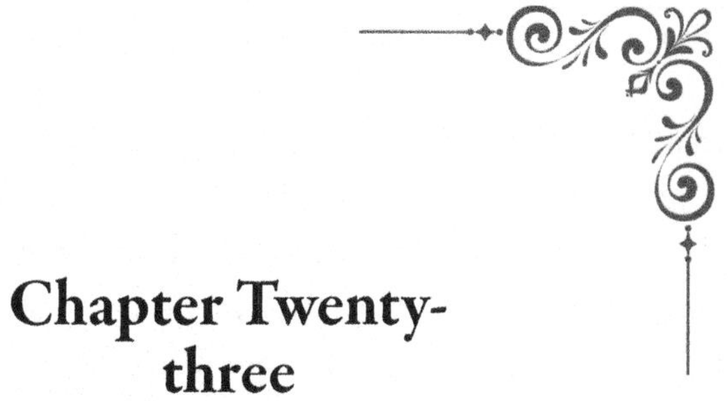

Chapter Twenty-three

Gold digger! If anyone would check the dictionary, Lily Vanderhoof would be the definition. But where was this woman who was after her man? Not on the grand pillared first-floor aisles of Livingston's, nor among the glass showcases of the second level housing women's clothing, shoes, and fashion accessories. Vivian shoved another dress to the side in the latest designs section. She might as well shop this afternoon while she waited. Arthur mentioned his sister worked every Wednesday and Saturday. Well, this Wednesday, today, she'd implement her plan to get Lily out of Benjamin's life for good.

Her parents had been useless. Mother's tactic of speaking with Benjamin's hadn't gone anywhere. Results should have come from the effort between now and a couple of weeks ago. Her patience had held on far too long. Especially after Father hid details of seeing Lily in Benjamin's arms weeks ago. Where was his loyalty? Her fingernails dug into her palms. How could Father have done this to his only princess? If she would have found out sooner, she could have stopped Benjamin's horrible behavior. And the embarrassment of their breakup never would have happened either. Two days ago, she had insisted Father do something about the predicament he allowed her to fall into. After all, things wouldn't have gone so far if it wasn't for his misguided self-serving ways. But whatever Father had said to Benjamin's father hadn't worked either. Her man should have crawled back to her by now begging for forgiveness.

She had only one choice. Take this matter into her own hands. If she was going to do something at least she'd get it done right. And the department store would be a great place to publicly scorn Lily. Fundamentally, that's how she'd been humiliated, so this would be perfectly fitting for little Miss Flower. The corners of her mouth curled with anticipation while her jittery foot tapped the floor. She glanced over her shoulder. *For crying out loud. Where was Lily?*

If only Arthur had told her something she could have used. The story of how Lily and her sister had taken candy from a store when they were only four and six wouldn't be enough to condemn her now. They hadn't even gotten in trouble since they took back what they'd stolen and returned the sweets with an apology. By the end of Arthur's rambling on and on, she figured he'd played her just as much as she did him. *Damned Vanderhoofs! Too smart for their own good.* She held up a yellow floral tunic dress and slung it over her arm.

"Would you like me to take that to a fitting room for you?"

Vivian glanced over her shoulder at a tall, skinny waisted lady who was the epitome of a phony catalog woman. "Sure." She handed over the item. "I'd like the private one in the corner."

"Of course, Miss. Is there something I can help you find?"

Not something. Someone. Vivian smiled slowly, "Do you know a Lily Vanderhoof who works here?"

"Yes, but she's not available right now. May I help you?"

Guess this woman will have to do for now. "All right." Vivian grabbed a red dress with double-ruffle butterfly sleeves. "Here, I'll try this one on as well."

"Lovely choice of evening dress. The material is silk chiffon which gives a shimmery smooth texture." She grasped the hanger. "I'm Winifred, by the way, and I'll help you with whatever you need."

Well, the woman at least had good taste. "Thank you. And I'm Vivian." She pulled a navy dress off the hook and held it up.

"That is top of the line for a day dress. The tailored fit is wonderful and every wardrobe needs a blue outfit like that. Should I add this with the others?"

The woman knew fashion. "I have one in this color, but not the style." Vivian passed her the garment. "I'll see how it looks on. I think this will do for now. I've checked through the entire section."

"All right. Come this way." Winifred glided in a straight line toward the fitting room.

She had to be wearing a girdle to make her waist so narrow. No one could be that small. Vivian placed her hands above her hips and gave a squeeze. If she'd wear one, her waist would be even tinier.

Winifred pushed the drape away and hung the dresses inside. "I'll wait right outside in case you need anything."

She entered the corner room and pulled the drapery closed. Each of the three sides had a full-length mirror and a chair off to the side where she laid her hat. Hurriedly, she disrobed and hung her attire. She pulled the yellow floral tunic off the hanger, tugging the dress over her head. The design was nice, but not her style.

"How's everything going?"

"Just fine." The silky red dress was her favorite. A neckline shaped in a *v* with a high waist falling just below the bustline where the skirt flowed long to the floor. She would have loved to wear this out on the town with Benjamin. They could have danced all night long while he held her in his arms. She twirled and let her imagination take over.

"Vivian?"

"Yes." She slid the drapery.

"Wow! That dress was made for you."

"I know, it's perfect."

"Your fiancé is going to love you in that dress."

Vivian glanced at her engagement ring. She smiled. After today, Benjamin would be hers again. "I certainly hope so. He's taking me dancing and now I'll look fabulous."

"Your husband-to-be won't be able to take his eyes off you."

"That is the plan." Vivian swayed her hips, swooshing the dress from side to side. "I think I'll need a chain with a pendant to accent this neckline, wouldn't you agree?"

"Oh, yes."

Vivian rotated on her heels into the fitting room. She shut the drapery and caught a glimpse of herself in the mirror. Her eyes sparkled with excitement. Soon, she'd put her plan into action. Everyone would finally see Lily for who she was...a conniving, money-hungry, fiancé stealing, undesirable Catholic from the wrong side of town. She couldn't wait to expose her. Once Lily was gone, Benjamin would see the error in his ways and he'd be back in her arms. She hung the evening gown and unzipped the day dress. The size appeared correct for her bust, although the waist seemed narrow. Tugging the garment over her hips, she slipped her arms through the puffed sleeves. She yanked the zipper and it barely moved a few inches. "Rats!"

"Can I assist you with something?"

"It's a bit tight." She must have gained a pound or two and that was all Lily's fault too. Sweets were irresistible when annoyances like Miss Flower were hovering around. "I don't think this is accurately sized."

"Do you mind if I come in and take a peek?"

Vivian hid behind the drapery as she let Winifred inside. "Maybe the zipper's just stuck." She turned her back toward the clerk. "I could perhaps try the next larger size."

Winifred heaved hard on the zipper, but it didn't budge much. She pulled on the dress fabric, holding the two pieces together. "Hmmm, another size up would be too baggy on you with this style. I didn't mention this before but I'm a trained fitter for undergarments. A corselette would define your figure and give you the little bit of extra room needed for this tailored outfit. Would you be interested in getting measured?"

"Yes." She didn't have to hesitate if something would make her hourglass figure even more shapely.

"Great, I'll need to take several measurements. By the end of the week, your custom order will arrive at the store. If you'd like, I can hold this dress for you. Then we can make sure everything will fit proportionately." Winifred stuck her hand in her pocket pulling out a cloth tape measure, along with a notebook, and pencil. "I'll jot down all your information just in case you'd like to place another order at a later date. Then we won't need to schedule an additional fitting."

Vivian wiggled her way out of the material.

"I like to alphabetize my clients." Winifred touched the pencil to her tongue. "What's your last name?"

She slipped the dress onto the hanger. "DuCate."

"All right, let's get started." Winifred tucked the notebook in her pocket. "I'll need some measurements around your bustline, waist, and hips." She unrolled the tape measure and wrapped the cloth around the first area. "These corselettes are very comfortable. I'm wearing one from the same company we'll be getting yours."

I knew it. No one could be so smoothly contoured without help. She held her arms away from her body while Winifred adjusted to the next spot. Standing here practically naked and exposing the slightest of her flaws had been a bit daunting. Although she would go through anything to keep up with fashion. Especially since Benjamin had always appreciated her stylishness. She grinned. With two new outfits, he could adore her even more.

"Please bend to the left. And now to the right." Winifred held the measuring tape against her waist on each side.

She slowly inhaled, holding her fluttery stomach taut.

"Just relax so we can have the right measurement. Good. Now forward." Winifred adjusted the tape. "Now backward. Just a few more and we'll be finished with the fitting."

Vivian gently rubbed her hands together. *Soon, I will find you.* If Lily were here like she was supposed to be, that is. She had no doubt outwitting Lily would be easy when considering the previous time they'd met. Lily must have been so intimidated by her she'd barely spoken more than a few words, even after being taunted with an insult. If Lily didn't comprehend that day Benjamin was already spoken for, she would make certain once and for all today.

"All done." Winifred rolled up her measuring tape. "I'll gather these dresses and meet you at the jewelry counter. I know the perfect lady who will be able to find you the right look for your evening dress."

Vivian pulled back the drapery, bouncing on her toes. "I'll be there shortly."

The clerk slipped out of the dressing room.

She should have asked Winifred the person's name. Wouldn't it be an amusing coincidence if Lily would be the one? She smirked. Her arms slid through the three-quarter length sleeves and she fastened the zipper. What would little Miss Flower know about high-quality taste when it came to choosing jewelry anyway? She faced the middle mirror, picking up her hat and situating it on her head. A few loose strands of her berry red hair curled under the brim. She stretched the elastic band around the nape of her neck, rechecked her hair, and quirked an eyebrow. *Let the fun begin.*

In the store center, tall wood cabinetry with built-in drawers was surrounded by glass cases filled with all sorts of rings, necklaces, earrings, bracelets, and watches. Winifred stood near the far end, blocking the view of the person in front of her. Vivian gazed at the jewelry, along with the faces behind the counter as she approached the ladies. So far, no sight of Lily. And the lady near Winifred was way too pretty to be Lily either.

"Vivian, this is Georgia. I've taken the liberty of showing her the dress you'd like the necklace for." Winifred placed her hand on the box. "I've kept the other one for the fitting. I'll call you when your order comes in and we can set up an appointment. Where can I reach you?"

"326."

"Wonderful, I'll leave you in Georgia's capable hands." Winifred wriggled her fingers as she walked away.

Vivian sat in the cushioned cloth chair. "I want a pendant to hang right about here." She pointed partway down her neckline.

"I would say this one seems to be the closest." Georgia held up a chain. "May I?" She opened the clasp and draped it around Vivian's neck. "Here, take a look in the mirror. Does this suit the length you'd like?"

"Yes."

"All right. I'm assuming by your engagement ring you prefer white gold to yellow." Georgia removed the sample from Vivian's neck. "Do you have something in mind for your pendant, like colored glass beads, or maybe a white on white appearance? Any particular shape? Like geometric, natural forms, or moon and stars."

"I'd be fine with almost anything." Vivian tilted her head. Georgia sure did ask a lot of questions without even taking a breath in between. "I just want to accentuate my neckline with the red gown."

"I'll gather some pieces then. Just give me a moment." Georgia stepped away.

The multitude of silver in Georgia's dark tresses implied at least fifteen years more senior than her. Hopefully, that meant the lady knew style.

A figure beyond moved near the opposite end of the display cases. She scrutinized the back of a teal-patterned dress. The height, figure, and hair color precisely matched that of the one she'd been waiting for. Vivian sucked in perfumed air as the woman placed some boxes on the counter and turned. *Lily!* Her hands tightly clenched the chair as her body stiffened. Lily was right where she wanted. Vivian opened her mouth, but Lily reversed direction without any eye contact and disappeared to the other side.

"Nooo!" Vivian shook her hands until the tingling subsided. She'd get that tramp next time. That couldn't have been her only opportunity slipping away so easily.

"Here we are. We can start with these and if they don't meet your needs, I've got a few more we can try." Georgia placed each piece of sparkling jewelry on a black felt cloth. "This first piece is filigree white on white."

"Hmmm. I like it but too plain."

"Maybe this one. Lots of colors."

"Too much of a statement for the dress." Her eyes shifted focus at the movement behind Georgia. Another woman approached with similar features as Lily, but it wasn't her. She depressed keys on the cash register while filling a bag with purchases.

"Here is a strand of onyx beads with an embellished tassel cluster."

Vivian glanced down briefly and back again at the woman behind who impersonated the jerkiness of a wind-up toy. "Not my style." Why would anyone move their body in that manner? The woman scouted every angle around her, pushed another key, and the till drawer opened with a ding. Instead of placing the dollar bills into the register, the woman's hand slid the cash into her pocket. "Did you see that?"

"See what?"

"Never mind. I'm sure you didn't." Vivian ran her finger across a red pendant surrounded by round diamonds. "This is the one I want."

Georgia draped the glistening chain over her wrist. "I think you've made an excellent choice. This is an art deco piece in platinum. The rectangular coral is lovely surrounded by thirty, quarter-carat diamonds. Would you like the price on this stunning jewel?"

"No, just add to Walter DuCate's account." Father owed her that much at least for all her troubles. Vivian rose from the chair. Her body tingled. "I would like to speak to the manager."

"Yes, of course. I'll get him immediately."

The woman from the register was gone. She must be on the other side where Lily had gone. What would make someone commit such a criminal act? Wasn't she afraid of getting caught? Or losing her job for that matter? Vivian peeked around the tall cabinetry and spotted her prey. Letting her out of eyesight now could be a huge travesty.

"Hello, Miss DuCate. Happy to see you again. There isn't a problem, is there?"

She'd never liked Oliver's one little beady eye poking through that monocle. "Actually, you have a thief in your employment. And as a concerned shopper, I felt it was my duty to inform you exactly who it is." Vivian's heart pounded as she directed the manager's gaze with an extended finger toward the accused. "I saw her with my own eyes swipe a handful of money."

"You're certain?"

This was turning out even better than she'd planned. Her words breathlessly escaped, "Yes, the woman in the teal-patterned dress."

Chapter Twenty-four

The wind whirled so strong on the rooftop Lily's tears dried quickly against her cheeks. If she could have turned the clock back twenty-four hours, her foot never would have stepped into the Claussen house or into work at Livingston's. But that would have just held off an inevitable chain of events. She'd been made a fool in so many eyes. Her soul ached from yesterday after the spiteful comments Benjamin's mother made, and today her difficulties compounded beyond her imagination.

Oliver wouldn't listen to a word she had to say. Nor did he believe her when she'd shown him her empty dress pockets.

His thin suspicious lips spewed, "You could have hidden the money anywhere."

"But I didn't." Her heart pulsated hard in her veins. "You have to believe me."

Oliver's chin jutted out, exposing his neck. "No, as a matter of fact, I do not."

Her body froze in place as his thunderous voice drew attention to their confrontation behind the counter. Why had he so firmly suspected she'd taken money from the store? He couldn't have seen her do it himself or he would have known she hadn't. Her accuser must have convinced him and the money for certain had to be missing. *This can't be happening.*

He sternly held his ground with a wide stance. "You will be an example so no one else thinks they will get away with this. Now go." His finger pointed her toward the exit. "And don't expect any more pay, you've taken enough money."

Lily's chin lowered, covering the faux double string of pearls surrounding her neck. The townsfolk below had seen the last of her. She'd never show her face again with this tarnished reputation. Mercifully, she was offered a solution thanks to her big brother. Arthur had been the only one home when she'd arrived jobless. Crying women had always made him uncomfortable, so instead he concentrated on the problem until he figured out a way to help. Now all she needed was the strength to follow through.

Why had she let herself fall deeply in love with Benjamin as opposed to taking her advice on going slow? Her bruised heart couldn't take another disappointment, but what alternative did she have? If Benjamin chose her, they'd be poor and she couldn't do that to him. She couldn't ask him to give up everything and throw his future away for her. That would just be too selfish. He was better off without her.

Snap. Startled, she pressed her hand against her chest as her heart raced and turned toward the sound. "What are you doing here? You frightened me."

Benjamin peered out from behind a camera. "I'm capturing this moment for eternity." He smiled. "You're beautiful in the sunlight with those curls framing your face."

"I could have fallen off the rooftop. Besides, I'm certain I look a mess."

"Believe me, you're not. Your appearance was so natural with that teal dress blowing in the breeze." He crouched. "Can I take a few more?"

"I'd rather not." Lily rubbed under her eyes and across her cheeks. "How did you know where to find me?"

His eyebrows rose. "Your brother told me."

She should have figured Arthur had opened his big mouth. After all, he'd told her waiting would make the situation even worse. "Is that all he said?"

"No. He also said you've had an awful day." He stood. "Hopefully, I'll be able to help make it better."

"I see." Lily turned toward the street. "There certainly are a lot of women out today in their expensive hats."

"I didn't notice. You're the only one who draws my attention."

She loved his charm. Or was it his money as some others would believe? The women below who flaunted their wealth and societal position by wearing hats she could never afford had always put her in her place. Just like Constance did yesterday. Her insides were breaking into pieces. Money wasn't everything, but it sure seemed like it when you didn't have any.

He wandered over, placing the camera on the ledge, and took a seat behind her on the rooftop edge. His hands gently touched her shoulders. "What happened today?"

She lowered her head toward the tightness in her chest. "I lost my job."

"Oh, no! I'm sorry." He slipped his arms around her waist.

Lily's back sank slightly against his chest. "Oliver said he had no other option."

"I know him, maybe there's something I can do." He rested his chin on her shoulder. "What reason did he give you?"

"You won't be able to get me out of this mess. I don't even understand how it happened." Her eyes stung with tears. "I didn't do it." She stuttered on each word. "You have to believe me."

"Of course, I will. What didn't you do?"

She sighed. "Steal the money."

"I believe you." He squeezed her tight and let go.

She twisted around toward him. "How can you know that for sure?"

Benjamin's brow furrowed. "I trust you." His fingers touched her jawline and gently inched her closer.

Her lips tingled against the warmth of his breath, tempting her to meet him halfway. He truly cared for her. She gazed into his softened face as time seemed frozen between them.

"Everything will be fine, you'll see." He whispered, "I love you." A smile sparkled through his eyes. Little by little he approached until his silky lips tenderly brushed over hers. He lingered there, peering at her while holding the side of her face in his hand.

She couldn't reciprocate those words. Tears prickled at the corner of her eyes. Why did he have to say them now? She caressed his arm with a trembling hand.

"Please don't cry." He kissed each salty tear that escaped and followed their trail down her cheek.

Chills ignited her body and her prior inhibitions faded away. All she wanted was to be closer to him. Closer to that sweet smell mixed with pipe smoke and earthy musk that could only be him.

She ran her hand across his shoulder and behind his neck. Gently, she pulled him toward her.

His mouth captured hers with an intense purpose.

The beat of her heart pulsated rapidly, flooding her body with warmth. She had to savor this moment one last time. One last passionate kiss. But her belly knotted and her conscience grounded her. She nudged him backward.

"What's the matter?" His brown eyes searched hers. "I can tell something's off in your kiss." He leaned until their foreheads touched. "I'm here, what is it?"

"I'm sorry." Her hands fell limp against her sides. "You said you trusted me."

"I do."

If he stayed with her, she'd for certain knock him to the bottom social rung. She couldn't do that to him. Her heart panged with disappointment. All hope for their happiness was crushed. "I can't destroy your reputation. It wouldn't be fair."

"You won't."

"I will. You have to trust me on this."

"I can handle anyone who has a problem with us being together." He held her face in his hands. "You have to trust me too."

"I don't fit into your world."

"But you do fit with me, you make me whole."

"It's not enough to be whole if you're not in control of your destiny." She backed away. "Don't make this any harder than it has to be." Her hands shuddered as she pulled his from her face. "We can't be together anymore."

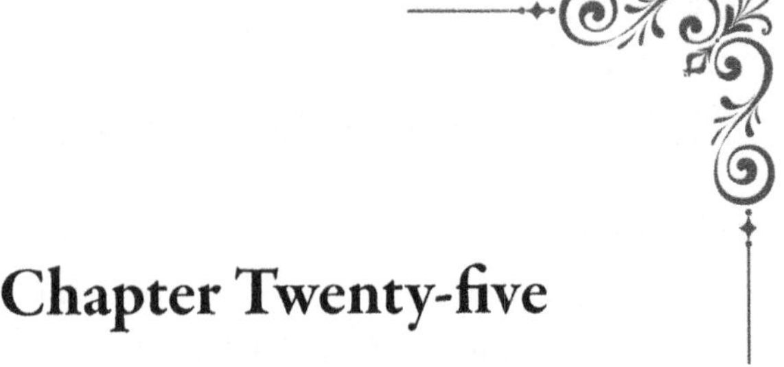

Chapter Twenty-five

Tap, tap, tap.

Benjamin jerked his head toward the doorway as Eva danced through gleefully and swung the door shut. He almost dropped the phone cradled under his chin and the pipe he held in his mouth. "All right, got to go, we'll talk again soon." He hung the receiver and puffed out a cloud of smoke. "What's got you in such a happy mood?"

"So glad you're still here so I can tell you. I'm not surprised though since you've been staying late almost every night."

If she had such good observation skills for how late he'd been staying, why hadn't she used them before interrupting his phone call? He spoke around the pipe hanging from his mouth, "What time is it?"

"Five-thirty, don't you check your watch anymore?"

His thumb slid over the pipe bowl, snuffing out the flame. "I'm not in any hurry these days. Nor in the mood to do much of anything. Except, tonight Louie made me give him my word for playing poker since I missed last week. We'll see, I could work on a few things here."

"Let me guess, you haven't tried to see Lily." She pulled the chair close to the front of his desk and sat on the edge of the seat. "Why not?"

His insides were crushed without Lily. He would do anything for another chance to make things right, but nothing in his life had changed. So what new did he have to offer her? "She made it clear we're through."

"You're going to let her go that easy?" She clutched several ledger books in her arms. "Maybe you ought to go over and tell her how you feel."

"It's not that simple. In case you haven't noticed, my life is an absolute disaster. And it's all my fault. Who could blame Lily for wanting to be free of me?" He set the pipe in the ashtray. "I've missed her terribly for the past two weeks. And I'm trying hard to come up with something to resolve the situation, keep my job here at Ebbe, and not marry Vivian all so I can have a life with the woman I love."

"You love her?

"Yes."

"Then you must go to her."

"I will, just give me a little time. But I'm sure you didn't come in here to talk about Lily. You haven't wiped that satisfied smile from your face since you've been in here. What's going on other than your heavy-handed matchmaking skills?"

Her gleeful grin spread wider. "Operation *Hold Your Man* is about to be executed."

His head jolted back. "What?"

"You know..." She glanced over her shoulder briefly. "...the botched blackmail scheme."

"I'd almost given up." He leaned forward in the chair. "What did you find?"

"I've finally connected the trail." She cupped her hand around her mouth and lowered her voice. "Well, the envelope written to Walter wasn't a check."

His shoulders dropped. "That's not good news."

"I didn't recall sending him out a check anyway. Besides, someone else could have easily put that envelope with my stack."

"I suppose. But if you didn't mail it, how do you know it's not a check?"

"Good point. I can only assume. But after combing through several years of ledgers and bank records I finally found what's been happening. It's rather ingenious really. And I'm going to take all the credit. Oh! That's a good pun."

"Could you save me the humor, please?"

Eva covered the giggle coming from her mouth. "First, I searched for checks written to Walter or his business, but I didn't find any. Of course, at that point, I figured your imagination had just gotten the best of you. But then, out of curiosity, I pulled all of the invoices for Walter's company and you know what I found?"

"He does a lot of business with us."

"You're right. The stacks each month were at least this high." She held her hand a few inches above his desk. "Anyway, that's one reason this has taken me so long. Besides all the invoices, there were numerous credit slips each month. I decided to do the math on each one and found some didn't equal the prices of the material returned. Which of course seemed odd. But what was staring me in the face was even worse."

"This is getting dramatic, but I'll ask. What was it?"

"Every slip that didn't equal contained the initial's *CC*."

"Christian Claussen?" He rubbed his cheek. "Father's always been a whiz at calculations." His brow furrowed.

"Right. Father repeatedly told us how fast he'd gotten through arithmetic problems on the board at school. He said he'd left everyone in his chalk dust."

He chuckled. "Maybe they were off because of the discount we give Walter."

"Nope. I checked that. And then I decided to add up all the credits by month with a separate line for those only done by Father. Glad I did, it helped me in the next discovery." She stood up, laying several ledgers on his desk. "For each month of credit slips done by Father, I found the exact total paid in earnings." She opened the books to the dog-eared pages. "See here, last month's credit to Walter was fifty-two dollars and seventy cents for these three slips. Then over here on this line, Father's income was the same."

"Seems coincidental, but that doesn't provide enough proof to ask Father about it. How many times did you find this? And did Walter use the credit when he paid his invoices?"

"Yes, Walter used each credit every month. I traced Father's wage going to Walter's business for at least one or multiple credit slips equal to one of Father's earnings checks. By the way, those checks of Father's which matched Walter's credits still all remain uncashed to this day. So, this was a way to move money Father owed through the business and to Walter almost undetectable except for this trail in the ledgers. And these are only the books from *this* year." She pushed up her glasses. "I went back for the last four years until I couldn't find a connection."

His eyes widened. "Twenty-nine?"

"Yes, precisely November of twenty-nine was the first time Father's earnings linked back to Walter's credits." She pulled her shoulders back and gave him a proud grin. "Operation *Hold Your Man* completed!"

"Not so fast. Your work may be done, but how am I going to find out why Father's been paying off Walter? How much more does Father owe him? Is Ebbe's future going to remain lucrative? We have a right to know."

"Well, it won't be now." She closed the ledgers. "Father took Mother out for supper."

He slumped back in the chair. "It will be soon. I'm not going to wait much longer. Why don't we grab a bite at Hotel Charles? I'll buy since you worked so hard to help me out."

"Sure. Let me put these things back and I'll be ready."

Ten minutes later, they were standing at the entrance of Hotel Charles. "Good evening, Mister Benjamin." The proprietor stood with his hands behind his back. "Would you like a table or are you here for a card game?"

He'd forgotten all about poker tonight. "We'd like a table, please."

"Right this way."

Benjamin placed his hand on the small of Eva's back and directed her forward. He'd have to stop by and give an excuse to Louie and Emmett. But right now, all he could concentrate on was what Eva had found out. If Father had given fifty-some dollars every month to Walter since the end of twenty-nine that was a whole helluva lot of money. What kind of trouble had Father tangled himself up in? Had this been the agreement Walter had come in and spoken to Father about weeks ago? If so, did Father and Walter's conversation have anything to do with Father's decision about him marrying Vivian?

"Here we are. Will this table do?" The proprietor pulled out a chair for Eva.

"Yes, thank you." Benjamin waited until Eva sat and positioned himself in the chair next to her. "I usually order the special and Thursday's are always fried chicken."

"My mouth was already watering when we came in. Sounds like the tasty choice." Eva unfolded her napkin and placed it on her lap. "Have you come up with an action plan before you approach Father?"

"I thought about it on the way over. Maybe it would be best to tell him what we found. If he knows we figured out his trickery, he can only confess."

"Or just tell you to mind your own business."

"I suppose." He tilted his head, staring at the ceiling for a moment. "What if we went to him together? What he's done has to do with Ebbe and he's always saying it's our legacy. I'm sure you're interested if what he's been doing will affect us in any way."

"When do you want to do it?"

"As soon as possible. Tonight even. I also have to find out if this money has something to do with our parents' insistence on me marrying Vivian." He winced. "Even if I don't persuade Lily we are meant to be together, Vivian could never be my wife."

A familiar tall blonde waitress approached their table and set a glass of water in front of each of them. "Are we ready to order?"

Benjamin smiled. "We'll both have the special."

"It comes with three pieces." The waitress winked. "Your choice between a breast, leg, thigh, drumette, wing, or back."

"I'll take a breast, drumette, and a wing along with a glass of iced tea." Eva set her menu on top of Benjamin's.

"And for you, sir?"

"The same is good for me."

"Are you both all right with coleslaw and potato salad for the sides?"

"Yes, that will be fine." Benjamin handed the waitress the menus.

"Wonderful, I'll be back in two shakes of a lamb's tail." She twirled around and sashayed toward the kitchen.

He chuckled. "She must use that saying an awful lot."

"Why do you say that?"

"She's the same waitress the night I broke the engagement with Vivian. And her mannerisms made Vivian insanely jealous."

"Or just insane." Eva winked. "I'll bet blondie's flirty little eye signal could put Vivian in a straitjacket." She snorted.

"I'm sure you're right." He picked up his water glass. "Cheers to Vivian not being your sister-in-law."

Eva giggled. "I'll drink to that." She tipped her goblet, clinking his. "Cheers to a narrow marriage escape from disaster, big brother."

He laughed. This night could have been even better if their brother was here too. "I don't think I told you earlier, but Robert called. That's who I hung up with when you came into my office before."

"Where is he now?"

"Chicago."

"He said he's doing better there selling door to door than the last place. There are a few outer city neighborhoods with some well-off folks."

"Good to hear. Is he staying out of trouble?"

"As much as can be expected." He grinned. "Robert mentioned there are some nice clubs playing jazz and blues. Said I should come down sometime and he'd show me around."

"You know Mother would say he'd only negatively influence your behavior, getting you involved with that type of crowd."

"I'm sure she would, but Robert had a lead for me. He met a man at one of the clubs and they're building onto a university up near Cumberland. One of those government deals. I told Robert I'd be interested and to get me the specifics for the proposal. If Ebbe could win a bid like this, that would be great. He's going to call me back early next week."

"That's nice."

"Here you go. Two specials." The waitress balanced her tray in one hand and served Eva with the other. "Careful, the food is really hot." She set the second plate in front of Benjamin and placed the tea next to each water glass. "Can I get either of you anything else?"

"No thank you." Benjamin winked.

The waitress grinned. "I'll be back to check again with you shortly."

"This looks good, doesn't it?" Eva inhaled. "And it smells even better. I heard they fry their chicken in pork lard. I'll bet that's why it's so crispy." She took a bite.

Jangle, jingle, clunk.

Benjamin angled his head toward the noise. A man in a white uniform was clearing off a faraway table but had his back turned. He figured by the short stature the man might be Lily's brother. If he got closer, this could be his opportunity to inquire about her. And if Arthur ended up telling his sister, he wouldn't mind. Maybe then she'd know how much he still cared. At this point, he needed any help he could get.

He slid a forkful of coleslaw into his mouth and glanced back in Arthur's direction. So far, Arthur was still in the same spot. The situation he was in had been his fault. His parents had controlled his life for far too long and now he was paying the consequences. He would give up his job at Ebbe for Lily if that's what it took. But first, he had to prove he could take care of her regardless of the outcome. He just needed her to give him the chance.

"How's everything tonight?"

Benjamin glanced over his shoulder. "Oh! Hello." He dabbed the napkin on his lips. "Eva, this is Arthur, Lily's brother. And Arthur, this is my sister, Eva."

"Pleasure to meet you." Eva smiled.

"Likewise. I'll bet when men meet you, they wish they had more than seven nights a week to see you." Arthur returned a whimsical grin and laughed.

Eva barely covered her giggle with her fingers.

"As long as you're here, do you have a few minutes?" Benjamin motioned toward the chair next to him. "You can have a seat across from Eva."

Arthur glanced around the dining room. "Sure, I'm caught up for now. We could chat for a bit." He set down the dishpan and sat. "Honestly, I stopped by because I thought your sister was your new girl. Glad she's not." Arthur waggled his eyebrows at Eva. "You two looked quite cozy sitting next to each other. But I'm glad to find out I was mistaken."

"I don't know what Lily told you, but I feel awful how things ended with us." Benjamin laid his fork down. "How's she doing?"

"She's doing fine under the circumstances." Arthur's eyes squinted. "You know I met your other ex at this exact place about a month ago. Seems like you're not having much luck with the ladies lately."

"You met Vivian?" He lifted a brow.

"Yes. She came back to retrieve a bracelet she'd lost. Coincidently, I was the one who she fell on the night you two broke your engagement."

"I see."

"I don't want to get in the middle of what you two have going on, but I sense things aren't over between you and Vivian."

Benjamin's nostrils tingled and his chicken smelled more like day-old fish. "What makes you say that?"

Arthur leaned forward, putting a white-clad forearm on the table, and lowered his voice. "She's still got her engagement ring on. And any woman who's wearing that sphere after this long hasn't let go. Besides, she thought she could pull one over on me and dig up information on my sister. I outfoxed the little vixen by the way, but Vivian's a feisty one. My sister better not get caught in any crosshairs between the two of you."

What lies had Vivian told Arthur? And why didn't she take off that ring? "You were with her one time and called her a little vixen. Just think if you'd taken her out for seven nights." Benjamin raised his chin. "I commend you, by the way, for watching out for your sister." He glanced at Eva. "I do the same for mine. Nevertheless, Vivian is my past. I'm in love with Lily now and I will find a way for us to be together."

"Don't be so sure." Arthur's head shook. "It's going to be a lot harder to do when she's in Milwaukee."

His pulse rose along with his curiosity. "How long will she be away visiting her sister?"

"She's not visiting. Lily took a job there with Celia."

His core froze. "At Childs?"

"Yes." Arthur stood. "And I think I've said more than my sister would have liked me to, but you seem like a sincere man. And who am I to stand in your way?"

He couldn't believe it! Lily had left without a word. His frozen heart cracked hard against his chest like a sudden temperature change on an ice-covered lake. How would he ever convince her to come back here now? She must have been completely distraught with what happened to her.

Benjamin took several deep breaths as his head cleared. "You're right. I truly have the best intentions for your sister. Whether you intended to let her whereabouts slip or not, I'm grateful for the chance to help her through this." He leaned forward and offered his hand.

Arthur shook Benjamin's.

"I'm going to make the trip this weekend and make certain she is all right." Benjamin straightened his posture against the back of the chair.

"Glad to hear." Arthur grabbed the dishpan. "Nice meeting you, Eva." He grinned and meandered away between the tables.

Eva pulled her glasses down and gazed over the frame at Benjamin. "Do you think there was more to Arthur's conversation with Vivian than he mentioned? Because I do. Why would Vivian discuss her relationship with you to Arthur? I don't like hearing this. Vivian always has a motive for doing something and

I told you before she wouldn't let you go without a fight." She shoved her glasses up. "You'd better keep your guard on high alert."

He rubbed at the back of his neck. Everything had wound his muscles into knots. "I don't know how things could get any worse than they already are. Lily's gone and we're no longer together. This is exactly where Vivian would want us to be." Benjamin picked at a piece of chicken.

"But if you win Lily back, what then? The waitress made Vivian insanely jealous. Those were your words. Not mine. You're wondering whether this scheme with Walter and Father has something to do with Vivian and it just might."

A throat cleared in back of them.

Eva grabbed Benjamin's arm.

Benjamin quickly glanced behind him. "Evening, sir." Father's face lacked his normal approachable appearance. "Evening, Mother." Her stern glare caused a lump to rise in his throat.

"Eva. Benjamin." His father pulled out a chair and his mother sat. "Before either of you say anything, I heard the conversation you were having." He seated himself next to Mother.

Benjamin's eyes shifted slightly in Eva's direction. Was she going to say something, or would he have to?

"What do you think is going on?" Father crossed his arms over his chest.

This was his battle. Benjamin swallowed the lump. "Why was Walter in your office the day you told me I had to marry Vivian?"

"That is a private matter."

"The matter isn't private if it involves me." Benjamin twisted the napkin between his fingers underneath the table. Father's answer had been rudely curt, but he hadn't denied the connection between the events. "Seems to me that you're admitting Walter has something to do with why I need to marry his daughter."

"We've spoken about this, Benjamin Kenneth!" Mother jabbed her index finger several times on the table. "You will not defy me." Her voice rose.

Father leaned forward and placed his hand on Mother's. "Constance, please. We are at a restaurant."

His parents were both hiding something. That was for certain. "We'll open up with what we know, and we'd like the same in return." Benjamin waved his hand toward his sister. "Go ahead and explain."

Eva breathed in slow and even. "We know about the credits every month you've been giving Walter." Her voice faintly quivered. "And we know that your earnings have been going to him to cover those credits since November of nineteen twenty-nine."

Mother gasped.

Father pursed his lips while giving Mother a stare like she'd given away a secret. "What right did you have to investigate me like a common criminal?"

"I'm sorry if I've upset you." Eva's voice softly spoke, "I didn't think I'd find anything, but I did. Telling Benjamin was the right thing to do especially if there are consequences affecting our futures."

Benjamin unclenched his jaw. "Why have you been paying Walter?"

"I legitimately owe him the money. It was a business deal about which I'm not going into details." Father's face reddened. "Walter wants all of his money now unless you marry Vivian."

A burning flame released a fury in his gut. "Tell him no." Benjamin's fist struck the table. "Why can't you just keep paying him as you have been?"

"The promissory note allows him to call in the debt whenever he wants. If he does..." Father squeezed Mother's hand. "...we will have to either give up the house or my half of the business."

"Please, Benjamin. Go to Vivian. Tell her you made a mistake." Mother's face was pained under her watery gaze. "It's for your own good."

The muscles in his neck tightened. "For my own good?" Benjamin unbuttoned the top button and yanked his tie loose. "Forcing me into an untenable situation is what's good for me? Making me choose between my entire family's welfare or my happiness is what's good for me? When will this controlling behavior of my life end? All of this is not for my own good. I didn't make the debt. Why on earth should I be responsible to fix this?" He shoved himself away from the table. "Come on Eva, I need to leave before I say something I'll regret."

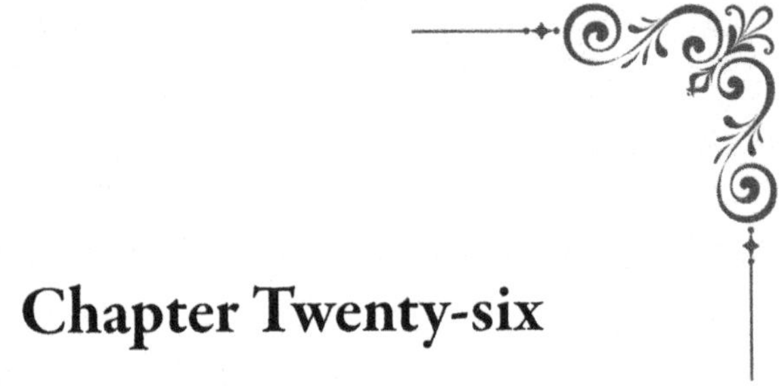

Chapter Twenty-six

The birds chirped eagerly this morning with as much enthusiasm as Benjamin had. Today, he'd arrive in Milwaukee and see Lily for the first time in over two weeks. He missed her and couldn't wait, but he also had the difficult task of explaining the events surrounding his parents' disapproval of her. However, telling her how he'd handled the situation might prove he'd taken charge of his life.

Honking his horn, he coasted into the filling station. An attendant dressed in blue overalls ran over and slopped a soapy rag across the windshield. Benjamin unrolled the window and hollered, "Fill 'er up and check under the hood."

Everything needed to be in tiptop shape before he left town. The entire trip would easily be four hundred miles. This was the first Saturday in months he hadn't worked at Ebbe for at least part of the day. Father hadn't given him any hassle asking for the day off, which didn't come as a surprise. For once, he had the upper hand over Father and planned on using it to his advantage. Even his mother had mellowed last night since the upheaval at Hotel Charles, which he figured was her way of hoping he'd decide to do what she wanted. One last-ditch effort on her part, he figured.

A flashy red car streaked around the other side of the pumps, stopping abruptly. Its horn had a long-drawn honk like a flock of geese flying overhead. The attendant waved from Benjamin's side of the car. He wiped the dipstick and stuck it back under the hood. The obnoxious horn continued in succession, but this time the attendant's arms moved around in a perturbed manner. The hood closed. Again, the horn sounded, and the attendant stomped away toward the other car.

Benjamin had his passenger window partially down, however, the conversation was barely audible. He leaned closer to the other side but still couldn't hear anything beyond a few mumbles nor could he be certain of the car model with the pumps blocking his view. What had been so urgent the person couldn't have waited until his service was done? He grabbed the roadmap off his seat and unfolded it. The best route was Fifty-one until Madison and then east on Eighteen into Milwaukee. He'd gotten a late start this morning after his alarm didn't go off. Now, it was almost eight and the drive would be around four hours.

"Mister."

He glanced over at the window obstructed by a pair of blue overalls.

The attendant leaned in— "She's looking for you." –and gestured behind him.

"Me? Who is she?"

"I'm an attendant, not a host at a soiree. But she's a doll, so if I were you, I'd get on over there before she changes her mind."

Certainly, not the doll he wanted to see since Lily was hundreds of miles away. Benjamin folded the map, tossing it onto the seat. *She* had best be quick. The longer he spent here, the less time he'd have with Lily. He got out, strolled behind his car and around the pumps. A luxurious red Duesenberg glistened before him with the back door open exposing a floral brocade interior. He'd never seen this car around the city before, but whoever sat inside certainly had good taste. As he approached, the large back compartment blocked the view of the occupants until he reached the swung-open door and stuck his head inside. "Vivian." He jerked back against the door. "I should have known."

"You look surprised."

A roiling heat thrashed in his gut. "The impatient horn blaring should have given you away. Why do you want to see me?"

Vivian leaned forward. "I always like seeing you."

Benjamin strained not to roll his eyes, but they had a mind of their own. "Where are you going this morning being chauffeured around?" Hoping he sounded more civil than he felt, he closed the door and rested his arm on the open window. Somehow having that door between them gave him relief.

"Funny thing is, I wondered the same thing about you. Louie mentioned you were out of town when I stopped by your office. As luck would have it, you weren't but a block away." Vivian touched her lip with her index finger. "Where are you going?" She batted her lashes. "Hmm?"

What right did she have to ask him such a question? His jaw tightened, but he'd have to be cautious until he could figure a way out of this debt fiasco. No sense in riling her without a plan. "Well, where I'm going won't be in as grand of a style as you riding around in this Duesenberg." He glanced down the side of the car. "Heard the straight eight-cylinder motor can do over a hundred. When did your Father get this beauty?"

Vivian twirled a red strand of hair around her finger. "He hasn't yet, but he's considering." Her tone softened. "And I've considered everything we've gone through." She gazed at him from underneath thick mascaraed lashes. "I want you to know I forgive you. And I know now you didn't want me to get so upset."

"Thank you, I appreciate your understanding."

"I still care for you...for us."

His hair stiffened on the nape of his neck and he turned away, staring at the ground. Where was this conversation going? Not where he wanted it to, that's for certain.

"We can still have a good life together." She reached for him, brushing across his forearm. "You're not seeing anyone anymore and I'm certain we can work out whatever we need to now."

Benjamin backed away while his mouth fell open. Yet he couldn't articulate one word or thought spinning through his mind. So he clamped his jaw shut hard.

Vivian pasted on her finest smile. "No need to worry. I didn't expect an answer right away. Thinking about all we've shared and what you potentially have to lose without me might take you a while. We'll talk again in a few days. I'm running behind for an appointment." She slid open the glass partition. "Driver, we can go now."

He took a few steps back away from the car. *Is she serious?*

Vivian's hand waved out the window as the car sped off.

What just happened? He gaped at the rear of that Duesenberg until it was out of sight. *Vivian's delusional. That's what happened.*

The attendant poked him. "Mister, that will be two fifty-five."

Benjamin handed the man a couple of dollars and sixty cents. "Keep the change." He wandered back to the car and got in. Vivian's sense of timing was uncanny. Or was it? She'd known he wasn't with Lily any longer. And she certainly had something to do with Walter all of a sudden wanting all his money now. Probably why Vivian insinuated he had a lot to lose without her. Didn't Vivian realize there were other choices he could make than surrendering to a shakedown? He turned the key in the ignition, shifted into gear, and cranked the volume up on the radio.

LILY SHUT THE DOOR to Room 820 at the Miller Hotel. A checkerboard pattern on the tiled floor led her like a hopscotch game ten doors down to Celia's door. They both had a shift in the hotel restaurant until one o'clock and had planned for a relaxing day at the beach afterward. She fisted her hand, and just as she was about to knock, the door swung open.

"You're right on time." Celia came through the doorway.

Lily yawned. "I'm surprised since I had another restless night."

"I've never seen you like this. You'd think as soon as your head hit the pillow, you'd doze off from working most every day these last two weeks." Celia pulled the door shut. "Are you questioning the decision of leaving Benjamin?" She turned around, parading backward.

Lily's chest tightened as an image of him flashed in her mind. "Don't you see? I did the only thing I could. His mother controls his life and even his ex tried to do the same. Forcing him to choose between me and his future position at Ebbe isn't right."

"Aren't you doing the same thing they've done?"

"That's not true. The situations are completely different. My past comes with too many burdens which will only make matters worse for him. Even if there might be a way to undo my tarnished reputation, our faiths will keep us divided. I've heard it from our mother and his."

"If you say so." Celia spun around and pressed the down button for the elevator. "However, from what you told me, you didn't even give him a chance. Maybe deciding to end your relationship on the same day you lost your job might not have been the wisest option."

Lily sighed. "Well, it's too late now. I'm here."

"I know you're hurting from the humiliation with Oliver and Mrs. Claussen. But the truth always has a way of coming out. You're not a thief and regardless of what Benjamin's mother says, you are good enough for her son. If Benjamin is who you want to spend your life with, then who cares what anyone else says?"

"I agree with you to some extent." Lily glanced above the elevator door at the half-moon brass dial. "Benjamin needs to get his issues with the family straightened out and find a way to support himself if he leaves Ebbe. And I have my problems to work through too." The hand inched its way from seven to eight. "His mother wouldn't have been able to make me feel inadequate otherwise. I'm trying my best right now, but I'll need time."

"All right, but don't take too long." Celia rubbed her shoulder. "Oma already thinks I'm too old. You don't want to end up like your old spinster sister." She grinned.

"True." Lily giggled.

The elevator car arrived, and a uniformed attendant slid open the door. "What floor, ladies?"

"Ground." Lily followed Celia into the wood-lined box.

The man tipped his round hat, slid the door back, and pulled the accordion gate closed. "Otis going down."

Lily smirked. Otis used that line every time they rode. Not only was it his name, but the elevator's brand name too. Riding inside the small, enclosed place with the clanking of the cables below could give anyone a cause for concern. But she rather liked the fluttery sensation in her abdomen.

Benjamin had given her the same delicate wisps whenever they were together. She did miss him terribly. So many things reminded her of him. The nights she couldn't sleep were happy what-if scenarios instead of how their relationship ended weeks ago. She could have handled the situation differently but turning back the clock was impossible. Reaching out to him now while his parents insisted on him marrying Vivian would be an act of desperation.

She would wait. Wait for word from her family about the rumors of her thievery subsiding. Wait for word about Benjamin's marriage to Vivian. After all, how would he be able to refuse? Wait for a new ending like in her scenarios. Wait for a miracle.

Otis opened both doors and they exited.

Celia grabbed hold of Lily's hand, swinging their arms back and forth. "The water's going to feel great after our shift. I can hardly wait."

They entered the grand main lobby emphasized with tall pillars and large vases holding artificial flowers. The door into Childs Restaurant was near the main entrance opposite the reception desk.

"Miss Vanderhoof. Miss Lily Vanderhoof."

Lily glanced toward the desk.

The clerk waved his arm in the air.

"Come with me." Lily tugged Celia's arm. "Wonder what he wants?" They took less than twenty steps to reach the corner curved desk. Along the sidewall, square slots were used for mail. That was where the clerk reached in and grabbed a yellowish envelope, holding it out towards her.

"A telegram for you, Miss."

Lily locked eyes with Celia for a moment. The message must be urgent to have been sent by telegraph. Something bad must have happened with her family. Her unsteady hands grasped the envelope. She slid the flap open, tugging out the paper, and unfolding it.

> July 21, 1933, 9:20 PM – Western Union Telegram
> MF 1 9 XC=J1=Hub City WIS 11 915 P
> Miss Lily Vanderhoof =
> Miller Hotel 723 N 3rd St Milwaukee WIS=
> Benjamin arriving Saturday=
> Arthur.

Celia leaned over. "Who's it from?"

"Arthur." Lily dropped her hand to her side. "Benjamin's coming today."

Celia rubbed her hand across Lily's back. "Breathe, you'll be fine. What else did he say?"

"Nothing." Lily swiftly gazed at the front doors. "But it has to be bad." Her eyes searched all the faces in the lobby. "If he's coming here to disclose his marriage to Vivian, I don't want to hear it."

"That possessive woman wouldn't let him come here. Perhaps it's good news."

"I hope you're right." Her stomach fluttered softly. This could be the miracle she'd waited for.

BENJAMIN HADN'T TAKEN into account the times he had to stop for gas, but even with the added minutes, it was only twelve-thirty. He drove around the block bursting with buildings four times taller than those at home. The streets were busy with the commotion of people and cars. Childs Restaurant sprawled out in the middle of the block just ahead. He pulled into a space near a small park.

The day was bright and sunny, so he left the windows open and exited into the street. His heart unevenly palpitated the closer he came to the entrance. Even though he'd rehearsed what he would say, his unsettled nerves weren't under his control.

The doorman greeted him with a smile while he walked through the open door and into the lobby. He followed a clear pathway toward the reception desk. A young man in his early twenties stood behind the desk.

Benjamin cleared his dry throat. "Morning. I'm trying to locate a lady by the name of Lily Vanderhoof. Do you know if she's staying here at the hotel?"

"Aah, yes! The pretty one with the blue eyes."

"Sounds like you know her."

The clerk leaned over the desk and lowered his voice. "Are you the one coming to see her from the telegram?"

Benjamin's eyebrows rose. Who would have sent her a telegram? It had to be Arthur. "Yes, that would be me. Do you know where I can find her?"

The young man pointed to the other side of the room. "She works at Childs. I saw her several hours ago head in that direction."

"Thank you." Benjamin's abdomen had an empty queasiness as he neared the restaurant. What if Lily didn't want to see him? She'd left, despite him declaring he loved her. But this time he would insist she hear him, even if that meant begging on bended knee. He stopped at the glass double-door. Inside, everything appeared clean and tidy against all the white on the floor, tables, and chairs. Even the waitresses dressed in white, but none of them were Lily.

He pulled on the handle and went through the doorway. More than half of the tables were filled, however one nearby in the corner was empty. He'd have a good view of the entire room from this spot. He slid the chair across the tiled floor and sat.

The food scent lingering in the air certainly had a nice aroma, but he'd best fill the empty pit in his stomach with some soothing tea. He placed his fedora on the chair next to him and opened the menu. Near the bottom of the page, the tea options were listed.

He gazed up from the menu. His heart quickened against his chest. The waitress coming toward him was Lily. She locked eyes with him and stopped momentarily in mid-stride. Her captivating face sent an icy sensation over his skin, prickling every fine hair heavenward. Her trim necktie knotted in a bow resembled a perfect present. She was beautiful. He swallowed the lump rising from his chest as she arrived in front of him. "Morning, Lily. Lovely to see you. I presume Arthur told you I'd be coming today."

She had an uncertain smile building as his presence became surprisingly real. "He did and I'm afraid he may have overstepped his brotherly duties. But it's nice to see you too."

"I didn't mean to cause any issues between you two. I will take all the blame."

"That's admirable of you."

His posture relaxed a bit. "I hope you go easy on Arthur for telling me you were here." Her widened eyes had softened in exchange for a widening smile. "I've missed you considerably."

She bit lightly at the bottom of her lip. "I've missed you as well."

"When does your shift end?"

"One."

"I've thought a great deal about what you said on the rooftop." Benjamin closed his eyes and sighed. "I have some news I'd like to discuss. Could we possibly go somewhere and talk?"

The smile disappeared, and her posture slumped. She tapped a pencil against her pad of paper. "I'll let you know after my shift. Would you care for anything while you wait?"

"Hot green tea would be nice."

"Comin' right up." She walked away.

A long counter with about twenty stools had been situated near the kitchen. Behind the counter, a blonde waitress was keeping a watch on Lily as she came back to the area with the brewing machines. Although her hair was lighter than Lily's, she had some similar features. And the way she huddled around Lily while getting his tea, he could only assume the woman was her sister.

Hopefully, the tea would settle his stomach along with his nerves. He still had to convince Lily to give him another chance.

Certainly, that would be a bigger hurdle than agreeing to speak with him or so he'd imagined. Why hadn't Lily responded right away to his question? Had he already botched his chance? And why was Lily's sister coming toward him?

"Here you are, one cup of tea. We haven't met but I'm Lily's older sister Celia."

"Pleasure to meet you."

Celia lowered her head, studying him. "And as the older sister, I need to watch out for her." She crossed her arms against her chest. "What are you doing here? Because if you've come to cause her more heartache it would be best if you just finish your tea and be on your way."

He shook his head. "No, I can promise you that's not my intention at all."

"Does anything you have to say involve Vivian?"

"Yes."

"Then I'm certain my sister doesn't want to hear it." Her lips pressed into a flat line. "I'm sure you somehow feel obligated letting her know of your marriage, but—"

"Marriage? Whoa!" Benjamin raised open palms. "I'm not marrying Vivian. Is that what Lily thinks? Trust me, that's not why I'm here. Please make Lily understand." He placed his palms together in a prayerful position. "I'm here because I love her and only her. Will you help me?"

Celia's green eyes twitched back and forth. "This must be the same approach you worked on my brother, but I'm tougher than he is. What are your intentions if she agrees to hear you out?"

"I want to work on the issues we have keeping us apart. And I want to have a future with her." His voice choked. "Please, Celia. I just need a chance."

"All right. I'll ask her to meet with you, however, the choice is still hers." Celia strode away.

"Thank you." His eyelids closed. Lily would have to agree or he'd be publicly pleading on his knees. He pulled out his pocket watch and flipped the lid. Only fifteen minutes left until one. He ran his thumb over the inscription—*Time spent wisely is time well spent*. On the way here, he had memorized three key items he needed to clarify, and now would be a good time to go through them again during these final minutes. He took a sip of tea, leaned over the table, and clasped his hands under his chin.

EXACTLY AT ONE, LILY approached the table. The knot in her stomach cinched tighter. "I'd rather not have the discussion here."

"There's a park across the street." He swallowed the last of his tea, laying a dollar on the table, and tossed on his fedora.

"That seems more private."

He stood, offered his arm and she slid her hand around into the crook of his elbow. They walked through the restaurant door, the lobby, and out the entrance into the sunshine. "I'm so glad you decided to talk to me. I wasn't certain you would."

"You did come a long way." The sensation of his touch warmed her. "Celia said it wouldn't be right if I didn't hear what you had to say. Although, I'm hoping the news isn't terrible." She glanced up at him, waiting for any hint of impending doom as her mind galloped from one scenario to another.

Benjamin smiled. "I wouldn't say terrible per se, but complicated." He placed his hand on hers which rested on his arm as they crossed the street. "An in-person explanation will be so much easier than sending you a letter. Besides, I'm sure you will have some questions." He motioned to a bench and they sat. "First, I want to put your mind at ease. I still have no intention of marrying Vivian. My mother had no right to put you in the position she did. And I know in the past I've let her dictate my life. But I can assure you that is no longer the case."

Lily briefly closed her eyes and drew a deep breath. Some of the tension unknotted in her stomach. "I'm sure that wasn't an easy decision, but I'm happy for you." She bit back a smile. "When did you come to this conclusion? And how has everything gone with your parents since?"

"I've known for months I shouldn't have allowed my parents or Vivian to control my life. Unfortunately, I should have put a stop to it back then. You wouldn't have ended up caught in the midst of it all. I'm truly sorry you had to endure the fallout. And losing you has been the worst." His shoulders drooped. "However, there are extenuating circumstances why my parents wanted me to marry Vivian, which I've recently become aware of, and this is where it gets complex."

Lily sensed the emotional strain in his words as her intuition danced the hairs upward across her skin. "Oh?"

"Ebbe does quite a bit of business with Vivian's father, Walter. So, besides my mother's friendship with Vivian's mother, my father has ties with hers not only through business but socially. Walter's business buys goods which equate to roughly fifteen percent of our earnings. If we lose his account, there aren't too many nearby to make up for the loss."

"Breaking off your engagement with Vivian certainly was risky on your part. I hadn't realized how she'd been interrelated with the business before. That's probably why you were hesitant." Her head tilted to the side as she studied his face.

"Absolutely. And my fears have come true more than I could have imagined." He shifted on the bench, slanting himself toward her. "What I'm going to tell you explains why my parents reacted the way they did but it is not an excuse for how they behaved. Nor do I condone what they did. However, I do sympathize with their predicament."

The situation appeared difficult for him, and whatever it was, he'd been cautious in his approach. "Of course, they are your parents." She patted his hand, hoping the touch would give him encouragement. "Do go on."

Benjamin stood, pacing back and forth in front of her. "Walter holds a promissory note with my father. The amount remaining is enough to jeopardize either the business or their house. And there's no way for Father to get a loan with the banking crisis." He heavily sighed. "As horrendous as this sounds, Walter stated he was calling in the note, which I'm certain he knew my father couldn't pay." He perched on the edge of the bench.

Lily raised an eyebrow. "That doesn't seem right for either their personal or business relationships. What would make Walter do such a thing?" She had a sneaking suspicion the personal relationship trumped the business one.

Benjamin rose, pacing again with his hands clenched together. "To get Vivian exactly what she wants...me!"

Her hand covered her mouth for a mere moment and slowly dropped back into her lap. An angered heat flickered within. "What kind of morals does her family have? No wonder your mother reacted the way she did to me. What's going to happen now? You said you wouldn't marry her." She tapped the bench. "Please come here and sit."

He sank beside her, placed his elbows on his knees and covered his face with his hands.

Lily rubbed his shoulder. "I can tell how much pressure you must be under. And I can understand how your parents were manipulated. But what gives them the right to do the same thing to you?" She huffed. "I'm glad you didn't just give in."

He glanced at her. "But I must help since what happened stems from my involvement with Vivian. By some means Walter's demand needs satisfaction. I just haven't found a reasonable solution, yet." He stroked the side of his face. "As far as I understand, Father doesn't have much time to come up with the money. Maybe another week or two at best. The way I look at it, if the business is protected somehow, we will all continue having an income. If not, no one in my family will have a position with the company anymore." He lifted his chin. "I have to try."

Her heart ached. "I know how hard you've worked to earn a place at Ebbe. This is a sad circumstance for your entire family." She reached out and took his hand in hers. "Is there anything I can do?"

"Yes, there is. However this turns out, I want to be with you in the end. You are my whole world and I can't live without you. I love you!" He picked up her hand, placing a kiss behind her knuckles. "All I ask is for you to give me another chance. I will prove to you that you do fit into my world. And I can fit into yours."

Lily wanted him to come back to her. But what he'd told her hadn't solved anything. It was worse than before. Her watery eyes blinked. "Aren't you worried about your reputation? Or finding a new job if you're not at Ebbe? What about my thievery and more importantly my religion?"

"I know who you are and you're not a thief. But I understand the importance of clearing your name and I promise we'll get to the bottom of it. If I don't have a job at Ebbe, I will find one somewhere." He squeezed her hand. "As far as our differing religions, we will need further clarification for our future."

"You seem so sure of being able to work everything out. I'm not." Lily slid her crucifix necklace slowly along the chain. "How your mother treated me brought back a lot of bad memories. Will she ever accept me?" A tear flowed down her cheek.

"My mother's tough, but she does want the best for me. And that's you. She will come around." He wiped the drops away from her eyes. "Can you trust me on this?"

"I truly want to believe we can solve all these issues. But I just don't know how." She tucked her chin into her neck.

"Do you love me?" He raised her head.

"Yes, Benjamin. I do love you." She peered through tear-soaked lashes. "But I don't know if I'm strong enough to get past all the shame. I can't go back home until these matters are resolved."

"I will be there for you and do what I can if you let me. We can accomplish so much more together than apart. I need your support to get through this too." His fingertips skimmed along her jawline. "Please, Lily. Say you will."

Her stomach ignited with millions of flittering wings. She leaned closer and softly touched his lips with her fingertips. "With you, Benjamin. I will try."

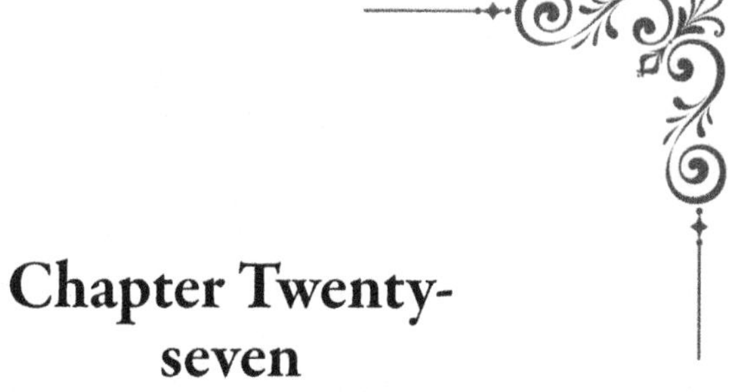

Chapter Twenty-seven

Benjamin counted the twelve steps it took to reach the doors of the post office again. Lily had promised to write after he'd left Saturday. But Monday came and went without a letter. If he didn't get one this afternoon, he feared she could have possibly changed her mind. He opened the door, went inside, and only a few people were waiting.

Luckily, Robert had called late yesterday with the details for the Cumberland bid. His mind stayed occupied for the rest of the afternoon tackling the plans and specifications. If Ebbe would be saved from the DuCate's clutches, this would be their best chance. The scale of the project was the largest he'd ever worked on and the deadline was set for Friday by five o'clock. He would for sure have some long days and nights ahead.

He filed in line behind a young woman with a boy around four or five. It didn't take the youngster long to become antsy. The child would peek out on one side of his mother, make a face, and disappear behind her skirt. After a second, the boy would reappear on the opposite side with another goofy facial expression. He hoped one day he'd have a son who'd be just as silly.

The next few windows opened and he waved as the little boy again peeked around his mother. The clerk was the same man from yesterday. "I'm here again." Benjamin smiled. "Did any mail come in for me today?"

"Yes, as a matter of fact, I saw one with your name on it this morning. One second, let me get it for you."

Once outside, Benjamin ran down the steps and across the street all in under a minute. He rested his shoulder against a tree. Carefully, he ran his finger under the envelope flap before pulling out the contents. He flipped up the top third of the letter to see she'd written two days ago. Unfolding the letter the rest of the way, he read the first paragraph. And grinned.

July 23, 1933 – Sunday

Dearest Benjamin,

When I awoke this morning, I had to pinch myself to make sure I wasn't dreaming. I'm still having a hard time believing you'd come all the way here for me, but I'm so very happy you did. You were able to ease my worries even though everyone and everything is against us. You've shown me you are standing up for what you believe in. I'm letting you know I'm never going to give up this time. As long as you are by my side, I'll be right next to you.

I hope your trip back was good. My week should go by fast as I have a shift every day, except Saturday when I finally have an entire day off. We had such a good time at the beach. Maybe the next time Emmett and Anna could come along. I'd enjoy the company. I've prayed for your family since you left, and I always add a special intention in sympathy for their plight. You are a good man for helping find a solution and I hope they'll appreciate your efforts no matter the outcome.

I'm going to close now and check at the front desk if they have a stamp so I can put this in the mail. Let me know when you receive it. I'm thinking you should have it by Tuesday or Wednesday at the latest. Hoping you write soon, looking forward to reading your letter.

Missing and loving you,

Lily

His body relaxed against the tree. Lily had written. The best part was she'd promised she would never give up. He read her words again and gently put it back into the envelope. *I miss you too.* Stuffing the letter into his pocket, he skipped down the sidewalk toward Ebbe.

Benjamin slipped into the side door and removed his hat. Dampness had formed under his fedora from the humid jaunt.

"You're back from lunch a little late." Louie popped out from around the feed sacks.

"I walked down to the post office and back." He pivoted on his heel in the hallway toward his cousin. "The car got a flat and I dropped it off at the station." He grabbed a hanky from his breast pocket, wiping it across his forehead. "Has my father made it in yet?"

"No. But if I see him, I'll send him your way." Louie tossed a sack on his shoulder. "Can't tell if that sweat of yours is from nervousness or this damn heat. Are you gonna tell me if Lily wrote to you or not?"

He tapped his pocket and smiled. "She sure did."

Louie stepped up toe to toe with Benjamin. "Great, now get out of my way. This bag is heavy."

Stepping aside, he let Louie pass into the hall. "I'll be in my office." He slipped through the doorway and swung it shut behind him. Piles of paper were strewn about on his desk mostly for the Cumberland bid. He slid a stack over, opened a drawer, and rummaged around for a few clean sheets of paper. If he could get his letter out and send it special within the next several hours, Lily could have his correspondence tomorrow. He sat, rolled his chair closer to the desk, and copied the calendar date onto the paper.

> July 25, 1933 – Tue at the office
> Darling,

He glanced up at the movement of his door opening and shook his head. Certainly, he shouldn't be surprised. She'd forewarned him the last time he saw her. "Vivian." He turned over the letter and stood up. "What can I do for you? I'm in the middle of an important project."

"Are you going to help me with the chair?" She took a few steps in. "This won't take long."

Benjamin rubbed across his rigid jaw. "Of course." He walked around and pulled the chair away from the front of his desk. "Please have a seat." Turning around he gathered notes, calculations, and other confidential information. He flipped them upside down on the corner of his desk, stiffly sitting in his chair. "I can spare a few minutes."

"Obviously, you're working on something secretive." Vivian grinned mischievously while scooting closer to the desk. "Anybody I know?" She bent forward and moved a few papers, lifting a piece for a peek.

Benjamin smacked the paper. "I doubt it. But I'm sure you didn't stop by to check on my abilities. If it's about the conversation you had with me the last time, I haven't had a spare minute lately." He didn't assume she'd let him off so painlessly, but what did it hurt to try? "Next week will hopefully be better."

Vivian glared with pursing lips. “Do you have any clue what trouble I’ve gone through since you ended our engagement? Don’t think for one second you’ll dismiss me so effortlessly.” She tugged at her gloved fingertips and pulled the covering from her hands. “Instead, let’s talk about the money your father owes mine.” She slapped her pristine white gloves on his desk. “If you show some effort, maybe my father will be a bit more tolerant of Christian’s financial position.”

His pulse sped at her smugness. Just as he suspected, she’d been involved with exercising the rights of the note. “My father’s debt has nothing to do with us and I resent what you’ve done. But I can say, I’m not at all astonished by your maneuver.” He couldn’t hold back providing an equally diabolical ploy. “Although, maybe I’ve been waiting for a reason to leave Ebbe and now might be my chance. Besides, if my father signs over his half of the company I’m out of a job.”

“You wouldn’t!” Her reddish-orange lips curled.

He hoped the warning penetrated her stubborn mind. Everything about her had always been the importance of what money could get for her. If he didn’t have any, he figured her shallowness would inadvertently be revealed. “Without my status, I’m not as attractive, am I?”

Her fingers fisted her gloves. “That’s far from the truth and you know it. Such a ridiculous comment.” She spoke in a tart, snappy tone. “Who would want to live poor? Aside from Lily who’s penniless and has no job. What kind of influence did she have on you anyway?”

His head drew back. “What did you say?” Had he heard her correctly?

“Well, she must have had some kind of effect—”

"Not that, you said she has no job. What do you mean?"

Vivian placed her hand over her mouth for a moment. "She got caught taking money at Livingston's. The manager fired her and rightly so. Haven't you heard?"

"How did you?"

Her lips tensed and her eyes glanced upward for a split second. "Sallie's Beauty Parlor."

The last time she'd worn that same expression, she'd lied to him. What was she trying to hide? Lily lost her job, that had been the truth. Which left who Vivian had heard the story from. But why make that up? Pressing her any further wouldn't glean a truthful confession. Besides, the sense something just wasn't right washed over him the instant she'd hesitated. He needed her to leave before he antagonized her further. After this weekend he'd have a better idea if this bid would be viable to save the company and get her out of his life once and for all. "I should get back to work. How about I send for you next week and we continue the conversation then?"

Vivian curled her fingers around her gloves, shaking them in the air. "I'm going to say what I came here for. Then you can mull it over until next week. But know I will require a firm decision from you one way or the other." She raised her chin high, exposing her neck. "I've been patient; the Lord knows. In so many ways I've reminded you of your commitment. You told me we were going to be together forever. A deep connection like that doesn't just disappear. There's been nothing that has gotten your attention, up till now. You've forced me to corner you like this." She edged closer. "You can save Ebbe. I know you want to. Marry me and Father will forgive the debt." Her tinted lips twisted cleverly.

Benjamin's nostrils flared while he drew the heaviness of the air into his lungs. This strategic game had to end. He wouldn't be her pawn and she certainly wouldn't be his queen. The sacrifice would be too much. "Such a tempting offer, but—"

Vivian pressed her finger to his lips. "Shh! Don't be too hasty. You've got your family and a business to think about." She slipped her finger down until it fell off his chin. "I'll await your call by Tuesday."

The sound of her heels clicking against the wooden floor mirrored a ticking time bomb for his future. She'd given him exactly one week. Everything hinged on this Cumberland bid and beating out some of the finest supply companies in the industry. For sure there would be a narrow margin between having a low bid and still making enough. But what was the dollar figure to pay off the debt? And when would his father be back, so he could find out? If there wasn't sufficient profit, his time spent would be useless.

Benjamin reclined into the chair, closing his eyes. His shoulders were heavily burdened, but he would use any amount of ingenuity he could muster. He wanted Lily to have a comfortable life. She deserved as much. He sat up, turned over the letter, and continued writing.

> I'm sure if you knew how many trips I've made to the post office, you would have written sooner. It seems more like a week than two days. I'm not going to make you wait too long so if I send this special, you should get this tomorrow.

Tap, tap.

Benjamin glanced up and motioned at his father. "Please come in and shut the door." He flipped the paper over, replaced the cap on the pen, and leaned forward.

"Louie said you were looking for me." Father walked over toward the desk.

"I wanted to let you in on some possibly good news."

Father pulled out the chair and sat squarely in front of him. "After my meeting at the bank this morning, I could use some. I realized a loan would be unlikely, but I had to try."

"Not even some of it?"

"What good would that do?"

Benjamin lifted his shoulder in a half shrug. "What if we came up with the balance somewhere else?" He grabbed the papers from his desk corner. "Robert gave me a lead on a huge project near Cumberland for a university building. I've been doing some preliminary calculating since yesterday. I think we could get this one, but the bid is due in three days."

"Let me take a look."

Benjamin passed Father his notes on the bid request. "It's going to take a great deal of work, but I'm willing to stay late every night to meet the deadline. If you're at all questioning my commitment, this should prove I'm trying. Please understand, I don't want to lose Ebbe, but I can't let you or Mother control my choices any longer." His agitated stomach gave him a sudden sense of nausea. But he had to present his option. He lifted his chin, attempting to appear more confident. "I have a proposal for you."

Father continued glancing through the papers. "So, what is it you want?"

"The size of this project might be enough to cover the debt. Can you tell me how much Walter's asking for?"

Father placed the notes onto the desk. "You do realize winning a bid like this is a long shot." He grabbed a pen, scribbled on a piece of paper, and folded it in half. "This is just between us." He held up the paper between two fingers.

"Of course." Benjamin reached out, slipping the figure from his father's grasp. He unfolded it. His eyelids blinked rapidly, and he took another glance. "That's a lot of money." He rubbed his hand over his eyes. "But this bid is our best chance at paying it off and getting out from under the reign of the DuCates."

"If anyone can make this happen, I'd venture it would be you. I should have recognized your abilities sooner. You are business-savvy and that always leads to a good outcome." Father quirked an eyebrow and smiled. "I'm proud of what you're trying to do. This time I'll assist you instead of directing you."

"Thank you, Father." Benjamin held a hand over his racing heart. "There is one more imperative piece to this whole bid." His voice faintly quivered and he cleared his throat. "No matter the outcome, you and Mother will accept Lily in my life without question and treat her with the respect she deserves." His chest tightened against his lungs. He could barely breathe.

Father's lips pressed into a thin line. "Son, if you want Lily in your life your mother and I will not stop you. Maybe in time, we'll be able to welcome her into the family. That is all I can promise. I'm certain you must know society won't conform so easily or quickly either." Father stood and firmly shook his hand. "Lily must be one special lady." He walked through the doorway.

"She certainly is." Benjamin pressed a hand to his throat where his bottled breath had at last released. He turned over the letter and removed the cap off the pen. He had the best news to tell her.

> If you didn't realize how much I loved you before, I sure hope you do now. It made me happy to hear you're not going to give up on us. I don't think I could go through that again. I want you to know, Darling, that I have never missed you so much and I wake up in my sleep with a lump in my throat thinking about you.
>
> I'll be busy this whole week working on a large bid that's due Friday for a company in Chicago. If we get it, we should have enough to pay Walter. Since we haven't done business with them before, I want to deliver our offer in person. I can stop by you for a visit. I'll see if Emmett and Anna can come along too. They can keep you company Friday until I get back. Then we can all spend the day together Saturday when you have off.
>
> The best news is all my efforts aren't going unnoticed by my father. He agreed not to stand in the way of us being together. I believe more than ever everything will turn out positively. I'm sure your praying didn't hurt. Keep it up, we'll need all the help we can get.
>
> I also wanted to tell you the trip back was very lonesome. I hope though soon, you'll be riding back with me and then it sure won't be lonesome.
>
> All my love,
>
> Benjamin
>
> P.S. Vivian stopped in to see me and I have some suspicions I'll need to look into. She knew about what happened with your job. I don't believe how she's claiming she heard the story.

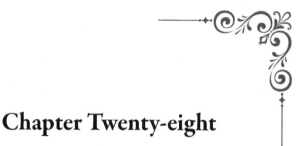

Chapter Twenty-eight

Benjamin dug through the top dresser drawer in his bedroom. The sterling silver box had to be in here. He tunneled under the socks and into the back corner. There it was, heart-shaped and bearing the initials of his grandmother, *KC* which stood for Kirsten Claussen. Or her middle name Corabelle as Grandfather had teased if she hadn't accepted. He opened the box and slid the ring onto his pinkie until it caught just before his knuckle. The diamonds appeared dull and Grandma's finger size was quite small, but he'd have the width adjusted if need be to fit Lily's. He slid the band back into the purple velvet fold and placed the box inside his suit jacket pocket. If everything with this Cumberland deal went as planned, he'd propose immediately and Lily would accept.

For the past two days, he had worked non-stop on the bid. Last night ended well after midnight while he rechecked all the figures with the Addiator. He was confident with the proposal but in less than nine hours he had to be in Chicago and deliver the offer. There were still a few errands he needed to do before picking up Anna and Emmett. He grabbed his suitcase and satchel off the bed.

As he headed down the stairs, he visualized the best route. He'd swing by the jeweler and drop off the ring for cleaning then head on over to the filling station. Stop by the telegraph office and have two telegrams sent. One for the Cumberland deal indicating their bid in case he didn't make it in time and the other for Lily. Her latest letter came yesterday, and he wanted to ensure she knew they were all coming. Hopefully, after the other stops, the jeweler would have the ring finished. He tossed his items inside the luggage trunk and got in the car.

Almost an hour later, they were on their way traveling south out of town. Benjamin gazed into the rearview mirror, eyeing Anna behind him. "We should arrive around lunchtime which will work out well since Lily said her shift would be done at one."

Emmett turned toward him from the passenger seat. "How long are you going to be in Chicago?"

"Not sure, but I'm meeting Robert by four at his apartment. We're going together so he can introduce me to Joey. He's the owner of the construction company we're putting our bid in with." Benjamin shifted into a higher gear and swung into the opposite lane going around a green Plymouth. "From what Robert told me, we'll probably end up at one of the clubs downtown." He navigated back across the center of the road and in front of the car. "I'll tell you this though, I'm going to do whatever it takes for Ebbe to get this job."

"You sure sound determined." Emmett angled himself at Benjamin. "What's driving your motivation?"

"Plenty is hinged on this deal. I can't go into the specifics, but our family business is in trouble. And if this materializes, I'll finally prove my worth for the company and show my parents I can make sound decisions. Not to mention securing my future." Benjamin glanced over his shoulder. "I do have a favor to ask you, Anna."

"Sure. What is it?"

"I have high hopes for this trip. Not only for the deal, but I'm going to ask Lily to marry me."

Anna squealed. "Oh, my!"

"Congratulations!" Emmett smacked Benjamin's shoulder.

"Please don't say anything though. If I don't get this project, I'm afraid Lily will say no. I won't ask her yet if we aren't the chosen bid. I'll send you a telegram and let you know what happened." Benjamin craned his neck. "Then I'm hoping you'll help get a surprise ready before I arrive."

Anna scooted forward toward Benjamin.

"I need you to arrange..."

ALL DAY THE RAIN HAD come down nonstop. The usual crowd outside Childs' flapjack window diminished to only those who could stand underneath the pinstriped awning. Lily filled coffee cups for the few remaining patrons perched on the counter stools. The afternoon rush was almost over. She lined up sugar, salt, and pepper containers on three separate trays. Scooping out the sugar, she let the crystals fall in a stream from side to side, filling each glass to the rim.

Several hours ago, she had checked at the front desk for word from Benjamin. He would be coming today, along with their friends. Ever since she'd read the telegram, she could hardly concentrate on her duties. Four words had repetitively played through her mind. *Found reason Vivian lied.* What did that mean? A few more words might have given her a better idea. She didn't like the fact his ex had found out about what happened to her anyway. When would the woman finally leave them both alone?

Lily twisted off the salt and pepper shaker caps. She sprinkled the salt over the glass bottles and repeated the process with the pepper. Once all the caps were screwed on, she carried the tray around, replacing the missing shakers on the tables.

The door opened and Celia approached in a freshly starched white uniform. "Have you heard from Benjamin?"

"He should be here soon with Anna and Emmett too." Lily balanced the condiment tray on her palm and rushed around the table, bumping into the edge. "Dang it!" She steadied the platter. "The telegram he sent revealed Vivian had lied about how she knew I lost my job."

"I'm sure the wicked woman jumped at the chance in spreading the rumor when she heard the news."

"I wish Vivian would mind her own business." The container slipped through her jittery fingers and landed with a thunk. The more she learned about Vivian the more she could understand why Benjamin didn't want his future with her.

Celia followed as she weaved into the next row of tables. "My shift ends at six tonight. Let's all meet for supper."

"That's fine with me." Lily spun to the last table and stopped short. "Benjamin!" Her heartbeat quickened. She'd been thinking so hard she must have conjured him. "You're actually here!" His smile was such a pleasant sight. She set the tray on the table, flung her arms around him, and squeezed tight. "Are you hungry? Do you have time to eat before you have to go?"

Benjamin returned a gentle embrace in his arms. "Yes, I can stay for a little while." He let his hands slip down her arms, staring into her eyes.

Celia cleared her throat. “Nice to see you again.” She grinned at them in a sweet-as-sugar way. “Why don’t you all sit back here. You’ll have more privacy in the corner and I’ll be back to see what you’d like.” She pointed to a nearby table. “Go ahead with them, Lily. I can finish up the trays.”

Benjamin removed his fedora. “Good seeing you again too, Celia.” He stepped to the side, allowing Lily to notice their friends behind him.

Lily rushed forward and wrapped her arms around Anna. “It’s so good to see you. I’ve got a list of places I can show you while you’re here.” She let go. “You can come along too, Emmett.” She smiled.

“Are you sure? If you’d rather be alone, I could take a nap after lunch.” Emmett pulled out a chair for Anna and she sat. “That’ll leave you girls to your privacy.” He rested his hands over Anna’s shoulders.

“That’s nice of you, sweetheart.” Anna looked up at Emmett and touched his hand.

Benjamin pushed Lily’s chair closer to the table.

Emmett took a seat across from Lily. “What do you recommend for lunch?”

“A sandwich if you’re not too hungry, otherwise the plate special which is turkey with all the traditional fixings.” Lily didn’t crave food as much as finding out what Benjamin had to say about Vivian. She trusted her friends wouldn’t repeat the story and gazed on her left side at Benjamin. “Can you elaborate on your message about Vivian?”

Benjamin draped his jacket over the back of the chair and sat. “Ah! Yes. I’ll just bring everyone up to date first. Let’s see.” He rubbed his chin. “Well, the last time Vivian came by she commented Lily lost her job. Right afterward, she covered her mouth, and when I asked where she heard the information she hesitated. Those actions caused me to doubt her truthfulness. So, the next day I went to Sallie's Beauty Parlor where she claimed hearing about Lily, and do you know what the owner told me?"

"Let me know if you'd like something other than water." Celia placed a glass in front of each person and passed everyone a menu. "Would you like me to come back? Or is everyone ready?"

"I'll have an egg salad sandwich." Anna handed her menu to Celia.

Lily nodded. "I'll have the same."

"Turkey special for me." Benjamin grinned. "I'm not taking any chances with the egg this time."

"Me either. I'll have the turkey special too." Emmett laughed.

"All right." Celia gathered the remaining menus. "Shouldn't be too long of a wait, the kitchen's not busy." She walked away.

Lily glanced at Benjamin. "Please, go on with the story."

"I spoke with everyone who worked at the parlor and no one had heard about any incident at Livingston's. At first, I thought maybe they weren't telling me the truth." Benjamin rolled the cuffs on his sleeves. "But then I asked Sallie when Vivian had last been in. I watched her flip back through the pages, and Vivian's name didn't appear until the week before Lily lost her job."

"That certainly is suspicious." Lily narrowed her gaze. "Now how do we find out where she heard it from? And why she lied about the circumstances?"

"Well, I knew better than to go ask Vivian. I decided the best place was where the story would have leaked from to begin with."

Lily touched her parted lips. "You talked to Oliver?" Her stomach churned as the appalling incident replayed in her mind.

"I did." Benjamin tenderly moved her hand away from her mouth. "I'm sorry Oliver let you go so publicly. I didn't know until he profusely apologized for his actions. Apparently, he thought I was there to teach him a lesson with my fists." He rubbed across the top of her hand. "At that point, I didn't think there would be any way to find out how Vivian knew since Oliver hadn't been discreet."

"But I can tell by the way you're caressing my hand, you did." Lily's heart pulsed faster at Benjamin's knowing grin.

"You're right. I did find out. Oliver of course knows Vivian, so I inquired if she'd been there that day." Benjamin's eyes sparkled with delight. "Not only was Vivian there, but she told Oliver you were the one who took the money."

Lily pulled her hand away. "What a cold-hearted, ruthless woman." A wave of heat stung against her skin. "Did you tell Oliver I didn't do it?"

"Yes." Benjamin shook his head. "But someone did take the money and even though a possibility exists the thief wasn't you, Oliver said he needed tangible proof. His career is on the line too and he won't exonerate you without someone else to lay the blame on."

"His career? What nerve! And how can I provide such a thing?" Lily's fingernails dug into her palms. "I should be deemed innocent. Instead, I'm guilty just because a high society woman claimed it so."

Anna brushed Lily's arm. "We will think of something. That woman won't get away with this."

Benjamin picked up her hand. "I'm sorry Vivian caused you all this heartache. I will do whatever I can to protect you from now on. There has to be a way to clear your name, we'll just need to find it. Everyone will know you are innocent. You have my word."

HOURS LATER, LILY STOOD at the edge of the rooftop above the Miller Hotel with her arm entwined in Anna's, pointing at all the interesting sites. "I'll give you a sneak peek of some of the sights we can go see. Over there is St. Mary's Church, the courthouse, the Pabst building, and on a clear day, you can view five different bridges." She twirled around indicating where to look for each. "The large area over there is Mitchell Park and if you follow the canal back here, you can see the harbor. Of course, the most incredible sight is Lake Michigan. I love coming up here to watch the sunsets. Don't you think this spot is beautiful?"

"Oh, yes! Just like your special place at home." Anna braced her hand against the cement ledge and sat. "Umm...so, I ran into Mary a few days ago."

Lily slumped as she sat, facing Anna. Memories of Ira slammed into her like a train stop at a dead-end track. She took a deep pained breath. "How's Ira doing?"

"His father built him a ramp for his wheelchair so he could get out of the house and even placed a set of metal bars outside. Ira's been using them to exercise his legs and regain as much strength as he can."

"I can't imagine how difficult this has been for him and his whole family. There will always be a place in my heart for him." Lily touched the ache in her chest.

"Mary wanted me to tell you she truly hopes you and Benjamin are happy." Anna tucked a strand of her caramel brown hair behind her ear. "She said she knows what Ira put you through with the other girl and respects how you were still willing to devote yourself to him."

"Mary would have made a sweet sister-in-law. But the way I see it, Ira made the ultimate self-sacrifice when he let me go." Lily touched her bare finger where the engagement ring used to be.

"He did redeem himself in my eyes too." Anna grabbed onto Lily's hand. "Now, how are we going to vindicate you?"

Lily wanted nothing more. Vivian had found a way to simultaneously strip her dignity and the slight amount of prosperity she had. "I tried to imagine who would have taken the money, but no one came to mind. If we knew who did it, we could make them confess."

"Whoever the thief is might try again since they got away with taking the money the first time." Anna shrugged. "At least then there would be some more doubt in Oliver's mind."

"Since he asked for proof..." Lily paused as brassy notes from a trumpet flowed across the wind. "...I don't think that will work."

Anna stood. "Where's that coming from?"

"Come on, I'll show you." Lily led Anna toward the front of the Miller Hotel building's roof. "See there, in the park, some musicians." A trombone joined in along with a mellow tone from a saxophone. "Last week, some of the same performers played. I love the sound of soulful jazz."

"I hear why." Anna swayed to the rhythm. "The melody is great."

"All the pieces are so different. Some notes long, some short while others are high or low and raspy." Lily moved along with the beat. "If you listen closely, you'll feel the emotions coming through the song."

"You're lucky you get to hear this type of music. If I had a phonograph, I could play songs like this anytime I wanted. Maybe someday, if we're ever rich." Anna laughed.

"One can always dream." Lily smiled. "Benjamin's mother had a phonograph. I noticed it in her front room the day we met."

Anna's eyes widened. "Can't you record on those?"

"Yes, on a wax cylinder. Why?"

"I have an idea of how we'll be able to corroborate your innocence."

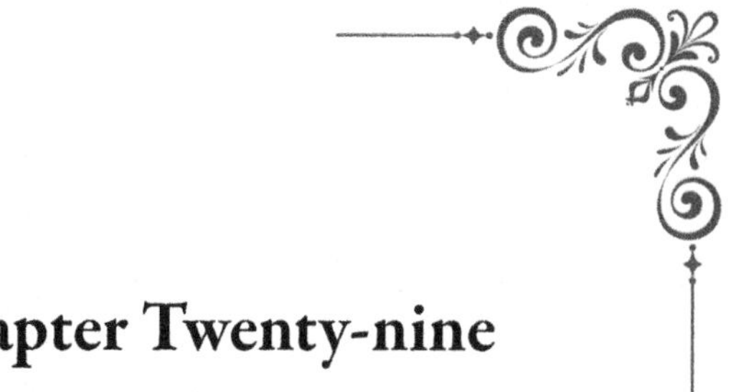

Chapter Twenty-nine

Benjamin slowed in front of a large white house on Fullerton Avenue. The number above the door matched what Robert had given him for the boarding house. He was a little early and although he hadn't seen his brother in almost five years, he recognized him walking off the expansive porch. His brother looked like a younger version of their father with brown hair, medium skin tone, equivalent six-foot-three height, and distinctively two different eye colors. One brown and the other hazel. But, most importantly, Robert had inherited Father's same authoritative nature. His brother was always in control of his own decisions. Maybe that's why Benjamin idolized him so.

Benjamin opened the door and ran around the front of the car, meeting Robert on the sidewalk. He pulled Robert into his chest, slapping his hand several times across his brother's shoulders. "I've missed you." He pushed him back, glancing up and down his frame. "You look distinguished in that pinstriped suit. A bit skinny, but great."

Robert knocked his fist into Benjamin's upper arm. "You don't look so bad yourself. Life must be agreeing with you. Or is that new gal of yours giving you such a sunny disposition?"

"Her name is Lily. I'm certain she has a lot to do with my chipper attitude. By this time tomorrow, if everything goes well here, she'll be my fiancée."

"Well, that's a call for celebration. I'll buy the first round at the Green Door Club." Robert grabbed the door handle and ducked into the passenger seat.

Benjamin hustled around the car, slipping in. "We need to stop by Joey's office before hitting the juice joint." He shifted into gear.

"Nah, Joey said he was skedaddling early from the office today. He'll meet us at the club." Robert laid his black homburg hat on his lap. "Go straight two blocks, then take a left. We'll head for downtown."

"I can't thank you enough for giving me this lead." Benjamin slowed at the intersection, checked the area, and sped up. "What's the man's last name? I should address him properly when we meet."

"Petrillo." Robert raked his fingers through his hair. "I've been laying some groundwork for how good of a company Ebbe is every chance I get. He's a reasonable man. I think he'll give you a shot."

"Good, let's hope your efforts pay off. But didn't Joey question why you left the family business?" Benjamin turned the corner. "I hope you didn't tell him Father and Mother manipulated you right out of town, did you?"

"Aah, well." Robert touched his chin. "You've got it all wrong. Mother and Father weren't the same with me as they are with you." He brushed the crown of his hat and avoided Benjamin's eyes. "This is my chance to help the company out for a change. I caused the problems. Father did his best, but it's time you knew." He placed the hat on his head. "I had trouble with gambling and Father bailed me out more times than I can count."

"What? You're playing me for a sap." Benjamin jerked his head toward Robert who revealed a solemn expression. "Why didn't you tell me before? And how didn't I know?"

"I'm five years older. You hadn't even grown facial hair when I started staying out all night. Besides, my addiction wasn't something I wanted to share with my little brother who looked up to me. I would have been a bad influence on you."

Benjamin glanced over at Robert whose cheeks were flaming red. "Mother's voiced that concern many times over the years. If our parents didn't make you leave, why did you strike out on your own?"

"Go right at the next intersection." Robert pointed. "I had to. There was a lot of strain I caused our parents financially. Father almost didn't acquire Ebbe because he had to pay off a loan shark. That's why our uncle partnered with him or there wouldn't have been a family business."

Benjamin smacked the steering wheel. "Holy moly!" Robert had even less control of his life than he did. And now he was putting all his trust in this big deal orchestrated by his wayward brother.

"Even after that, Father still gave me another chance in the business. He probably shouldn't have. Less than a year later, I racked up some more debt and that's when I left."

Benjamin turned. "Did you quit gambling then?" He tried shifting, gears ground, and he thrust the clutch back in with his foot.

"No, not then. I tried, but something always seemed to suck me back into the thrill of it all. For years, I got good at counting cards playing blackjack and poker. Much easier tallying blackjack than poker by the way. Father bailed me out again about four years ago. After that, I got my act together, but I still gamble once in a while. Although my betting is limited to the amount of cash I can afford to lose." Robert looked away out the window. "That's why I've got to help get you out of this mess with Walter. It's all my fault."

Benjamin couldn't believe he'd never heard anything about his brother's problems and the crisis his family went through. But then again, Father had kept other secrets like the loss of money four years ago. "How are you responsible?"

"I informed Father I'd gotten in over my head, but he didn't have enough dough. Instead, I went on the run from the loan sharks and hid out until he did."

Two events in the same year couldn't be coincidental, could they? Benjamin's guts squeezed rock hard. He sensed a bombshell about to explode and braced for it. "Where did the money come from?"

"Walter convinced Father that stock with the railroad would be a sound investment and make a huge profit. Since Walter had already made a fortune, he offered Father a low-interest loan to purchase shares. Once those shares were worth more than the debt, Father could sell and have plenty to get me out of my predicament. Or so Walter told him. I did eventually have my tab paid off, but the ironclad contract stated only a certain portion of Father's stock could be sold every quarter. Walter knew if Father's entire stock investment were cashed, there would be trouble with the railroad stock values dropping because of how many Father had."

"Good grief! Walter made Father stay invested."

"Yes, until the crash in twenty-nine happened and everything tumbled. For years when Walter and the other directors of the holding companies wanted more investment money, they would form another holding company that would buy out the first."

"Wow!" Benjamin rubbed his hand over his mouth. "So, they took in more investors and sold more stock to buy out the existing holding companies. Sounds like stacking a catawampus pyramid."

"You're right. And as the market began to crash, the sale of goods dropped because people couldn't afford to buy. The operating companies which sold the goods couldn't support the holding companies without the sales, and in turn, the holding companies couldn't pay the investors. Stock values plummeted. The whole structure collapsed and Father along with everyone else lost everything."

"I'll bet that's why to this day Father owes Walter. You know, I asked about the loan and all Father would state was he owed it because he'd made a legitimate business deal. He not only safeguarded his secret but yours too." Benjamin's knuckles turned white as he girded his fingers on the steering wheel. There was one more question he needed to ask. "And after all these years of hiding the truth, why should I trust you?"

"Pull over in here." Robert waved his hand toward the parking lot. "I can understand why you'd question my character. I'd have my doubts too, but I could have kept quiet and you never would have found out. Confessing the worst thing I've ever done and seeing how you're looking at me now causes great pain and all I can do is apologize." He hung his head. "The whole family has risked a lot for me. When the opportunity presented itself with Joey, I saw a chance to finally repay my gratitude. I'd like to make things right and not be so ashamed of my actions. Maybe if this bid works out, I could come home once in a while. I've changed for the better and my life is under control. Please let me prove it to you." Robert's tone pleaded with him. "I'm tired of being the outcast."

"I'm sorry you feel that way and you had to go through everything alone." He wanted to believe Robert was sincere, but he couldn't. Not just yet. Benjamin drew in a deep breath, slowly exhaling. "No matter how this turns out, you should come home and explain how your life has changed."

"We'll see." Robert's shoulders wilted as if with a release of tension. A slow smile unfurled, and he reached for the door. "Are you ready?"

"Yes, just have to grab my satchel from the trunk." Benjamin understood why Robert had at last confided in him, and now the bid became even more pivotal for their family. Not only could they save Ebbe and secure his and Lily's future together, but this deal could bring his brother home.

A few minutes later, Benjamin stood with Robert at the Green Door Club. Taking a breath, he focused on the task ahead and the door that would soon open. He wasn't surprised the painted door was green with the speakeasy beyond. The colored door's meaning for illegal booze had spread just as fast as a nosy switchboard operator's daily exposé.

Robert knocked. The metal door creaked ajar and a doorman peered through the crack. His brother spoke softly near the doorman's ear, "Last call." And the door opened.

They walked through the entrance into the dimly lit place, heading down a narrow hall. Smoke swirled in the air along with the sounds of clanking glasses and murmured voices. But the end of the passageway opened into a large square room. The perimeter held rows of tables with a dancefloor in the center. To the far edge, a raised platform surrounded by drapery framed a stage. The opposite side housed a lengthy mahogany bar. Behind, a man with a thick curled mustache awaited in a black vest and bowtie.

Robert leaned on the edge of the bar railing, looking at Benjamin. "What's your preference of giggle water?"

"Gin's fine with me." Benjamin laid his satchel on the bar and placed his fedora on top.

"Two gin fizzes, Mac." Robert drew a wallet from his breast pocket. "I'll buy."

Benjamin glanced behind the bar at a row of booze bottles lined from one side to the other. "I've never seen so much sauce."

"Those containers are sitting on a trap door. It's quite clever actually. The bottom falls out with a push of a button and they land in a compartment underneath. Not once has this place been nailed by the fuzz." Robert laid a dollar on the bar and turned around. "I've scoped everyone on the way in and Joey's not here."

Benjamin flipped open the lid on his pocket watch. "It's four-thirty." He glanced at the bartender who continued to jiggle a cocktail shaker. The bid deadline was fast approaching. He rocked back on his feet. "Is Joey usually behind schedule?"

"Could have gotten tied up in traffic." Robert leaned back against the bar and crossed his legs. "There's one thing you need to know about Joey beyond his love for the dolls' gams in scanty dresses." He chuckled. "He's a gambling man like me and likes to have a little fun once in a while. That's why I figure he'll take the risk with Ebbe as long as you've given him a good bid."

Benjamin imitated his brother's posture. Robert appeared calm, collected, and in control as he'd always pictured. Following his brother's lead would keep his nerves steady. "I think I made it fair enough where we should both come out lucrative."

"Well if we get into a game, we should have a few gestures between us so we know if one of us has a good hand." Robert grinned while motioning between them. "I've played Joey before and he'll have some type of signals prearranged with his partner."

"Ah? I hate to say this, but I'd rather beat him honestly. Trust me, no matter if Joey cheats or not, he'll have more respect for doing business with us if we're not caught with trickery. Besides, after all these years of experience, you should know the odds of winning a hand." Benjamin reached over and grabbed his highball glass the bartender placed next to him. "And as a matter of fact, I'm usually quite lucky when it comes to playing cards. Although, not high-stakes." He tipped his drink toward his brother, hoping the pep talk provided some credence. "Here's to securing this deal for our family."

"I'm fine letting you have your way." Robert elbowed him and grinned. "We'll keep the wheeling and dealing on the up and up." He clanked his glass against Benjamin's. "Cheers!" And took a drink. "Well, here Joey comes now. The other fella is his right-hand man, Phil. Don't be fazed, Phil's a man of few words."

Benjamin took a sip and licked the froth from his upper lip. "Great drink." He straightened his stance as Joey and Phil approached. Both men were well dressed in posh suits. Compared to him and his brother, they were short and appeared ordinary except for Joey's long, slightly crooked nose and Phil's limp.

Robert stood square with his shoulders pulled back. "Joey, this is my brother, Benjamin."

Joey firmly squeezed his hand. "Pleased to meet you. Robert speaks highly of you and your family. In my opinion, family is paramount."

"I agree. Pleased to make your acquaintance, Mr. Petrillo." Benjamin smiled. "I heard Robert filled you in on the company owned by my father and uncle. You're welcome any time to come by. I'd be happy to show you around Ebbe and all the products we offer."

"Robert insists you're quite the salesman." Joey touched Phil's shoulder. "This is Phil. A friend and employee of mine."

"Pleasure." Phil stuck out his hand.

Benjamin firmly pumped his arm once. "Good to meet you. You're welcome to come along to Hub City too."

"I'll keep that in mind." Phil let go of Benjamin's hand.

Joey walked up to the bar. "What are you two drinking?"

"Gin." Robert waved at the bartender, held up his drink, and indicated two more with his fingers. "I'll buy."

Five minutes later, they walked through a hidden door located behind a false wall and into a card room. A dozen or more green felt tables were scattered about with three occupied on one side. Green-shaded light fixtures hung above each of the tables. Joey led them to the opposite side in the back and they tossed their hats on the rack next to the table.

Benjamin sat directly across from Robert with Joey to his right. He took another sip of his drink, quenching a dry mouth. Asking outright about the bid didn't seem like the right thing to do. But what if Joey hadn't received the telegram? He pulled out his pocket watch, which revealed five minutes until the five o'clock deadline. His heart raced along with the second hand. "Mr. Petrillo?"

"Call me Joey."

Benjamin grinned. "Joey, did you receive my telegram with our bid for the Cumberland project?" He tapped against his satchel. "Otherwise, I brought an official written proposal with me."

"Sure did." Joey shuffled the deck of cards one-handed. "As of four o'clock, you were the lowest bid."

"Wahoo!" Benjamin pumped his fist. "This is the best news ever. The next round is on me."

"Hold on there." Joey cut the deck, moving the cards through his fingers with one hand. "Phil, call the office and see if any more bids came in." He motioned with a jerk of his head behind him. "There was one I still expected."

Phil got up and hobbled away.

Benjamin met Robert's eyes and then darted his gaze to Joey. "How many bids did we beat out so far?"

"Three. But I hate to say the one I'm waiting for we've already done business with." Joey formed a ring with his index fingers and thumbs on both hands, facing his palms toward each other. "To be precise, the lowest bid may not get the job."

"I anticipated you may have some apprehension." Benjamin shuffled through his satchel. "Here is a list of references we've supplied similar materials."

Joey's brow arched. "Impressive."

"May I ask how close the second and third lowest bids were to ours?" Benjamin slid his chair forward.

"Within five percent."

"The variation sounds like we all put in a reasonable offer. I would be willing to give you a line by line itemization to compare our figures." Benjamin flipped through the papers in his satchel.

"I appreciate that, but it won't be necessary." Joey laid the deck of cards on the table. "Your eagerness and ingenuity of salesmanship have convinced me to give your company a chance."

"Thank you." Benjamin grinned as a peacefulness soothed his stomach. "I guarantee you won't regret the decision."

"Not so fast. How about a wager?"

The airy sensation he'd had in his stomach tangled into a knot. He shouldn't have assumed victory just yet. Not by the way Joey masterfully shuffled those cards. "What did you have in mind?"

"A friendly game of poker. What do you say? Yes or no?" Joey raised and lowered his palms like a balance scale indicating which reply. "Should be fair odds considering at the moment I don't know if the other company beat out your bid. If you win, the job is yours." He moved the card deck in front of Benjamin. "Dealer choice."

An icy chill shot up the back of Benjamin's neck, lifting his hairs. He didn't like being cornered one bit. Gambling for his future seemed wrong on so many levels. He would have rather gotten the job using his salesmanship skills. But what alternative did he have? None. Especially if this is how Joey wanted to do business. He'd just have to play along. The bid against the other company left him with a fifty-fifty shot, but a card game would only leave him twenty-five percent. The odds weren't in his favor. He needed to even his chances. "All right. I'll agree only if either Robert or I win, we get the work." He glanced at Robert who gave him a wink. His brother better be good. He wiped the sweat forming on his palms across his pants.

"Agreed."

Phil pulled out a chair and sat.

Joey flashed his palm at Phil. "Don't tell me what you found out. We have a serious challenger to a game of..." He gestured with a wave.

"Five-card draw, aces high, and no pot limit." Benjamin liked his probabilities the best with this game. He rested his satchel on the floor, tugged his money clip from his pants pocket, and tossed in a dollar. "Ante up." He dealt a wobbly card to each player while they placed their share into the middle of the table. Clearing his throat, he hummed along to the song "We're in the Money." If that didn't help boost his confidence, maybe the tune would annoy the other players enough to throw them off their game. His hands flicked the cards steadily from one player to the next until everyone had five.

On the first betting round, Phil tossed in another dollar. Robert added one, Joey matched, and he slid one more into the pot. "Looks like we are all still in the game." Benjamin picked up the dealer deck and gazed at Phil while fine-tuning his observation skills. "How many?"

"Three." Phil discarded his trio onto the table.

Benjamin dealt Phil three more and moved the thrown cards into a pile in front of him. Getting rid of so many exposed Phil's weak hand. The likelihood of him ending up winning was slim, and his odds went up by twenty-five percent. He hummed another verse of the song. "How many, Robert?"

"One."

A sudden wave shot through Benjamin like a fast car ride over a sloping hill. *This must be the excitement of high-stakes that pulled a guy in.* He bit the inside of his lip, gave Robert one card, and placed the rejected card into the pile. If he understood his brother's actions accurately, their chances just got better. He glanced at Joey. "What will it be?"

Joey knocked on the wooden table. "That's for good luck. I'll take two." He tossed his rejected cards into the pile. As he placed the new cards into his hand, he slightly curved them inward.

Benjamin surmised the gesture of Joey's reaction as an instinct to protect a good hand. He laid two from his hand onto the discarded stack. "I'll take two as well." Adding them into his hand, he fanned them out. A pair of one-eyed jacks stared back at him. The next highest card, a king. Not the worst hand, but certainly not the best.

Phil eyeballed the cards in his hand. He threw two dollars into the pot. "I'm in."

The bet caused Benjamin to reconsider he may have counted out Phil's hand too soon. Or maybe the move was a way to entice someone to fold. He shifted his gaze on Robert's straight-face. For a fraction of a second one tiny facial twitch curved his lip. First impressions which include a faint smile usually mean a good hand. He had to keep his composure and he pressed his lips together, humming the intro.

Robert matched the two-dollar bet. "And I'll raise you another two." He lifted more money from his short stack.

"I'll see your four dollars..." Joey pitched his cash into the pot. "...and raise you another two."

Benjamin debated what he should do. His hand wasn't great. Although, both Joey and Phil could be bluffing. Even Robert for that matter. If he stayed in, at least he'd still have an opportunity to win. If he didn't, he would be throwing away any hope of saving Ebbe. "I'm in." He pitched in his six dollars.

Phil tossed his cards on the table. "I fold."

Just as Benjamin suspected. Phil had nothing.

Robert grinned. "Count me in." He placed another two dollars in the pot.

"The two of you are quite the players, but I'm afraid the odds are against you." Joey spread his cards out on the table. "You see, three of a kind is most likely the best hand one can get while playing five-card draw and even if either of you has the same, my aces will win."

Benjamin's optimism plunged just like the stock market did that day in twenty-nine. Joey was right. He tossed his losing cards face down on the table and swallowed the sour taste of defeat.

"I guess you're correct, Joey." Robert bit at his fingernail. "The probabilities are not in my favor. Though losing eight dollars is a small price to pay especially if the outcome could better my family." He let his cards fall one by one face-up onto the table.

After the last card dropped, Joey laughed.

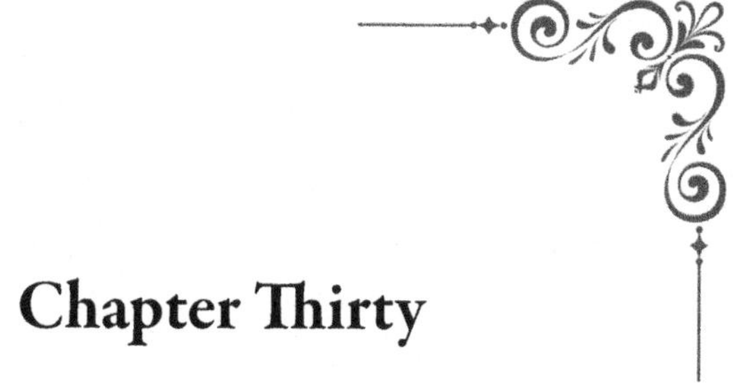

Chapter Thirty

Lily's foot jittered under the table. Almost eight already and still no sight of Benjamin. The night had been another busy one for Childs' Friday fish fry. But as soon as Celia and Emmett's plates were empty, they dashed off, each giving an odd excuse. She didn't mind spending more alone time with Anna, although they all seemed to be hiding something. A few times while they ate, she caught them glancing and grinning at each other like they knew something she didn't. Then there was the whispering between Celia and Emmett on the way here. No sense in asking Anna what they were hiding, she assumed whatever it was had to be a secret.

"I wonder how much longer we'll need to wait. It's been about three hours since the bid was due. I'd hoped Benjamin would be here by now."

"Emmett said Chicago is at least a two-hour trip." Anna squeezed a wedge of lemon over her iced tea glass. "I'm sure he'll be here soon."

"I've got a whole list of places written down and things we can do tomorrow. I thought maybe we could go through them and all decide tonight what we should do." Lily unfolded the paper. "See, there are so many places. But my vote is going to be for the festival at Mitchell Park. They have a wonderful sunken garden there you'd like."

"Sounds delightful." Anna took a sip. "The last celebration we were all together was at a park too." She set her glass on a napkin. "Oh, I almost forgot to tell you. Remember that day you mentioned the church wouldn't allow a marriage to someone who wasn't Catholic?"

"I do, my mother told me."

"Right, that's what you said." Anna laid her arms on the table and leaned forward. "I asked my mother why they had such a rule. And you know what she said?"

"What?"

"My mother had never heard of such a thing. Then she even named a local man who married a Presbyterian woman a few years ago." Anna reached across and touched Lily's hand. "The next Sunday after mass, I asked Father Toeller if a Catholic and a Presbyterian could marry." She took a deep breath. "They can, but there are church decrees that must be followed and Benjamin would have to meet with Father Toeller too."

"Mother lied to me?" Lily's hand flew over the heaviness in her chest. "She told me I'd be excommunicated from the church. Why would she do that?"

"I don't know. Maybe she completely misunderstood."

"Malarkey!" Lily's voice rose. "Mother just wanted to keep us apart. What if she hadn't given Benjamin another chance when he came back to her? How could Mother manipulate her like this? I can't believe it!"

"Perhaps your mother should speak with Father Toeller." Anna's voice faded to almost a whisper. "That way he'll be able to answer any questions she may have and you won't be caught in the middle."

"I'm sorry. I know you're trying to help, but I could have lost Benjamin forever if I believed Mother's lie." Lily rubbed at the throb in her temple. "Why didn't she tell me the truth?"

"Surely you have every right to find out. But don't you see the bright side?" Anna smiled. "Now you can marry the man you love."

Lily tipped her head. "Is there something you know that I don't know? Don't think for one moment I didn't notice how all of you were acting." Her eyes narrowed on Anna. "Are you going to tell me what's going on?"

"I can."

Lily whirled around. "Benjamin!"

"I made it back as fast as I could." He leaned over, placed a kiss on her cheek, and sat in the open chair next to Lily. "The traffic in Chicago was horrible."

"Sorry to hear." Lily fiddled with her necklace. "Don't leave us in suspense, what happened?"

Benjamin scooted his chair forward. "I've never been through anything like that before in my life. I couldn't stop my heart from pounding against my chest. Nor my palms from sweating. The only thing I could do to calm myself down was hum." He crossed his arms on the table. "Robert was the epitome of a cool-headed big brother. I'm glad he let me know about the deal. And Joey, what can I say. He talks a lot with his hands and is a shrewd negotiator."

"By the sounds of it, your evening must have been exciting." Lily's fingers quivered as she let her crucifix fall against her chest. "But, please tell me. Did you win the bid?"

A smile spread across Benjamin's lips. "We did!"

Lily jumped up and threw her arms around his neck. "I'm thrilled for you and your family. You should be proud of yourself. I know, I sure am."

Benjamin embraced her. "I couldn't have done it without my brother." He gazed at her as she let go. "There are a lot more details about what happened tonight. However, I'd rather fill you in later."

Lily eased back into the chair. "All right. We could decide which places to go tomorrow. I wish Emmett and Celia were here though."

Benjamin glanced across the table at Anna.

"I know where they are." Anna got up. "Why don't you follow me?"

Lily's eyes darted between Anna and Benjamin. Both of them stood while she remained seated. "Where are they?"

Benjamin held out his hand toward her. "It's a surprise, Darling." He bent down and kissed behind her knuckles. "You do like surprises, don't you?" He peered down her arm and into her eyes.

Lily's knees were weak as she firmly gripped his hand and stood. The enthusiasm in his voice bubbled on the air between them. Her heart fluttered. "I don't even get a hint?"

"No, nothing." He grinned and tucked her hand around his arm. "You're just going to have to trust me. Do you think you can do that?"

"Most definitely." Lily let him lead her into the lobby of the Miller Hotel. She searched the faces in the wide-open area. Neither Celia nor Emmett were anywhere. Not standing around any of the pillars or sitting on any of the seats.

Anna handed Benjamin a long, narrow black cloth.

"What is that for?" Lily pinched her brows tight.

"It's part of the mystery." Benjamin walked behind Lily and held the fabric in front of her eyes. He leaned in next to her ear. "Will you allow me to blindfold you?"

The warm breath against her exposed neck sent a chill, shivering her body. "I..." She sucked in a quick breath. "I suppose."

He laid the material over her eyes, gently making a knot behind her head. "Can you see anything?"

"No, it's pitch-dark." Lily inhaled a deep breath, hitching momentarily on the exhale. "Could each of you please take hold and walk alongside?" She raised her unsteady hands. What did they have in store for her? Benjamin and Anna grabbed her hands, slowly moving forward.

"Let us know if we're going too fast." Anna squeezed her hand.

"All right." Lily's feet shuffled across the tiled floor. "How long have all of you been planning this?" She trudged a few more steps, but no one spoke. "I'm not even getting one small clue."

Benjamin chuckled. "You'll find out soon enough."

Lily let her mind wander while they guided her to some unknown place. The only thing that made any sense was he planned to show her something. Otherwise, the blindfold wouldn't be necessary. They must have headed in the opposite direction of the front of the hotel or they would have been outside by now. All she could do was rely on her senses.

"We'll stop here." Benjamin touched her shoulder.

Lily turned toward him. "That was a short trip."

"We still have a little way to go, but soon we'll have help."

Chains rattled, a screeching metallic sound scraped, and a buzz of whispers passed by her. She couldn't be fooled too easily since she'd ridden the elevator at least twice every day. A touch on her back ushered her forward.

"Everything all right with you, Miss Lily?"

"Yes, Otis." She smiled. A situation like this wouldn't be something an elevator operator saw every day. Hands pressed on her shoulders, turning her halfway around. The elevator rose but came to an abrupt stop. Chains jangled beneath her feet. They could have only gone one or two floors at the most. *Eek*! The noise must have been the door opening. Benjamin pulled her into his side.

"Oh, dear! We need to call the police," a woman's voice shrieked.

"No, no, no." Lily raised her hands in the air. "I'm fine, they're just trying to surprise me. They're friends of mine."

"Go ahead." The woman's voice sounded calmer. "I'm going to take the stairs instead."

The door squealed and the elevator rose again. She hadn't heard Benjamin or Anna tell Otis what floor, so they must have used a hand signal. The ride she took every day from the eighth floor without stopping was under thirty seconds. And with only nine floors in the hotel, they wouldn't be in here too much longer.

Benjamin's robust arm held her tight and stable. The scent of his pipe smoke and earthy muskiness drifted in the confined air. She breathed in the intense essence of him. Never before had she blindly accepted such a plea for trust from a man. But with him, all her inhibitions were gone.

The elevator shuddered to a stop and she proceeded forward with Benjamin at her side. Anna's heels clicked in front of them as they curved slightly to the left. A door creaked on rusty hinges, the familiar sound from a heavy metal door at the end of the hall.

"We're going up some stairs, so we'll go slow." Benjamin rested one hand on Lily's waist while the other he held above the crook of her arm. "The first step is directly in front of you and the railing is on your right."

"All right." She grabbed hold of the bar, raised her foot, and stepped up.

"Good, there are five more until we reach the top."

Lily had an idea where they might be going, but she didn't want to spoil his surprise. They climbed another step. "You sure are going to a lot of trouble." She placed her foot forward and went up. "This must be quite an event."

"Well, I can't take all the credit."

"Just as I suspected, my sister and our friends were involved." She rose another stair. They had to be close now. "How spontaneous was this plan?" And up another.

"Patience." Benjamin laughed. "One last step and we'll go through the exit."

The click of Anna's footfalls ceased and a door opened. A gust of air rushed over her. "Can I take off the blindfold?"

"Here, let me take you a little farther." He moved a few more paces forward. "I'll untie this for you."

The cloth dropped from her eyes. She blinked rapidly. Strings of lights hung overhead crisscrossing atop a small table covered with a white cloth, a place setting for two, and an unlit pair of candles next to a bouquet of red roses. The overhead lighting illuminated the dim sky sparkling like stars above the rooftop. "This place looks gorgeous. How did you know I liked coming up here?"

"I have my ways." He smiled. "And the best assistants anyone could ask for."

Lily beamed at her friends and sister standing off to the side. "Thank you for helping Benjamin make this surprise special for me."

Celia walked over and hugged Lily. "Our pleasure. We'll leave you two to the romantic setting." And she went toward the door.

Anna kissed her cheek. "Have a great night." She grinned. "You can tell me all the details tomorrow."

"You've got a good fella." Emmett rubbed her shoulder and followed the ladies out the door.

Benjamin escorted her to the table, pulling out the chair. "Please, have a seat." He went around to the other side and sat facing her. "I'm hoping this will be a night you'll remember for a long time." From the pocket of his jacket, he pulled out a lighter, setting the flame to both candles. "There is a tasty dessert made just for you under that silver cover. Why don't you take a look?"

Lily removed the lid. "Oh, my! Red velvet cake. One of my favorites. Is the frosting cream cheese?" She slid her fork through the piece and slipped a morsel into her mouth. "Mmm. Yes, it's cream cheese."

"You're looking exceptionally beautiful under the moonlight." He smiled. "I must say there isn't another person in the world I notice as much."

"I think I might be blushing."

"You're right. Your cheeks are a gorgeous rosy pink." Benjamin cut his fork into the cake. "Maybe if I keep up the sweet-talk, you'll turn as red as this cake." He chuckled. "On the day we met, I remember the frilly yellow dress you wore. And when you looked at me with those beautiful blue eyes, I fell hard."

"Oh, is that so? And how about the next time we met?" She dangled a cake piece on her fork. "Do you remember then?"

"That's a tricky question. You were covered in a slicker."

"Ah, no. I was covered in water." She laughed.

"After that clumsy mishap, I'm astonished you even agreed to go out with me."

"If you recall, it took some convincing but I'm glad I eventually did." Lily dabbed a napkin on her lips. "I'll let you in on a little secret. You are the one who physically met my dreams of a tall, dark, handsome man. However, you are so much more." She placed her palm over the drumming of her heart. "The day we met I knew you were someone special. Although I was led to believe we didn't belong together by most of the world, I'm glad I didn't listen." A tightness nipped at her throat. "I could have lost you forever." She blinked away tears. "I've grown to love you more now than I ever could have imagined. All of this is possible because you've made me worthy of your love."

"You deserve nothing less from me. We've both endured so much to be together. I can only hope the rest of our moments will always be as happy as right now." Benjamin stood, moving toward Lily. He smiled and lowered one knee, facing her. "I've realized with you how valuable love is and how much stronger we are together." He wiped the tear from the corner of her eye. "I'll admit I took much too long arranging my life properly. I'm truly sorry for the heartache you've experienced because of me.

If you'll allow me, I want to make it up to you for the rest of my life. Will you give me the honor of being my wife?" He drew a small, silver box from his jacket pocket.

A warm rush of adrenaline awakened her senses. He offered her a new life. A life of endless possibilities with him by her side.

His fingers fumbled while pulling the ring from the purple velvet. "My darling, I love you." He presented the ring. "Lily Rose, please say you'll marry me."

Oh, Benjamin! Why did you have to ask this now? Her stomach sunk. "No, I can't." She shielded her mouth under her hands.

Benjamin guffawed. "You know, that's not funny."

Lily slid her hands from her face. She was going to hurt him, but it had to be said, and it had to be said now. "It wasn't meant to be."

"You're serious? But why?" Benjamin's expression pained, and his backside collapsed onto his heels.

Lily folded her hands prayerfully, asking for strength and hope he would understand. She sighed. "It's easy for you to feel everything is resolved. But for me, it's not. You've protected Ebbe and secured your career." She pushed her shoulders back. "What about me? My life is still in shambles. I can't live in Hub City without being vindicated. And more importantly, we've never discussed whether you'd be willing to marry me according to my church guidelines."

Benjamin exhaled while his gaze looked upward at her. He returned into a kneeling position, and his face seemed to shine with a new plan. "You're right. I was so wrapped up in my good news all I wanted to do was get you alone and tell you how much I love you." He glanced at her, at the ring, and back at her. "We'll clear your name and I will seek guidance with your priest.

Come back with me Sunday. We'll devise a strategy to fix everything." He extended his hand, offering the ring. "Let's make a new promise. Please accept this ring knowing you can hold me to my word now and forever."

An overwhelming joy ignited inside like a flower bud blooming under the fiery sun. "I most definitely, positively, absolutely will hold you to your word. And yes, I want to be your wife." She held out a shaky hand.

Benjamin slid the ring onto her finger.

She recognized now more than ever they were meant for each other. In others' eyes, they might be wrongly suited. In hers, they were imperfectly perfect. A peacefulness settled her soul and she laced her fingers through his.

A glimmer of candlelight sparkled through Benjamin's eyes. He nudged her gently from the chair. In one swift move, he rose and whisked her into the safety of his arms like a bride being carried over a threshold.

She tossed her head back and lightly laughed.

He twirled her.

The more she laughed, the more he whirled around the rooftop.

Benjamin's breathing quickened while his pace slowed and he teetered slightly on his feet. "I'd better sit down." He carried her to the chair and she rested across his lap.

"I have just the cure for your dizziness." She pierced a sliver of cake with her fork and held it toward his lips. "Sugar's the perfect remedy."

"Is that so?" He panted. "What if I don't like cream cheese? Then what will the future Mrs. Benjamin Claussen do?"

Lily grinned. "Have it your way." She tilted her head, inching closer. "Trust me. I'm only doing this for your own good." The cake piece clung to the tines between their lips. "Open up."

His eyes and mouth widened simultaneously.

She fed him, sliding the fork out, and covering his mouth with hers. The flavor on his silky, sweet lips sent layer after layer of sensations right to her core. And her skin tingled all the way down to her curling toes. If this was any taste of his affection, she would surely get used to it.

He ran his hands up her back and into her hair. Holding her head and guiding her lips, as he kissed every inch of her mouth.

She melted like icing on a hot cake in his arms. Nothing existed but them. And at that moment, her heart and breath were stolen away in unison.

"You sure are a sweet diversion," Benjamin whispered breathlessly. "But you may need to feed me some more. I'm still a bit dizzy."

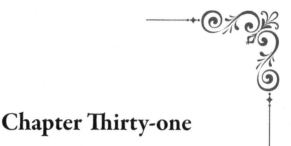

Chapter Thirty-one

Lily still had a hard time believing Benjamin proposed. But the gorgeous fiery orange opal flashed a hint of teal blue and neon green, reminding her of its passionate existence. Eight diamonds surrounded the gem, creating a clustered flower appearance. She loved the ring and the man who supported her.

They'd just finished their meeting with Father Toeller and Benjamin had pulled around the block, parking in front of her parents' house. On the one hand, she couldn't wait to give her family their wonderful news. And on the other, the announcement would force her into addressing Mother's dishonesty.

Benjamin turned, facing Lily in the passenger seat. "I know you're disappointed we can't get married in the church." He picked up her hand. "However, I will try to make our wedding the most special day you'll ever have."

"You're right. It was a letdown, but I understand the church's laws since you're not Catholic. Our marriage is about you and me. Not the location we say our vows. I'm sure a priest's house will be a pleasant setting." She smiled. "Besides, I'm grateful Father Toeller agreed to meet with you so quickly for the necessary faith sessions."

"I hope these next thirty days go by faster than the last." He rubbed his thumb across her skin. "If you didn't already know, I'd marry you tomorrow if I could."

"August thirtieth will be here before we know it." She patted his hand. "Especially with all the preparations we need to get done."

"Tell me what's on the list and I'll make it all happen." He took both of her hands, placing a kiss on each and one on the ring. "You know, I don't think I mentioned the story behind my grandmother's ring."

"No, you haven't."

Benjamin let their hands fall into Lily's lap. "After Grandpa died, my mother sent me over to handle all the handyman chores. Whenever I finished a job, Grandma would always have something prepared for me. We'd eat and talk for hours. Some days I'd come over and there wouldn't be any work. But still, she'd always have a story or two to tell."

"I'll bet she just wanted your company."

He nodded. "She said I reminded her of Grandpa. That's probably why most of the stories were about him. I heard about how they met, their courtship, how he had proposed, and interesting anecdotes throughout their entire marriage."

"Was their proposal as romantic as how you asked me?"

"Not even close." He chuckled. "But Grandma did say there wasn't a day that went by she didn't feel the love Grandpa had for her. She hoped someday I would be as lucky."

"I wish I could have met her. She sounds like an amazing lady."

"I know she would have loved you." He winked. "After one of our visits, Grandma told me how she enjoyed our time getting to know each other and how it meant the world to her. That's when she mentioned leaving her most precious gift to me. And when the time came, I'd know what to do with the ring."

"I'm so glad you saved this ring for me." Lily blinked away the tears forming in her eyes. But had she been the only one he'd ever given the ring to? She had to ask. "You mentioned you had it hidden at home. Did you ever consider giving it to anyone else?"

"No, I didn't. Although, I made the mistake of letting Vivian see it once. After I told her the story, all she wanted to know was what it was worth. I wished I hadn't because she never stopped dropping hints about how good all those diamonds would look on her finger. I knew her reasons weren't sentimental ones." He scowled. "When I proposed to Vivian, somehow it just didn't feel right giving her my grandmother's ring. Instead, I purchased one from the jewelry store. My grandmother was right, I did know when the right woman would come along."

Lily smiled. "I'm honored you chose me to wear your grandmother's ring."

"It's yours now." He squeezed her hands. "Let's go show off your ring."

A few minutes later, they walked through the front door and into the foyer. The voices hushed from inside the sitting room. She peeked around the corner. "Surprise!"

Ruby ran toward her. "Sissy!" And dove into her legs.

Lily knelt and embraced Ruby, kissing the top of her head. Directly behind, Frankie stood like a statue. She wiggled her fingers, motioning him toward her until he came close enough and drew her brother into a hug.

Frankie put his arm around her neck. "I missed you."

"I missed this sweet little face too." Lily pinched his cheeks.

Ruby gazed at Lily. "Mommy didn't tell me you were coming."

"I wasn't sure until yesterday. Celia took over my shift at Childs so I could come back with Benjamin." She stood and peered into the room. Mother and Oma were seated in the matching chairs with identical perplexed expressions. "I've missed both of you too." She figured the statement wouldn't smooth out any of the lines creased between their brows. "Is Father here?"

"I'm right here," Father called out from the hallway. "This is a pleasant surprise seeing both of you."

Lily slipped her hand into Benjamin's. "Now that we're all together, we have an announcement." Her voice excitedly rose. "Benjamin proposed." She bounced on her toes. "And I said yes."

Ruby squealed and grabbed Frankie's hands, jumping around Lily. And just as quickly, Ruby stopped. "What's proposed?"

Lily laughed. "It means we're getting married."

"Like Mommy and Daddy?"

"Yes."

Father leaned in and kissed her. "Congratulations, sweetie." He turned toward Benjamin, offering his hand. "Take good care of my little girl."

"Thank you, sir. I will."

"Ruby, Frankie. Go to your rooms." Mother pointed toward the staircase.

"Aw, come on!" Frankie fisted the air.

Ruby stomped her foot. "Sissy just got here."

"Now!" Mother leaned forward as if she were getting up.

The children ran up the stairs.

Mother stiffened her posture. "Lily, Benjamin. We need to talk."

Father crossed the room to stand beside Mother's chair, placing a hand on her shoulder.

Lily had warned Benjamin their news would undoubtedly cause concern with her mother. She squeezed his hand and took a deep breath. "I want to speak with you too. Before coming here, Benjamin and I met with Father Toeller."

Mother's brow abruptly curved. "Oh?"

"Yes. And I was surprised to find out we can marry even though Benjamin is Presbyterian. I'm almost certain you told me the church forbids marriage with someone who isn't Catholic." Lily held her mother's gaze. "I'm just trying to figure out why you don't want me to marry Benjamin."

"I..." Mother glanced at Oma. "I didn't know." She rubbed her forehead. "I truly believed no one in our faith could have a legitimate marriage unless they were both Catholic. At least, that's what was repeatedly drummed into me." Mother cast an accusing glance at Oma. "Why is that, Mother?"

"You know very well, Ruth, that man wasn't for you." Oma pursed her lips. "And if I hadn't intervened you wouldn't have this family now. You should be grateful."

"I am thankful for my family." Mother glanced across the room at Lily, then up at Father. She grasped the hand he'd laid on her shoulder before returning a sharp gaze to Oma. "But you took my choice away. How could you do that?"

"Marriage is hard enough the way it is." Oma wrapped yarn around her left finger. "Why would you want to add more complications?"

Lily couldn't remain upset with her mother in light of the recent information and her eyes narrowed on her grandmother. "Oma, I respect your opinion." She walked a few steps closer and Benjamin followed her. "But you've always asked us for truthfulness. If your beliefs aren't coming from church laws, where are they coming from?"

Oma pulled the last loop from her finger and sighed. "When we arrived here, your Opa and I longed for a good life just like anybody else. But those who were not of our faith made it...difficult. Many of...many of our Catholic parishioners were refused jobs, or decent apartments, or loans, and newspapers blamed us for the rise in crime." Her voice choked with tears. "Others said Catholics were committed more to the pope in Rome than we were to America." She laid the knitwork on her lap and dabbed her eyes with a tissue. "Americans who were already here thought our religion was wrong and we felt the same way about theirs. For fifty years we've had these fears and insecurities to overcome, and look how little we've managed."

Lily lowered herself onto the footstool in front of Oma. "I'm sorry you had such an unpleasant experience." Her grandmother was right about the last half-century, not much had changed. People had viewed her religion or lack of wealth as inferior. She patted Oma's knee. "And I understand why you feel the way you do."

Oma touched her chest. "I've held onto this hurt for so long. After telling the story I can see how unfair I've been." Her face sagged, making all the lines of her age more pronounced than ever. She glanced at Mother. "I'm sorry, Ruth. Please forgive me."

Mother drew in a long breath while Father rubbed his hand over Mother's back. "Your heart may have been in the right place, but…" She closed her eyes briefly. "I think we should talk about this later." She focused her gaze on Lily. "I'm more concerned right now what the two of you will do when your religious beliefs contradict each other."

Lily lifted her chin. "Mother, you know our relationship hasn't been without its difficulties and we're still here together. I'm not naïve in thinking from now on our lives will be any easier. However, I do believe we are meant for each other. We have similar values and strong faith in God." A hand rested on her shoulder. She reached up and touched Benjamin. "We will continue going through life step by step, discussion by discussion, and decision by decision."

Benjamin squeezed Lily's shoulder.

Lily sensed Benjamin's warm supportive touch. "Mother?" She rose from the stool, stood next to Benjamin and laced her fingers through his. "I came here to ask for your blessing before we get married. Father gave us his. Are you able to do the same?"

"Well…sweetie, I…um…wish I could say yes as easily. This whole situation has been a lot to take in." Mother closed her eyes and rubbed the middle of her forehead. "Let me pray about it."

Lily and Mother's situations were identical, didn't her mother see that? Her stomach churned with nausea. No matter, she'd said what she'd come to say. She and Benjamin approached her mother. "I'm leaving in a few hours on the train. We've set our wedding date for the thirtieth of August. I would like your blessing, but the next time I see you we will be married. I do hope your prayers are answered by then. Goodbye, Mother." She leaned over and kissed her cheek.

"EVERYTHING IS SET HERE." Anna peered out from under Benjamin's walnut desk. "How does it look from out there?"

Lily paced backward until she reached the doorway. "Benjamin will have to stand right in front of the desk opening or Vivian will be able to see you." She motioned with her hand. "Come out and help position the chair to cover the gap."

"I can't wait until we catch Vivian in her lies." Anna crawled out. "Let that vindictive woman try and deny she was at Livingston's. Winifred has proof with her dress order and the charges made on the DuCate's account." She slid the chair over. "How's this?"

"I appreciate you asking the women on the floor for me. I thought if she was there someone might have remembered seeing her. A little more to the right. No." Lily pointed. "My right, your left." She laughed. "That's good." She peered out of the doorway and down the hall. Benjamin stood at the side door, awaiting Vivian's arrival. "That woman is going to be furious when she finds out why Benjamin called her here."

"Have you figured out how you're going to get her to confess?"

"Well, Vivian likes to talk about herself, especially if she thinks she's the one in control. I'm hoping if I let her ramble on, she'll delight in how she's humiliated me." Lily glanced in Benjamin's direction again. He hadn't moved. "Do you have any suggestions?"

"Mother would always use silence to her advantage. She'd ask a question, let us answer, nod in agreement, and then wait. Sometimes she would even nod during the quiet time. Usually, her actions would prompt another response and that's when you'd slip up. I can't remember how many times I fell for it."

Anna brushed her palms together. "The tactic is rather clever. I think you should try it."

Benjamin hollered, "She's here!" He came rushing toward Lily. "Get ready."

Anna scooted under the desk.

"Quick, Benjamin, go stand in front of the desk." Lily backed up against the office wall, next to the open door. Her fingers gripped the paneled walls.

Benjamin left the chair in place and leaned against the desk edge. "Is this a good spot?"

Bang! The outside door must have swung shut.

Lily nodded, giving him a thumbs up. Heels clicked upon the hall floor and her heart raced faster. Vivian would soon understand she'd tangled with the wrong person. All of that woman's nastiness, along with those grade school bullies, and everyone else who'd ever made her feel inadequate roiled a fiery ball within. No one would ever define who she was again. Her nails bit into her palms.

The clicking stopped inside the doorway.

"You're looking as handsome as ever, Benjamin." Vivian took a few more steps into the office. "I've always liked that bold-striped suit."

Lily rolled her eyes. This woman thought she had Benjamin right where she wanted. Vivian had even dared to wear the evidence of the fitted blue day dress from Livingston's.

"Thank you for coming on such short notice." Benjamin tugged at his tie. "I thought today would be more private since we're closed." He wriggled the knot loose.

Vivian swayed her hips as she made several more paces inside. "Don't you have a compliment for me?" She ran her hand across the curves of her snug waist.

Lily shoved the door shut. As the wood slapped against the frame, a wallop rattled the glass. The whiff of sweet lavender mixed with vanilla didn't match Vivian's true essence one bit.

Vivian spun on her heels and met Lily's eyes. "What are you doing here? Didn't you run out of town with your tail between your legs?"

"I'm here because the little stunt you pulled didn't scare me for long." Lily moved away from the wall, taking strides toward Vivian.

"What are you accusing me of?" Vivian presented a playful grin.

Lily stepped closer. "I can understand why you tried to push me out of Benjamin's life. I am the other woman after all." She half-shrugged.

Vivian tossed her head back, laughing boomingly. "That's right. You never had a chance."

"I see now, you were only protecting your relationship with him." Lily gave an easy nod.

"From you? Don't be ridiculous."

"But you do know that the real thief got away with another crime now, don't you?" Lily moved directly in front of Vivian. "There's been more money missing."

"I'm not following your story." Vivian propped her one hand against her hip and swung the other in a widely dismissive fashion. "What in the world does this have to do with me and...?" She pivoted toward the desk. "...Benjamin. Why don't you tell her to leave? We have important things to discuss."

Benjamin crossed his arms over his chest. "Lily isn't going anywhere. We know you have some information and I suggest you cooperate."

Lily took a few wide steps, standing on the left of Vivian. Having Benjamin's support helped relax the tension in her neck muscles. "What is your side of the story then?" She held her hands behind her back while taking a few easy breaths. "Do you remember where you were the day after Independence Day?"

"Well, of course. What kind of question is that?" Vivian tapped her shoe against the floor. "Do you remember what you were doing that day?" The tone of her arrogant voice stung like a cornered venomous snake.

Lily could spit equally poisonous words if this was how Vivian wanted the conversation to proceed. "Amazingly, both of us occupied the same second level of Livingston's." She raised her chin. "I didn't know you were there though, until recently."

"Who said I was there?" Vivian bit her lower lip.

"Oliver."

Vivian's high-pitched laughter went on and on until abruptly stopping. "He's wrong." She slid her other hand onto her hip. "That little man has a very untrusting character, mine is impeccable."

"Impeccable?" Benjamin choked out a mirthless laugh. "There is no way you can stand there and say you are blameless in this situation."

Lily's heart pounded with the rush of excitement in her veins. If this conceited witchy woman needed more proof of being caught in lies, Lily would happily oblige. She glanced up and down Vivian's frame. "The dress you're wearing is awfully familiar. Didn't you buy that from Livingston's recently?"

"Yes." Vivian slid her hands down her sides. "And it fits my flawless figure like a glove."

"With some help." Lily pushed her shoulders back, standing tall.

Vivian's eyes narrowed and her upper lip tensed.

"Winifred keeps very good records of all her clients and the store does as well for account charges." Lily glared directly into Vivian's eyes. "If you continue insisting it was me and the thief gets caught, which we all know is likely, then it's going to appear you knowingly hid the crime." She nodded. "Couldn't you possibly have been mistaken on who you saw take the money?" She had laid everything out and Vivian had to realize, whether she admitted her guilt or not, these games were over.

Vivian's cheeks transformed from pale pink to blood red. "And if I say there might be a possibility the thief wasn't you, what then?" She turned her head toward Benjamin as if she were making an emotional plea for help.

"Possibility?" Benjamin scoffed. "Stop being evasive and concede your involvement."

Lily breathed deeply and savored this moment. Whether Vivian admitted her guilt or not, she'd stood her ground and was proud of herself. "Honestly, for me, it doesn't matter. I know I didn't take the money. But, for you, it's only a matter of time until everything unravels and the real truth comes out. With your reputation, a blow like this could become quite a scandalous tale if people thought you did it out of spite. Is that how you want this to turn out?" This time she would remain quiet like Anna suggested and keep nodding.

"Frankly, I don't care one way or the other." Vivian held her palm up and out. "I'm tired of this conversation. If it will get you to shut up so you can leave, there was someone behind the counter who had similar features as you. Maybe I did mistake that woman for you. But that doesn't change anything with me and Benjamin." She waved her hand. "Now go away!"

Lily laid her left hand over her heart as her chest lightened with relief. "I appreciate you saying that. I'd like to put all this animosity behind us."

Vivian's lip curled. "What is that?" She snatched Lily's hand. "This is Benjamin's grandma's ring. Why do you have it?"

"We're engaged."

"I take back everything I said." Vivian pushed away Lily's hand. "You did steal the money and I'll swear to it." Her face reddened.

Benjamin moved to the end of the desk. "It's too late."

Vivian bared her teeth. "What ludicrous drivel are you talking about?"

"Anna, did you get all that?"

Vivian swung around in the direction Lily pointed.

A hand appeared out from under the desk, holding a cylinder. "Every incriminating word!"

Lily poked Vivian's shoulder with a pointed finger. "That little roll has our whole conversation recorded. If you go back on your word, I'll be forced to play it for everyone."

Vivian's mouth fell open. "You're bluffing."

"And just so you know..." Benjamin mischievously grinned. "...your father's debt will be paid in full."

"I'm not standing around listening to any more of this." Vivian whirled around and stomped toward the door.

"You're right about that." Lily rushed past Vivian and blocked the exit. "We are all going to Livingston's. Oliver is waiting for us."

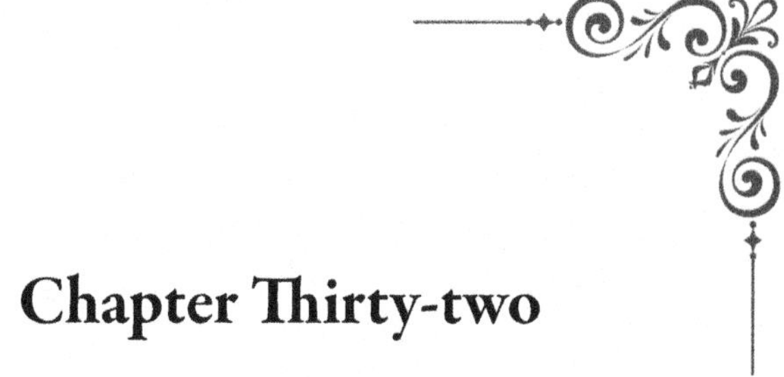

Chapter Thirty-two

July 31, 1933 - Mon evening at home

Darling,

I don't know what else to say other than this being in love sure is nice but has its drawbacks. I wish you would have let me see you off since I didn't get the sleep you thought I should anyway. I was in bed when your train pulled out last night and I listened to it go till it was gone. I had quite a time trying to doze off. The lumps in my throat kept me awake, but of course, the swell weekend we had offset that some.

Do you remember the day I took your picture on the rooftop? Well, now it's sitting on my desk in a gold frame while I write to you. At least I can look into your beautiful face while we are apart.

It seems all I can think of is how long it's going to be till I see you again and when one thinks about it now it seems like a long way off. I know we agreed to save all the money we can before the wedding, but not being able to hold you in my arms is going to be tough. I suppose the wait will make everything worth it. Looking forward to seeing you in thirty days.

All my love,

Benjamin

P.S. Also wished all day you had missed the train.

August 4, 1933 – Friday

Dearest Benjamin,

I feel the same way you do. If you would have stayed with me at the train station, I'm afraid I wouldn't have been able to tear myself away from you. The next time we see each other, we'll be promising to be together forever and I hope that will be many years more than these days apart.

My trip back was good and mostly uneventful. On the train, a boy was traveling alone who reminded me of my little brother. He was on his way to visit his grandparents and asked me how many children I had. I laughed and told him none...yet! Which reminded me, we've never talked about how big of a family you'd like to have. I'm hoping for two boys and two girls. How many would you like?

Celia and I are going dress shopping tomorrow afternoon. I'm excited to see all the styles they have and be able to mark this one item off my long list. Hope to hear from you soon.

Missing and loving you,

Lily

August 8, 1933 - Tue at home

Darling,

I hope this past weekend you were able to find the dress of your dreams. Will you describe it to me or will I need to wait? I did a little shopping last night and I'm having a couple of suits sent out for my approval. Would you like to know what my suit looks like after I pick which one or do you want to be surprised? Just a hint if you don't tell me about your dress, I'm not compelled to tell you about my suit.

Good news! My father paid off the entire debt with Walter and has severed all ties. I'm relieved because that means Vivian for certain is out of our lives too. I'm sure you'll agree we deserve some tranquility after what we've gone through.

Speaking of even more surprises, maybe I should have mentioned how many children I would like. Hold on to your hat...I would love to have a dozen. Growing up with my brother and sister was one of the best memories I ever had. Even now, I don't know what I'd do without them. I want all my children to have the same kind of experience with their siblings and the more the merrier.

Tonight is the first meeting with Father Toeller and I have to say I'm a little jittery. He seems like a nice fellow but I don't want to say something to mess things up. I'm going to run down to the post office so this gets in the mail before I go. I will let you know how the meeting went in the next letter. Only twenty-two more days until I see your beautiful face in person.

All my love,

Benjamin

August 11, 1933 – Friday

Dearest Benjamin,

Oh, my! A dozen children. I can't imagine how full of a house we will have if that comes true. We may need to compromise how many little ones we have depending on the size of house we can afford.

Great news about your father's debt and especially the ties with Vivian's family. I'm so relieved, for us and your family. I still can't believe how we bamboozled Vivian into admitting the truth. The best part was after she'd confessed, you got Oliver to publicly announce my innocence. Now the whole town will know the truth.

I did find the perfect white dress for our wedding, but I've decided not to describe it to you. I'd rather be surprised when we see each other. Although I will reveal I've found the ideal hat, gloves, and shawl that complement the dress well. And I'll also understand if you don't want to tell me anything about your suit. However, the colors blue or brown look the best on you but whatever you decide to choose will be fine.

Mother still hasn't contacted me at all and I'm bothered by her lack of response for us getting married. If anyone should understand, she should, especially after what Oma put her through. I'm going to speak with the priest here at the parish this Sunday and ask if he would be willing to perform our ceremony on the thirtieth. I think being married before returning to Hub City would be better for both of our families. Will the change be all right with you?

Missing and loving you,

Lily

August 14, 1933 - Mon at the office

Darling,

I will be happy to marry you anywhere. The meeting went swell with Father Toeller. We discussed how God would be a part of our marriage and Father Toeller said he liked what I had to say on the matter. Will be seeing him again tonight and toward the end of the week.

My father asked me this morning if I wanted to rent the house next to the warehouse because I guess the renter is going to move, told him I'd think about it. I don't want to live there unless we can't get anything else. I have a few places I've looked at and will leave it up to you when I bring you home.

Sure wish this was three Friday nights ago because I am starved for a flock of your kisses. Waiting sixteen more days till I see you seems so long and I know when we are finally together kissing you every night isn't going to be enough. We will have to kiss every morning, noon, and night before I'll be satisfied.

All my love,

Benjamin

P.S. Oliver deserved the humiliation after what he did to you. So thankful all this is over.

August 17, 1933 – Thursday

Dearest Benjamin,

Time seems to have slowed for me too and I can't wait until I see you again. You are always on my mind no matter what I am doing. I've tried keeping busy by picking up every extra shift, but even that doesn't work lately. At least we will have a little nest egg to start with from the money I make at the restaurant and what you've been saving.

I'm sure the places you looked at are very nice. Besides, anywhere we can be together will be fine with me. Your father sounds like he is accepting of us getting married. How is your mother coming along? I spoke with Father Heller at St. Matthew's Parish and he agreed to marry us. He will be contacting Father Toeller to make sure everything is ready by the thirtieth. I also sent a letter off to Anna asking for her and Emmett to make arrangements to come along with you.

I can't believe in two more Thursdays we'll be married for one whole day. I've been marking each day off my calendar right before I go to bed thinking of you. Sometimes I dream you are right here next to me.

Missing and loving you,

Lily

Hotel Charles "strictly fireproof"

Every room with running water and toilet

Owned and operated by CE Blodgett & Son Co

Rates $2.00 with bath $2.50

August 21, 1933 – Monday

Darling,

I'll bet you can guess where I am by this paper. This afternoon Al Myles came into the office, he's a cement salesman and we had dinner at the Hotel. So now I'm up in his room and we're having a few drinks.

You're right about father accepting our marriage. Don't worry about my mother, trust me, she will come around. It may take some time but she's no match for your kind heart. I'm certain your mother will accept me too. We just have to keep showing them how much we love each other, and eventually they will both realize our happiness is what matters the most.

I agree it's important for us to have a little and every bit helps. I've saved even more dough by walking everywhere and keeping my car in the garage lately. When I come down, I want to make sure I pick you up in style. Last night, I cleaned the whole inside and this weekend the outside will be polished. I'm returning some hairpins I found in my car because I've heard you say that it's the little things that count and I figure that is a little thing.

I'm getting the fishing bug again since it's been quite a while. Wish you were here to go along but you'll be back soon–only nine more days! There's no one else I'd rather go fishing with or should I say get tangled up with?

All my love,

Benjamin

P.S. Anna and Emmett are all set to come with me.

August 25, 1933 – Friday

Dearest Benjamin,

The things you notice are one of the many reasons I love you so much. Don't ever change. It's true...it is the little things that count and your actions show me how much you love me too.

My mother sent me her blessing and I am so happy. Everything is coming together wonderfully and I'm glad our friends can come along to celebrate. This weekend I'm planning a trip to Mitchell Park and I'm going to wander through their sunken gardens. I'd like to find some places to take pictures of us after the wedding. Could you please bring along your camera?

I can't believe our wedding day is less than a week away. It seems like yesterday when you proposed on the rooftop. That day was so special to me and the place you'd chosen couldn't have been any better. I feel close to God when I'm there and I know he will always be with us. The next time I see you we'll be together forever.

Missing and loving you,

Lily

August 27, 1933 - Mon at the office

Darling,

We had our names in the newspaper tonight and everybody, especially our crew, has been giving me plenty. They are keeping track of the hour closer than I am, but I can take that easy enough.

You'll never guess who gave me the paper I'm writing on—my mother. She handed me a wrapped box. Inside was a set of matching stationery and envelopes. I didn't have the heart to tell her this was my last letter to you. But I hope you see the gift the way I do as her beginning to accept our relationship.

I met with Father Toeller for the last time tonight. Last week he said we should be on track for the thirtieth so that is one more thing we can check off the list.

I was thinking this afternoon how when I come down this time to get you, it will be for keeps. No more distance between us will be nice. Don't know of any more to tell you outside of loving you just as much as ever which is more than anything in the world. I'll be seeing you soon.

All my love,

Benjamin

P.S. I look forward to waking up next to you every morning and falling asleep next to you every night.

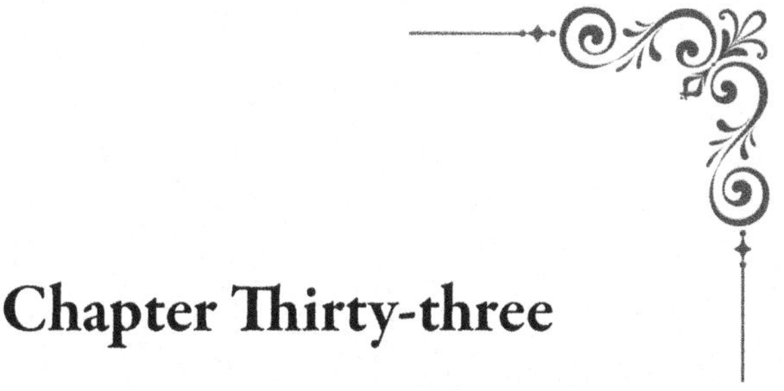

Chapter Thirty-three

Lily stood inside the quaint room within the rectory. Sunlight sparkled through the decorative prismed glass window, creating a spectrum of colors. Her image reflected an equally radiant complexion in the long mirror—from her white two-inch t-strapped shoes, to her pleated white tea-length dress, and to the top of her fashionable white veiled pillbox. She slipped a few more pins around the sides, securing the fancy hat.

By her own judgment, the grandeur of her new style defined a higher societal class. Or did it? If that was her thinking, how had she behaved any better than the people who'd treated her poorly? Labeling people by how they dress, where they live, the amount of money they have, or the way they worship their God simply creates an unfair overgeneralization. Today would be a new beginning. Not only in a marriage with Benjamin but with a new perspective on life where she would always try to treat people uniquely as individuals.

Lily's fingers trembled as she untied the bow from her shawl, draping the garment across the chair. Her skin had turned a rosy shade of pink from the warmth and her eager heart pounded at a rapid pace. Celia and Anna had left a few minutes ago to ask if the men were ready. The anticipation of catching sight of Benjamin dressed in a spiffy suit stirred all kinds of sensations.

Tap, tap, tap.

Lily twirled around. "Who is it?"

"It's me, Benjamin."

She rushed over to the door. "Is everything all right?"

"Yes, can you let me in?"

"We're not supposed to see each other." She braced her hand on the door frame. "It's bad luck."

"I have something I want to give you before the wedding. If you let me in, I promise not to peek."

"Just a moment. I have a gift for you too." Lily hurried over to the chair, picked up the box, and returned. "All right, turn around. We'll keep our backs to each other." She opened the door. "Hold my hand and I'll guide you." She grasped his fingers and an exhilarating tingle flowed across.

Benjamin's feet shuffled across the carpet until they stood back to back. "I've missed you."

"I've missed you so much too." Lily leaned into him and her stomach flip-flopped. "You do know..." She took a few breaths. "...being this close to each other is going to make it difficult not to look."

"If I can promise to wait a little longer, you can too." He squeezed her hand. "I decided to write you a letter. After this last month, I've got this composing down pat." He slipped the envelope to her.

Lily exchanged the letter for her gift. "I hope you like it."

"Please open your present first."

She slipped the stationery out.

August 30, 1933 – Our Wedding Day

Darling,

The first time we met, your beauty made me wordless. If you remember the day, I couldn't stop gazing at you. As we got to know one another, your compassionate loving nature drew me closer. It didn't take long for me to fall in love with you so deeply I couldn't ever see my life any other way. It is the reason I followed you to Milwaukee and I would have traveled anywhere till the day our eyes met again. Thank you for being who you are and encouraging me to take hold of my life.

Our love has brought us to this joyous day. Today I become your husband and you my wife. We will walk together, face many happy, and hopefully not so many sad times but we will do it as one. I know our love will endure through it all. I want to make a written promise today. In the event I falter, you'll have this in writing to remind me. From this day on, I promise to love you with all my heart and soul for as long as God allows us to be together on this earth. Each day, I will make every effort to let you know how much you mean to me. I can't imagine loving you more than I do today but I hope and pray our love will multiply over the years. The vows we will be saying soon to one another are on the enclosed paper. On our anniversary, I thought we could say them to one another as a renewal of our commitment.

I am eager for us to continue our journey so don't make me wait any longer. I think we've waited long enough.

All my love from your soon to be husband,

Benjamin

Lily blotted a handkerchief under her eyes. "Your letter is as sweet and charming as you are and I'm excited for us to be together forever too." She sniffled. "Please open your present."

The paper crumpled. "Let's see what we have here." The lid squeaked as the box slid open. "Wow! This minnow looks real. It's great."

"I'm glad you like it. I thought a fishing lure would be an appropriate remembrance of our first date and our first kiss." Lily turned around. "If you can keep your eyes closed, I'd love a kiss before we say our vows."

"You've got me hooked." Benjamin whirled around and drew her close. "Every time I use this fishing, I'll be reminded of how you reeled me in."

Lily laughed. "Is that so?" She placed her hands on Benjamin's chest. "I'm never going to let you go. You're absolutely the catch of a lifetime." Finally, she had found the man she craved. The one she could not live without.

~I hope you loved Lily and Benjamin's journey to a happily ever after. If so, you can make a big difference. When it comes to getting attention for my book, receiving a review is significant. If you've enjoyed this story, I would be very grateful if you could spend a few minutes leaving a review on the book's Amazon page.

Thank you very much for your time and consideration.

~What makes writing the best career choice is building a relationship with my readers. I occasionally send newsletters (about once a month) with details on new releases, special offers, and personal interests (cooking/baking, gardening, dogs). If this sounds like fun, sign up for my newsletter at

https://www.lorioestreich.com/newsletter-sign-up/

I hope you'll join.

~Here are a few more ways you can connect with me,

My online home:

https://www.lorioestreich.com/

On Facebook:

https://www.facebook.com/LoriOestreichAuthor

Or follow tweets:

https://twitter.com/LoriOestreich1

Instagram:

https://www.instagram.com/lorioestreichauthor/

I love hearing from my readers!

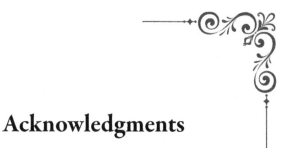

Acknowledgments

Creating a novel truly takes many talents. I am so grateful for the people in my life that have helped me accomplish my dream. This story is personal to me because the hero and heroine are based on my grandparents. The photo on the cover is my grandmother, and some of the words written in the letters (chapter thirty-two) were from my grandfather. There are over three-hundred and fifty letters he wrote to my grandmother while she was in Milwaukee.

I'd like to thank my husband, Tim, who has been supportive of my new career choice. He listened to me talk about my characters as if they were real and gave me the "male" point of view when I asked. I'm giving him credit for this line in the book: *"Besides, any car that's fast enough for Bonnie and Clyde is good enough for me."*

For my three daughters: Jessica, Jennifer, and Jayme who gave me encouragement and vigilant prodding to keep me going and finish. It took many years, but the time is here, and I hope your mom has made you proud.

To my writing group, you are the best: Amy, DeAnn, Helen, Lyn, Marlene, and Steve. Your encouragement and successes gave me the drive to stay on the publishing journey.

To my editing team, Chantelle at Paper Mills Editing, Helen, and Amy. The invaluable insight all of you contributed with your time and talent is immeasurable. All of you helped me create the words I longed to write. Thank you from the bottom of my heart!

To my cover design team, Katie at TrūCreative. For your graphic artist talent and an eye for creating a cover that embodies the story inside. Mac Bailey, for the wonderful photo you captured and the hours you waited until the precise light appeared for that perfect shot. I love the cover!

To all my family and friends, I'm glad you are in my life, and I wouldn't be where I am today without you.

For my readers, without you, there would be no one reading my novel. Please stay in touch with me. I look forward to your reviews and messages. As long as you read, I'll write. Thank you for giving me the privilege to share my story with you!

About the Author

Lori Oestreich's 1930s romance debut novel "Darling, All My Love" entwines historical events into the emotional lives of two characters based on her grandparents. Lori makes her home in Wisconsin, where she and her husband raised three daughters and are now enjoying an empty nest. When she's not creating stories, she's either reading, walking her rescue dog Charlie, gardening, or spending time with family (including her five grandchildren) and friends.

Read more at https://www.lorioestreich.com.